I0768117

On Principle

BOOKS BY BONNIE CALLAHAN

REMY VS. ROME

ROAD OF STARS AND FLAME

ON PRINCIPLE

On Principle

BONNIE CALLAHAN

A DESERT GRACE NOVEL

This book is a work of fiction. Names, characters, places, and incidents are either the product of the author's imagination or are used fictitiously, and any resemblance to actual persons, living dead, business establishments, events, or locales is entirely coincidental.

No portion of this book may be reproduced in any form, scanned, or distributed without written permission from the publisher or author, except as permitted by U.S. copyright law.

ON PRINCIPLE Copyright ©2024 by Bonnie Callahan

All rights reserved.

Desert Grace Book One

FIRST EDITION

Cover design by Gia Thompson
GIACREATIVE.CA

ISBN 979-8-9860846-4-0

For my favorite Bump in the road of life, Lord of Humanities, and absolute world-changing, life-changing, brilliant gift of a human being and best friend. I love you so much, Nat, and I am so damn proud of you.

And for everyone finding their way through the storm.
I'm really damn proud of you, too.

On Principle

Author's Note

While this is a love story, and though there is a lot of humor in the text, the book also touches on heavier themes, including depression, parental abandonment, loss of a parent to suicide (off-page, in the past), thoughts of suicide, PTSD, drug overdose (off-page, in the past), school violence threats, dementia, chronic people-pleasing, divorce, and in addition, contains religious references. Be gentle with yourself and consider not reading if these topics might be triggering to you.

One

OCTOBER

A GAP OPENS UP in the mass of writhing, sweating bodies, and I bolt for the edge of the room, bouncing off someone's sharp hip and pushing away stray hands. The pulsing lights make it feel like I'm moving in stilted, broken steps through a poorly designed video game. Bursting through the crowd, I lean against the grimy glass bar and take a deep breath.

It is official. I, Emeline Jones, do not love Las Vegas.

Like most high school teachers, or at least the ones who work in schools like mine, I spend my days taming the inhibition and irrationality of others, trying to channel those impulses and shape them into something productive and beautiful, or at least something unlikely to warrant a visit from the police station. Vegas celebrates the same impetuous recklessness I strive to squash in my daily life.

Which is ironically why I agreed to come when Leila invited me.

I climb up onto the nearest unoccupied barstool. It isn't even 8 p.m., and my entire chest is soaked in something red and sticky that smells disturbingly like my childhood drenched in vodka. This is what I get for wearing my work clothes out on Halloween...on the Strip. If my employer were to see me, they would fire me on the spot. But given my salary, dressing up as a slutty teacher seemed like the most cost-effective way to celebrate the holiday and broadcast the fact that I need to get laid.

If I don't have sex soon—the kind that includes another human being—I might implode.

My habitual celibacy is not deliberate. My job consumes all my time and brain space. And when it isn't work specifically demanding my attention, it's a problem related to work, and those problems often qualify as emergencies. Emotionally, physically, spiritually, there is no remaining energy in my life to seek out potential partners and endure pre-coital formalities, much less pursue a relationship. Thus, Vegas.

Picking up random guys is not my *modus operandi*, and it is not something I am exceptionally practiced at. But I promised myself I would try, because as much as I love my job—emergencies and all—I also really enjoy being naked with another person every once in a while.

I pull my shirt out at the collar and peek inside. The cherry liquid has leaked through to my white Victoria's Secret lace bra, which is older than my bachelor's degree and the only piece of sexy lingerie I own. With a sigh, I unbutton my shirt to examine the full extent of the damage, taking in the view of my unspectacular, syrupy cleavage.

"Fudge it all," I mumble, dropping my face into my hands.

The guy beside me laughs, and I glare at him from the corner of my eye. He shrugs, clearly unbothered, and takes a sip of dark beer from his pint glass.

"Hey." I reach up to gesture down the bar. "Can you hand me those napkins?"

He turns slowly in his seat, taking in my face and then my open shirt. He smirks. "Jaysus, Mary, and Joseph, a vision from the Almighty himself," he says, stacking his hands above his heart on the black fabric of his...cassock?

"Funny, you're a priest." I roll my eyes. "Now do me a solid, Father, and pass me some of those napkins."

He grabs the entire pile and rests it in front of me, cocking an eyebrow as his gaze flits to my bra. "Need any help with that?"

I shoot him my best side-eye and go to work on the Dirty Shirley dripping into my demi-cups. He politely looks away.

"What's that accent?" I ask, keeping my eyes on my chest.

"I'm Irish," he answers. "More so when drinking."

I glance up, angling my head to better consider him. Medium-brown hair verging on auburn, a splash of freckles across the bridge of his nose and top of his well-defined cheekbones. His eyes are an indeterminable shade of non-brown in the club lights. He has a gorgeous mouth, and my less-sober parts have some thoughts about what they'd like to do to it.

Attractive, alone, and Irish.

He grins.

And immune to scrutiny. Serial killer?

"Did you have any pets growing up?" I ask, narrowing my eyes.

The Irishman chuckles and stares at his beer as he contemplates the question. "I did."

"How did they die?"

His eyebrows are high on his forehead when he faces me. The lights flash in his eyes. I'm pretty sure they're green. "Mostly of old age," he says. "Though, Gur went out with a bit of a bang."

I knew it. Only serial killers have exploding pets. But he *is* very handsome, and despite my professional qualms about hooking up with people in clerical clothing, he might be my last chance to get some action. "Your dog exploded?"

"Cat. And no." The Irish stranger rubs his brows. "Gur was hit by a lorry carrying Bang energy drinks."

I grimace as his eyes drop, his teeth pressing into his quivering bottom lip. My heart sinks. I am officially a horrible person for making this man relive the tragic death of his beloved feline on Halloween. At a bar. In Vegas. This is not what Vegas is for.

There has to be a way to fix this. Maybe kill two birds with one stone? I'm considering apologizing by inviting him to bed—I'm not well-versed in the art of seduction, but I imagine being direct is best—when I realize he's laughing.

I slug him lightly on the arm, and my knuckles meet a well-muscled bicep. What else is he hiding under the cassock?

"Awful, I know. I truly did love that cat. God rest him." He crosses himself and then chuckles again. "But it's a feckin' hilarious story."

"Are you always this weird with strangers?" I ask, wrinkling my nose.

"Ah, sure look it." He winks.

Whatever *that* means. My lips turn up into a smile.

I can do weird.

He beams back with those lovely Irish lips—a cute, slightly crooked bottom tooth peeking out between them. "She smiles," he says, shifting his body toward me. "Does she also have a name?"

I have to tilt my head back to look him in the eye. "I've understood approximately one-third of what you've said in the past five minutes."

"Probably for the best."

"Do women usually fall for the whole Irish schtick?"

"Always. But generally, we've had a drink before my Irish stick comes up."

"Ha ha," I say, grateful for the grenadine hiding the blush that blooms across my chest at the innuendo. God, I am so horny.

He reaches out his right hand. "Tommy Flynn. A pleasure to make your acquaintance, Mrs....?"

"Ms. Silva. Emmie Silva," I say, lying only a little bit as I take his hand in mine and give it a solid shake. In addition to an aversion to bad words, a powerful desire to do right, and a strict adherence to on-time arrivals, my stepdad also imparted the value of a good, strong handshake.

"Quite a grip you've got there, Ms. Silva. Careful showing that off around these parts." He looks out at the crowd and adjusts the collar on his habit. "Never know what kind of scoundrels are lurking in these places."

"As it happens, handling troublemakers is my particular gift."

"Is that so?" Tommy Flynn's gaze wanders over me again, a hint of mischief on his lightly freckled face.

I lean back in the seat, gesturing to myself. "Small but feisty."

Tommy's almost certainly shamrock-colored eyes sparkle. I bite my lip. Maybe I'm not so bad at this whole picking-up-strangers thing after all.

"Can I offer you a beverage?" he asks.

I smile. "One. Sure." Tommy already confessed that one drink is all the prelude he needs, and with a flight back home to catch in eighteen hours, if he is willing to break my dry spell, I don't intend to waste precious time flirting over beers. Plus, it's now past my bedtime, and I'm not sure how much longer I can stay awake.

"What are you having, then?" he asks, grinning faintly as he rests an arm on the bar.

"Corona, please." My alcohol preferences have remained relatively unchanged since college spring breaks. I'm not ashamed of my unsophisticated choice of drink, but I do feel better asking this Irish priest to purchase one rather than someone like the hotelier I was talking to earlier, which is how I ended up covered in a cherry-colored cocktail and not Corona.

Tommy nods. "Never tried one. I'll give it a lash as well."

The bartender brings over two cold Coronas with limes, and Tommy and I clink our bottles together. He holds my gaze as he brings the bottle to his lips. I cross my legs a little tighter.

"Not bad for what looks like a bottle of piss," he admits after his first swallow.

"This beer is delicious and tastes like sunshine on the beach," I correct.

"Fair enough, but Guinness tastes like last call with your rat-arsed best mates in the alley down the road from Copper Face Jack's the night of Paddy's Day, so far off your trolley you don't remember your own name. Can't beat that."

"You are a verifiable Yeats, Mr. Flynn."

"Sláinte, Ms. Silva," Tommy says through a grin, draining the rest of his beer. Despite the sweet crinkles in the corners of his eyes, there is something naughty glinting in his pretty green irises.

All of my blood rushes low into my belly.

Forgive me, Father, for I am about to sin so hard.

Tommy Flynn is hot, funny, and foreign, basically the trifecta of one-night stands, and when I finish my beer, I set the bottle down purposefully on the bar. Time to shoot my shot.

Pushing my long chestnut hair back from my face, I lean toward him. "What do you say we get out of here?" I ask, going so far as to point a thumb over my shoulder. "I've got a room at Caesars." And if we hurry, we can get there before Leila makes it back. The non-refundable Groupon booking saved us a lot of money, but the Julius Deluxe, double queen, non-smoking room I'm sharing with my best friend does not afford much in the way of privacy.

Tommy mulls over my invitation, chewing his cheek. I resist the urge to squirm as my mind shouts that I've made a terrible, embarrassing mistake. I probably should have made sure he was single before propositioning him. Or straight. Or interested in me, for that matter.

If this fails, I'm giving up. Every other guy I've talked to or danced with since arriving in Vegas has been a bro-y finance type or a sleaze. Tommy, though maybe a bit strange, managed to keep me laughing through an entire drink, and even though he is dressed like a priest and wearing a cassock, his shoulders are broad enough to make it troublingly sexy.

Nobody else will do now. I want this Irish clergyman or nothing at all.

Taking a deep breath, I sit up a little straighter. I can do this. Maybe if I explain my situation in all its pitiful detail, he'll be more willing to help. Not that I intend to coerce him into pleasuring me, but I don't want him to feel bad about it, either. I don't want him to think he's taking advantage.

"Well, mot," Tommy says, interrupting my near eruption into what would surely be a dumpster fire of a conversation, "we can't leave and have you traipsing around the Strip all undone."

He hooks an arm around the back of my stool. The breath goes out of me as he pulls it up against his, leaving mere inches between our bodies.

Oh, god. He smells terrific, even over the perfume of spilled liquor and sweat that permeates the bar. This close, I can see the golden flecks in his alarmingly hard-to-look-away-from eyes.

"What's a mot?" I ask in what I hope is an endearingly breathy voice.

"You are, you muppet." Tommy smiles as his hands find the open buttons of my shirt, and with deft, delicate fingers, he puts me back together. My chest heaves closer to his face with each inhale without my permission. He straightens my red satin tie and flattens it over my breasts with the palm of his hand.

I shiver and almost ram my mouth into his right then, but Tommy pushes his chair back and stands, offering a hand and a devastatingly charming lopsided grin. "Let's have a little walkabout first."

My hand slides into his, and I relish the way they fit together, the way his fingers hold mine in place. All big and broad and masculine. I imagine that hand pinning my wrists above my head and have to clear my throat before I answer.

"A walk sounds nice." After all, getting back to the hotel will require walking anyway, so I just have to make sure our stroll sends us in the right direction.

Using Tommy's arm for support, I hop off the barstool and onto the floor. The black pumps I primarily wear for fundraising events offer a bonus three inches of height. Still, I barely come up to Tommy's chest. His eyes widen. I roll mine.

"If you make a leprechaun joke," I say, glowering up at him, "I promise you will live to regret it."

Tommy's mouth twists. "Even if it's a really good one?"

"You've been warned."

He presses his lips together.

"Good boy. Now, how do we get out of here?"

Tommy squeezes my fingers, our hands still twined between us, and I feel it in every neglected recess of my body. My face must show as much because his ears turn pink before he pulls me after him and toward an exit only he can see over the mob of costumed partiers.

Once we're out of the bar, there are still a series of casino areas, lounges, banks of ticket redemption machines, and very fancy boutiques and jewelry stores to navigate before we reach the outside of the hotel. When we step into the night, Tommy stops walking and drops my hand.

"Much better," he says, followed by a deep inhale of brisk desert air.

I cross my arms against the chill breeze, unsure how to proceed. Do I give him a gentle nudge toward Caesars Palace? Or wrap my arm through his and pull him the full ten minutes to my room so he doesn't have a chance to question my commitment? I know where I want this night to go; I just have to get us there.

To our left, the Flamingo Road pedestrian overpass that leads to Caesars extends above the street. Tommy turns, facing the other way.

Apparently, my night isn't going *there* yet.

"So," Tommy says, smiling down at me. "I take it you're not from around these parts?"

Oh, no. Small talk and getting to know each other were not part of my plan of seduction. I should have gone straight for the kiss when I had the chance.

But he's cute, and if I'm being honest, I'm kind of curious about him too—this Irish fellow all alone in Vegas on Halloween—so I give enough of an answer to hopefully get some of my own in return. "Nope. Just here at the behest of my far-more-socially-adept colleague."

Who is currently watching her "it's not that serious" boyfriend's talk on architectural conservation in the Southwest dressed as a sexy ghost (though she claims her costume is Paranormal Distribution). Leila did tell me the hotel room is mine until midnight and that I best take advantage, but I don't think Tommy needs to hear the part about me coming to Vegas explicitly for the possibility of sex.

Tommy assents his head in the direction of the intersection in invitation. I follow as he sets a leisurely pace. He seems to be good at managing the circus that is Vegas, and it's probably in my best interest to let him take the helm, though I liked it better when he was holding my hand. We turn right onto Las Vegas Boulevard, taking the tree-lined path along the viewing area of the Bellagio Fountain—still heading away from Caesars.

"And what brought you to Vegas?" I ask as Tommy gazes up at the few stars shining through the haze of light and exhaust.

"Work meeting."

"Ah," I respond, hesitating to ask what kind of work. Mostly because I don't want Tommy to do the same. Luckily, he provides the information without prodding.

"I'm the guy the board goes to when..." He pauses, looking toward the fountain where brilliant white jets of water erupt like fireworks in the night. "When businesses aren't doing well. They bring me on for a year or two to cut extra weight, straighten out budgets, manage staffing issues."

"Sounds like a blast."

"Yeah. A whole bunch of people in this country probably have slightly ginger voodoo dolls tucked under their pillows."

I glance at Tommy's face, his tall body hidden under the cassock. Sure. The far more likely reality is that those people keep printouts of his LinkedIn profile shot in the drawers of their bedside tables for inspiration while they pleasure themselves. I find it hard, if not impossible, to believe someone like Tommy Flynn is capable of making people hate him.

"How long have you been in the States?" I ask, running my hand along the cold metal railing that lines the sidewalk.

"We moved to D.C. for my mum's job when I was sixteen. I was at university in Boston when they went back to Ireland, and after, I just...stayed."

Tommy's smile turns soft and maybe a little sad. I'm tempted to ask him if he misses his family, his home. But perhaps that is too personal for a random hookup. I'm not sure what the proper etiquette is for prying into the private life of your one-night stand.

A group of college-aged boys overtakes us on the path. They make a show of checking me out as they walk by. One of them grabs his crotch.

"I've been a real bad boy, miss. Wanna come back to my room and teach me a lesson?"

His friends cheer. I sigh. Tommy catches my gaze, arching an eyebrow—a question, an offer. I shake my head. I've fought plenty of these battles before. I'm basically the modern-day Menelaus of shutting down inappropriate come-ons.

Pushing my lips into a pout, I give the kid a little tut-tut. "The men I sleep with don't need lessons, honey." I lean into Tommy and pop my hip, shaking my hair over my shoulder. Tommy's hand slides around my waist. "But if you're having trouble finding *it*"—I wiggle my pinky finger—"I'd start with an anatomy book."

He throws a "fuck you" over his shoulder as he stalks off with his guffawing friends.

"I pray you find Jesus, son!" Tommy shouts before turning to me, his big hand still resting on my hip, warm and firm. "Impressive work."

"I've had some practice."

"What's with the costume, anyway?"

I am willing to share some details of my life with my new favorite attractive stranger, but I shudder to share this one. "I had it lying around," I answer honestly. "What about you, Father Flynn?"

He winks. "Same."

My brows draw together. "You don't mean you're actually—"

"No." Tommy chuckles. "God, no."

A shiver of relief runs down my spine. Or maybe it has more to do with the way his fingers have splayed above my bottom.

"Are you cold?" he asks.

"What are you going to do if I am? Offer me your cassock?"

He bends slightly to whisper in my ear, his warm breath a caress against my neck. "If I took this off out here, I'd be arrested."

"Nothing underneath?"

"Completely bare," he admits.

I grin at him. I won't judge myself for being turned on by a free-balling man in a dress. Not when he is sweet and has such a great face, and not when I'm in such desperate need of relief. The only problem is, we've somehow walked the entire edge of the fountain and are now standing at the Bellagio's main entrance.

"Well," I say, disappointed. "This is not Caesars Palace."

Tommy stares up at the hotel. "True indeed," he affirms. I shift my feet, and Tommy brings his free hand to my face, brushing my hair back behind my ear. "However, this *is* where I'm staying."

I cross my arms, hoping the move comes off as flirty and not like I'm pissed that Tommy just wasted fifteen minutes of my time not making love to me. "Why didn't you say so earlier?"

"Ms. Silva, the first question you asked me was about my childhood pets. For all I knew, you were some tiny, beautiful, copper-eyed siren come to rob me of my identity."

Tommy Flynn gives wonderful compliments, though I'm not sure he intended this as one. "And the walk?" I press.

"If you had asked for the last four digits of my social security number, I'd have run away screaming."

I step closer to him. Rising onto my toes, I rest a hand on his chest and tilt my head back. Tommy gazes down at me, his lips opening just barely.

"I'm not interested in your bank accounts," I say, grasping the front of his cassock.

Tommy drags his bottom lip between his teeth. "I know," he breathes against my mouth. "You're just after me lucky charms."

Two

"Your hotel room has a foyer," I say with more than a hint of incredulity as Tommy swings the door open. His fingers press into the small of my back as he steps into the room behind me. My skin tingles beneath them.

"And a guest bathroom ahead on the right if you need to hit the jacks." He reaches his arm over my shoulder to point the way, his chest a warm, inviting wall of man behind me. This is more physical contact than I've experienced in months. He smells so good, all close and musky and masculine. I want to bury my face in the sleeve of his cassock and get a good, solid whiff.

But that would be crazy, right? I swallow. *Cool your jets, Em,* and make the mature decision to step away and not sniff the stranger. Yet. "Easy there, high roller. Two bathrooms?"

"Plus, they tell me the carpet is organic," Tommy adds with a wink as he sets his wallet and room key on a gilded credenza near the door.

"Be still, my environmentally-conscious heart," I tease, resting my hands over my actually fluttering heart—though I'm confident my racing pulse has very little to do with the carpet.

A sudden rush of nerves threatens to launch me back into the elevator. Now that I've gotten this far, I'm not entirely sure what comes next. Should I just tear my clothes off and get straight to the point? My skin is hot with anticipation, but he doesn't seem to be in as big a hurry to get naked as I am.

"Can I offer you anything?" he asks as we pass through to the bar.

"Water, please," I answer, pulling my phone out to text Leila as I round the large L-shaped couch. I linger by the floor-to-ceiling window. In the glass, I can see Tommy behind the bar, his hand ranging through his auburn hair. Even his reflection is handsome.

I take a deep breath to fortify my composure, resting my fingers on the cool glass beside the echo of Tommy, a blur of man against the view outside, and turn my gaze to the Strip stretched out below. Constellations of city lights blink up at me, and from up here, the city is almost beautiful—a nebula of pulsing neon, colorful blazes ranging out into the darkness.

Away from the chaos and the exhaust, Vegas is kind of...romantic.

When I turn back to Tommy, everything but the top of his head is hidden behind the bar. "This room is really—"

"Absurd?" Tommy suggests, peeking up at me from where he crouches in front of the fridge. "Offensive to the very fabric of humanity and the concept of worldly justice?"

I shrug. "Yeah. But also, totally amazing."

Tommy reappears with a glass bottle of sparkling water in hand. "I hope you're okay with bubbles. The only other option is a very expensive half-liter of virgin melted iceberg from Greenland."

"In that case, bubbles are great."

Tommy fills two glasses and comes to stand beside me at the window.

"You must be saving some pretty important businesses to end up here." I take a sip of water, glad to have the cold fill my belly. I need something to counteract the stubborn, desperate heat that is settling there the longer Tommy stands in front of me with that adorable sideways grin on his face and those sparkling Emerald Isle eyes.

"I'm really good at my job," he says, somehow managing to make his assertion not at all cocky. His words sound true, and I suspect they are if he is sleeping in a thousand-plus-dollar-a-night suite at the Bellagio.

Tommy smiles and wanders into the bedroom, returning with something black hanging from his hand. I watch as he settles himself on the velvet couch, his long legs stretched out in front of him under the cassock. So much concealed beneath the fabric.

He laughs, low and deep, and I realize I've been staring indelicately at his lap. He pats the spot beside him on the couch. My breathing quickens as I walk in front of him, sliding my heels off before sitting down, one leg tucked beneath me, skirt pulling tight against my thighs.

Tommy's gaze sweeps over my body, and I do my best to stay still. "You're a lovely little thing, Emmie Silva," he says, green irises flashing as he leans forward. But instead of crushing his weight on top of me like I'm desperately hoping he will, he reaches down for my foot and draws it across his thigh, slipping an impossibly soft black sock over my toes.

"Cashmere?" I ask. The only cashmere I own belonged to my mother before she died and now lives in the freezer where the moths can't continue using it as a mating ground.

Tommy nods, wrapping his hands around my foot.

He can't know that the one and only reason I would consider involving myself in a serious relationship is the possible promise of regular, free foot rubs.

I spend so much of my life standing. During lunch, during meetings, and even at my desk, mostly because I look exceptionally tiny in chairs. I don't rest, and I don't often allow myself the luxury of just sitting.

My arches crumbled long ago. My heels splintered. Tommy presses his fingers into all the right places, kneading and coaxing. I might not get sex tonight, but I will still leave mostly satisfied.

My body sinks into the cushions as he works between my tired toes.

"Do you like your job?" I ask to keep my mouth from asking something stupid like if he would be interested in moving in with me and Leila.

His brow furrows. "I don't dislike my work. But I do wish I could do something more. Something good. Is it ridiculous if I were to tell you I'd like to make a difference in the world?"

"Not ridiculous," I reply, my breath hitching at the end as he massages along my ankle. "I want the same thing."

"I just accepted a new position." He glances at my outfit then meets my eyes, looking sheepish. "I think maybe it will be an opportunity to help people, create real change." His hand pauses before he brushes his knuckles up my calf and along the inside of my knee.

"That's nice," I manage to eke out before my head drops back and my eyelids flutter closed. My moan falls between us, loud, raw, and hungry. My eyes fly open, and Tommy chuckles, releasing my foot and gesturing for the other.

He watches as I adjust myself to release said foot from under my body, his teeth running over his full bottom lip as I tug the hem of my skirt down when it rides up. Our eyes lock, and I pop my foot into his lap.

Only to discover the big surprise he's been hiding under his cassock.

"Oh," I murmur, my voice unrecognizably husky. If foot rubs count as Irish foreplay, I've been living in the wrong country.

Tommy's eyes dip to my mouth and trace a line down to the very tips of my toes. Slowly, he rolls the second cashmere sock over my foot. He smooths his strong hands along the bottom of my sole, then up my leg.

"Would you like me to continue, Ms. Silva?" he asks, his fingers pressing into the skin just above my knees.

"Please," I respond—*beg*?—my voice a reflection of the thrill firing through my nervous system.

Tommy's hands slide up the side of my legs and to my hips. He yanks gently at the waist of my skirt, and I fall back onto the pillows, laid out over the velvet cushions.

"Comfortable?"

"Very," I breathe.

Tommy works my skirt over my hips and down my legs. I let my knees fall open as he crouches between them, the bright green of his eyes giving way to the blackness of his pupils. He leans over me, and I feel him hard against my hip as his tongue runs a cool line up the column of my neck. I push against him when he hovers his mouth over mine, and he pulls back, smirking as he unbuttons my top.

I tug at the fabric of the cassock as Tommy kisses his way along the tops of my breasts, the fingers of his left hand dipping into the grenadine-stained cup of my bra. My legs wrap around his waist when he gently rolls my nipple before readjusting and flicking his tongue over the sensitive pink tip.

"Holy smokes," I gasp out, my body quaking with a year of pent-up sexual energy.

Tommy raises his face above mine, smiling, then rakes his gaze over my bare skin. "Holy smokes, indeed. You're bleedin' massive."

What the frick?

I shove Tommy off and crawl onto my knees, crossing my arms and giving him what I know is a very powerful glare. "I'm *what?*"

He reaches out, his hands encircling my hips, and hauls me directly onto his lap so I'm straddling his thighs. I feel him through the fabric of the cassock, hard and wanting, and can't help but arch against him, my desire exceeding my need for justice. Or even explanation.

I can be massive tonight.

Tommy grits his teeth, pulling me harder against him, his thumbs digging into the skin on the inside of my thighs. "It means," he grits out as I rock myself into him again, a soft cry escaping my mouth, "really fucking sexy."

I grab hold of his strong shoulders. "Thank god," I say, slanting my mouth against his.

His lips part for me, and before I know it, we are an urgent tangle of tongues and teeth. I am panting into his mouth as I dry hump him like I'm a teenager with a purity ring, dragging the fabric of the cassock between us and against the lace panties covering my aching clit. Then, Tommy's mouth drops to my collarbone, his arms winding around my back to hold me tighter, our bodies grinding eagerly together.

My eyes close, and the next thing I know, light bursts behind my lids, and I am entirely breathless and coming apart on a man dressed as a priest. I cry out, and Tommy takes my mouth with his, his hips bucking against me as I ride out my release.

I whimper as he slows, drawing out my pleasure, and then melt into him when I can't take anymore, burying my face in my hands. "Sorry," I mumble.

"Emmie," Tommy says, prying my fingers away. "What's wrong?"

"I just…" I gesture to our laps. "On your dress thing."

"I almost just…*in* my dress thing."

I snort, but he's still hard beneath me. I lean forward and kiss him, and when our tongues meet, another wave of want rages through me.

"How do you get this off?" I ask into his mouth as my hands search his cassock for buttons or a zipper or anything that will provide access to Tommy's naked body.

His eyes are near-black when they meet mine, and he grabs the neck of the cassock and tears it down the middle. I push the fabric off his shoulders and stare at him, sucking in a breath as I trace a finger along the deep creases on his chest and stomach.

"Oh, dear, Tommy. How does this happen to a human body?" I ask, trying to fit my hands around his bicep.

"Crew," he answers.

I nod. "Massive," I say, before running my tongue over the stretch of warm skin and up to his lips.

He grins against my mouth, his hands gripping my bottom as he stands, my legs wrapping around his waist. He carries me to the bedroom, falling on top of me on the king bed, and our kiss is so delicious and so perfect that I think I must have won the one-night stand lottery. He pushes me further onto the mattress, and his lips trace the oversensitive skin behind my ear.

"Tommy?" I rasp between kisses.

"Yes?" he murmurs, his faint hint of a five o'clock shadow tickling my jaw before he looks at me.

I guide my hand between our bodies, taking his fingers and pressing them into the damp fabric of my panties. I bring my mouth to his ear. "Tonight," I say, arching as his palm presses against me, eliciting a whimper, "my pot of gold is all yours."

He leans his head back and finds my eyes. "Glory be, a leipreacháin álainn," he whispers, taking my mouth with his before I can ask him what he said. He kisses me languidly, savoring my mouth as he pushes the fabric of my panties to the side. He grazes the slickness there with his fingers, and his body tenses. "You're so fucking wet," he growls, and his jaw pulses when I buck against his hand.

He teases the hungry spot between my legs, and I squirm, shuddering as a torrent of need, heady and wild, tumbles through my system. When he slips his fingers into me, my entire body clenches around the sensation. I moan, digging my fingers into his back.

"Jesus Christ, Emmie," he huffs, working his fingers as I writhe against his hand for more. "I don't think one night is going to be enough for me."

I SMILE, SIGHING INTO the pillow. Tommy's chest is curled around my back, one of his arms slung over my waist. His fingers trace circles on my bare skin.

I did it. I got laid. And not just once.

I've officially had my first successful one-night stand. With zero—I squeeze my eyes shut, ignoring the deep hum Tommy makes against my ear as I shift in his arms. With zero emotional attachment. And so many orgasms.

I do have to wonder how a stranger could know the exact path his tongue should take up my belly to make my body arch without tickling, the perfect pressure to ease my need just enough to make me ache for more.

Maybe that is the joy of having lots of sex with someone you don't know and never have to see again, the excitement of having your sexual standards subverted by a tall, handsome Irishman.

It is probably totally normal to cuddle your random hookup, wrapped up in each other's arms, waiting to watch dawn break over fake Paris and a half-scale replica of the Eiffel Tower. Normal for it to feel like the man you haphazardly picked up understands you better than most of your childhood friends.

The moments in between our lovemaking—no, our *banging*; it was just meaningless sex—were laced with quiet conversations and laughs. Surely, it isn't out of the ordinary to discover a seemingly endless list of shared passions and interests after cunnilingus and multiple orgasms. I mean, it can't be that strange that we both enjoy octopus documentaries and collect different translations of *The Odyssey* that we read while eating Nilla Wafers with Nutella.

Right?

I tilt my face, looking up into Tommy's.

His eyes are soft hills I want to roll down. The crinkles at the corners sweeter than most smiles. Why is he staring at me like that? Like he sees me so clearly. His lips curve in a smile as we gaze adoringly into each other's faces.

Oh, *sugar.* I'm suffering from some sort of oxytocin-fueled post-coital high.

I turn my head away and frown.

"What are you thinking about?" Tommy asks, brushing a strand of my hair from the side of my face.

What am I thinking about? Definitely *not* the fact that my relationships with men are still stilted by the fact that my gaping anus of a father left me and my mother when I was six. That the person who replaced him is the best human being ever to walk the earth.

No one I have ever dated could even come close to comparing to George Silva, the man who fell in love with my mother and took on me and all of our baggage—not to mention all of the difficulties that followed—with so much grace and goodness that I sometimes still wonder if he is real.

I absolutely am not thinking about my nagging wish to fall in love and my tragic inability to do so. Not in a hotel room in Vegas with someone I met hours ago on a barstool.

"Emmie?" he asks, pressing a kiss to my cheek.

"Everything bagel!" I blurt out. "Garlic cream cheese. Lox. Pickled onions." *There*. That should send the troublesome hint of romance bubbling between us to a shallow grave.

Tommy rises on his elbows, bracing himself above me. I slide onto my back to face him. His brow wrinkles. "You're hungry?" he asks, his voice filled with so much concern that I question if I've been wrong my whole life and eating smelly bagels isn't one of the reasons I am perpetually single. "I can order you something."

"The only thing I'm hungry for is this," I respond, wrapping my arms around his back and digging my nails into the flexed muscles of his shoulders. I pull him down over me, tugging his bottom lip between my teeth like some sort of professional seductress.

I am here for sex, after all, not to fill the enormous void in my heart where love is meant to go. No, I can shove other things in there to lessen the expansive emptiness. Work, tacos, stopping people walking their dogs on the street so I can cuddle the pups and tell them I love them, time with Leila, and visits with George at the care home. That is enough. I can survive with a half-empty heart; I always have.

Better that than broken.

Tommy breaks the kiss, nuzzling into my neck with a groan and then sitting up. He checks the fancy watch he tossed onto the bedside table last night and grins. "Half an hour until sunrise," he says, pulling the covers over my shoulders.

I watch as Tommy stands from the bed, the shape of his naked body highlighted by the soft orange glow of Strip lights that blanket the city and flood through the open windows.

"Stay here," he whispers into my hair before leaving me alone in the room.

I stretch out in the warm spot Tommy left behind on the silky sheets and close my eyes.

When I open them again, the sun has risen, and I am still alone in bed. My palms are sweaty, the last bits of a bad dream dissipating as I blink the images away. I roll over to check the time. He's been gone for an hour and a half.

"Tommy," I call, rolling out of the softest bed sheets I've ever slept in, covering myself with a pillow as I wander to the door. I'm not nearly as convinced that the giant windows lining the walls are made of one-way glass as I was last night. Then again, last night I didn't really care.

I peek out into the suite.

Empty.

My heart thumps uncomfortably inside my chest. Tommy hasn't come back.

My skirt and shirt are folded on an armchair in the bedroom, my bra resting over the back, shoes side by side beneath. I get dressed, ignoring the heaviness of the dark cloud building over me, the familiar sadness that has trailed me since childhood.

My underwear is conspicuously missing, and my shirt is still damp from trying to wash the stain out. I look myself over in the full-length mirror and wince. My outfit is decidedly embarrassing, even for a Las Vegas walk of shame. I snag Tommy's Boston College Crew sweatshirt off the dresser to throw over my ensemble.

I'll have it returned to the hotel. The last thing I need around is a reminder of how I'm so hungry for intimacy that I let myself imagine, just for a little bit, a life of foot rubs and Irish-accented sweet nothings.

Poor Tommy. He was too kind to kick me out, so he was forced to escape instead.

I check the suite anyway, for a note, a number, anything, just in case I'm wrong. After scouring the bathrooms and counters and the credenza by the door, I laugh at myself, at the suggestion of something *more* I'd thought I'd sensed between us, my eyes stinging just a little. I was so desperate for connection that I invented affection where there was none. Nope, it isn't the bagels that render me lonely. It is my complete and total lack of emotional literacy.

I make the bed and put my water glass in the sink before leaving, my throat tight as I shut the door of the suite behind me.

The only part of the encounter I plan to hold on to is the way he made me come. It will be handy to remember the feel of his body on mine as I face the next year of involuntary celibacy with nothing but my vibrator.

Three

January

THE FIRST OFFICIAL DAY back to school after winter break is, historically, my least favorite of the entire academic year. The kids are coming down from unlimited, unmitigated screen usage—social media, sociopathic video games, porn (probably). They likely have consumed no actual food for the past two weeks, despite the care packages the faculty had prepared from Desert Grace's Family Pantry and sent home with them. Most survived the holidays on a strict diet of Spicy Takis and caffeinated soft drinks. I know because their fingers are stained red, and their behavior is aggressively obnoxious.

I observe the students filtering into the small auditorium that doubles as the school's chapel. They are loud, occasionally inappropriate, and sometimes so stereotypically moody that it's hard not to laugh in their faces. But they are also curious, sweet, and full of hope and promise. I love each of the ninety-eight teenagers who attend Desert Grace High School with every fiber of my being.

I clutch my school ID badge, the lanyard it hangs from digging into my neck as the three pens dangling on the attached key ring splay against my chest like armor. My nostrils flare.

If the new head of school does *anything* to make things even remotely worse for them, I will give him hell.

Mr. O'Connor, the recently hired interim head of school, failed to return to campus when the rest of the faculty did a week ago to prep for the students. The board said he'd been attending to family business. Based on everything else they'd told the teachers about him and his

MBA from Harvard, I assumed that probably meant he was skiing with his very blonde wife and two private-school-educated children in Aspen and couldn't be bothered to show up.

Leila grips my arm, pulling me toward the rows of plastic seats. "You're scowling."

"I just know this guy is going to be a giant wiener, and I hate him already," I mutter under my breath so the kids elbowing their way past won't hear, before a much, much louder, "Tuck your shirts in, scholars!"

They groan, and I step in front of one of our seniors who towers over me. "All the way, Amari."

"Ems," Leila says, gesturing to the swell of adolescents in navy-blue uniforms. "Mr. O'Connor probably won't even make it through the end of the year with these assholes." She doesn't have the same hang-ups about swearing in front of (or in reference to) the kids that I do, probably because Leila didn't grow up with George Silva.

I cross my arms. "Do you think I can ask Chaplain Peters to include that in our prayers at afternoon worship?"

"Come on," Leila says, assessing the room like she's preparing for battle. "You take the right wing, I'll take the left. Mr. Duarte looks like he's already reconsidering his decision to show up today, and we can't lose another science teacher."

"I'm on it," I say before drifting down the aisle. As I pass, I give Mr. Duarte a pat on his shoulder and a sympathetic smile. When you're in charge of instructing over eight dozen students, some of whom have been kicked out of every other school in town, camaraderie is a pivotal aspect of survival—and teacher retention.

I slip into an empty seat, and all the conversations around me turn to whispers. The kids are adequately intimidated by my presence.

The silver-haired board president, Mr. Edmonds, comes out onto the makeshift stage, wearing a suit that costs more than some of these kids' parents make in a year. I resist the urge to give him the middle finger.

The only requirement for our students to attend Desert Grace is eligibility for the Department of Education's free lunch program. If you qualify for free lunch, your family is hovering at, or below, the state's poverty threshold.

You'd expect that after years as board president, Mr. Edmonds would be slightly more self-aware, or thoughtful, or just generally not awful. But he's not. Which is why I give myself permission to dislike him without feeling bad about it.

He checks his shiny gold watch before he taps the microphone, clearing his throat. The kids do not give a single hoot about who he is or why he is here. In fact, his call for attention causes the overall volume in the hall to increase. One of my juniors yells, "Penis!" And the chorus quickly spreads.

After a full minute of false starts at the microphone, Mr. Edmonds starts to look like a panicked President Snow, the districts revolting around him.

I stand up. "Zip it, all of you, or Ms. Bashar and I are taking over study hall this week, and you better believe you'll regret it."

A collective moan echoes across the hall. When Leila and I are in charge of study hall together, these kids study so hard. No phone time, no flirting. They hate it.

"And Marco," I add, swinging my focus to the back row, "if you so much as utter the word 'penis' again for the rest of the semester, I'll hack into your TikTok account and post a photo of your graded first trimester Latin final."

This is an empty threat. I don't have the slightest clue how TikTok works, and I don't intend to find out, but Marco smiles guiltily. "Yes, Ms. Jones."

I clap my hands together, the crowd quiet and under control. "Good. Now back to you, Mr. Edmonds."

"Yes, well, thank you, Ms. Jones. Is that right?"

I keep my back straight and nod. I've been teaching at Desert Grace for six years, which is four years longer than he's been involved with the school. I know every inch of the campus. I know which students come to school hungry in the mornings and which ones have nowhere to go in the evenings when they leave. I have given these kids the literal clothes off my back.

But the board only cares about numbers. And I'm just a history teacher with a penchant for demanding more than the higher-ups care to offer, which I assume is the reason Mr. Edmonds could never be bothered to learn my name.

I see Leila glance at me from the other side of the room. "What a fuckface," my best friend mouths. I groan in agreement.

"Today," Mr. Edmonds goes on, "I would like to introduce you to someone very special. He will fill the position Mrs. Torrez left and help us steer our school into the future." My gut does something funny. I do not like the sound of that. The threat of change. "Please welcome Mr. O'Connor, your new head of school."

Mrs. Torrez, our previous head of school, announced her retirement in October, and after the news broke that she was leaving, our principal followed suit. Since our school basically operates as a school *and* an independent school system in one, we need both. A head of school to oversee the board, policy, and finances, and a principal to work directly with the teachers and students and manage student affairs.

The position of principal has yet to be filled, but Mr. O'Connor will likely be the one to make it happen.

My new least favorite person rises from a chair in the front of the room with his back to the audience, trailed by paltry applause as he strides onto the stage. He, at least, had the wherewithal to dress like he didn't just leave his Mercedes with the valet. A crisp white button-up, khakis that fit well but aren't tailored. He has the sort of casually put-together air of the other teachers, just less frazzled—for now.

I know the school needs help. The budgets were demolished when we had to buy tablets for the students during a facility closure, and the maintenance of the old building, in general, is a constant weight on resources. Most of our funding comes from private donors, but when the new, shiny Episcopal school opened on the other side of town, we watched a lot of that money disappear. At some point, people want to see a return on their giving. They want to see that their money is making a difference.

Apparently, keeping the kids out of juvenile detention and off the streets isn't good enough.

I turn my attention back to the lectern, and my insides twist.

The man standing behind it stares right back at me, his mouth caught open in surprise. My heartbeat ratchets up so hard and fast that my whole body vibrates. I wrap my hands around the edge of my chair.

He shakes his head, auburn hair falling over his brow, and tears his gaze away, looking out over the sea of students. He introduces himself in a charming Irish accent that makes my blood run hot. Or cold. I can't decide.

But I know it is a bad thing. Just like I know the twitch I feel behind my ribs and below my belly at the sight of Tommy Flynn—the guy who told me in Vegas that his job is to cut extra weight and straighten out staffing issues—standing in *my* school auditorium is not related to desire. Except for the pressing one I have to get him alone in his office so I can find out what the actual heck is going on.

I DON'T MAKE IT to the head of school's office until after the last bell, and when I'm finally there, I freeze, my back pressed against the door across the hall—the empty principal's office—as an infuriating blast of heat and indignation makes my legs shake.

I recite the Desert Grace motto in my head: "Per ardua ad astra." *Through adversity to the stars.*

This is my turf, my world that I've worked so hard to build. I push my hair behind my ears and stand up straighter. I won't let Tommy—a not-at-all-consequential one-night stand—make me feel insecure in *my* space.

The door to his office is slightly ajar, and I rap my knuckles twice, hard and fast, on the cracking wood.

"Come in," he calls with his deceptively sweet Irish lilt. Angry hairs rise along my arms.

I push the door open and step inside.

Tommy has his head bent over a stack of papers. His hair has grown out since Halloween and falls over his forehead. I hate that I know how it smells (warm and musky with a hint of spice) and how it feels (soft and thick enough to lose yourself in). I blink and take another step forward, shutting the door behind me.

When I clear my throat, Tommy's head snaps up. Good. I've gotten his attention. But now that it has landed fully on me, I'm not sure what to do with it. *Melt*?

No. Wrong answer.

"*Thomas O'Connor?*" I whisper-hiss, narrowing my eyes as I sit in one of the chairs in front of Tommy's desk.

"Hello, Ms..." His eyebrows rise as he pretends to flip through the employee directory. "*Emeline Jones.* I was wondering if you'd be by."

"It's still Emmie," I say, crossing my arms.

"In that case, it's still Tommy. And look." He pulls out one of his new business cards. I have *never* gotten business cards. "Thomas F. O'Connor. Flynn is my middle name. So, it wasn't really a lie."

I grab the card and make a show of crumpling it in my hand before shoving the wrinkled paper into my dress pocket. "Well, Silva is my stepdad's last name, and George Silva basically raised me. So I guess I didn't lie either," I retort, sounding especially adolescent. I glare at him harder.

Tommy's mouth quirks up, all lopsided and cute.

Oh my God. Why am I telling him these things? And why are we arguing like high school freshmen? I used him for sex. Tommy left me in a hotel room. Now, he is my boss, and the only thing I need to worry about is making sure my kids are taken care of.

I take a deep breath and sink back in the seat. "I just came by to say that if you need any assistance getting settled into your new position, I would be happy to help. Show you around, make introductions."

Tommy's eyes sparkle at my proposition with something verging on hope.

I drop my gaze. *Don't be silly, Emmie.* Those sparkles only ever existed in my imagination. People whose eyes sparkle at you don't proceed to abandon you in glitzy Las Vegas suites after a night of—

"Thank you, Ms. Jones. Some family stuff came up over the break, and I haven't been able to familiarize myself as much as I'd have liked to with the school. Or the town." He bites his stupidly full bottom lip and shrugs. "I might have to take you up on that offer."

I raise a hand between us. "The school, I can help with. The rest, you're on your own." There is no way I am playing tour guide for Tommy Flynn.

O'Connor.

Whoever the *hedge* he is.

"Of course." His smile seems a little sad. But what do I know? I only managed to get in one cup of coffee today, and I'm not capable of understanding men on my best of days. His green eyes settle on my face. "I'd appreciate that. Truly."

"Right then." I lurch to my feet, knocking the chair sideways. I scramble to grab it before it teeters over, take a breath, and decide it's probably best I stay seated. "For starters, ignore anything Mr. Edmonds told you. He knows nothing about this place. I'll run you through the classrooms tomorrow. Then we can talk about the staff. They are good—amazing, actually—but they are tired. Last, I'll introduce you to the students. One on one. They need to trust you. You have to make them feel safe." My voice trembles. I've gone from taking charge to pleading in the course of seconds. But for the kids, I would get down on my knees in front of him. I'd...

I press my palms into my eyes.

"Are you okay, Ms. Jones?"

I clear my throat. "I'm fine."

"Good."

I peek at Tommy through my fingers. Is he smirking?

"Good?" I ask, dropping my hands. "*Good* as in *we're done here?*"

Tommy's rolled sleeves tighten at the top of his forearms as he folds his hands on the desk. "Almost. Before you go, there's something I'd like to ask you about."

I tense. "What?"

"The St. Patrick's Day Talent Show Fundraiser used to be organized by Mrs. Torrez, correct?"

"Yes," I answer slowly, watching as he picks up a pen and starts rolling it between his fingers.

He leans back in his chair. "Would you, perhaps, be interested in taking over?"

The St. Patrick's Day Talent Show Fundraiser is one of the biggest public fundraisers the school hosts all year and provides nearly the entire budget for our arts programs.

"Take over?" I repeat, shaking my head. "No way." I take on a lot for the school. Have already taken on so much, in fact, that there is no way I could find the time to head the talent show.

"Would you consider helping me, at least? Lead me in the right direction?" He taps a stack of folders with the pen he's holding. "We're just about three months out, and there is nothing lined up. I'd hate to see the school miss out on all that money because I'm an incompetent organizer of talent shows."

Maybe if he is incapable of organizing talent shows, he shouldn't have accepted the job. "Why me? Can't you find somebody else?"

Tommy rises from his chair and walks around his desk, coming to stand in front of me, so I have to look up, way up, at him. "Because if you don't, I'll tell the board you're a thief."

I scoff. "Excuse me?"

"I know you stole my sweatshirt in Vegas, Emmie."

Dang it. I did. And I've worn it way too often since. I am a horny, sweatshirt-stealing bandit. Which doesn't reconcile well with my no-nonsense-but-wholesome high school teacher persona. But even though I'd been dressed like a slutty teacher in Vegas, the new acting principal of my parochial school got a boner for me while wearing a cassock. In my book, that means we are equally depraved.

"Don't worry," he assures, a mischievous twinkle in his eyes. "I kept a little souvenir myself."

My mouth falls open. He didn't!

"Though I must say, these lace knickers are far less comfortable than my college crew shirt." His eyes hold mine as he adjusts his waistband, shining so bright and green my insides flip-flop.

I clench my hands at my sides. Tommy reaches for one and chuckles.

"The little lady's hands make little fists," he observes in his teasing accent, holding my hand between us.

I stand and push him in the chest before I realize what I'm doing, my palm growing hot where it presses against Tommy's shirt. His hand tightens around my wrist, his thumb grazing my pulse. I am outraged, and almost definitely *not* turned on.

I step closer so we are just inches apart. "I should have stolen your fancy socks, too."

Tommy drops my hand and bends at the waist, his breath trailing my neck as he bows down to lift his pant leg. "You mean," he says, gazing up at me, his face so close to the hem of my dress that I squeeze my legs together as I feel a flush creep up my chest, my neck, my cheeks, "these socks?"

"Uh-huh," I murmur, my toes curling at the memory of the soft fabric. At the thought of his big hands on my feet. I catch my lip between my teeth. *Pull yourself together, Emmie.*

He stands, setting my skin on fire as he brushes by me to open the door. "I look forward to tomorrow," Tommy says, gesturing to the hall, not afraid to kick me out of his space this time around.

I fumble past him with uneven breaths, happy to oblige.

Four

I'M SO OVERWHELMED BY the idea of stopping and getting gas that it feels easier to take the streetcar home and leave my mechanically neglected Prius in the parking garage. Maybe I'll get lucky, and someone will steal it. I lean my head against the window, turning my conversation with Tommy over in my mind the entire ride.

I can't believe he blackmailed me into helping with the talent show. And did he really keep my lacy panties?

Enraged warmth sinks low into my belly as I remember Tommy dragging them down my legs and tossing them behind him. I imagine him finding them in the hotel room the next morning and packing them in his luggage, maybe wrapped in his torn and tainted cassock.

Did he wash them? Where does he keep them?

And why, *why*, would the man who ditched me in his suite keep my underwear like some sort of prize?

"Weirdo," I huff under my breath, biting my bottom lip hard between my teeth.

In a fair and equal world, I'd be able to blackmail Tommy right back. Demand he spring for the all-natural juice boxes in the cafeteria and update the computers in the tech lab if he doesn't want me telling the board about him playing pervy priest on Halloween. But things don't work that way, and someone as haughty and privileged as Mr. O'Connor clearly knows that.

Another reason for me to hate Vegas: dishonest advertising. What happens there doesn't stay there. In fact, it shows up at your work looking unwelcomely attractive and making wisecracks about your undergarments.

I get off at my stop, hesitating to cross the street. Somehow, I managed to go the entire school day without telling Leila that Mr. Thomas O'Connor is *the same* Tommy that masterfully wrecked my vagina in Vegas. But I will have to come clean sooner rather than later. Leila is bound to put two and two together eventually.

I'm not looking forward to the conversation for a host of reasons. I know my best friend well, and she will have many thoughts about distressing things like *feelings*. She will ask me absurd questions like, "Are you okay?"

Which, lo and behind, is the very first thing that pops out of Leila's mouth when I get home and confess to the unfortunate reality that I had a one-night stand in Las Vegas with our new head of school.

I sigh and lean over the edge of the balcony, gazing at the red solo cup-littered lawn of the frat house next door. Nearly nine years ago, before our second year of college, Leila's dad bought this condo on University Boulevard, where Leila and I have lived ever since with her discerning and occasionally vengeful Manx cat, Fib. We are by far the oldest people in the building, and I am not proud of the number of times I've called the cops on our undergraduate neighbors, but the rent is right, and the building is close to Desert Grace.

More and more often, I come home to find Leila's long-term, sweet, supportive architect boyfriend, Benji Green, in the condo too. Benji is great, but I sigh in relief every time I open the door and he's not here.

Because, deep down, I am a selfish, horrible friend. Unlike Leila, who right now looks like she's both about to burst into tears and put Tommy in the hospital.

"Of course I'm okay," I say in my most okay voice, even going so far as to roll my eyes to prove the question is truly exasperating. "I'm great. Vegas meant nothing."

And seeing Tommy again hadn't been *all* horrible. Outside of the part about my missing knickers, our meeting went kind of well, I think, courteous and to-the-point.

I scrunch my eyes closed, hearing Tommy's voice, low and very Irish, in my mind.

You mean, these socks?

Okay, *overall* courteous and to the point, if maybe not entirely professional.

"Tommy's interest in getting to know the school and the kids seemed genuine," I go on, my knuckles tight on the balcony railing. "Which is the only thing that matters in this whole mess. The only thing that matters to me. Really."

Unconvinced, Leila hums into her wineglass.

I whirl toward my friend, pointing a finger at her. "I. Am. Fine. Don't you even insinuate otherwise."

Leila shrugs, mumbling something about a Boston College sweatshirt under her breath.

Clearly, taking the sweatshirt was my grossest mistake in this whole debacle. One, however, that I can now remedy. My eyebrows cock up. "I'm giving that back," I announce. "It's not like I've had a chance since Vegas."

Leila frowns. "You haven't taken the damn sweatshirt *off* since Vegas."

"It's so soft." I pout. The sweatshirt is by far the coziest item of clothing in my possession, even if it technically is not mine. This fact alone should reassure all involved parties that my attachment to the old piece of clothing is purely a question of human comfort.

"Keep the sweatshirt," Leila says, filling my glass with cheap red wine from Trader Joe's before bringing it to me at the railing. "But be honest. Are you sure you feel all right about the fact that the man who deserted you in a hotel room after fucking your brains out is now your boss?"

"My interim boss," I correct. "And yes."

"Em, he's in charge of the thing you love most in the world. A guy who jilted you, my best, most awesome friend, is responsible for overseeing everything you care about. And that doesn't bother you?"

I take my glass from Leila's fingers. "What happened between us does not reflect his ability to run a school," I say with more confidence than Tommy or the situation warrant.

"Well, if he so much as looks at you like he's thinking about you naked, I'm going to kick his ass."

I laugh to fill the hollow in my chest. "I don't think that'll be an issue."

Logic would dictate that a man who left you high and dry in his bed after hours of sex stuff doesn't think about you nude months later. But then again, he probably doesn't keep your dirty underwear as a keepsake.

Tommy Flynn, a perverted paradox indeed.

I clear my throat and don't mention the panties to Leila.

Unfortunately for me, I've thought about Tommy naked loads since Vegas. If the index and middle finger on my right hand developed a consciousness, they'd probably think they were named "Please, Tommy, yes."

I will just have to start watching more *Bridgerton* in bed.

No. Something with fewer accents.

I take a deep swig of wine. "I've weathered worse storms at the school than Tommy O'Connor," I say to Leila, lifting my glass in a toast. "I have no doubt I'll be able to ride this one out."

Leila snickers as she raises her glass to mine.

I SIT IN BED later that evening—the frat boys across the street loudly debating what happens if you use lighter fluid on Match Light charcoal while Leila mutters something in the hall about dying in her sleep—and type up a list of all the things I don't want to forget to tell Tommy about the school.

My eyes sting as I write, fingers pounding out row after row of points, from the occasionally trivial (which toilets tend to clog) to the other times serious (how mandatory reporting laws affect the kids and how the school staff can support them).

But I struggle to do the school justice on paper. With everything written out as bullet points, our systems look disorganized and un-professional, even if *I* know those systems have evolved and have been refined by years of experience and, in many cases, mistakes. How can I convey to Tommy how important Desert Grace is? To the kids. To the community. To *me*.

Not that he cares, or should, that the school is my whole world.

But in Vegas, he did say he wanted to do something good. Make a change in the world.

Maybe he can start with Desert Grace.

Four pages in, I sigh and shut the laptop. This will have to do for now. I don't want to overwhelm the guy. I want to make him understand, to see the possibilities. I need him to fall in love.

With the school.

I bite my lip and look down, *Boston College* written across my chest in faded red letters. Wearing Tommy's sweatshirt felt far less creepy when he wasn't my boss and I knew I wouldn't have to see him almost daily for the indefinite future. I'm giving myself one last night with my favorite item of clothing.

My cheeks warm as I trace the letters. I'm giving myself one last night with the fantasy that is Tommy Flynn, too. A girl has got to blow off the soul-crushing steam of having her life upended somehow.

I dim the light and sink into the covers, reaching into my bedside table for my handiest little assistant as I let my mind wander back to Vegas. The feel of the cold glass behind my bottom as he took me against the window. The way his huge hands wrapped all the way around the back of my knees when he hauled me to the end of the bed and straight onto his face. *I'll miss these moments*, I think, as I slip my hand into my sleep shorts and pull up the memory of Tommy's green eyes.

"Nope," I murmur, shaking my head. "Not that one." But there it is again: me standing chest to chest with Tommy in his office just hours ago. His eyes fiery bright as he tells me he stole my lacy panties. He's so handsome, more so without the cassock, even.

Is there a lock on his office door?

Bad, Emmie. No, no, no.

I readjust my knees and mentally return to the velvet couch in Tommy's suite at the Bellagio, the foot massage, and the cashmere socks.

The ones he was wearing at school!

I groan in the opposite of pleasure. It's official. I hate Tommy. He hasn't only come in to take over my school after ditching me in a hotel room, but he has denied me the one respite I had from it all: guilt-free masturbatory moments with his hot face and smokin' body.

The duvet suddenly feels way too warm. I sit up, pushing the covers to the side, preparing to tear off Tommy's sweater and toss it directly into the laundry machine for delivery to his desk tomorrow when my phone rings.

The number is unfamiliar, a D.C. area code. God, I hope the kids haven't been trying to hack government emails again. It was a little funny the first time when they thought they could use the .gov addresses to convince the board to send them to Disneyland on their senior trip, but today, I'm not in the mood to be lectured by some senator's twenty-year-old intern about misconduct in our computer lab.

"Hello?" I answer, sitting on the edge of my bed.

"Emmie?" the deep voice on the other end of the line asks, and a deluge of adrenaline threatens to make my heart explode. "It is still okay, right? That I call you Emmie?"

I curl my legs up onto the mattress and hug my knees. He doesn't know what I was doing. He couldn't know. Could he?

"Yes?" I respond, a hint of panic edging my answer.

A relieved sigh sings through the receiver. My mouth wants to quirk up at the sound, but I stop it.

"Hi, Emmie."

"Hi, Tommy. Can I help you with something?"

"No. Yes. I mean, I'm so sorry to bother you after hours."

I make myself stop playing with the loose thread on the sleeve of his sweatshirt. "How did you get my number?"

"It was in the teacher directory."

"And so, you thought you would just call at..." I check the clock, only to be reminded that I have the same bedtime as an actual toddler. But how else would I compensate for the hours I lie awake in the middle of the night after the bad dreams? How would I make up for the time I spend angsting over the school, the state of the world, and the wasting away of octopus moms after they lay eggs all before the sun comes up? And George, of course, who I really need to visit. "Seven-forty in the evening?"

"I've made a right bags of this call, haven't I?"

"I'm not sure how to answer that question without an interpreter."

Tommy laughs, and unwelcome goosebumps lace my skin. "Well, to the point, then. I noticed you took the streetcar today when you left the building—"

"You *noticed?* Were you watching me?" Am I under audit by the board or something? Am I the extra weight that Tommy is here to cut?

"Not quite like that," he answers, not making his comment any clearer or making me feel any less worried that he's come all the way to Desert Grace to sack me. "I just meant that, if you'd like, I could pick you up tomorrow before opening."

"You called to offer me a ride to school?"

"Maybe we could grab a little something on the way, and you could fill me in a bit about the school before we get there. Just a quick coffee. Or, if you prefer, bagels?" His voice is playful, and holy moly, did my new boss just call to mock me about my apparent lack of transportation and the fact that I drove him away with everything bagels in Vegas?

"Seriously?" I ask, my voice hard and cold, a well-honed weapon that I've sharpened in countless classrooms.

"I just..." he fumbles.

"I will see you tomorrow in the teachers' lounge before first period, Mr. O'Connor. Be prepared to take notes. Lots of them." I hang up, exhaling a rage-filled breath, and crawl back into bed.

I'm keeping the sweater. And tonight me, my hand, and imaginary Tommy are going to enjoy our first round of hate sex.

Five

I GET TO SCHOOL extra early to set up for the faculty meeting. And to organize the library, and vacuum the tattered carpet of the hallways, and pick the gum off the bottom of the cafeteria tables. (Based on the sheer number of Juicy Fruit wads I recover, I'm pretty sure I'm the first person to do so.) I stop myself just shy of Windexing the walls, and that is only because the school's cleaning supplies are running low.

At a quarter to seven, I lean against the back counter in the teachers' lounge, rolling my fingertips over my temples.

I want to impress Tommy. *Need* to impress him. Not for my sake, or the sake of my pride—that he ground into dust by smiling at me with those green eyes and then vanishing from the bed while I slept—but for Desert Grace. If I can make this place sparkle a little, he might see the potential and be taken with all the possibilities, at least enough for him to want to try and make it better, to fight for the kids and the resources and education they deserve.

The more he cares, the more he'll do. And if that means I have to wake up before dawn to clean hot sauce off of communal countertops, then so be it.

I grab a damp paper towel and get to work on a red stain on the peeling Formica laminate.

"Top of the morning to you, Ms. Jones."

"*Buckets!*" I shout, dropping the paper towel. "You scared me." I thought I had at least another twenty minutes until anyone else showed up, and that person was supposed to be Leila with my mocha latte.

Taking a deep breath, I turn around to face the intruder, using the back of my arm to push the strands of hair that have fallen out of my bun off my face. "Good morning, Mr. O'Connor," I say, a little breathless from the heavy scrubbing. Hot sauce dries like cement.

Tommy clears his throat and scans the room, assessing. I hold my breath.

"Smells better in here than it did yesterday," he says at last, examining the cupboards.

The teachers' lounge does have a habit of smelling bad in that sort of ominous, uncertain way where there might be an overripe apple forgotten in a drawer or something worse festering, like a dead mouse under the refrigerator.

I cross my arms, propping my hip on the counter. "It always smells fine in here," I lie. I don't want him adding *chronic stench* to the list of things he associates me with.

I shake my head. *That he associates with the school.*

"And," Tommy says, spinning in a small circle as he takes in the space, "the floor is much cleaner."

Apparently, his attention to detail extends beyond the bedroom. His gaze lands on me. I swallow.

"Did you do all this?" he asks.

Why couldn't Tommy have shown up a week ago when he was supposed to, with the rest of the teachers? A week ago, the scent of Clorox still hung in the air and the fridge was free of questionably edible leftovers. Instead, his first impression of the school was based on seven days of use by a bunch of overwhelmed educators. What will he think after he sees what the kids manage in that same amount of time?

Now he's probably going to threaten to fire the janitorial staff for not doing their jobs properly, and it will all be my fault.

Maybe I'm going about this all wrong. Maybe I should be trying to get rid of him as soon as possible. What if I make it so nice that he wants to stay? That would be fine in the short term, but I can't imagine we'll get on well forever if he always holds my panties over my head, so to speak.

We might both be adults, but he made it clear in his office yesterday that we haven't moved on entirely from whatever happened in Vegas, and the sooner all six-feet-something of lean muscle and gorgeous face that is Thomas Flynn O'Connor is gone, the better.

"Listen, I—" I start.

"Emmie, I have to tell you something," Tommy interrupts.

His tone makes my heart rate speed up. "What?" I ask as I simultaneously squash the inappropriate quiver of hope in my chest, a stupid hope that I couldn't even articulate and makes no sense and…

"I didn't keep your panties."

Heat rushes to my face. "Excuse me?"

"Yesterday I made that terrible joke about keeping your underwear. I don't know what compelled me to say such a thing, but it was entirely out of line. I'm truly sorry."

I grit my teeth against a problematic flash of disappointment. "Okay…"

"It would appear that the surprise of seeing you again made me go a bit…" He shakes his head.

I stare at Tommy. He fidgets.

"Anyway, I wanted you to know that I didn't. Keep them, I mean. Sure, I might have considered it when I found them." He chuckles and looks at me. I blink at him, and he drops his gaze to his feet. "But it seemed a bit perverse. And beyond that, unhealthy."

Um, rude. "You thought my underwear was *unhealthy*?"

"No, god, not like that," he says, raising his hands and taking a step toward me like he's going to grab my arms. I shiver.

"Like what, then?" I demand, forcing my voice not to shake.

Tommy scrubs at his blushing face. *What is happening?* "Unhealthy for me, emotionally," he explains.

I shake my head. "I don't understand. How could my underwear be emotionally unhealthy for you?"

"My therapist," he begins, then sighs. "I mean, I've been looking—"

The door bursts open, and Leila pushes her way in backwards with a drink carrier and school bag in her hands. "Good morning again, my little sex-starved history slut. When's the head of school supposed to be here to ruin your day?"

Tommy hurries over to hold the door for her. "Surprise," he says as she turns around and comes face to face with him.

"Well done, Em. He's even better-looking up close," she says, peeking over his shoulder at me. "My one-night stands never hold up in the daylight."

I gape at her as Tommy bows his head like he's embarrassed, but the hint of a smile on his face screams, *Who, me? Little ole perfect me?*

"Your eyes look like they're about to bulge out of your head." Leila hands me my coffee, and we all suffer a moment of awkward glances—never mind, my best friend looks delighted—when it becomes apparent that Tommy also brought me a coffee. And not just any coffee: it's the locally roasted, ethically sourced stuff from the boutique roaster in the old barrio.

"I'll just pop this here, then," Tommy says, leaving the coffee on the counter and scribbling a little note beside it, which, I observe with pursed lips, is more than he left for me before fleeing from his hotel room.

"Come on, Mr. O'Connor," I say as I dig the list I wrote for Tommy out of my bag and push it into his hands, shoving Leila hard with my hip as I walk by. "You have a school to meet."

T OMMY AND I HEAD back to his office before first bell, so I'll have enough time to get to my classroom downstairs for homeroom and attendance. I smile at him at his door. I'm chuffed—and yes, I just learned what that means during my fifty minutes wandering the halls with Tommy—but he *did* take a lot of notes, and he asked thoughtful questions about the kids and not just about how we spend our money.

Then, he even listened to my answers. Closely. Like sometimes so closely, I had to step back before all I could smell was him. Before I forgot what I was saying.

But I have given myself a sliver of permission to hope he can do some decent things for the school. Or at least not to let anything bad happen.

"That was the most enlightening hour I've spent in a while, Ms. Jones," he says, leaning against the wall beside his office door so a couple of seniors can pass between us in the hall. "When can I see you again?"

My smile falls as I parse his meaning. Enlightening? In a good way? I feel my face starting to think out loud, my nose wrinkling, eyebrows drawing together. *Ginger snaps.* Does he want to see me again because he's already going to fire me?

Tommy reaches for my shoulder, and I could swear we both start a little when his fingers graze the cotton of my shirt sleeve. He pulls his hand back. "I'd like to talk to you more about the after-school ESL program," he clarifies. "I might know someone who can find us a volunteer interpreter to better connect with the Farsi-speaking families."

"Yes," I say, my voice high because of this incredible possibility and not the fireworks still coursing through my arm. "That would be..." I squeeze my eyes shut against excited tears, shaking my head. We had a wave of Afghani students arrive in the fall, refugees, and connecting with most of the families has been difficult.

A dedicated interpreter would change everything.

I exhale, trying to center myself, and open my eyes. Tommy is watching me, his head tilted to the side, expression unreadable—probably glad he left me in that hotel room and didn't wait to find out I'm totally nuts. I clear my throat and force a normal-sized smile. "Ms. Conn handles all of that and would be so grateful to have someone onboard who can help. She shares an office with Mr. Duarte and Mx. Brown. I can take you there now."

Tommy's grin is considerate and crooked, and I look away. "I'd appreciate that, but I have a meeting in"—he checks his watch—"four minutes. But maybe after school? I'd love it if you could be there too when I talk to her."

Do I want to act as Tommy's buffer? His agent on the inside who vouches for him with the tried and tired staff. *Sure.* Happily. If it means getting the kids the services they need.

"Right after school, I have exam practice with the juniors," I recall aloud. "Then graduate support meetings."

"Graduate support meetings?" he asks while I scan my brain, trying to think of somebody I could ask to cover for me. Perhaps it makes me a horrible person, but I'd love to get out of my meetings. It's not that I don't enjoy seeing the kids again after they've left the school, but graduate support tends to fill me with Sisyphean despair.

We spend four years trying to prepare our students as best we can for college or tech school or the job force, pouring love, time, and tears into them before freeing them into the wild world beyond. And sometimes, when they come to see us, they have amazing things to share about successes, big and small. But more often than not, they still face the same struggles they did in high school, desperately trying to stay afloat. We push and push, struggling to the top of the hill, just for so many to tumble down the other side.

I don't have the power or means to help them in the way they need, the way I wish I could. But Tommy...

Tommy knows business things and businesspeople, he's good at that stuff, and perhaps he could offer our alums wisdom I cannot. Or at least begin to appreciate what we are truly up against.

"You should come with me. If you can."

"I'll be there," he promises, and my heart pings around in my chest at the sincerity in his green eyes.

"Great." I grin. "I'll meet you here, and we can walk to classroom seven together. I'll organize something with Ms. Conn for tomor—"

Tommy's office door creaks open, and a familiar face splits into a very white, straight smile on the other side. Big, bright hazel eyes framed by silky dark hair.

Audrey Wyn Edmonds.

The beautiful, brilliant valedictorian of my high school senior class and our board president, Mr. Edmonds', niece.

Audrey comes from money, like her uncle, but she's not nearly as obnoxious about her wealth. She donates a lot of her time to the school, and unlike most of our other affluent volunteers—who we often suspect stick around because they have a savior complex or feel guilty about their incomprehensibly deep pockets—Audrey seems to actually enjoy working with the kids.

For a person whose first car was a brand-new Lexus, she's good at relating. She's even spent time working in retail, which is not something most of the students who graduated from my small private upper school can say. A school I only attended because George was the school's daytime security guard and got a heck of a deal on tuition.

Guaranteed, I was the only kid there who ever did their back-to-school shopping at Goodwill. Though, after we moved in with George, he made sure all my first-day-back outfits were fresh off the rack.

Audrey is kind and was when we were teenagers, too. Just like she's always been gorgeous. It wasn't lost on the student body that her initials spell AWE.

She is a wealthy, well-educated unicorn. And now she and Tommy are beaming at each other, and I'm the awkward fifteen-year-old girl in hand-me-down, out-of-style skinny jeans who is always on the outside once again.

What's worse? Audrey only takes morning meetings with the head of school when Mr. Edmonds needs her to break bad news.

Six

A UDREY'S VISIT SETS ME on edge, and not just because she and Tommy would make a gorgeous couple and pop out impossibly beautiful, freckly, dark-haired babies together. Or because they could hang their complementary MBAs—social impact and general management; adorable—in his and hers frames above their mantle.

Faculty lounge hearsay corroborates my suspicion that Audrey spent most of the morning in Tommy's office. The last time she was here this long, we found out that the county was cutting a portion of the funding for our meals program despite every single one of our students being food-insecure—which happened to be the same week Mrs. Torrez stepped down as head of school.

Leila catches me in the hall between fifth and sixth periods. To ease my anxiety, I've been spending the five minutes between lessons jogging between the classrooms to refresh the teachers' dry-erase markers. "Dude, you look like you did that time you prepared Christmas dinner at the Ronald McDonald House and thought you gave all the families botulism because the green bean cans were dented. What is up with you today?"

"Audrey was in Tommy's office this morning." I grab the red grading pen on my lanyard and start clicking the top. "And I've been in a tizzy ever since."

"First of all," Leila says, grimacing as she extracts the pen from my fingers, "never use that word again. It gives me the icks."

I snort. "Tizzy?"

"Gross. But more importantly, Emmie, what are you worried they were doing in there?"

"Drafting a list of people and programs to cut from the budget?"

Her eyebrows rise.

"What? It's true." Well, that and gazing admiringly into each other's eyes while fantasizing about angel investments and vacationing together in Bora Bora.

She pulls me into a hug. "Worse storms, remember? We've got this. The school is going to be okay when he leaves. And so are you." I squirm, but she holds me tighter. "Now, go teach the hell out of some history because, after that, we have something legitimately shitty to face."

"*Corn nuts,*" I groan as she lets me go. "We got the sample test scores back."

She nods. "And they are *ugly*."

"Has anyone else seen them?"

"Only Mr. O'Connor."

"Can we bribe him not to tell anyone?"

"Based on what you told me you got him to do to you in Vegas, you might have a chance."

"Yeah, right." I put my hands on my hips and give Leila my best Marilyn Monroe. "The good ole 'Mr. Headmaster, I will Schoolhouse *Rock* your world if you don't tell the board about those test scores just yet.'"

"Gets them every time," Leila wheezes through a laugh as she glances over my shoulder.

"*Every time?*" Tommy asks, and I'd very much like to play dead.

"Coming from this little wildcat?" Leila pinches my cheek. "How could it not?"

I glare at her even though I know she's one of the few humans immune to my meanest mugging. Then I turn to Tommy, who smothers his smile into something verging on professional.

"You saw the scores?" he asks, leaning closer as a throng of students file past us down the hall.

"Not yet." My shoulders slump, and I swallow. "But Leila mentioned they aren't good."

"Do you run all the exam practices?" he asks, and my stomach drops.

Oh god, he's going to think I'm the reason the kids did so poorly. And he's not entirely wrong. I could only get my hands on sample tests from two years ago, and even the copies I made of those are technically illegal, but the students and the school can't afford those fancy testing teachers who come in. I don't know if it would make a difference if we could. Some of our kids are still learning how to read in English.

"No," Leila says, nudging me with her shoulder. "Emmie took over in October. She only had three weeks with the kids before the test. And frankly, we should all be horrified by the idea of her teaching anyone arithmetic at any level. In college, she took Math in Modern Society instead of Algebra, and she still doesn't know how to calculate a tip."

"Thanks, Lei," I mumble.

"Then why do you?" Tommy asks, his eyes scanning mine as he slips his hands in his pockets. "How'd you end up taking on exam practice?"

"She's a saint," Leila answers for me. "We might get paid more than the average high school teacher, but we also have longer days, longer weeks, and significantly shorter summers. Plus, loads of unresolved emotional trauma and the weight of one hundred fragile futures saddling our souls. Most of the teachers have families and partners to get home to after school. And Emmie…" She trails off, gesturing to me.

Is it too late to fake my own death? My best friend telling my new boss and former lover that I have *nothing* and *no one* is humbling at best and making me vaguely murderous at worst.

"Emmie," she says, eyes soft, glancing at me and then Tommy, "is all that is good in the world."

"I see." Tommy clears his throat. "Ms. Jones, how would you feel about me joining you for exam practice today? Then we can go from there to the graduate support meetings."

"Sure. That works," I say, resigned. Maybe I can find a way to coax out some information about his visit with Audrey while we're at it and uncover what horrible news she came to deliver.

"Excellent. I'm looking forward to getting to know our alums," Tommy says to me. "See you after the last bell. And Ms. Bashar"—he nods to Leila—"I appreciate your frankness."

"At your service," she says before turning to me as I watch Tommy disappear down the hall. "Speaking of being frank, there is something else I wanted to talk to you about."

I frown, shifting my full attention to Leila and away from Tommy's behind, which is actively defying the laws of how good a butt can look in khakis. "Did Fib poop on my bed again?"

"No. Way worse."

"What's wrong?" I ask, reaching for her hand.

Leila hesitates. She never hesitates.

Panic twists my middle. "What, Leila?"

She chuckles, then winces. "I wanted to talk to you about Benji. I want to ask him to move in."

I'M SO DISTRACTED DURING my next class that I only realize I've been detailing an episode of *Game of Thrones* and not the Battle of Bannockburn when one of my sophomores raises her hand—startling in and of itself—and asks if Tyrion Lannister fought for Robert the Bruce or Edward II.

"Wow, you were really paying attention, Harper," I say, biting my lip as I try to recall what in the sweet sugarplums I just told the class.

She blows a giant pink bubble, nodding as it implodes in on itself with a snap. I give her a pointed look, and she spits the gum into its silver wrapper with a guilty shrug.

I turn my attention back to the rest of the class, who are all now actively trying to appear as though they are not also chewing gum. "Great. Well, surprise, nothing I said today will be on the test, so you can just"—I mime scribbling something out, then pretend to tear up a piece of paper—"whatever notes you took. In fact, why don't you break into your discussion groups for the rest of the period and brainstorm some thesis statements for the compare-and-contrast essays we'll be starting at the end of the week?"

"Miss," Jarreau says, eyeing the wall clock. "We've still got like, thirty minutes until the bell rings. I don't think our brains have that much storming in them."

Shoot, he's right. Not only am I turning into an increasingly ineffectual teacher, but now I am an ineffectual teacher who isn't even teaching. I'm basically firing myself at this point. But all I can think about are test scores and Audrey.

And the fact that my best friend wants a whole man to live in our condo.

Her condo.

Oh Lord, what if she means she wants me to move out? I *should* move out. It is weird if I don't move out, isn't it? Leila and Benji and Fib. And Emmie. Does that make me the fourth wheel? Is that better or worse than being the third?

The mental storm clouds darken, my eyes pricking as a strangled laugh lodges in my throat when I consider the possibility that I might lose my job and my home in the same month.

Come on, Em. Don't cry in front of the kids.

My shoulders drop on a long exhale.

"If you'd prefer," I say, hardening my gaze as I sweep it over twenty-five confused faces. "I am happy to give a quiz on the succession of the Angevin kings."

"No, thank you, Ms. Jones," they all echo, finding their way into their groups.

"That's what I thought." I raise my eyebrows, face steely. But inside, I am a soup of sixty percent panic and forty percent nausea.

I try to be reasonable. Leila is not going to kick me out, even if she should. Tommy would have a heck of a time filling my position on short notice, so I at least have the security of knowing I won't be going anywhere soon.

But, ew, there it is again. *Change.* Big change.

I do a few laps of the classroom, mostly to work the nervous tension out of my limbs and try to focus on how I should play exam practice. Do I take the fall for the kids' bad scores and hope that Tommy somehow works some budgeting magic and brings in someone qualified? Or do I try to convince him I'm capable in case he tries to wrangle some poor, exhausted teacher on our staff to take over for me?

By the time the bell rings and the kids are getting packed up, the tizzy has worsened. I'm sitting at my desk, *in my desk chair*, for the first time since school started in August, shaking my hands out when Harper comes over and hands me a pen.

"I stole this yesterday," she says, looking bored. "When I couldn't find mine."

"Keep it," I tell her. "And feel free to ask first next time."

"Thanks," she says, picking up the pen and twirling it between her manicured fingers. So much glitter. She heads for the door, pausing before reaching for the handle. "Ms. Jones, this medieval history stuff is kind of cool."

And that's all it takes—the quirk of her lip as she says it, the sincerity of her comment—to re-fan the fire that keeps me going, to ease the weight of fear and failure that has built a home atop my shoulders. I bounce to my feet, closing my hands in a single clap.

"Harper! You are so right. This medieval stuff *is* kind of cool. Maybe even more than kind of? I'm so glad you're enjoying it." And hopefully not just the accidental recap of Westerosi warfare I delivered at the beginning of the period.

She regards me in that scanning, assessing way that teenagers sometimes do, like they can see right through you, and my skin prickles.

Here goes. "What is it, Harper?"

"Do you think Robert the Bruce's accent was as hot as Mr. O'Connor's?"

"Oh, um." I was not expecting that. "You know, Robert the Bruce was Scottish. Obviously. And their accents are different from the Irish. I don't know what they all sounded like seven hundred years ago. But since there was some crossover between Scottish-Gaelic and

Irish-Gaelic, I suppose it is possible that Robert the Bruce's and Mr. O'Connor's accents wouldn't be altogether dissimilar."

"So you agree?" she says, cocking an eyebrow.

"What do you mean?"

"That Mr. O'Connor's accent is hot."

My chest and neck and face can't be more than a single degree away from whatever temperature melts flesh. "No. What? Harper, that is entirely inappropriate. He is the head of school." *And you are a* child, I don't add.

"In art class, Mx. Brown told us it's important to appreciate beautiful things."

"I don't think they meant Mr. O'Connor," I admonish while trying not to smile.

"Mr. O'Connor's *accent*," Harper corrects as she walks out.

Seven

TOMMY DOES NOT MAKE it to exam practice or graduate support that afternoon—or any afternoon that week—because of emergency board meeting after emergency board meeting.

Needless to say, Mr. Edmonds got wind of our not-so-stellar test scores, and before they are released in the quarterly report, he is devising a crisis containment plan to keep all our donors from jumping ship.

The fact that our major concern about the scores is that people will stop giving the school money makes me sick to my stomach. That anyone with a heart would pull resources from a bunch of underprivileged students when they need them the most is one of the world's cruelest jokes.

Then there is the issue of our conspicuously nonexistent principal. Mr. Edmonds, for the time being, seems content to be saving on another faculty salary. The current faculty, however, is gearing up for revolt.

A good principal helps mitigate the pressure on the teachers. A principal makes the calls home, organizes extracurriculars, supervises additional programs—hello, exam practice—and ensures teachers have the necessary equipment and resources to do their jobs. Now, all of that is falling to the teachers.

And they are drowning.

Tommy hasn't mentioned anything about a job search to fill the position. Perhaps his hands are tied, but if something doesn't happen relatively soon, between a depleted staff and the possibility of dwindling endowments, the whole ship might go down.

The clouds are dark and heavy, but I keep scooping, bailing bucket after bucket. Just enough to keep me from throwing myself overboard.

Nine days after Tommy's second-day tour of school, I finally get him together with Ms. Conn. Two days after that, we have a part-time volunteer Farsi translator on staff. The following Monday, Tommy is able to join me after school for graduate support.

Our first meeting goes so well that my excessive grinning makes my cheeks ache. Nilo Lopez graduated from Desert Grace my second year at the school and is completing a master's in education after graduating with a B.A. in history. (Do I flatter myself and assume I had something to do with that decision? Sometimes, a little, when I need the morale boost.)

Our second meeting involves a lot of cheerleading on our part, and the third is canceled because recent graduate Levi Barker forgot he had double scheduled with his probation officer. Overall, it is a good characterization of our alums.

Tommy walks me to the small office I share with Leila.

"This afternoon gave me a lot to think about," he says. For better or worse, Tommy missed exam practice because the girls' toilets on the second floor backed up, and apparently, no one else on campus knows how to use a plunger. He rescheduled for next week.

Desert Grace did not nail the good-first-impression thing, my efforts be damned.

"I bet," I reply, trying to sound positive even though his words terrify me. "Like, what, though, exactly?" I prompt, unable to stop myself.

He considers me as he rubs his jaw. "Some reorganization."

"Of things or people?"

"Both. But I think the latter, more so."

When Tommy leaves, I spend ten minutes standing in the middle of the room unmoving, my eyes glazing over as I stare at Leila's posters—a collection of math puns I don't understand despite her having attempted to explain them multiple times—before I shake the staggering numbness from my center and google the word *reorganization* in a business context. I whimper when the results pop up. It's just as bad as I expected.

I slowly get my things together and drag myself out of the building. I'm doomed. The school is doomed. It only took two weeks for everything to go sideways, and somehow, I'm in the middle of everything that is going wrong.

But there is something I can do to make today suck less. Leila and I have barely had a chance to talk about Benji since she told me she wanted him to move in, and I know part of that is because she doesn't want to push or make me uncomfortable.

But right now, I can go home and tell Leila I'd love for Benji to live with us. I can write his name on the fridge with alphabet magnets and buy a third wineglass. We can celebrate with takeout and watch a movie—we'll let Benji pick—together in the living room.

And then, when I'm sure she knows I mean it, I can cry myself to sleep under the covers.

I stop at the base of the parking garage steps when I see Otis with his bag propped under his head and a stack of creatively decorated cardboard signs at his side. Otis is one of the only humans who has consistently told me *good work* at the end of my school days, though I'm not sure we've ever really discussed what I do, and I try to repay his kindness with whatever I can muster. Sometimes, that's no more than a premade, plastic-wrapped PB&J from our school pantry. But today, after patting myself down, I come up short. Not a cent or snack on me.

"Don't bother," he tells me as I become increasingly intense in my search for spare change.

My shoulders slump as I add another failure to my day. "Sorry, Otis."

He laughs. "You're a good friend, Miss Jones."

"I try."

"Well, you'll be happy to know that some strange-sounding fellow handed me a hundred-dollar bill about two minutes ago and asked if I would like a hotel room for the night. Maybe it's time I treat you to dinner."

My eyes narrow. "I don't know if I like the way that sounds, Otis. Maybe his intentions...were..."

Otis raises his eyebrows. "Nah, miss. I don't think I'm his type. But thanks for looking out for me all the same."

"Have a good night, Otis. Stay warm."

"Good work today, Miss Jones."

I smile and hike up the three levels of stairs to where I've parked my twenty-year-old baby-blue Prius almost every day since I started working at Desert Grace. I'm panting by the time I get to the driver's door, squeezing in between the shiny electric luxury vehicle parked beside me that screams *gentrification, but make it eco-friendly!*

My clicker doesn't work no matter how hard I press the unlock button, so I spend a frustrating few minutes trying to figure out how to get the physical key out of the fob. When I finally get the door open and toss all of my stuff onto the passenger seat, I close my eyes, trying not to cry.

What a day.

Tommy. The tests. The bathrooms. The uproar about the principal (or lack thereof). Leila and Benji. My darn car key.

I take a deep breath and press the start button.

Nothing happens.

I try again.

"No, no, no, no," I plead with the car. "Please start."

The car does not give a flying *fudgesicle* about me and my rising desperation. It's silent, and in that silence echoes the flash of the "Check Hybrid System" warning light that has been on for the past month.

Tears spring to my eyes, almost as violent as the unbelieving laugh roaring through me. I bury my face in my hands. This can't be happening. If I could afford a therapist, they would think I made it all up for sympathy.

But I can't afford a therapist. I choke on a wail.

I'm impossibly, unbelievably pathetic.

A knock at my window jars me from my crying, and I scream—a tight, awkward, only half-afraid scream. But Tommy, who is bent forward on the other side of the glass, throws up his hands in apology, mouthing a dramatic "Sorry" through a wince.

My finger goes to the window button, which obviously doesn't work, and I stifle a sob as I crack the door open, wiping frantically at my leaky mascara with my free hand.

"You all right?" Tommy asks, his voice soft and kind and terribly annoying.

"Fine," I say, my voice sharp through the tears. "Just great."

"Need a ride?" he asks, tilting his head toward the fancy car at his back.

Figures.

I clench my jaw. My nod is as embarrassed as it is reluctant.

Tommy holds the door for me as I collect my things, and then I remember that my lesson plans for the rest of the week are in the trunk. I start to cry again when I realize I can't get it open.

"May I?" Tommy asks.

"Be my guest." I gesture toward my useless, dead car and the useless, locked trunk.

Tommy folds his whole body into the backseat as I stare in disbelief. He somehow lowers the actual seats before disappearing halfway into the trunk, but not so far that I can't see the stretch of skin where his shirt has come dislodged from his pants.

Holy *shnikes.*

I hear a mechanical *pop,* and he pulls his head back out. Why is this person so sexily capable?

"H-how?" I stammer.

"My uncle had a small car repair shop in Drogheda," he says as he extracts his amazing body from the Prius. "You only allow your cousins to lock you in a trunk so many times before you figure out how to get yourself out."

He's breathing a little heavy from the acrobatics and standing very close—close enough for me to imagine what a trunk full of Tommy would smell like. No, that's not right. But I can't tear my eyes away from where his shirt is still bunched up above his khakis. He's staring down at me. He said something. I'm supposed to respond.

A faint whimper echoes against the concrete walls of the parking garage, and we both turn toward the front of my car.

"A dog," I say quietly. *A dog?* In the parking garage?

"A puppy, I think," Tommy murmurs in a low, soothing voice. We both lean forward to get a better look at the source of the sound.

Against the wall, between the cars, is a shaking, shaggy, reddish, large-pawed...

"Doodle gone wrong?" Tommy wonders out loud, finishing my thought.

I nod. "A puddle?"

"A pitoodle?"

"I'm sure Google would know. Definitely part poodle, part pit bull, and part—"

"Chupacabra?" Tommy questions.

I frown at him, eyebrows scrunched. For an Irishman who just moved to the southwest, he seems well-informed about our legendary local wildlife.

"Ethan was telling me about some horrible episode with his pet goat this morning," he explains. "During his counseling session. You all really need to hire a professional. I am in no way qualified to guide children through these sorts of losses."

"I believe that's your problem now. But yes, I've been telling the board for years that a bachelor's degree in education does not a high school counselor make. Or whatever degree you got before your MBA, for that matter. A B.S. in bleeding small not-for-profit schools dry to fill the pockets of its wealthy benefactors? Is that what they offer at those fancy East Coast colleges?"

"That's exactly what they printed on my diploma, in fact."

"I thought so."

As we talk, the dog creeps closer.

"Poor baby looks hungry," I say, bending down.

Tommy squats beside me. When we're both nearly sitting on the asphalt, the dog approaches, sniffing, butt waggling sideways. We both reach out, and she licks our hands in one long swipe.

"What should we do?" Tommy asks.

"Help me catch her, and I'll take her to the vet. See if she's microchipped." The pup is growing increasingly friendly and increasingly excited. She puts her paws on Tommy's legs, and when we pet her, she pees a little.

Tommy laughs. "The girl's gone and wet my trousers."

I clap my hands to draw the dog into my lap instead, but the pup seems torn, bouncing between both of us like we're raw steak and peanut butter, and she can't decide what she wants to eat first.

"If you get in the car," Tommy says, "I think she'll follow."

I stand, reaching into my pocket to grab my keys.

"My car," Tommy says, ushering me toward the door of his Tesla. Because mine won't start. Right.

"Are you sure you want to put a dog in this thing?" I ask, eyeing the leather interior through the window.

"It's just a car," he says, smiling as he gives the metal roof a little knock to prove his point. "If you'd prefer to drive, I'll sit in the back with Este."

"With *Este*?"

The dog barks when I repeat the name.

"It suits her." He shrugs and smiles, and I open the rear door, call the dog, and wrap an arm around her when she hops in beside me.

Eight

WHEN WE ARRIVE AT the vet's office, Tommy comes around to open my door, and I pass him the puppy so he can carry her in. A tech brings the scanner out right away and tells us she isn't chipped. Tommy and I release simultaneous sounds of delight at the news that Este is potentially up for grabs, my squeal a countermelody to his deep exhale. Este cocks her head at us, and Tommy immediately asks if they have time to do an exam. He smiles, and the receptionist says yes.

She hands us a clipboard, and we sit next to each other on a small, padded bench while we wait for the exam room to be ready. Tommy fills out the intake paperwork while I cuddle the dog.

I see him write his name under owner information and elbow him. "Put me on there too." If I keep the dog—which I can't, can I? In my yard-less condo? With Leila's finicky fourteen-year-old cat? And Benji? The dog nuzzles my cheek with her nose. I don't care. I'll figure something out. My information needs to match hers.

"Okay," he says, chewing his lip for a second before writing *Thomas and Emeline Jones-O'Connor*. He looks at me. "Does that work?"

"Um?" I say.

"Here, you do it. I don't want to mess anything up." We do a little shuffle, transferring the puppy into his arms and the clipboard into mine.

I lift the pen and get to work. "Phone number?"

"I thought you'd never ask."

I roll my eyes, forcing my mouth to contort into a definite not-smile as I write it down.

"Species?" I ask next. We both study Este, who looks up at us with what I believe is the equivalent of a doggy smile.

Tommy points to her awkward, knobby legs. "Donkey." Then, her feet. "Tortoise."

I kiss her broad face, and we both gaze into her deep brown eyes. "Seal." Then I whisper, nodding to her tail, "Rat."

Este barks.

"So," Tommy ventures, "a dog. Probably."

A dog. Probably, I scribble, and then under *Pet Name*, I write *ESTE*.

"Este?" he asks, peering over my shoulder.

The receptionist peeks up at us from behind the counter for the third time. I can practically see her brain trying to make sense of this weird dynamic.

"It was your idea," I point out.

"Este?" he repeats, a laugh in his voice.

"What?" I ask, exasperated.

"I said *S.T.*"

"And what the heck does S.T. mean?"

"Short for Shirley Temple," he says. "The dog is a ginger, and I thought it was a sweet callback to the first time we—"

"All right, E-S-T-E it is, then."

We both look up when the receptionist chuckles. "You sound like my parents," she says. "The doctor is ready to see your pit boodle now."

We stand, and Tommy leans down to whisper in my ear as we head for the exam room. "I preferred puddle."

It isn't until we get back in the car with Este's rabies certificate and pockets full of puppy treats that we swiped from a jar in the exam room to make her feel better after her shots that I discover I left my cell phone in the back seat. Tommy tells me Este and I should just sit up front, but I insist this is safer for the puppy.

I have a single text from Leila: **Am I gonna have to go full Liam Neeson on some motherfuckers?**

Not abducted, I text back. Found a dog. Hitched a ride with Tommy.

In this scenario, is Tommy the dog?

I snort. Running a quick errand, and then I'll be home. See you soon. Yay, Benji! Has he moved in yet?

"All good?" Tommy asks, glancing at me in the rearview mirror when I keep staring at my phone screen after hitting send.

"Yes." I force a smile. "Everything is great." I mean, my life seems to be unraveling around me, but my friend is happy, and Tommy seems like the kind of person who can find a way to save the school, which may or may not include me losing my job.

Este nuzzles into my hand, and I feel my shoulders relax.

Tommy's eyes soften in the reflection when he sees us snuggling in the backseat. "Your place or mine?"

"Oh, I, um...I thought we were—"

"I mean, where should Este spend the night?" he clarifies, the tips of his ears vaguely pink. "Would you like to keep her with you?"

"I wish I could," I say, bending down to kiss Este's scraggly ginger head. "I should talk to Leila first. Her cat, Fib, doesn't love other furred creatures as much as I do."

"You know how we handle troublesome cats where I come from..."

"With a Bang!" I say, giggling. "Poor Gur."

"Ah, you remember."

"Of course I remember," I say, flicking his shoulder.

He grins at me in the mirror, and I smile back, my cheeks pleasantly warm. I open my mouth to make a joke about priests picking up schoolteachers in bars when it dawns on me that I am flirting. Or about to attempt to.

I school my features back into Teacher Emmie and clear my throat. "Are you sure I can't help cover the cost of the vet visit?"

Tommy raises an eyebrow at me in the mirror without saying anything in response and parks in front of the pet store.

Since Este is not fully vaccinated, he won't let her paws touch the ground outside of the car. He gives me permission to choose a collar and leash, a tag, and toys at will while he carries her down the aisles.

I settle on a moss-green leash and collar set, which (not at all on purpose) complements Tommy's eyes. I try the collar on her, and he holds her up beside his face. The two of them look matchy and precious together. Este also gets a collection of vet-recommended goodies, chew toys, a bed, a crate, a bag of premium puppy chow, and a laser-engraved tag shaped like a heart that has my number and Tommy's etched forever one on top of the other, making whatever this dog co-parenting situation is feel very official.

"I hope there's no one out there that loves her as much as I do," Tommy says in the car after checking out. He pulls the paper tags off her new toys. "I don't think I could give her up."

At his words, a ridiculous twinge of dejection makes my fingers fumble as I struggle to attach Este's pink heart tag to the collar. I look up to see Tommy's eyes on me.

What would it be like to have someone feel that way about you, to be desperate to take care of you? To never leave you?

Tommy clearly has no intention of deserting Este in a hotel room.

"Yeah," I say, turning my focus back to the tag, finally getting the metal ring to slide over the D-ring on the collar. I clip the green band around her neck, and we both admire her. "I feel the same way. Are we terrible people if we don't put up 'Found Dog' signs?"

"Maybe, but it's a risk I'm willing to take. Though, if Este is missing her human..."

"We can put up a couple to ease our consciences."

He nods thoughtfully. "With very vague details."

"Found: Canine. Has fur and paws. Size of 3.5 smallish watermelons."

"Please call 1-800-TOO-LATE if yours."

I laugh. "Perfect. I'll type something up tonight and make copies at school tomorrow—" I pause, eyes wide. "I mean, with my own materials. Or I'll pay the school back. I just don't have a printer at home. The teachers all know not to use the copy machine for personal reasons, of course."

"I'll pocket some tape from the supply closet, and we can hang them during lunch," Tommy says, smiling.

WHEN TOMMY PULLS UP in front of the condo, I smother Este in cuddles and whisper sweetly in her ear about the threat of future baths. Our new street dog still smells like an unsavory mix of motor oil, dank water, and mystery fustiness from the parking garage.

"I'd try to wash her on my own"—Tommy turns around in his seat to face us, blatantly eavesdropping—"but it might be a two-person job to get this one cleaned up. Someone's going to have to get in with her while the other one lathers her up."

Hm, add that comment to the list of things that shouldn't make me clench my legs. I blame the accent. "I'll ask around about a professional. A groomer with some know-how might be our best bet."

"You're no fun," Tommy says, the shadows from the streetlights making his eyes look extra dark.

I wrinkle my nose. "You really want to get into the bathtub with a dirty dog?"

"Well, not that, exactly." He runs a hand through his hair. "It was more... never mind."

"How would you prefer to be reimbursed for her expenses? I've got all the money transfer apps. With Leila's help, I can probably even figure out how to use them."

He waves me off. "Emmie, please. I was happy to pay for that stuff."

"It was *a lot* of stuff, Tommy," I say, trying to sound stern even though his *Emmie, please,* turned my guts to mush. "If we get to keep this dog—"

He nods. "We are keeping this dog."

I nod back and hope he's right. "Well, in that case, you can't insist on covering all of her expenses. It's not fair."

"We'll see." He reaches out a hand to rub Este's face.

Lord, he's stubborn. There has to be something I can do to repay him.

"Is maith an cailín tú, a Este," he says to the dog, then glances at me. "Beagnach chomh hiontach le do mhamaí."

I added Irish to my Duolingo line-up weeks ago, but I still have no idea what he's telling our dog. I will have to buy the premium subscription when it goes on sale this St. Patrick's Day so I can make sure he's not teaching Este anything inappropriate.

Ha. That's it!

St. Patrick's Day.

"If you're going to be like this," I say, leaning forward, "there's something you have to let *me* do for *you*."

His eyes shoot up to mine. He swallows. "What's that?"

"Chair the St. Patrick's Day Talent Show," I answer in a shallow voice, suddenly wondering if there was something else I could have done for Tommy to make us even that would have required a lot less of my time and been a lot more fun.

"Ah, sure, the talent show." He chuckles. "I need the help and would be a fool to say no. But it wouldn't be fair to you."

"Sort of like how paying for everything is not fair to *you?*"

He shakes his head and doesn't have to bother saying he has much more money than I have time. "Co-chair," he offers.

"I don't think you're going to find any volunteers to fill that role if you haven't already," I argue.

"Me," he says. "And you. We will co-chair the talent show."

"We will?"

"If we can successfully raise a puppy together, I'm sure we can manage a high school performance showcase."

"The jury is still out on the puppy. This was just day one." I give Este one more big squeeze. "Text me and let me know how she's doing later," I say, backing reluctantly out of the car.

"Will do." Tommy holds Este's collar to keep her in the seat. She whines when I close the door, her sad cry carrying out the cracked window. "Wish me luck. She's already sad to see you go."

"Good night, Tommy. Good luck."

"Good night, Emmie," he answers, and I turn away before he drives off.

When I open the door to the condo, I find Benji and Leila making out on the couch.

"Finally," Leila says, hopping off of Benji's lap, which he scrambles to cover with a pillow, offering me a strained wave.

Ack. "Were you two waiting up for me?"

"Isn't that obvious?" Leila asks, running a hand through her hookup-tousled hair.

"Ah, yes, just like my mom and George used to do it. Humping away their apprehensions while they waited for me to make my return."

"Don't lie. You never went out in high school, and you definitely never gave your parents anything to worry about."

"Except for maybe the fact that *I never went out.*"

"That happens to be a concern I share in the present. Now tell me what happened?"

I outline—in what is probably unnecessary detail, but I need Leila to know everything so she can make sense of it for me later—what happened from the second the last bell rang at school up until I walked through the door of the condo, complete with a slideshow of all thirty-two photos I took of Este.

"So what you're telling me," Leila says slowly, handing me my phone, which is open to a photo of Este licking Tommy's cheek while he carries her around the store, "is that you and our head of school, whom you f—" She glances at Benji in the kitchen and lowers her voice to a whisper before it goes extra high and loud. "Whom you fucked, are sharing custody of a puppy?"

"Yes, I think that is what I am telling you."

Benji, who has wandered in and out of the room since the beginning of my story, ambles over and offers us some tortilla chips from a bowl.

"Can you believe," he says, feeding one to Leila, "that guy left a high six-figure position in DC to be stuck in that dilapidated building with one hundred teenage assholes."

"Excuse me, Benji," Leila says, shoving his shoulder. "Only *we* are allowed to call our students assholes."

"High six figures?" I hiss. "Like, more than five hundred thousand?"

"Like two hundred fifty thousand more," Benji confirms, popping a chip into his mouth.

"No wonder our budget seems tighter than ever," I groan. "The board must have had to offer him a fortune."

"Those assholes probably did," Benji concurs. "I can call them assholes, right?"

Leila and I nod.

Benji sighs in relief and then shrugs. "But Tommy wouldn't accept more than what the previous head of school made."

I grimace. "*Seriously*?"

"I know," Benji says, passing Leila another chip. "What an idiot."

He tries to hand me the bowl, and I shake my head, worrying my bottom lip. "Are you absolutely sure? About the money?"

"Micah told me. He's got some in with Audrey." Micah Green is Benji's younger brother, who "graduated" last spring from college at twenty. "Graduated," as in he invited his family to the giant university ceremony, walked across the stage with the other students, and forged a diploma, which he offered his father in exchange for a new pickup truck. Essentially, Micah is a hot, perhaps marginally unethical genius who is naturally good at everything and capable in ways that make him useful to important people.

If he told Benji that Tommy accepted peanuts compared to what he's used to earning to run our school, it's true.

"What an unwelcome insight." I frown as I drop onto the couch and then scooch further away from where I just caught Benji and Leila going at it on the cushions. This is *bad*. Really bad.

Well, bad for me.

Almost all the evidence would suggest that the odds of Tommy being a good person are in his favor. Every single little thing except for...Vegas.

He's maybe even an extraordinarily good person. He's not the money-grubbing, corporate hound I assumed he would be when the board announced they were bringing him on. Nope. He's the guy on the couch rubbing my feet, telling me how he wants to make a difference in the world.

And he is my boss. And now we have a dog together. And I have...*oh no*.

I have pretty big—verging on ginormous when I think about his laugh and his eyes and the way he snuggled Este—feelings.

"*Cheese and crackers*," I moan, dragging my hands down my face.

Benji gawks at me, bewildered, and Leila puts a hand on his arm.

"I thought..." he says, glancing between us. "I thought it was a good thing. You know, finding out that your new head of school isn't a terrible person. He seemed pretty cool when I met him yesterday. I thought I'd invite him out to drinks with Micah. Maybe we could all—"

Leila cuts him off, shaking her head.

"Sorry," he murmurs.

"No, Benji," I say, standing. "You're right. The school deserves someone great at its helm. And Tommy has the education and the background to be the captain we need to steer our sinking ship to port."

"Stop immediately," Leila says. "You're doing that thing you do where you like, dissociate, and turn into a character from *Mad Men*. A boring one, not the sexy, alcoholic kind." She sits down next to me on the couch, and Benji takes the other side, his eyes still a little wide and vaguely nervous.

"I can have Micah poison him?" Benji offers.

"No," Leila and I both say in unison, with varying degrees of conviction.

"For now, he lives," I say, taking both their hands. "And moving on to more exciting things, Mr. Benji Green, Leila has something she'd like to ask you."

Nine

B ENJI SAYS YES. AND Leila is only moderately mad at me for bringing it up to him before she and I had a chance to talk.

"Leila," I tell her when she corners me in the hall bathroom as I'm getting ready for bed, "I would ask the entire cast of *House of the Dragon* to move in here if I thought it would make you happy."

She leans against the door. "A shame they'd probably say no."

"A shame," I repeat, setting my electric toothbrush on the charger. "Benji will have to suffice." I smile at her in the mirror.

She frowns back at me.

"What?"

"I worry about you, Em. I love how kind and generous you are, but sometimes I wish you were less of a d—"

I whirl to face her. "Do not say it."

"Do-or," she says, dragging the word out. "Ma—"

My face heats. "I am not a doormat, Lei!"

"You sort of are, sometimes."

My heart pounds in my ears. "Why?" I ask in a sharp whisper, extra glad that I intentionally forgot to mention that I volunteered to chair the talent show while recounting my evening earlier. "Because I want my friends to have everything they want? Because I like to spend some extra time at school helping the kids when I can? Because I—"

"Because you're whispering right now even though you are wildly pissed off, so you don't make me or Benji feel bad about the fact that you are human and also have emotions and needs."

I roll my eyes at her, afraid to speak, but the wetness building along my lids makes the gesture less convincing.

"Em, other people's happiness and well-being do not rest on your shoulders or depend on your sacrifices. You are not responsible for all of us."

"I know that," I say, blinking away tears. "But if I can help make someone's life better, and it doesn't cost me anything, then why not? What's wrong with that?"

Leila sighs and puts her hands on my shoulders, looking down at me with deep brown eyes. "It's costing you, Em. It's costing you *your* happiness. Your life, really." She pulls me into a hug and kisses the top of my head.

When she pulls back, my eyes are so full of tears that I can't make out her expression. I don't try, ducking my head to stare at my feet instead. I don't want her to feel bad for making me cry.

"This conversation isn't over," she says softly. "You know I love you, right?"

"Love you too," I murmur. I fight the urge to tell her she should be locked in her bedroom with Benji, celebrating this new relationship milestone, and not locked in a bathroom with me. I want to tell her I'm fine, fine, fine. That I love my life. That I don't feel sad and empty on the inside at all or worried that one day the dark cloud that trails me between smiles, hovering at the edge of every merry moment, is going to swallow me whole, like it did my mom.

But she'd know I'm lying.

Leila hugs me one more time before sliding out of the bathroom. When she's gone, I reach for my floss, my dentist's words from last year's checkup echoing in my memory, just like they do every night: *Good work brushing, Emeline. But I would like to see you take better care of your gums.*

I've been flossing twice a day ever since so when I see her again, I don't disappoint her. I want to make my dentist's day a little better. I want her to feel like she's doing good things and that people respect her and listen to her dental advice. I want to make my dentist...happy.

Leila's wrong.

I'm not a doormat.

I'm something much crazier.

My face is frozen in the mirror, and I blink at myself, considering if there is anything I truly want or need in my life. I make enough money to cover the necessities and help with George's housing, even with the care facility upping its rates this year. I don't need a bigger house or a nicer car. I think about Este, and yes, I would like a puppy in my life. But that doesn't mean she has to live here in our second-floor condo with poor Fib, who would be miserable. If Tommy can keep her at his place, I can wake up extra early to walk her in the mornings and take her to the park on the weekends. Tommy and I could work out a schedule for visits. And when she's with him, I can rest easy knowing he will spoil her rotten.

I smile, thinking about Tommy scooping Este into his arms when a chihuahua started barking at her in the vet's office, the gentle sound of his Irish reassurances.

"One day," he told her, "you'll be big enough to eat that little yapper." He winked at me, grinning, when I gasped beside him. "But you won't, Este. Because you're our best girl."

My reflection shakes its head at me, and I turn on the cold water, splashing my face.

Este, I confirm. *Este is what I want and need.*

Then I floss between every tooth—twice—and go to bed.

M Y ALARM GOES OFF at five, and as soon as I turn sleep mode off, I find an invite to a shared album titled *Baby Este (not S.T.): January.* I open it immediately and scroll through all the photos Tommy took of the dog when we were together, way too many of them featuring me holding and kissing and petting her, and all that he took after dropping me off. Este eating. Este playing. Este sitting in the crate, her big, sad puppy dog eyes staring up at the camera through the bars.

And last, a photo of Este no longer in her crate but instead passed out on a very comfortable-looking bed, snuggled deep into a (likely real) down blanket, captioned, *Oops.* I'm still laughing as I pad into the kitchen to make coffee.

I lean against the counter while it brews, reading the series of corresponding text messages Tommy sent, hourly updates about the puppy, how she misses me but he's keeping her busy, how he hopes he's not bothering me by texting too much, how the puppy doesn't want to sleep alone.

I scroll back to the photo of her curled up in Tommy's covers. And why would she want to sleep alone when that is the alternative?

I'm up, I text. Let me know if you need any help with the puppy this morning.

Then I add, Thanks for the photos and the updates. I was only a little jealous when I saw her in your bed. I hope you both got some sleep.

I press send, and the coffeemaker beeps. I pour a cup, add some milk and maple syrup, and take a big sip, looking out the kitchen window where the moon still hangs high in the west, glowing between bands of silver clouds above the Pi Alpha Kappa frat house. The *Tears of My Students* mug—Leila's favorite—heats my hands, and the coffee warms my insides, and I'm filled with a sense of okayness, about Tommy, school, Benji. Everything.

What Leila said yesterday in the bathroom wasn't wrong, but that doesn't mean it's bad. I'm pretty sure my life will turn out all right, which is good enough for me.

I pull my phone out again to scroll through the pictures of Este, and my text thread with Tommy is still up. I reread my last message and almost spit out my mouthful of coffee. *What the frick were you thinking, Emmie? I was jealous when I saw her in your bed?* Even if Tommy's awake, too, it's not a surprise he hasn't responded. What do you say to that? Your one-night stand and current employee coming on to you.

But I wasn't! Was I?

Jealous of YOU, I meant, I type furiously. That you got to sleep with Este.

And not alone.

Not that you necessarily sleep alone.

Oh my god, is there another woman in bed with my puppy?

I didn't want you to think I was jealous of the dog. That would be weird. You can sleep with whomever and whatever you want.

I need to stop.

It doesn't matter at all to me what happens in your bed.

Obviously.

Eight individually-sent text messages, all before five-thirty in the morning. If that doesn't scream *unhinged,* I don't know what does. As long as he doesn't fire me, we are good. He can't fire me for this, can he?

I'm pacing the kitchen when my phone buzzes.

I haven't had enough caffeine yet to decide if I should be offended by these messages, but all the same, I'm happy to report that Este and I slept great, just the two of us, in my bed, and that she has only chewed through one sock so far—not cashmere.

He closes the message with a winky face.

My exhale sounds suspiciously like a giggle.

Our best girl would never chew through the cashmere, I respond, wishing I could be there with them to watch Este wake up in her new home.

I can swing by and grab you after I shower, he texts, remembering before I do that my car is still dead in the parking garage.

There are so many reasons I want to say yes to his offer, but instead, I tell him not to worry and to enjoy his morning with Este. Hopefully, if I can get the car thing figured out, I'll be able to see her after school.

About that, he says, I made a couple of calls last night and found someone who can replace the hybrid battery in situ, so you won't even have to have the car towed.

I gape at my phone, slightly panicked about how much this kind of car service will cost.

Wow, Tommy. Thank you.

He'll be there at eleven. Since you have the juniors for Latin at that time, I will plan on meeting him in the garage.

A thrill goes through me that Tommy knows my schedule, but this is outrageous. Perhaps, since all the proof points to Tommy being an exceptional person, he feels guilty about the hotel situation and is trying to make it up to me—a fresh start now that we are dog parents together. I appreciate the sentiment—actually, *appreciate* isn't the right word. The "sentiment" makes my body flood with heat and my heart skitter between *all* of my pulse points, but for my sake and his, we will have to secure some boundaries before I'm so head over heels that I ruin things between me and him and Este.

I can't ask you to do that, I write back.

You didn't. Besides, the fella owes me a favor.

You've lived here for two weeks! How can someone already owe you a favor? And please, don't use that favor on me. I am grateful for your help, but I can figure it out on my own.

He sends back: Too late.

I reply with a paragraph about how I am capable of taking care of myself, and I've done it for years, and I don't need his help, all in the politest way possible. In fact, I add that I should be assisting *him* with the puppy—which reminds me that I never typed up those missing signs or googled groomers. So basically, while Tommy was helping Este adjust to an entirely new world and finding someone to save my car, I was doing nothing at all.

In lieu of an actual response, Tommy sends me a picture of Este on his couch with one of the toys we picked for her: a squeaky plush shaped like an octopus. We'd had mixed feelings when we found it at the pet store, and Tommy's *phew* emoji that follows the photo tells me that he is as relieved as I am to see her cuddling and not destroying the cephalopod.

I chug my coffee and jump into the shower before the water is warm. I'll take Leila's car to school—she can hitch a ride with Benji—and by the time Tommy pulls into the parking lot, he'll find a bunch of beautifully typeset "Found Dog" posters. Plus, I'll have a call into the best dog bath place in town and an Excel sheet prepared for the talent show.

I'll even stop and get him a flat white with whole milk and an extra shot of espresso on my way in—and hope he doesn't ask how I know his order. (I happened to see his to-go cup in the teachers' lounge trash can and absolutely did not mean to study it long enough to memorize what was written, but I had to check twice that I hadn't imagined the heart drawn in Sharpie under his name.)

So there.

Take that, Tommy.

Ten

When I finally manage to sneak out of the school to check on the status of the Prius, it has started raining. I hurry past the building that just went up for sale next door to Desert Grace and pray they don't put in another smoke shop, covering my head with my arms when I'm past the overhang. By the time I'm half a block from the parking garage, the gentle winter drizzle has turned into a full-blown desert whopper, making me regret leaving my cardigan in the faculty lounge. My boots slide sideways beneath me as I round the corner, and when I finally make it to the covered stairs, my clothes and hair are plastered to my skin.

I don't regret my lifelong resistance to umbrellas (three hundred and fifty days of sunshine a year do not justify the purchase of rain gear) until Tommy does a double take when I walk up to him.

"Hey," I say, hoping my nipples aren't so hard from the cold that they've defied the padding in my bra. I know that my rain-drenched shirt will do nothing to counteract their pertness. I glance at my Prius, parked where I left it while someone tinkers under the hood. "I hope you haven't been stuck out here this whole time."

The car repair was supposed to begin at eleven, and it's now past one.

"My guy was running late, and since I'd been distracted thinking about Emmie all morning, I ran home to check on the dog," he whispers.

I scrunch my brow, shivering when a gust of cold air whistles through the concrete walls.

"*Este,*" he corrects, handing me the jacket he has hanging on his arm. "Thinking about Este."

"Right, of course. How is she?" I whisper back, not sure why we can't talk openly in front of the mechanic.

"Good. I closed her in the laundry room, but she has everything she needs." He grins and slips his hands in his pockets. "She even did her business on the puppy pad and again when I let her out in the yard."

"Such a good girl." I glance back toward the staircase to the single "Found Dog" flyer we taped on this level and briefly let myself entertain the idea of tearing it off the wall.

"The best," he says, taking the jacket from my hands and opening it for me. "Put this on. You look like you're freezing."

"No, I'll be fine," I protest, but he's behind me, working my arms through the sleeves. "Honestly, Tommy, I'm sopping. It's going to get all—"

"Emmie Jones, is that you?" A puckishly attractive face and two bright blue eyes peer at me from under the hood, dark curls escaping from a backward baseball cap. "I've never seen you wet before, though I've definitely thought about it."

"Hi, Micah," I mumble. My blush is almost painful; Micah's joshing always makes me turn red, probably because it tends to center around him poking fun at my well-established lack of sexiness.

Beside me, Tommy crosses his arms. "You two know each other?"

"I live with his brother," I say in case it wasn't already clear that there couldn't possibly be anything between me, Micah Green, and his alternatively very well-established *abundance* of sexiness.

"Is that so?" Tommy asks, his eyebrows about shooting off his forehead as his mouth tightens.

"With him and Leila," I hurry to clarify when I realize I'm not doing a great job making my point and before Tommy turns any paler. "Mostly with Leila, really."

"I heard the big news," Micah says before using his very tight white T-shirt to wipe his face, exposing his ridged abdomen and a swath of tattoos to me and Tommy. I look away. "We should go out and celebrate."

"Yeah, maybe," I offer, trying to determine whether I should be concerned that Micah somehow already owes Tommy a favor. Micah is usually the one eliciting debts.

Micah laughs. "Careful with this one, Tommy. She might look all sweet and innocent, but I'm convinced that somewhere in there..." His gaze drags over my soaking wet clothes and lands on my very wide eyes. Tommy tenses. "Is a wild little thing waiting to get out."

"Ew, Micah. There is no wild thing in here."

Tommy chuckles, and I stare at him in disbelief. Micah doesn't miss the exchange.

"I wouldn't know, would I." He shifts his attention to Tommy, setting his hands on his hips so his biceps look extra big. "I've been trying to get Leila and Benji to set us up on a double date for nearly a year, but Emmie refuses."

I scoff. "What are you talking about? That's definitely never happened."

"So you'd consider?" Micah teases, twin dimples appearing on his cheeks.

"Oh my god, Micah," I mutter, mortified that hot Micah is doing such an easy job of demonstrating to dreamy Tommy that the idea of dating me is a big joke even my friends are in on.

Tommy steps forward, seeming a bit more self-satisfied than I'm used to seeing him, and takes my hand to bring me around the front of the car, where I find myself standing between him and Micah.

"The battery is installed bond good to go," Micah tells me, smiling as he flips a wrench in his hand.

"I tested it," Tommy says, releasing my hand and rolling the sleeves of his linen button-down up above his elbows. I bite my lip as he leans over the fender in a way that I find troublingly sexy. "I was just going to check the oil and give the rest of your fluids a once-over."

"My fluids," I repeat stupidly.

"I can manage her fluids," Micah says, his mouth quirking at the corner as his shoulder brushes against mine when he reaches under the hood. "You head back to the office, Tommy boy. I'll make sure she's well taken care of."

Tommy clears his throat and leans across me to look Micah in the eye. "Kind offer, mate, but my afternoon is quite open, and I'm enjoying the fresh air. I'll be in touch. Thanks for the help today."

Micah chuckles and backs away. "I assume you know how to use the dipstick."

"I've known how to use a dipstick since I was twelve," Tommy says, reaching for something in the engine.

"Then have at it, man." He turns to me, lifting his cap to run a hand through his black curls. "I'm helping Benji move some stuff with the truck later this evening. See you at your place? I'll grab some of that Mexican beer you like."

Tommy's hands fist. I gape at Micah. We've hung out approximately five and a half times since Benji and Leila started dating. How could he possibly remember—

"Is it Modelo or Corona you keep stocked in the apartment?"

I shake my head and laugh. He remembers because he finishes at least half of our six-pack every time he comes over.

"Actually," I say, "I'm not sure I'll be home. I—we, um—I sort of got a puppy, and I have to—"

"Next time, then." Micah winks at me before giving Tommy a hard pat on the shoulder. "Feel free to call me if anything comes up with the car, Em."

"Thanks," I say, tugging at the sleeve of Tommy's jacket. Neither of us says anything until Micah drives off, flipping his baseball cap forward before waving out the window of his pickup with a smirk plastered on his face.

"So," I ask when his taillights disappear around the corner. "What's a dipstick?"

AFTER SCHOOL, TOMMY WAITS for me to wrap up exam practice—which I am pretty sure absolutely no one on the faculty or board thinks I should still be leading—so I can follow him to his house in my perfectly functioning car and play with Este.

The clouds have rolled on, and I lower the windows to let in the sun-soaked air, a *No Such Thing as A Fish* podcast episode blasting through the speakers while my still-squishy socks dry on the passenger seat.

How's this for living my life, huh, Leila?

Tommy, it turns out, lives surprisingly close to school. In a mere six and a half minutes, I'm parked along the curb of a very familiar-looking home. I work my damp socks over my toes, stuff my feet in my boots, and hurry up to where he's parked in the driveway.

I gasp when I realize where we are. "Tommy!"

"Yes, Emmie?" he responds as I pull the door wide so he can step out of the Tesla.

"Is this *that* house?"

"And which house would that be?" he asks, digging a set of keys out of his brown leather briefcase.

"Oh, you know, just the one that a certain world-famous, three-time Album-of-the-Year-winning popstar remodeled and sold."

He glances at the beautiful pink plaster adobe walls of the home he lives in, the perfectly xeriscaped front yard. "Cece never sold. I'm renting."

"You call her *Cece?*"

"She asked me to."

"You've met Cecily Prior?" My voice is so high I barely recognize it.

He laughs as he walks to the antique, carved mesquite front door. "We've only spoken on the phone, but she seems as lovely as the public imagines. You're a fan, I take it?"

"Did you know she has a Master of Social Work? And if it weren't for her, there never would have been enough pressure on Congress to pass the Education Advancement Act last year. I'm not just a fan—I *love* her."

"Ah," he says, his sun-bright green eyes holding mine. "So that's your type. Good to know."

I purse my lips at the carefully curated cactuses in the yard. "Cecily Prior is *everyone's* type, Tommy. After all, you're the one living in her house."

"On that note, are you happy admiring the exterior, or would you like to peruse inside as well? I know Este would be happy to see you."

I clasp my hands, rolling onto the balls of my feet. "Oh, yes, I want in, please."

Tommy glances down at me as he works the key into the bronze lock. "She left all her furniture, linens, even some shampoo. It's basically the exact same as when she lived here."

I make a noise between a squeal and a snort. "Leila is going to be so jealous when I tell her my tush and Cecily Prior's tush have touched the same surfaces."

"I hope that means you'll stay a while," Tommy says, swinging the door open. "There are a lot of surfaces."

I smirk. "I'll sit on all of them so I can really rub it in."

"Excellent." He gestures into the house, an invitation. "Where shall we begin?"

I hesitate outside the door, my mind going straight to places it should not, like the bedroom, and... "Oh my god, Tommy, do you sleep in her bed?"

"I suppose I do."

"On the same mattress?" I ask, crossing my arms.

He chuckles. "I can neither confirm nor deny that."

"Either way, her essence is still there. Can you feel it?"

Tommy's eyebrows furrow. "Is it strange that you are much more excited about me sleeping in Cece's bed than I am?"

"It's…" I study him as he pushes the door wider, holding it for me. "It's kind of nice, actually."

"Make yourself at home," he says, smiling as I step over the threshold and into the home of the only celebrity I've ever really cared about. But once I'm standing in the entry hall, which is even more incredible in person than it was in *People* magazine, I hear Este whimper, and all of my fantasies about sprawling myself across Cecily Prior's seats and couches vanish.

I turn to Tommy, and he nods down the hall. "Go ahead," he says. "I have to take a call, and then I'll come find you girls."

I run my hand over the gorgeous furniture as I walk through the house, following the sound of Este's cries, noting a box of Nilla Wafers on the kitchen counter. When I open the laundry room door, I crouch, and the puppy launches herself at me with so much love and abandon that I burst into tears as she licks at my face, squirming in my lap to get closer, every inch of space between us a thousand miles too many. I hold her to me as tightly as possible, breathing in the smell of her suspiciously less stinky fur, feeling her little heartbeat pound against my palm.

Sobbing is a normal reaction to Este-levels of cute, right?

I'm still crying when I carry her out to the yard, depositing my cardigan and lanyard—which keeps hitting Este in the face when I bend down to pet her—on a small table. The space is edged with old-growth trees, making it feel like I'm in the middle of a magical forest and not the middle of town. A magical mesquite forest, with a full outdoor kitchen complete with a wet bar, a raised, stone jacuzzi that spills into a lap pool, and a sitting area under a canopy of fairy lights that forms a circle around a stained-concrete fire pit.

I let Este down to do her business and sit on a chaise lounge that is probably worth more than my car, wiping the mascara smears off my cheeks and pushing the escaped gloom back into the recesses of my awareness. I fleetingly question why a little bit of affection from a dog was enough to rust the rock-hard bars of the cage I try to keep the shadows in, but there's not much to wonder about.

The fullness and force of being so implicitly and unabashedly loved, of belonging to another person, is not something I've felt since I lost my mom. It isn't something I want, either. I saw what it did to George to lose his person, the way it both literally and figuratively broke his heart. And he was strong. So much stronger than I am.

My mom was strong, too. But all of my love and all of George's love still wasn't enough to mend her broken pieces or ease the storm inside her heart—a storm that's followed me, too, for as long as I can remember.

I sniffle, watching Este stalk something in the gravel before she bounds back to me and jumps up on my thigh with her front paws. I lean down, and she licks my face. "Are you the love of my life?"

"Ah, *a spéirmhná*. There you are," Tommy calls as he comes through the back door, carrying cans of sparkling water in either hand, each a different flavor.

I take the raspberry when he joins us.

He pops the lime for himself and sits down across from me on the other chaise. "Sorry about that. I promised Mr. Duarte's biology class I'd make them Báirín Breac if they all passed the test, and I had to call my sisters' brother, Cormac, for Nan's recipe."

"How come every time you talk, I only end up with a million more questions?"

"Shall I start at the beginning?"

I nod.

"Yes, every single student passed the test. And yes, Mr. Duarte only included questions they had heavily reviewed in class, but to see how good they felt about themselves after, we both decided it was worth it."

"I one hundred percent support everything about this."

Tommy grins lopsidedly at me, and I accidentally sigh. "I told Mr. Duarte you'd say as much. You really get these kids."

"Was he worried I'd be mad?"

"The staff is nearly as intimidated by you as the students, Emmie. But I think we should keep it that way."

I huff out a laugh. "Yes, I'm terrifying."

"You have no idea," he says, shaking his head.

I roll my eyes. "So, what is this thing you're making for them?"

"Báirín Breac, or barmbrack."

"Which is?"

"A sweet bread with dried fruit that we Irish mostly eat around Halloween."

"Well, then, of course it makes total sense that you'd be preparing it for our students in January."

"They asked what my favorite holiday was." He shrugs, the tops of his freckle-dusted cheekbones a light pink. "Which is how we landed on the barmbrack."

"I see," I murmur, looking away from Tommy because all I can *actually* see after he said that is him sitting below me in a torn cassock.

"And as for my siblings, in total, there are seven of us."

"How very Irish Catholic of your parents."

He raises his eyebrows. "Aye, but it's a bit more complicated than that. How are you at family trees?"

"Try me." I bite my lip. As excited as I am about finding out Tommy sleeps in Cecily Prior's bed, I am far more excited that he is about to share intimate details about his family life. Because even if I know I'm not made for the kind of love my mom and George had, I can let myself appreciate Tommy and his easy laugh and smiling eyes risk-free, knowing that he's not interested.

I offer a sympathetic murmur when he talks about his parents' divorce, and I cuddle Este while he attempts to explain the confusing dynamics of his family. He tells me, with a smile that doesn't reach his eyes, that his parents remarried right away. His mom went on to have three daughters, and his stepdad had a stepson from his previous marriage who spent a lot of time with their family, thus his sisters' brother. His dad had two more sons.

He tells me more about his sisters, who he's grown incredibly close to over the years. And he tells me the reason he didn't arrive at school with the rest of the faculty the week before the students came back is because the oldest of his sisters, Neeve, is now going through her own divorce, and he flew to Dublin to help with her kids.

"She's tough, though. So are her girls," he says, his voice a little scratchy. He reaches forward to pet Este, who has fallen asleep beside me. "She'll figure things out."

When our fingers graze, I want so badly to take his hand in mine. To squeeze it. To kiss it. To take some of that quiet pain from him. "Is it hard being so far away?"

"It is," he confesses, resting his forearms on his legs. "But hopefully we won't be apart for too long."

I worry my lip, dropping my gaze to Este as I consider the very real possibility that Tommy is already planning his next move. And that it might be somewhere very far from here.

Eleven

As I click the unlock button on my Prius keys and hear the car door do exactly what it is supposed to, I admit to myself I was very, very wrong.

Spending time with Tommy is full of risks. The more I know about him, the easier it is to entertain the fantasy of conversations and foot rubs on the sofa, a lifetime of sideways smiles as we learn each other's secrets. That is an incredibly dangerous hope to harbor for your boss, who is also likely only in your town until his next best job offer comes along.

Especially when he's already made it pretty clear he's not interested in spending morning-afters together.

My arms still shake with the effort it took not to hug him when I left his house.

Instead of going straight home, where Benji and Leila—and heaven forbid, Micah—are probably celebrating, I drive to George's care home on the other side of town. I haven't visited him since school started back up again, and I feel guilty about it every day. But at the same time, every time I see him it feels like coming face-to-face with an emotional cave-in that I don't have the strength to dig myself out of.

I sign in at the front desk and wave at a few familiar faces as I get in the elevator. Hopefully, George will be asleep, and I can give him a kiss and leave a note. Hopefully, he'll remember who I am when he reads it.

I take a deep breath and enter the code to his wing. There is a group of people in wheelchairs and on couches watching Turner Classic Movies in the common room. The air smells like lemon essential oil and bleach and decrepitude, and I get mad at myself for the revulsion I feel, trying to replace the visceral distaste of being here with empathy.

All I manage is pity, which makes me feel worse.

Light floods out from under George's door, and I steel myself before knocking.

"Come in," he calls, his deep Brazilian accent, the innate friendliness of his voice, making me smile.

"Hi, George," I say, stepping into his room and shutting the door behind me. "It's me, Emmie." This part is always the hardest—wondering where his mind is and if I exist in that space.

"Emminha," he says, beaming at me. "I've missed you. How is school?"

"I've missed you too," I say against the tightness in my throat, bending to hug him in his bed. He has a book resting upside down on his chest. "And school is good."

His mouth flattens, his expression serious. "Don't worry about what anyone else tells you. There is nothing wrong with a degree in the humanities."

I laugh, even though my eyes sting. On the ten-year anniversary of the day George met my mother, just six months after we said goodbye to her, he had a heart attack. After, the doctors told me that George had suffered a severe lack of oxygen, and essentially, his coronary had caused such acute vascular damage in his brain that it resulted in the sudden onset of dementia.

Maybe that's what happened.

But I sometimes suspect he just didn't want to exist in a reality that didn't include my mom. For a long time, I was mad at him for leaving me alone with my grief. I was resentful that he got to exist in a fiction where everything was still okay, while every day I had to wake up and try to make sense of a loss I couldn't even begin to articulate. I had to fight every morning and every night, struggling to stay ahead of the regret and shame and dread that hunted me. And I had to do it all by myself.

I've forgiven him, though. I wouldn't wish the past ten years of pain and loneliness on anyone. Especially not George.

"You'll declare in history, right?" He pushes, sitting up straighter in bed. "Don't listen to that advisor. *Siga o seu coração, minha querida menina.*"

Follow your heart, my sweet child.

He said the same thing the week before he ended up in the hospital. And I followed his advice then. I ache to tell him how much it paid off, how much I love my job. I still grieve the loss of his guidance, of being able to let him know that his belief in me, his acceptance and love, helped keep me working through that history degree when I would have rather let myself waste away under the covers.

"Best advice you ever gave me," I say, taking his hand, the skin dark and warm against my own. "I declared my history major. It's official."

"You did good, *filhota*. You *are* good. And we are so proud of you."

When I hug him, I bury my face in his shoulder so he can't see my quivering lip, the tears building in my eyes. "Thank you, George," I murmur against his soft, forest-green sweater as he rubs my back.

George has been telling me this since I was eight years old. And since I was eight, I've been determined to keep being good. There were times—while George was growing up in Brazil, and when he first came to the United States, working nights to pay for school—that George didn't have much. Other times when he didn't have money for food or a place to sleep. "But Emmie," he'd tell me, "as long as I held on to my principles, I always had those."

And now I have them, too.

I pull away and reach for his book. "What are you reading these days?"

"*A People's History of the United States.*"

"Ah, yes. A nice, light examination of the horrors humans have inflicted upon one another before bed always helps me sleep, too."

I flip the book open to where he's marked his page with a precisely folded paper napkin.

He laughs, his hand rising and falling with his belly. "Ignoring the world's ugliness doesn't make it disappear. It just makes it more likely to catch you unaware when it rears its head."

"Don't I know it." I sigh.

"You're too young to talk like that."

For George, I will be forever eighteen, but inside, I feel like I've lived hundreds of lifetimes worth of hurt and worry: my own, and that of my students and their families. I wish I could hold more. I wish I could keep everyone's pain where they didn't have to feel it.

I think of Tommy and how devastated he appeared while talking about his sister and how the divorce has taken the entire family out at the knees. I hate myself for being so selfish that every time I looked at him these last two weeks, I only saw the bruise he'd left on my feelings and none of what he was carrying.

And still, he is endlessly kind and thoughtful, which I don't deserve. I'm not another abandoned puppy that Tommy has to care for.

I kiss George on his forehead and pull the covers up to his shoulders. "Ready for your good night story?"

He smiles and closes his eyes, and I read until he falls asleep.

I STAY UP WAY past my bedtime hanging out with George, and when I show up at school the next morning, I'm tired, grumpy, and sad in an impossible way. The kind of miserable where the tears are always waiting to fall, and the weight in my chest feels so massive that I worry the gravity of it will suck others into the gloom, that they will be forced to orbit my gratuitous despair with no hope of escape, which is why I actively avoided Leila and Benji before leaving the house.

I know the drill. I just need to ride out the melancholy until it's replaced by something different, like numbness or anger.

All I can do is hope it's a short ride this go-around.

Ah, *depression*. One of the few things I have left of my mother.

At school, I discover I don't have my lanyard, and therefore my access key to the door, and cry until Mx. Brown arrives and lets me in. I sob for the entire thirty minutes I spend packing boxes in the Family Pantry for our students and alums to take home, tears dripping down the donated cereal boxes and the toilet paper packages, because why do *I* have a right to be sad when these kids can come to school with smiles on their faces?

Then, I cry when Marco hugs me in the hallway because he's so excited about his excellent grade on his Latin project, and I'm so proud of his hard work.

He pulls a bruised apple out of his backpack, probably from that morning's school breakfast because there is nothing less appealing to these kids than an unedited piece of fruit, and hands it to me. "Thanks for believing in me, Miss J."

I cry again, and I'm still crying when I enter my office and see my red cardigan draped over the back of my chair, my lanyard hanging over it.

A big, gentle hand rests briefly on my shoulder. "Este and I came by to drop those off last night, but Ms. Bashar told me you hadn't come home yet," Tommy says.

I try. God, I try. I sniffle, I swallow, I do everything in my power to suck the tears back in, to Uno reverse my mental breakdown. All to no avail.

"You did?" I ask him, wiping my eyes, clearing them enough to see that he looks horrified. But not horrified in the way a man might when a woman starts crying. I am now well aware that he has too many sisters to be troubled by those things. He looks horrified because he has no idea *why* I'm crying, and now he's probably assuming it's because of him, and all he did to make me cry in reality was be...was be...

He strides past me and picks up the lanyard off the chair as I watch, then returns, standing in front of me with a soft, crooked smile as he drapes it around my neck, freeing my hair where it gets tucked under in the back.

I sob, dropping my face into my hands.

Why does Tommy have to be so perfect?

He pulls me into a hug, and inevitably, I cry harder.

"Let it out," he says, petting the back of my head.

And I do. Because *I am* the abandoned puppy. I hate to admit how nice it is to be held, to let another person bear some of this heaviness for me, to feel like there is something keeping me upright besides my own willpower and resolve. The relief of not feeling alone with it all is almost overwhelming.

Which is so unfair. This is my burden, and no one else's.

"You left the lanyard on the table outside when you were playing with Este." His finger grazes my neck, tracing the curve of the lanyard. "I wasn't sure if you'd need it, so last night, Este and I decided to take a walk and bring it by in case."

My chin trembles. "You guys walked all the way to my house?"

"Well, *I* walked. Este mostly napped in my arms and barked at a few passersby. You're quite close. Took us less than an hour there and back."

"How did you know which condo was mine?" I ask, risking a peek up at his face.

Tommy's gazing down at me, the green in his eyes deeper than ever. I press my face back into his shirt.

"We had to do some investigating," he admits. "Luckily men with puppies aren't terribly suspicious-looking. Unless they're in vans, I suppose."

I laugh, and he squeezes me a little tighter.

"Anyway, the door with the dead succulents out front and the #RedforEd sign staked into an empty pot of soil felt like a safe bet."

"Are we that transparent?"

"I fear so." His fingers twist the ends of my hair, and I shiver. "Micah answered the door when I knocked, told me you weren't home yet, and that Leila and Benji had already, well, retired to the bedroom."

When I arrived home after visiting George, Micah was still on the couch watching a YouTube program about building houses out of plastic. He tossed me a lime, and I missed it. Then he yelled, "Second time's the charm!" before pretending to chuck a beer at me. I crossed my arms and wished him good night before he actually threw the bottle and I was forced to spend the next thirty minutes picking glass out of the rug.

"Micah is almost charming when you're not around," Tommy says, his tone vaguely amused.

"Yet more proof that I have the unique gift of bringing out the worst in men," I mutter.

Tommy pulls back, angling his face to look into my eyes. He bites his lip.

"Sorry," I say, shaking my head. "That was—"

I cut myself off. What is there to say? That it's true? Every time Micah and I interact, he acts like he's four Jäger shots deep at a frat party. And Tommy left me in a hotel room, even though he is also *this* person: caring and thoughtful and holding me so close I can feel his heartbeat. Holding me so close that for a minute, he blocked the clouds.

How can a man who ditches someone after sleeping with them be such an amazing...

Oh. *Oh.*

I press my forehead against Tommy's chest. I can't believe I didn't see it.

I have this exact conversation with at least fifteen students a year.

I have been friend-zoned.

I push myself off Tommy's perfect body and take a step back, my eyes still volatile wells of tears. "Thanks for bringing the cardigan. I was visiting my...George."

"George Silva? Your stepdad, right?"

And just like that, I'm crying again, but this time I walk away. I'll go up to the roof and cry myself dry and be in class on time, looking perfectly sane and excited to be alive another day.

For the kids.

And for Este.

And because I have to believe that maybe one day there will be a tomorrow without clouds.

Tommy follows me out the door, but I'm around the corner before I have a chance to change my mind.

This will pass; it always does, and then I can go back to pretending. I can prove to myself again and again that my heart is strong enough to keep on beating, even when only darkness lives there.

Tomorrow will be better—because it has to be.

Twelve

L EILA AND I STAND with our backs to the faculty lounge door, heads bent together as we read our neighborhood association emails on our phones. The residential area right off the university campus is a combination of young kids with wealthy parents and old local holdouts who are unwilling to give students free rein of the historic housing, which means that the listserv emails are generally hilarious.

"'Bush and Bulky,'" I giggle.

"Oh, god," Leila says, putting her phone in my face. "Mrs. Kammemeyer called it 'Bulky and Brushy.'" She makes a wheezing sound, bending at the waist.

"Leila," I groan. "This one." I try to catch my breath through laughter. "This one says, 'Bushy and Burly.'" I snort so loud my face hurts.

Someone clears their throat behind us, and I freeze. How can even his throat-clearing have a hot accent?

"Sorry, ladies, but there is a strict 'No erotica in the teachers' lounge' policy in place." He catches my eye, and my chest bursts into flames. "I know, if only it weren't so."

"Don't worry, Tommy," Leila says. "We're just checking the Brush and Bulky schedule for our neighborhood. It's an American thing. We put out all our big trash for other people and the sanitation department to collect."

"Who knew garbage could sound so pornographic?" he asks, warily eyeing the coffee he's just poured into his mug from the stained Mr. Coffee pot.

"Actually," Leila says, "Emmie and I have a tradition." She looks at me, and I shake my head so hard I make myself dizzy, only stopping when Tommy glances at us with his eyebrows raised.

I've been excellent at keeping a healthy physical and emotional distance from Tommy since I had a mental breakdown in his arms last week. A lot of pieces came together as I sobbed on the roof, and as a whole, they presented the very clear picture that a.) Tommy is a hugely compassionate person who feels the need to take care of vulnerable creatures, i.e., me and Este b.) if I use his kindness as a brace while he's here, when he leaves Desert Grace and moves on, I might not remember how to stand on my own and c.) if I let him continue to take care of *me*, I'll never be capable of being what he's actually looking for: a friend.

Communication has been mostly limited to emails about the talent show (no, I will not dress up as a leprechaun just because I'm short, and for the kids' sake, it makes more sense for him to do it and prove to them we are all capable of subverting expectations), brief conversations about Este when I come over to walk her, texted photos of Este between visits, and the occasional FaceTime so I can tell the puppy good night. Plus, a whole lot of purely school-related things.

Tommy dumps his coffee in the sink and then pivots back to me. "And what does this tradition entail?" he asks, holding my eyes.

"See," Leila starts, "the school doesn't have much of a budget for furnishing classrooms. The stuff they buy tends to fall apart pretty quickly. I assume you've noticed. So"—she grins at me—"Emmie and I spend a couple of weekends a year scavenging the Brush and Bulky piles on the curbs. You wouldn't believe the things these college kids leave behind when they graduate."

"Huh," he responds, face unreadable, while I sink deeper into the shame of this man realizing the absolute dire straits that are our school and its survival.

Leila pushes on. "Yep. And then, when our spoils runneth over, and we know the school library will weather another year without collapse, we get really drunk and go dancing."

"Leila, what the *chuckwalla*," I hiss.

"I see." Tommy's mouth quirks into an adorable smile. "And when does this Brush and Bulky quest you speak of occur?"

"This Saturday," Leila responds, *oof*-ing as my elbow hits her ribs.

"And where do we meet?" he asks.

Leila gives him all of the details, and when he leaves, she reassures me that this does not go against my "no Tommy on private time outside of Este visits" policy because we are doing it for the school, so it is actually work, and therefore it makes absolute sense that Tommy should be there, too.

"And when we all go to the Budgy Pony after for beer, do we still consider that a professional context?" I ask over my shoulder, checking the expiration dates on the condiments in the faculty refrigerator.

Leila drags the trash can closer. "What, are you worried you're going to seduce him again if you get him somewhere seedy enough?"

"No," I say, tossing a questionable ketchup into the bin. But I'm extremely worried I am going to try.

Leila leans against the counter beside me. "It'll be great. And we'll have Benji and Micah as a buffer. You know, Micah—"

"I already told you, there's nothing there," I state over the sound of the now-beeping fridge alarm.

Leila scooches me out of the way and shuts the door, blocking me when I try to open it again. "You also told me he looks like a shorter, darker Chris Hemsworth."

"We all know Micah's hot," I say, putting my hands on my hips. "But that is your type, thus Benji, and not mine."

"It is *such* a good type, though." She sighs dreamily. "But Em, it's been since October. And spending so much time with the last guy who gave you an orgasm while not getting any can't be healthy. Just think about it. I know Micah would be down."

"Has he said something?" I ask, lowering my voice. I think about Micah in his white, muscle-hugging T-shirt leaning over the engine of my Prius. If Micah is interested, that would change things a little.

Is it possible he actually *did* care about my fluids?

"He might have mentioned to Benji, on an annoying number of occasions, that he thinks you're hot, in like a feral cat sort of way."

I shake my head. "Is that a *good* thing?"

"I think you make him nervous."

"And again, is *that* a good thing?"

She shrugs. "It isn't bad."

"Are you sure this isn't a trick, another way for him to mock the fact that I have the sexual energy of a wrinkly apple?" I ask, raising an eyebrow.

Leila pushes off the counter. "He said you have the sexual energy of a wrinkly apple? I'm going to kick his—"

"No, he didn't say that explicitly. I just assumed all his quips about being wet and getting drinks were, well..." I trail off, looking at my feet.

"You mean, all those times he was brazenly flirting with you, you believed—because you have the most deranged sense of self of anyone I know—that he was *making fun* of you?"

I tug on my lanyard. "Pretty much, yeah. Exactly."

"Surprise." She raises her hands, wiggling her fingers. "He was not making fun of you, Emmie. He was trying to get in your pants."

"We're sure?"

"Positive," she answers, crossing her arms.

I narrow my eyes at her. "Maybe you're in on the joke. I am reasonably confident I know the difference between flirtation and ridicule."

"You are hopeless."

"But Lei, wouldn't it be weird for you and Benji if Micah and I..."

Leila raises her eyebrows at me. "If Micah and you what? Hook up? Bang? Date? Start a furniture business together?"

"Any of the above."

"No. You would never date Micah. Both of you are horrible at relationships and are more committed to your coffee orders than you've ever been to another person."

I scoff.

"Romantically," she clarifies. "So a future messy breakup isn't in the cards. It would just be a way for you to blow off some steam and for Micah to add *cougar* to his list of conquests."

"I don't turn twenty-eight until June; that hardly makes me a cougar."

Leila rolls her eyes. "Fine, make it less exciting."

"That's what I do best." I grin at her, and she pokes me on the shoulder.

"Listen," she says. "No pressure, either way, but he's coming Saturday. You should just have fun and see what happens."

"Right, with Tommy there," I say tightly.

"Sounds to me like an opportunity to really expand your sexual horizons. Tommy might get jealous having to share you, though. I've seen the way he pouts when you're all over Este."

I scrub my hands over my face. "Would that it were so simple."

"You're lucky you're cute," Leila says, depositing a granola bar wrapper she grabs off the counter into the garbage can as she slides past me. "Because sometimes you are so impossibly fucking stupid."

"If it weren't for me and my vague knowledge of everything in the universe, we would never have won all those rounds of Hooters trivia in college!" I call after her as she heads for the door.

"That is true. But next time you decide to fall down a Google rabbit hole, do us all a favor and make it about something like 'how to read my hot boss' body language,' or better yet, 'how to tell if I'm too stubborn for my own good.' Okay? Thanks."

I throw my hands in the air. "Fine. I'll see Micah naked if it will make you happy."

"It would be a start. Even better, you could do it to make yourself happy for once."

B Y FRIDAY AFTERNOON, THINGS have gone off the rails.

Benji can't borrow Micah's pickup tomorrow for Brush and Bulky because Micah has some mysterious Micah-esque thing he has to do with it, though he swears he'll make it to the Budgy Pony for drinks after. But there will be no after, because without the truck, we have no way of collecting our treasure trove of trash.

I immediately start to panic that a child's leg will be crushed under the janky desk in the computer lab before we can replace it. After Leila assures me, with a detailed plan and list of materials, that we can secure the desk long enough to keep all limbs in our school safe, she leaves me in our office with orders to find Tommy and tell him that Brush and Bulky is off.

For a reason that neither Leila nor I fully comprehend—okay, Leila claims she *definitely* fully comprehends the reason and insists that I intentionally refuse to, but she is wrong on both counts—Tommy is unwilling to concede defeat and says he'll figure something out, which makes me even more upset.

Tommy now feels responsible for collecting literal garbage for his place of work. On a Saturday.

And because Tommy is Tommy, he texts us at seven the next morning and tells us he's all set and ready when we are.

"Holy shit," Leila murmurs, peering out the window. "We are going to be able to fit so much street furniture in that thing."

I hurry up beside her, and there he is, parked outside our condo, waving from the cab of a U-Haul rental with Este in his lap.

I drop my half-finished coffee in the sink and run out to the curb. "The board is going to be furious," I tell Tommy by way of greeting. "They never would approve this kind of spending."

"I figured as much." He shrugs. "I rented it myself."

"You…" Este leaps across Tommy's legs and licks me in the face through the open window. "You did?" I don't know why I'm surprised.

"Yeah, I—" His eyes catch on my top and then track down my body. I realize I left my oversized sweater inside and hug my arms over my middle. He clears his throat. "I did."

Every year since we were eighteen, for our not-so-secret Santa, Leila and I buy each other a cute workout ensemble in the hopes that one day we will feel inspired to, well, work out. So far, in the past six years, we've managed one and a half yoga classes. (We had to leave halfway through the second because the shiny leggings I splurged on for Leila made a queefing noise every time she bent forward, and we couldn't stop laughing.)

We've rededicated most of our athleisure to Brush and Bulky, which means today, all I have on is a white long-line sports bra and a pair of skin-tight Belgian Blue pants. I might as well be naked.

"Thank you, Tommy."

"Sure." He scratches his jaw and chuckles when Este tries to leap out the window for me. "This little booger slept on my head last night. It was unsettling, and yet, I've not slept so well in decades. She's missed you, though."

When Tommy opens the door, I very carefully grab Este off his lap and give her a big kiss on her forehead. "I just saw her Thursday."

Este squirms in my arms, twisting her body to sniff my face.

"Well, it obviously wasn't enough Emmie time."

"I feel the same way about you, Este. Never enough time," I say through a giggle, the dog's cold nose tickling my neck.

"You know," Tommy says, keeping his eyes on the puppy. "I meant it when I said you were welcome whenever. I think I have an extra key somewhere, and if you had your own, you wouldn't have to worry about my schedule. I know you think you're disturbing me or some nonsense, but it's nice to have you around. That's too big a house for a man and his dog."

We look at each other at the same time, and all I can do is blink. For Pete's sake, does this man's goodness know no bounds? Is he trying to ruin me with his kindness?

"Oh shite, sorry, not that she's my dog. *Our* best girl." He laughs, running a hand through his hair, and I notice for the first time that he's wearing a tight crew T-shirt that matches my...his...crew sweatshirt. I imagine my face is almost as red as the *Boston College* written across the front.

"Anyway, think about it. If I can't find the other key, I'm happy to have a spare made, and I'll give you the alarm code, even though I never remember to—"

"Hey, friends," Leila says, throwing an arm over my shoulder. "What are we talking about?"

"N-nothing," I stammer. "Just, dog. Dog things. Look at Tommy's great chest. *Truck*. Look at Tommy's huge truck."

Tommy smirks, sliding a hand over the steering wheel. "*Huge*," he confirms.

"Don't worry, Tommy," Leila assures. "Emmie always gets hot and bothered over the promise of a good secondhand file cabinet. The bright red cheeks are to be expected."

"Good to know," he says, studying me a little too closely. "You Rubbish Rousers prepared for the best dumpster diving of your lives?"

"Been working on that one a while?" Leila asks.

Tommy gives us one of his lopsided grins, and I fidget under Leila's arm. "Days."

"We love it," Leila says, dragging me around to the other side of the truck and shoving me in. "Onward, Rubbish Rousers! Benji and I will follow in the Honda."

"Wait," I say, reaching for her as she shuts the door. "My sweater!"

"I'll grab your things!" she shouts at me through the window. "And Tommy, turn on the A.C. before she combusts."

Thirteen

B Y THE TIME WE turn onto 3rd Street five hours later, Leila has been wholly taken by trash fever. She and Benji are no longer following us. He is driving, and she is making me keep a call open on speakerphone so she can apprise Tommy and me, in the much slower-moving truck, of their whereabouts.

Leila brought a map with a highlighted route of all her favorite houses in the area. She did not, however, bring me *my* sweater.

She brought me Tommy's.

"Turn left down the alley. Now!" she orders through the receiver.

Tommy jerks the wheel so hard I slam against his side, grabbing his thigh when I try to right myself without dropping Este on the floorboard. But there's no time for embarrassment. As soon as the truck straightens, we see Leila fly out of the passenger side of her CRV like it's on fire, racing to a gorgeous armoire before the people in the cargo van behind her can get there.

"To the victor belong the spoils!" Leila yells as they roll past with their windows down, looking understandably bewildered.

We park along the curb and help her and Benji load the enormous oak piece into the back of the almost-full truck. We all put our hands on our hips and admire our work.

"No prisoners," Leila says, glancing down the street at another huge pile of trash being visited by a couple of young kids walking a dog. Este barks. "Good girl. Let's go."

Benji reaches for her hand and slowly draws her back to him. "Maybe we should eat, babe. Refuel."

"One more bookcase," she demands, holding all of our eyes in turn.

"I second Benji's plan," I tell her. "I'm sorry, Lei, but it's taco time."

She looks at Tommy, glaring in challenge.

"Forgive me, Ms. Bashar, but I'm with Emmie."

"Quitters," she huffs. "See you at La Pasadita." I turn to go, and she pulls me in by the elbow. "By the way, our hot boss has been staring at your ass all day."

"Are these pants completely see-through?" I whisper-hiss, covering my butt with my hands.

"Just see-through enough, I'd say," she answers, opening the driver's door of her car.

"You're not funny," I tell her before crawling self-consciously back into the U-Haul, where Este is already falling asleep on the bench seat next to Tommy.

I give him directions to the best taco stand in town, and Tommy hums appreciatively as he starts the engine. "You know," he says, "I wasn't sure I had a full picture of Leila as a person before today, but it's all starting to come together."

"You mean, you thought maybe there were other sides to her outside of what you see at work, but you've now realized that this *is* Leila's side."

"Exactly." He smiles, pulling the gear shift into drive. "I get why you two are such good friends, being how you complement each other so well."

My brow scrunches, and I want to ask him what he means, but his phone rings.

"Excuse me," Tommy says apologetically as he opens the call. "Top of the morning, Audrey. It is still morning, right?" He winks at me.

Audrey?

Calling on the weekend?

I turn my focus to Este, trying to pretend like I'm not desperately straining to hear what Audrey's saying. The fuzzy sound of her laugh through the receiver makes every muscle in my body tighten.

"So far, I'd say we've been quite successful. You agree, Emmie?"

"Oh, what?" I ask, as if I wasn't giving his conversation the fullest attention.

"Audrey asked if our hunt for quality furniture has been successful."

"Yes, very," I answer. I feel my smile wobble. Why did Tommy tell Audrey about Brush and Bulky? Do they talk all the time, about everything? That's fine, of course, but he doesn't have to share things like this with her, does he? What if she tells her uncle? Can the board fire us for filling the school with garbage? What if it's a health violation?

Tommy chuckles and listens for a second before uttering some of the most unsettling words I've ever heard in my life: "Thanks, Aud. Yup, noon is great. Excellent. See you then."

Oh, dear, here comes the nausea. I wrap one arm tighter around the puppy and the other around my belly.

From my lap, Leila's voice rockets through the cab of the truck. "*Aud?* What the fuck was that?"

I fumble to hang up the phone. "Sorry," I mumble. "I didn't realize the call was still open."

Tommy flicks on his blinker with a laugh, pulling in behind Benji and Leila in the right-hand turn lane. "I think you two would get on quite well with Audrey. Maybe I could arrange a little dinner at the house. You and Leila could bring someone, if you'd like, as well."

"Like a triple date?" The words launch from my mouth without my permission, propelled by the frantic beating of my heart.

"A date?" Tommy responds, sounding amused. "A work date, perhaps. Do those exist?" That calms me down just barely. He seems to pick up on my weirdness, probably because I haven't taken a full breath in approximately three minutes. "Audrey's been very welcoming since I arrived."

Of course she has. Look at you! I want to scream in his pretty Irish face. But deep down, I'm glad someone has been there for Tommy. I sort of wish it wasn't Audrey, but...

"I think the board stuck her with me," he goes on. "They wanted to make sure I didn't immediately pick up and leave as soon as I realized what a quandary they'd gotten the school into, so she's been showing me around, trying to sell me on the town."

I swallow the bitterness that rises in my throat when I remember he'd asked me to do this on his first day, and I refused.

For the better. For *his* better.

I shake my head. "Wait. Did you say quandary?"

"Nothing to worry about," he assures. "Anyway, we've been to some nice restaurants, a couple of museums, a gallery opening."

Great. And here I am about to feed him street food after rifling through refuse for hours. Geez, I don't think I even brought my hand sanitizer.

"Sounds fun," I tell him in the cheeriest voice I can muster.

"I'm not much for such things, but it sure beats staring at my walls."

"Cecily Prior's walls," I correct at the same time a brick of guilt settles in my gut.

"I'd say it beats staring at most any walls. Exceptions being, of course, the Sistine Chapel and the refractory of Santa Maria delle Grazie. I'm sure there are a few more."

"The whale mural on Presidio Avenue?"

"I've not yet seen that one."

"But you've seen the other two?" I scoff, blinking at him. "The Sistine Chapel and DaVinci's *The Last Supper*?"

"Part of the convenience of living in Ireland is that it takes you as long to get to Italy as it takes someone here to get to Vegas." He looks at me, his eyes bright and playful, then turns back to the road.

"Not many great walls in Vegas," I say. "But the windows are nice."

His gaze shifts to mine again, a little darker, and my chest heats to boiling.

"I don't know why I said that," I mutter. *Dear god, what is wrong with me?*

La Pasadita comes into view, and I exhale, pointing to where Leila is waiting for us with crossed arms in the parking lot.

Tommy maneuvers the U-Haul into a tight end spot and clears his throat. "You're not mistaken, Emmie. The view in Vegas was grand."

As we sit at the plastic picnic table waiting for our food, an older couple, arms wrapped around each other's waists, approaches Tommy.

"May we?" one of the women asks, nodding toward Este, who is out cold in Tommy's lap.

"Certainly." He adjusts her so they can pet our puppy, the smile of a proud parent on his face as they admire our best girl. Este's tail wags in her sleep.

"Is it..." the other woman asks, giving a slight shake of her head as she takes in the puppy's collection of confusing features.

"A dog?" Tommy offers.

I give Este's nose a kiss. "Probably."

Tommy grins at me, and I grin back. The couple laughs, and I don't miss Leila's raised eyebrows across the table. Luckily our order is called up, and I don't have to take my friend aside to explain to her that it is perfectly normal for two people who co-parent a puppy to say cutesy little things about the dog in public and find it terribly amusing.

After scarfing down one of everything on the menu, Tommy proclaims to our delight that La Pasadita is the finest food he's had since he's been here.

"Best taco you've ever eaten, right?" Benji asks.

"It may well be," Tommy responds, picking up his glass of water.

Leila snorts. "Really. The best, Tommy?"

He takes a sip of his drink like he didn't hear her. The pink tips of his ears would suggest otherwise.

"You are officially the worst," I mutter, kicking her under the table.

Leila leans across the empty paper plates. "Jealous of the carne asada?" she whispers.

"No! I just want you to stop comparing my vulva to my favorite Mexican food," I hiss at her.

Leila smirks at me. "Does Audrey like tacos?" she asks, shifting her attention to Tommy. "Maybe you should bring her to try them sometime."

I freeze, gaping at her.

"I'm sure she'd love a lunch here with you and Emmie one of these days," he says, and Leila eyes me like she's caught a scent and won't let it go until she learns where it leads. Which, frankly, feels precarious in this case. I'm not sure I want to know.

Leila rests her elbows on the table, folding her hands under her chin. "Why do you think that?"

"You two might not be aware," he says, looking first at Leila and then at me with raised eyebrows, "but Audrey cares about Desert Grace near as much as you do."

"Impossible. No one cares about the school as much as Emmie," Leila says at the same time I ask, "What do you mean?"

Tommy shrugs. "Talk to her, then you can see for yourself." He licks a bit of hot sauce off his finger, and I shiver. "Should we head to school?"

Leila proclaims that our mission is not yet complete, and to appease her, we hunt down one last bookcase before going to campus to offload our plunder.

From there, sore and tired, we return the rental, Tommy gets his Tesla, and we all drive to Tommy's place under the pretense of dropping off Este. Only Leila, having been told that the house belongs to Cecily Prior, spends forty-five minutes absolutely freaking out as she investigates every little detail, including the sheet count on Tommy's bed—information I could have done without—and doesn't stop until Micah calls Benji to tell him he's on his way to the Budgy Pony.

"Splendid," Tommy says, crossing his arms. "Micah's going."

"The whole gang." Leila walks to the door, stopping to pout before she steps out. "But I'm coming back, Tommy. Me and this house are not through."

"Any time. Feel free to bring this one with you." He nudges my shoulder.

I cross my arms. "You make it sound like I'm a negligent dog mother, Thomas."

"Oh, Thomas, is it now?"

"I can do worse."

"Let's have it."

"Thomas *Flynn* O'Connor."

"Aye, just how my mum used to say it when she was giving out."

"Giving out what?" Benji asks.

"Good question, Benji," I say, and we both stare at Tommy.

"All right, friends," Leila interrupts. "We'll have to have our lesson on questionable Irish expressions another time. If I can't spend the rest of the evening in Cecily Prior's bedding, I'm going to need a margarita ASAP."

Benji and I file out the door behind her, and Tommy smiles at us. "Thanks for the lovely day. Be safe. Benji, until next time."

My heart sinks to my feet, but I tell myself it's relief—relief that I can't say anything stupid or, to be more accurate, *continue* saying stupid things to Tommy if he's not there.

The windows in Vegas?

No wonder he doesn't want to come.

This way, there will be no battle between me, my beer, and bad decisions involving my behavior toward my boss.

"Good try, man." Benji laughs as Leila pushes her way back inside, hooking an arm through Tommy's.

"Not today, sir," she says, dragging him outside. "Budgy Pony or bust!"

"I don't want to get in the way. I realize it might be weird with your head of—"

Leila lays a gentle finger on his lips, and it might be the first time she's ever made me feel jealous rage. "Stop. Talking. You are as bad as she is." Tommy's eyes flick to me, and I grimace. "You two, in the back seat. Now."

"Are you sure you're all right with me being there?" Tommy asks quietly as we trail Leila and Benji to the car.

There is nothing I want more. Which is such a problem. "You have to be there," I tell him. "It's Brush and Bulky tradition."

Tommy nods. "First round's on me," he calls to the others.

"I knew I liked this guy," Benji says, kissing the side of Leila's head.

Same, Benji. Same.

Fourteen

Micah is standing outside the door of the Budgy Pony in a tight shirt, looking like he just box-jumped off the cover of *Men's Health*. He's surrounded by a group of super cute co-eds in country western boots.

I'm in sneakers, my hair is sweaty, and I'm wearing Tommy's Boston College Crew sweatshirt, which Leila forced me to put on when I started shivering in the car.

Tommy grins every time he looks at it.

"Finally," Micah says, peeling away from the girls. He tugs off his baseball cap and shoves it in a butt pocket, running his free hand through his curls. "First rounds on me."

Tommy, who has a good four inches on Micah, pats his shoulder. "That's nice of ya, son, but I've already offered."

Leila nudges me, smirking. *Son,* she mouths.

Micah tenses for a quick second before tossing his head back and laughing. He throws an arm around Tommy and leads him to the bar. "All right, then, *Pops*, but I call the second."

I hustle to the bathroom so I don't have to hear what Leila has to say about that one, and when I come back out, a series of shots are lined up on the bar.

Here goes.

The first one flows down fine, but I gag on the second, spit most of it on the bar, and order myself a Corona instead. Tommy, Micah, and

Benji are four Tequila Slammers in before Benji throws his hands up in defeat and disappears with Leila.

Micah turns to Tommy, standing beside him at the bar. I think he might be on his tiptoes because he can almost look him straight in the eye. "What do you say, old man? Can you handle another?"

Tommy glances at me, two vacant seats down the bar, lobbing popcorn in my mouth between sips of beer. "I think I'll take a break. You've done it, Micah. You've out-drunk your middle-aged Irish mate. Well done."

"Fine," Micah says, "but you're not getting out of the karaoke competition."

"Wouldn't dream of it."

"Em," Micah says, leaning over Tommy to meet my eyes. His smile is so sweet it's almost boyish. "Want to dance?"

I take a quick look at the dance floor and laugh. Every muscle in my body aches. "Micah, I can barely move."

"Massage, then?" he offers, and Tommy frowns down at him like he might knock his head into the bar top.

I cough out a kernel of popcorn. "I'm good. But thank you. Go have some fun."

Micah grins and heads out into the press of attractive dancing people.

Tommy watches him go and then takes the seat next to me. "Having a good time?"

"Are you?" I counter.

"Pretty sure I can get Micah to end up in the toilet if I wait out the last shot."

"How fatherly of you."

Tommy chuckles, and dang it, I've done it again. Tommy beside me at the bar.

Tommy, my boss.

"I'll take a Corona," he calls to the bartender.

Boss. Boss. Boss.

"So, no dancing at all?" he asks when his beer arrives.

"Seriously? You could dance right now?"

"I could do a lot of things right now," he says, looking from me to his beer before taking a long sip.

Boss! I scream in my head. "Aren't you tired from all the heavy lifting today? Because holy *shish kebab,* I'm exhausted."

"Can you turn anything into a swear?" Tommy sets his beer on the bar top and turns to me.

"It's *not* a swear," I say, smiling. "That's the point."

He eyes me, one brow higher than the other. A day of too much sunshine, mild dehydration, and the effects of rapid-fire tequila shots loosen his features. "I'd argue that the 'sweariness' of a word is inherent in how you use it, not the word itself."

"That's ridiculous. A bad word is a bad word because it is bad." Okay, maybe the sun has gotten to me too. I clear my throat. "The essence of a word, which decides whether or not it is a swear word, is dictated by thousands of years of linguistic evolution and usage."

"That's a load of *horseshoes,*" Tommy says.

"And *that* did absolutely nothing to prove your point," I respond, laughing as I cross my arms.

"Okay, let me see if I can make this clear another way."

"Let's hear it.

Tommy grins, leaning closer. "If someone says, 'fuck you,' we can both agree that's a swear, right, Ms. Jones?"

"Yes," I murmur.

"But..." His voice drops.

"But?" I say, my heart beating in my ears.

"But if, in a film, for example, someone were to say, 'I want to take you to bed and fuck you for hours,' it surely isn't—"

"Still a swear," I interrupt, swallowing.

He pulls his bottom lip through his teeth. "Hm. I see."

"A swear word is a swear word is a swear word," I say, grabbing my beer with trembling fingers and looking around to see where Leila and Benji ended up. Tommy's gaze follows mine, and we both see them at the same time, making out against a wall.

"Can I try again?" Tommy says, and I swing my eyes back to him.

"You can try, but—"

"You are so fucking beautiful, Emmie Jones, that I have not stopped thinking about you for months. My mind is on fire with the memory of you, and every time I walk into school, it takes every single shred of my goddamn willpower not to bend you over a table and rip your clothes off. Every time you talk, I want nothing more than to taste your lips with my tongue. You have fucking ruined me, and it is the best and the worst thing that has ever happened to me."

Heat floods everything, all of me. Even my fingertips are on fire.

I gape at him, my breath catching as he stares into my eyes.

Is he trying to make me lose my mind? Because it is working.

What *was* that?

The hottest, most sexually thrilling thing anyone has ever said to me?

Yes. Definitely that.

A red stain appears on the tops of Tommy's cheeks, and he turns away, taking a sip of his beer. His head sags as he studies the glass bottle. "Yeah," he murmurs. "Pure profanity."

I stammer out a sound that neither confirms nor negates his assertion, but the slump of his shoulders has me reaching out my fingers and grabbing his hand before I can stop myself.

"Tommy," I say. "What. The. Hell?"

His head snaps up. A grin momentarily replaces the weariness on his lips, then fades again. "I'm so sorry, Em," he says, shaking his head. His auburn hair falls into his eyes, and I want to brush it off his face so I can try to read what's written in them. "It's just been sitting there in my mind, these memories and thoughts of you, and I've not known how to get past it. I hoped that if I laid it out between us, if we could both laugh about it, it might help. That I could move on. But every time I've tried to joke about it you get mad, and the feeling just wouldn't let up. Damn those Tequila Slammers for making it impossible to keep my yammer shut. But look at you, *a chroí*. A man was bound to break eventually."

"You left me, Tommy. You left me in your hotel room."

"Righto, I left. You wanted bagels."

"But you didn't come back," I insist.

"Emmie." He stares at me, the lines between his eyes deepening. "I came back. I came back with a half dozen everything bagels. Garlic cream cheese. Lox. Pickled onions, even."

"You didn't leave a note."

"A note? You said you were hungry. I told you to stay."

"It was hours. I thought—"

"Just under two hours, to be precise. Took me a bit to get a car, being before dawn and all. I googled *best bagels in Vegas* while I waited. The drive was just under thirty minutes, but I figured you could use the extra shut-eye. When I got to the bagel shop, the everything bagels weren't in the bins yet, so I had to wait a bit, call another car, make the ride back. All said and done, it was quite the adventure. Unfortunately, I ate them all myself and think I've rather lost my taste for lox."

I shake my head. "You mean, you didn't run away?"

"Run away from *you*? Are you daft? Those were the longest two hours of my life. I've never wanted to get back anywhere more in my life than I did to that damned suite. Only, once I got there, you weren't in it."

My knuckles are white on my beer when Micah runs up and slaps Tommy on the back. "Your song is up next, man."

"Thanks," Tommy says as he scoots his stool back, and I don't stop him because my brain is still too tangled for emotions to process.

He brought me bagels. I left! And I have been such an...an...asshole.

Tommy bows his head, smiling sadly before walking away toward the karaoke stage. Someone announces the song: "Next up, we have Tommy Flynn performing 'I Believe in a Thing Called Love.'"

I stare at his back as lyrics play across the screen. I'd cry if I wasn't so angry. At myself. At the world.

Oh my god. What have I done?

Leila slips onto Tommy's empty barstool. When she pulls it closer to me, the wooden legs scratch across the Saltillo tiles. "Well, Bushy and Burly did not disappoint this year."

"I need another shot," I tell her.

I DANCE.

I dance *a lot*. I dance with Tommy. I dance with Micah, who is still standing after their fifth shot and not in the toilets as Tommy predicted. I dance with a group of girls celebrating a twenty-first birthday who tell me they love me and that they wish I were their little sister (short people problems).

I dance because I do not know what else to do with the knowledge that Tommy brought me bagels.

That Tommy still thinks about me naked.

I dance because I am happy, confused, and furious all at once, and I have to keep moving, or I'll be forced to think about what it all means. I dance away George's voice, telling me I'm a good person.

Good people don't make unethical choices.

But what if Tommy *isn't* an unethical choice?

He's only my interim boss, in the end.

I dance off the feeling I get at the thought of Tommy leaving.

I dance until I am so hungry, Tommy feels my stomach gurgle under his hand when he's swaying behind me, an arm wrapped around my middle.

"Time to go," he announces, and to my dismay, a very sober Leila appears at once to drive us home to the condo, where, I decide, I will be making pasta for everyone.

Everyone, in this case, includes Micah, who squeezes in beside me in the back seat of Leila's car, so I am smooshed between him and Tommy in a delightful Emmie sandwich.

It turns out some very attractive people really *do* want to have sex with me.

"I'm going to make the red sauce from scratch," I declare, settling back into the pair of strong shoulders bracing my own.

And maybe tonight, I will have sex with one of them.

Tommy checks all the boxes he did the first time we slept together, plus, like, a thousand more since I've learned about his family, how generous he is, and seen what he looks like snuggling a puppy.

He's not my *real* boss; he doesn't have the power to change my salary or my class load or suddenly make my insurance plan compatible with human life, so I have nothing to feel guilty about.

And we've already done *it*.

Besides, the school employee handbook contains zero fraternization policies—I might have double-checked. In fact, we are so free to fraternize that last year, Desert Grace's chaplain married our P.E. teacher. Neither of the involved parties was fired or forced to quit.

Revisiting the bedroom with Tommy isn't necessarily a good idea, but it's not the worst. And I'm pretty sure I'm not just telling myself that because he's perfect, and if I were ever going to seek a real-life committed relationship, I'd want it to be with him.

Oh, nope. I shake my head, sighing through my nose. *Easy there, Em.*

"All good?" Tommy asks, his face so close that I have to bop his nose with my finger to keep from kissing it.

"Great!"

"I love homemade red sauce," Micah adds, pressing his shoulder tighter against mine.

He smells pretty good. But I can't have sex with Micah. And not even for a lot of little reasons. Just one big one.

I want Tommy.

"Do we even have pasta at home?" Leila asks from the driver's seat.

"Spaghetti noodles," Benji says.

"Just spaghetti, no noodle," I correct.

"Spaghetti," Benji says.

"Why do they call it a wet noodle and not a cooked noodle?" I ask, dropping my head back onto the seat. "It makes no sense. A wet noodle can still be hard. But what about *penne*? If the root word is *penetr*—"

"Drunk Emmie," Leila says. "Compelling us all to confront the hard-hitting questions of our time."

"Wet noodle," Micah says, chuckling.

"Am I drunk, though?" The dancing would suggest yes, but in total, I only had two shots and one beer over the almost four hours we were at the Budgy Pony. And all that was tempered by a whole lot of popcorn and ice water.

Maybe I'm drunk on nerves, assuming that's a thing. Ever since Tommy told me he wanted to bend me over the desks at school and tear my clothes off, I've felt like my insides are pure static.

"Tell them about the premise for your fantasy novel and let them decide," Leila suggests.

"Ugh, it's so good, you guys." I take a deep breath before the big reveal: "Every character is named after an NPR correspondent."

"I'd vote tipsy," Tommy says.

Micah hums. "I think she needs another Corona."

Fifteen

WHEN WE GET HOME, Leila and I supply blankets and pillows from our beds to make the couch extra comfortable while the boys decide on a movie to watch. Benji is determined to put on *The Big Lebowski*. Tommy and Micah are huddled on the couch debating which is better: *Raiders of the Lost Ark* or *Indiana Jones and the Last Crusade*.

(For a spaghetti party after tequila shots? *Neither*. Obviously, we need to watch a western.)

While no one is paying attention, Benji presses play and settles in.

And since making a marinara is pretty difficult if you have zero tomato product available, I serve everyone bowls of wet noodles in olive oil with a dusting of grated parmesan. All we have left is a small sliver attached to the rind. Leila is the only one of us who doesn't eat her spaghetti.

About a quarter of the way into the movie, I look down to see Tommy, who is sitting on the ground, his back leaning against the couch next to my legs, hugging *my* pillow.

The one I sleep on at night.

I almost whimper when he sniffs it on a long inhale. There is no way I am going to be able to sit through the rest of this movie.

"Hey." I tap Tommy on the shoulder. "You think Este is okay? She's been alone for a while now."

He turns back to face me. "You think I should leave? Go check on her?"

"No. I mean, I thought *we* could go. That way, I can...say good night."

Tommy stands up so fast everyone whirls to stare at him.

"Where are you going?" Leila asks from the other end of the couch.

Micah perks up from where he's dozing in the armchair and scratches the golden strip of skin above his waistband, where one of his tattoos peeks out. "Emmie's going somewhere?"

"To see Este," I say, taking the hand Tommy offers to help me off the couch.

"I'm not letting either of you drive," Leila says, glaring as she cuddles deeper into Benji's side.

Tommy has his phone out in a flash, his fingers already flying over the keys. "I'm calling a car."

"Nope," I say, pushing his phone down. "We're walking. Less than half an hour, right? Come on."

I give Leila a hug, and Tommy and I slide our shoes on. Before we even have the front door shut, Benji shouts, "Fuck yeah, I told you it would be Tommy! You owe me twenty dollars, babe."

Followed by a depressive, "Dude, that hurts," from Micah.

Tommy chuckles as we head down the sidewalk. "Should I be offended that Leila bet against me?"

"I feel like that was more of a bet against *me*."

"Do they often gamble on who you go home with?"

I shrug. "They've never had a chance before."

"So, then," he says, gazing up at the dark blanket of sky above us. The stars are particularly bright tonight. The air bracing, but not biting. "You and Micah aren't..."

"Spending figurative time under each other's hoods? Checking each other's fluids? No." I shake my head. "Nothing. Never."

He exhales, and I look at his profile. The muted wails of a siren echo from somewhere in the distance.

"You and Audrey?" I venture. "Is 'a new gallery opening' actually a veiled reference to her, I imagine, fancy private parts?"

"You mean like the taco conversation at lunch?"

I wince, and he grins at me, lopsided, irresistible. "Leila," I groan.

He laughs. "But no, Emmie. Nothing. Never. Audrey is just a colleague and a friend."

We both fall silent, and in the space of a few breaths, our fingertips find each other, then our palms, and soon our hands are twined between us, his hand engulfing mine.

My heart sighs, or maybe I do, but I've missed this since Vegas. I've missed this since he let my hand go after leading me out of that terrible bar and out onto the Strip. I need a Real Doll, but one that is just Tommy's hand and based on a mold of the real thing, so I can hold it all the time.

"Do you date much?" he asks when we stop at a red light.

"Me?" *The girl fantasizing about making a prosthetic of your hand to sleep with?* "Date?"

He looks at me, his eyes sparking over my body. "Are you being coy?"

"God, no. And no, I don't date. Ever." The light changes, and he shifts his hand to my lower back as we cross the street. His touch is warm and solid, and the heat ripples through me. "Absolutely zero dating," I add, my voice a little lower.

He bites the inside of his cheek, taking my hand in his again. "I see. Are you ethically, or otherwise, opposed to dating? Commitment? Putting up with men, or whomever, for longer than necessary?"

"None of that. I don't have the energy to be righteous about relationships."

"Then why?" he asks, his voice deep and gentle.

"Because..." I feel my eyes burn and blink. A car passes, the headlamps bathing us in temporary technicolor, the halogen-brightness exposing me. I duck my head to hide my face.

Tommy's hand tightens around mine, a squeeze that feels like a thousand hugs I've desperately needed over the last decade.

"Because," I start again, shielded once more by the shadows, "it turns out most guys aren't content to receive the dregs of my attention. I have the school and the kids to focus on, and those are my priority.

Filling someone else's glass is impossible when you're pouring from an empty bottle."

"Why would it be your job to fill their glass?"

"I assume in an equitable relationship, you do that kind of thing for your partner."

He stops walking. "Maybe in an equitable relationship," he says, waiting for me to meet his eyes, "the relationship itself is cup-filling."

"Perhaps." I shrug. "But probably not if you're dating me."

He tilts his head, considering me. "Why do you say that?"

Why did *I say that?* I mean, I know why I think it, but Tommy doesn't need to be given my entire tragic backstory and a glimpse into my Pandora's box of unaddressed mental disorders. I glance at our hands and then up into Tommy's face.

Is it weird, though, that he looks like he *wants* them? All the dark and twisty things?

I shudder as something inside me tries to rise up. Oh, no, lots of *somethings*. Like Tommy's stupid, kind words were the key to the dungeon where I keep all my monsters hidden.

I swallow, willing them back down, into their cages, deep, deep inside. When they're all properly locked up again, I exhale. Geez. I really need to start saving up for a therapist.

We've gotten closer, and Tommy's free hand cups my face, his thumb grazing my jaw. "Emmie?"

I tip my face into his hand. "Yeah?"

"You didn't answer my question."

I bite my lip as my brain scrambles for something to say, as I try to deduce the least crazy response I can give him as to why I think I'd be terrible to date.

Self-effacing: A gentle laugh and poorly accented, "Let me count the ways."

Self-deprecating: A slightly manic laugh to hide the panic, and a joke about how if *whomp-whomp* were a person, it would be me.

Honest: No laugh, direct and instant overwhelm. Tell him I'm a disaster of a human being with loads of unresolved childhood trauma and that I'm not sure I've ever really been truly happy, or felt genuine joy, once in my entire life.

All terrible options.

Instead, I smile, pull his hand up to kiss his fingers, and tell him that it was just a stupid joke. He does me the courtesy of not calling out my lie, and we continue the rest of the way in silence, our fingers laced between us.

When we get to Tommy's, we tiptoe inside so we won't wake Este after a long day of cruising in the U-Haul. She's asleep beside his bed, and he lifts her onto his pillow. She opens her eyes briefly, wags her tail when she sees me, and then falls back asleep, nestled in the feather down.

"Good night," I say, kissing her very soft ginger ear.

We sneak back out of the room and shut the door.

"Well, mission accomplished," I tell Tommy. "Guess I'll head out now."

His eyes widen, then shrink beneath his drawn-together brows. "Oh. Okay," he says after some lip chewing.

I stroll over to where he's standing in the kitchen and hop—with some effort; I am just over five feet tall after all—onto the kitchen island in front of him. "Tommy." I reach out for his shirt and pull him closer until he's standing between my legs. Look at me go. "I didn't walk all the way here with you, way past my bedtime, to say good night to our dog."

His eyes rake over my face, his hand moving to my waist as his gaze settles on my mouth. I shiver, but my body fills with heat.

"Then why did you?" he says, his voice hoarse.

"To make up for the two hours you spent buying bagels?" I offer, barely breathing.

He grins and leans over me, taking my mouth with his, gripping my back with a broad, warm hand as he bends us over the counter, pressing closer, but not close enough. I wind my arms behind his neck, fingers in his hair, and lock my thighs around him, bearing myself against his body as our tongues get reacquainted, the kiss so familiar but filled with the ache of waiting months instead of minutes.

I graze my teeth over Tommy's perfect bottom lip, and he reaches a hand under my sweater, his fingers teasing my peaked nipples through the sports bra. I fumble at the hem of his T-shirt, desperate to rub my hands along the bare skin of his stomach, his chest. His other hand wraps around my ribs, and I arch into him, into the length and the want of him.

I moan, reaching between us to work my hand into his pants. My core aches at the feeling of him against my palm as I stroke, my breaths quickening at the memory of him inside me. He moans into my mouth, wraps both hands around my hips, and lifts me off the counter.

He pulls back to study me like he's making sure this is real. His green eyes hold mine, and my heart stutters so violently I'm sure he can feel it. But I think I can feel his, too.

He smiles, and I smile back. His teeth glide over my jaw, and we kiss again, desperate and wild, the hunger of our mouths so intense that Tommy stumbles a step before continuing down the hall with increased urgency.

We get to his bedroom door, and he freezes.

"What's wrong?" I ask, gripping him tighter with my thighs as I pant against his neck.

"Este."

"Right," I say, relieved that he didn't just now realize he doesn't actually want to tear my clothes off and do it on the desks at school. "Guest room?"

"Guest room," he confirms.

We are down the hall in six long steps, and I relax my legs enough to let him set me on the floor in front of the bed. I shimmy out of his sweater and pull his Boston Crew shirt over his head, whimpering at the sight of his skin. His fingers find the waistband of my pants, and he tugs.

"Were you trying to kill me today with these fecking pants, Emmie?" He runs his hands along the fabric, then one between my legs. My entire body trembles. "Every time I was behind you, I had to think about Sister Pierre, my awful third-grade teacher, to keep from getting hard."

His hand glides between my legs, his mouth by my ear, and my entire body quakes. I sink against his touch, planting kisses on Tommy's chest. "You don't have to think about her now," I rasp.

He brings his other hand to my hip and pushes against me. I can feel his heat and want through our clothes. "I wasn't."

I reach up pulling his mouth to mine. I bite him, lick him, anything to taste more of him, as his hands work my pants down my legs. I peel off my sports bra and reach for the button of his jeans, running my tongue up the inside of his thigh as I rise after tugging his pants and his briefs to his ankles.

Tommy growls, and the space between my legs throbs.

"Get up here," he orders, and I scramble onto the bed, raising up on my knees to face him. He kisses my neck, rolling my nipples against his palm, pinching them as my head falls backward. His mouth dips to the bottom of my breasts, trailing down to my belly button as he kneels in front of me. His lips skim the inside of my hip, then his tongue finds my slit, and my fingers dig into his shoulders.

"I can't take much playing around tonight," I say through heavy breaths as he grips my ass—I say *ass* tonight, apparently—with both hands, hauling me onto his face.

Tommy chuckles against my center and I fist my hands in his hair. I think he knows. He licks along the length of my entrance, flicking my clit with his tongue, sucking, devouring me until my legs quiver so hard they can barely hold me up. "Turn around, Emmie," he orders as he stands

I turn, and Tommy rubs his huge hand up and down my spine once before gently pushing me forward so my ass in the air. He massages the top of my thighs, his thumbs working toward my entrance as he uses a knee to push mine further apart. I brush my hair out of my eyes and glance back, and the way he's biting his lip, the way his eyes are gleaming at the view of me, exposed and open before him, is almost enough to undo me.

I back myself into him and clench the sheets in my hands when he leans over my body, his erection nudging into my skin. He's so big that he can kiss my temple and run a hand up from my toes and along the length of my leg without shifting. His fingers find my sex, and the competence and intimacy of his touch, the headiness of his smell and his breath, makes my body seize, curl into itself at the force of the pleasure.

"Tommy," I plead.

"You're beautiful," he says in my ear, his voice a barely contained thunderstorm. "So fucking beautiful."

"I want you," I pant out. "Like, immediately."

He smirks. "I've waited this long. Now I want to take my time with you." He drags his fingers over me, slow and torturous, and I squirm into the sensation, moving myself against his hand for more. He slips in one finger and another, and my muscles clench, fluttering around them. He hums his approval.

"I haven't been with anyone since Vegas," I say, squeezing my eyes shut as he reaches his other hand around to circle my clit.

He drives his fingers into me again, pumping, curling them as his cock grinds against my ass. "Neither have I."

"Tommy," I beg, writhing, the pressure already mounting inside me, building and climbing so quickly I feel like I might shatter without him in me, without the anchor of his closeness.

"Em," he rumbles back, kissing my shoulder blade before pulling out his fingers and bracing my hips with both his hands. Then he's pushing against me, and as I tighten around him, I cry at the fullness and the rightness of him inside me.

"You sure you want to do this?" he asks, taking his sweet time moving inside me, probably trying to drive me crazy. But his voice is rough and deep, and I know he's driving himself crazy, too.

"Is ea, is maith liom arán," I rasp.

Which, based on my five minutes of Irish Duolingo a day, I'm pretty sure means, "Yes, I am very sure I want to do this. Thank you for asking. Please proceed."

It must be close enough because as soon as I say the words, he sinks his teeth into his bottom lip and slams himself in to the hilt.

Tommy goes still when I cry out, his hand flattening against my spine. "You okay?"

I can feel the tension of his muscles behind me, the barely contained restraint of his body. I rock back into him, pure need zinging through my bones like lightning. "More, Tommy. I want more."

And he gives me more, and more, and more.

Sixteen

I WAKE UP TO Este's face resting on my face. Tommy is wrapped around me, breathing gently, still asleep, but very hard against my thighs. I think I'd love to wake up like this every day.

Without the urgent need to pee, preferably.

Tommy's arm is heavy over my waist, and I try to work my way out from under him, untangling our legs and sliding out of the bed without waking up Este. The second my feet hit the floor, they both sit up.

"Go back to sleep," I whisper. "I'm just going to use the bathroom."

"Shower?" Tommy asks, blinking at me and then rubbing his eyes. His gaze darkens when he focuses on my very exposed, naked body.

"Pee first?"

"Este too," he says, scooping the puppy off the pillows and bringing her around to me for a quick kiss before he disappears out of the bedroom. I'm sure my eyes are doing the dark thing now, too, as I watch his bare bottom and chiseled back walk away.

I use Tommy's mouthwash, swishing for the full sixty seconds. After I spit, I examine myself in the mirror—the evidence of a day of trash collecting and a late night of dancing written everywhere—and wonder if Tommy was implying I *need* a shower or inviting me to shower with him.

"Este is fed and enjoying a beautiful Sunday morning out of doors," he tells me, coming up behind me and brushing my hair from my neck so he can run his tongue along it.

"And we are dirty?"

"Very," he answers, pulling me tight against him.

And since he is such a good host, he offers to give me a shower.

Once we are clean, shining, satisfied, and incredibly out of breath, he offers to make me a traditional Irish breakfast, too.

The morning is chilly, but Tommy ignites the gas flames in the concrete fire pit so I can sit outside with Este and drink my coffee while he cooks. He wraps me in one of Cece's patterned Pendleton blankets and kisses my head before returning inside.

I laugh as Este hunts a rock, nestling into the soft wool. This is good—waking up in a beautiful home, in a warm bed, with Tommy and Este. And if this is as good as it ever gets, this unexpected little moment where I co-own a dog with an Irishman who is only temporarily in my town, I won't be sorry it happened.

I could survive on this one morning for years, but I wouldn't be mad if it happened again—maybe a few times.

Tommy comes out a while later with a tray of eggs, beans, tomato, potatoes, and pork three ways. He grabs my mug, goes inside, and comes back with my coffee refilled, precisely how I like it.

Is this what happens when a man is raised with three sisters?

"My apologies," he says, gesturing to the beautiful spread. "I know you fancy a good loaf, but this is the best I could do on short notice."

"I enjoy bread as much as the next person, but toast or no, this looks amazing."

"Is that so?" He smirks.

"Did I give you reason to think otherwise about me and bread?"

Tommy bends down and whispers in my ear, "Is ea, is maith liom arán." The same words I told him last night. Heat floods my center. I am not opposed to making love in Cecily Prior's backyard.

"What about it?" I turn my face up to his.

He leans closer. "You told me," he says against my lips, "'I like bread.'"

I shrug. "It obviously got my point across."

Tommy looks at me, his expression tender, then brushes his thumb over my cheek and kisses me again before sitting down on the wicker chair beside me. "What are your plans for next weekend?"

"Next weekend?" I ask through a bite of sausage, hoping it will disguise the way my voice hitches. "I don't believe I have plans."

Tommy smiles. "In that case—"

"Oh, *fork*. You know what? I have Saturday School."

"Since I can easily check your schedule, I will assume that you are being honest, and this isn't a way to weasel your way out of what's coming next."

"What's coming next?" I ask, eyes wide.

"I'm going to ask you out, Emmie. On a date."

"I'd like that." I meet his gaze and hope my pupils aren't shaped like hearts. "I'd like that a lot."

"Me too," he replies, brushing my hair behind my ear. I know the size of my grin is ridiculous, but I don't care. "But here's the thing: I have a dinner with Audrey that evening, and I know you won't be available for lunch if you're running Saturday School."

I stare at him, my insides preparing to dispel all of the delicious sausage I've shoved inside it. "Pardon?" I pull back. "I thought we moved past this last night when you made it definitively clear that you and Audrey's *gallery* were not involved."

"Em," he says, shaking his head and chuckling. "There is only one gallery in this town I want to see more of." I blush. Tommy likes my gallery. "However, as I had not let myself hope that there might be a chance to take you out on a Saturday, possibly ever, I thought it was as good a day as any for a *business* dinner."

I swallow. Business dinner. Nothing to do with her gallery, just like Tommy told me last night. Because Tommy is a good guy.

"If you're up for it, I'd love for you to join Audrey and me to talk about the school," he says, rubbing the back of his neck. "There is something she was hoping to discuss with you."

My heart pitters and patters at the chance to speak with Audrey—who might have some sway over her uncle's decisions and thus the board—about the kids, our programs, and whatever mystery thing she wants to talk over. (Please let it be a counselor.) "Spending half a Saturday with one hundred teenagers who would rather be anywhere else can be draining, but with a decent nap, dinner is more than doable."

"We're going to Massa." He winks. "Best food in town, I hear."

"It's a date," I say. A weird date, but I'll take it.

"Excellent." He grins, a lopsided one, and reaches for my hand. I might as well be floating I feel so light inside. "And maybe we can squeeze in a *real* date, just you and me, and maybe Este, before then."

"Maybe we can." I smile back. And I wonder if that little tickle behind my ribs is something important, maybe life-altering, sprouting within me, growing.

I wonder if it's happiness.

I SPEND THE NIGHT at Tommy's again on Sunday, but we take separate cars to school in the morning. On Monday evening, after the sun sets, we take a very quick dip in the still-freezing pool and then watch the stars spark to life, cuddled together on a chaise beside the fire pit. Tommy pours us wine—not the cheap stuff Leila and I usually drink—and asks me about my mom and George.

I hesitate, sitting up and taking a gulp of the heady Amarone to buy myself time. These questions are always difficult to navigate, and most people get the least detailed answer possible, sparing all the particulars.

It's just easier.

Tommy listens as I recite the usual monologue about how I was eighteen when I lost my mom, how it was unexpected but not entirely a surprise. I touch on what happened to George after and tell Tommy where he is now. I compliment the care George receives at the facility and say I try to visit him every couple of weeks, so not nearly often enough.

Then, I drink the rest of my wine and refuse to look Tommy in the eyes because I don't want him to see more, to see *me*. I brace myself for the usual *I'm sorries* and the long, uncomfortable silence that always follows.

"What was her name?" Tommy asks, and my heart catches.

Her name. My mom, the person. It feels like an eternity has passed since my mouth has formed the word. "Lara."

"Lara," he repeats softly, and when he says her name, it feels like something comes together inside me. "What happened to her?"

I stare into my glass. Of course, other people have asked. I usually say she was sick, which is true. But not the whole truth. The only person I've ever told the whole truth to is Leila.

Tommy takes my hand, holding it in both of his like it's something precious and delicate, the first bud on a thorny bush. "You don't have to tell me. I'm sorry for prying."

I take a deep breath and gaze up into his face, and the thing is, I want to tell him. My insides ache to share this story that feels so alive where it dwells within me but never sees the light.

And before I realize what is happening, I do. The freedom of it makes me feel drunk. The words spill out of their cages: *depression, recovery, insomnia, addiction, intervention, regression, suicide.*

An elegy of hopelessness and loss.

Tommy's face—the tightening of his jaw and pursing of his lips, the bobbing of his throat, and the slow blink of his eyes—illustrates the emotions for me so I don't have to feel them. Not again.

When I'm done talking, I reach for my wine, but Tommy reaches for me first, pulling me onto his lap, snuggling me under his chin.

"Do you have family around?" he asks gently.

"Just Leila. My grandparents stopped speaking to my mother when she married George. A classic case of interpersonal racism winning out over wanting the best for your child. George's mom still sends me birthday cards, but she's in Brazil."

"Do you ever get to speak with her?"

"Despite what my nine-hundred-and-thirty-two-day Duolingo streak would lead you to believe, I am zero percent proficient in Portuguese."

"Is that what you were doing in the bathroom last night?"

"Guilty."

He pulls me tighter and runs a hand along my back. "I'm sorry, Em," he says into my hair. "That's too much for one person."

"I'm fine," I say, and I think we both know it's a lie, so I turn and kiss him so neither of us has to think too much about it.

Tuesday, Tommy puts a key to his front door on my "Keep Calm and Pretend It's on the Lesson Plan" key chain. On Wednesday, I grab Thai takeout after school, and Tommy rubs my feet while we watch *My Octopus Teacher* on Cecily Prior's big screen. Thursday, he kisses me in my office, and when we are back at his house, we make quesadillas and eat them while swinging our legs in the jacuzzi. We have Nilla Wafers and Nutella for dessert.

Friday, after a rough day at school, I fall asleep on the couch with my head in Tommy's lap and his hand in my hair. When I next open my eyes, blinking against the hazy unease that lingers from my dream, I'm in his bed. Moonlight filters through the linen curtains, and I can make out the curve of Tommy's shoulder, the mess of his hair. Este's paw is pressed into my cheek. She rearranges herself when I shift, curling up so her nose touches Tommy's.

I smile and let out a small sigh, wondering how I survived all these years without these moments to help keep my heart going.

"Emmie," Tommy whispers. "Everything okay?"

"Great. Sorry I woke you up."

"You didn't." He runs the back of his hand along my hip. "It was Este's breath. Stinky little mutt."

I giggle and pet her. "Those Snickerpoodles Leila bought have not been kind to her."

"The questionable pun should have clued us in." He shudders. "The cannibalistic implications are incredibly unsettling."

"What's more unsettling is they smell so good, I'm always tempted to eat them, too," I say.

"Truly appalling, Emeline. I won't speak a word of this to Este, for several reasons."

I reach up to pet the puppy. "I appreciate that."

We are quiet for a minute while Tommy works his fingers through my tangled hair. He kisses my temple. "You want to tell me what's on your mind?"

"Cinnamon-flavored dog?" I offer.

"Anything else? Like maybe what happened at school today?"

I sigh. "It was nothing big."

I can feel his eyes scanning my face even in the darkness. "You were exhausted when you got home."

Home. For a second, I forget to breathe.

Tommy reaches out for me and draws me into him, against his warm, bare chest. Against his heart. *Home.* "Three hours later than you'd planned to. Which is fine, of course, but you were so knackered, you barely ate dinner."

"Mr. Duarte's daughter was sick, so I took over his study hall. Then Gianna—"

"Gianna," he murmurs. "Senior, red streaks in her hair, likes horses and anime?"

I grin. Tommy's been trying to get to know *all* the students. He's doing an outstanding job. "Nailed it," I say. "She needed a ride home because Bus 11 wasn't running."

"Is that it?"

"No," I confess. "After that, I stopped by Lucas Bower's house." I pause to give Tommy a chance to show off. He doesn't disappoint.

"Curly faux-hawk, good at math, only eats Oreos and string cheese."

"Year?" I quiz.

"Freshman. No..." he wavers. "Sophomore. Freshman?"

"Freshman," I confirm. "At the end of class this morning, he asked if he could use the school bathroom after closing to wash up and do laundry. His mom, who I know works a ton, does cleaning jobs all over town, horrible hours, was delinquent on their water bill for the third time, and the water company cut them off."

"What did you do?"

"I told him no."

"You paid the bill, didn't you."

"Maybe."

"And?"

"And after I dropped Gianna off, I went by to make sure the water company had reinstated service and to drop off some boxes from the school pantry."

I prepare for what's coming next, what Leila has told me one hundred million times. *I can't save the world. I can't fix everyone's problems. I'm not responsible for everything.*

"Em?"

"Yes," I mumble.

"You don't need to carry all the apples."

"What?"

"You don't need to carry all the apples."

"No, I heard you the first time. I just don't get what you're trying to say."

His fingers squeeze mine. "I think you do."

I sit up, my chest tightening. "Fine. Let's say I do understand. It doesn't change anything. These kids need help. They need love and care and support."

"I know. I agree."

"But Tommy," I say, tears stinging my eyes. "Who else is going to make sure Lucas has food and water, that Gianna doesn't make a horrible decision just for the sake of getting home, and that Mr. Duarte doesn't quit because he can't take off a few hours to be with his sick daughter? If I don't carry the apples, who will?"

He kisses my forehead and runs a thumb against my wet cheek. "What if..." He pauses, raises my chin, looks into my face. His eyes gleam with the silver light of the room. "What if someone else wanted to help you carry the apples?"

I shift back, the sheets whispering beneath me. "I couldn't ask you to take that on."

"You didn't ask. I'm offering."

"But—"

He presses his forehead against mine. "I want this, Emmie. I want this so much."

"I don't think it counts as an equitable relationship," I argue, sniffling, "if I'm filling your cup with other people's apples."

"I get to be the one who decides that." He lowers his mouth, brushing his lips against mine. "But I have one request."

"Let's hear it," I murmur.

"I want *your* apples, too, Emmie. The bruised ones you hold close, the ones that feel too heavy, the ones you've been carrying too long—I want those most of all."

I shake my head. "I think those apples are meant for a therapist."

"Good. Yes. Talk to your therapist, but while you're working through things, let me help lighten the load."

I sigh, dropping my head back onto the pillow. "Might be a long while. Our insurance doesn't cover that kind of care."

He pulls away, sitting up straight. "What complete and total bollocks. Seriously? None of you have mental health coverage included in your benefits?"

"If we did, I like to imagine I'd be slightly less emotionally and mentally unstable."

Tommy pushes away the covers and gets out of bed.

I admire the silhouette of his tush against the curtains, resting my chin in my hands. "Did I finally scare you off?"

"Never." He takes three long steps back to the bed, leans over, and kisses me so deeply I moan. "I just have an email to write."

"At three in the morning?"

He cradles my face in his hands. "The fact that the students at Desert Grace don't have a counselor is unacceptable. And the fact that the teachers don't have access to mental health services is just as egregious."

"Can't argue with that."

"I'm going to fix it."

"Godspeed, sir. I've been trying for six years."

"I believe it, which just makes me angrier." He bends down and kisses me again. "Get some sleep. I'll be back soon. And by the way, I'm terminating your role as co-chair of the talent show."

I should protest, but I don't. Who am I to look a gift horse in the mouth?

Seventeen

I N THE MORNING, TOMMY has me read over the email he drafted to the board. It is a proper dressing down, and he really digs into Mr. Edmonds.

"They can't fire you, right?" I ask, worrying my bottom lip.

"Not for this."

I turn in the desk chair to look at him. He's standing behind me with his arms crossed, jaw hard. "You're sure?"

"Very."

"Send it," I tell him. "No one else has been able to get through to them, and it would be totally weird, of course, but who knows, maybe they'll listen to a cishet white man with a couple of flashy degrees and a fancy car. I'm sure stranger things have happened."

He leans over my shoulder, and I lean back into him. We both smile when he presses the send button.

And yep, that thing growing in my chest? That tickle that's become bigger and warmer, that's burgeoning with hope and possibility? I'm ninety-nine percent sure it's happiness. And maybe, even, a little something more that I'm not ready to name yet.

We get breakfast on the way to school, and after I finish my everything bagel with lox and pickled onions, he kisses me in the faculty lounge, quick and sweet and not overtly workplace inappropriate, before heading off to make our school a better place.

"I saw that," Leila says, interrupting my daydream about a world where Tommy is the Alexander the Great of education, but instead of conquering subcontinents, he's conquering the hearts and pocketbooks of mega-donors, convincing them to buy us the building that's for sale next door to Desert Grace for student housing, persuading them to fund food pantries and utility services for our kids and their families who need assistance.

"Which part?" I ask, twirling the strap of my lanyard around my finger.

"You mean that PG-13-rated kiss or the moon-eyed way you stared off into the distance after?" she asks, placing her Benji-made lunch in the faculty fridge.

"I guess you saw both, then."

"I did." She grins, facing me. "And I liked all of it."

"He's on a mission, Leila. To get the kids a counselor. And to get us…"

She looks at me, her eyes soft. She knows I've lived in fear of my depression since I lost my mom. She's offered to help with therapy. I think it scares her a little, too, knowing what happened.

"Mental health coverage? Fucking finally," she says, wrapping me in a hug.

"You need it, too," I tell her. "A professional diagnosis of know-it-all-ism would make me very happy."

"Of course I need it, Em. We all have our sore and shattered pieces, and don't you forget it. But you know what?"

"What?"

"I don't think you need a doctor to tell me I can be an asshole for you to be happy," she says, lowering her voice when Ms. Conn pops in to grab a Ziploc from the cabinet. "I think you're on the right track already. I think that with therapy, you might even be able to start speaking like a normal adult and sound less like you're in an episode of *The Good Place*."

"Never," I argue. Well, at least never outside of the bedroom with Tommy.

Leila gives a little eye roll. "Yeah, yeah. George Silva and his principles."

"See, there it is." I point at her. "Right there. You're such a wise*ash*."

She's also correct.

But not swearing seems like a fair sacrifice to honor the man who did so much for me and my mom. He might not be around to see it, but I still want to make him proud, to always be the good person he thinks I am. A little inflexible integrity and an unwavering moral compass never hurt anyone, right?

That evening, after six hours of Saturday School, a long afternoon nap with Este, and much convincing that arriving together is not shockingly unprofessional, I get in Tommy's car and let him drive me to Massa to meet Audrey for dinner.

The restaurant is in a beautiful white stucco building, the brick patio illuminated by string lights, and an actual band is playing romantic jazz covers of well-known seventies songs in the corner of the dining room. I have not eaten at Massa, or anywhere like Massa, because spending thirty-five dollars on a Caesar salad never appealed to me.

As the host leads us to our table, the warm air perfumed with fresh bread and herbs, the golden light pooling on heavy oak tables with bouquets of wildflowers at their center, I wonder if deep down, I might be an overpriced greens girl after all.

Audrey is already seated and stands to greet us, giving us both a friendly but undeniably bougie kiss on the cheek.

I don't dislike it as much as I should, even coming from Audrey.

Oh, no, I might be a cheek-kiss kind of girl too.

"I'm so glad we're finally going to have a chance to talk outside of school, Emmie," Audrey says, sitting back down.

Tommy pulls out my chair for me and then takes the seat beside mine. I'm already starting to squirm when Tommy's arm wraps around the back of my chair.

I throw him some serious side-eye but try not to make it obvious. He drops his arm. Audrey's lip quirks up

So much for being discreet.

"Me too." I smile. "Thank you for letting me join."

Audrey gives a little laugh. "Besides the fact that we wouldn't be having this meeting without you, Emmie, it's unthinkable that you and I have known each other for, what has it been now? Almost fourteen years? And we've never made it to dinner. It was way past time to rectify that oversight."

"Agreed," I say brightly. Not that Audrey was at all aware of my existence in high school. But it is kind of her to pretend.

"And we have big things to discuss tonight, so it's even more special."

We do?

Tommy clears his throat beside me. "How about we order some drinks and get the appetizers rolling before we jump straight to business?" He hands me my menu. "Audrey, how was your visit to the historical society yesterday? I'm sorry I couldn't join."

"I know you've been busy," she says, grinning at him in a way that makes me squeeze his knee hard under the table. "And thank you for asking. It was great. I found some documents about the history of the land Desert Grace was built on."

That gets my attention. "I'd love to see them." I close my menu. "I've been wanting to integrate a section on the history of our downtown and being able to talk to the kids about the historical uses of the space, the people who were there before..." I make a noise that sounds slightly like I'm feeling things I shouldn't about history. "It would just be so cool," I finish.

"I had the *same* idea," Audrey says, leaning across the table and grabbing my hand before letting go just as fast. "Especially since so many of our students' families have a long history in the area. Maybe we could get coffee and go over it all together? Or better, meet at the historical society and see if we can dig up more?" Her eyes are bright, and I think she may be as excited about this prospect as I am.

"Dream weekend," I declare. And I mean it. I glance over at Tommy, who has told me multiple times that Audrey and I would get on well, that we should hang out, and that I'd enjoy her company.

His eyebrows rise a little in a very clear *I told you so*. He seems pleased. His expression makes my insides tingle.

When the waiter comes by, Audrey selects a bottle of California cabernet from the drink list. I tell Tommy that I'd happily eat anything on the appetizer menu, which I've barely looked at but have great faith in, and when the server returns with the wine, he orders one of *everything* for the table to share.

"Did you hear about the board's most recent bad idea?" Audrey asks conspiratorially as the server fills our glasses.

"It's hard to keep track," I quip, reaching for my wine. I take a sip and panic, freezing with the glass to my lips. Audrey is *on* the board. Her uncle is the president *of* the board. One of her close friends, Adesh Jain, is the secretary.

Booger.

She laughs, and her cheeks turn pink. "You're not wrong. This one was just a particular favorite. They discussed rebranding the school."

My heart stops. "Like the name or the entire vision?" I wouldn't put it past them to decide it was all for naught and turn Desert Grace into some elitist preparatory academy.

"Name," she clarifies. "They wanted to go with Hand of God." She regards me knowingly when I grimace.

Tommy chuckles. "Where Jesus touches us all."

"Horrible," Audrey says, swirling her glass on the table.

"Not to mention," I add, "we'd have dozens of teenagers running around with *HOG* emblazoned on their uniforms."

"That bit might've been a tad funny," Tommy counters.

"I'm glad you shut it down," I tell her, smoothing my napkin in my lap. "I'm not sure the faculty's morale would have survived the fallout."

Audrey nods. "I think it's pretty apparent the board needs some shaking up, which leads me to my first point of business." Tommy straightens beside me. "We are officially launching our principal search next week."

I literally slump in relief, well-timed applause filtering through the dining room as the band finishes up a song. "This is such great news. When do you plan to fill the position?"

"By April at the latest," Audrey answers.

I bite my lip, calculating. Two more months of teachers pulling more weight than they should be isn't ideal, but at least it will be easier knowing there is a light at the end of the tunnel. Knowing things will get better. I can find ways to fill the gaps in the meantime.

Audrey lifts her wine glass. "Hopefully sooner."

"Do you have candidates in mind?" I ask, going through possible options from the local pool of education administrators in my head.

"I know that face," Tommy says, his green eyes twinkling when they meet mine. The familiarity of it all makes my breath hitch. "You're already scheming."

"I am," I say, grinning back at him. "There's a great principal at one of the public schools on the east side of town who I'd love to poach. Maybe I should bake her cookies this weekend and start laying the groundwork. Make a casual after-school visit."

"Actually." Audrey glances at Tommy. "We're hoping to fill the position internally."

I clap my hands together. "Even better!"

"We think so, too," Audrey says, tapping her fingers on the base of her glass. "And based on what I've witnessed during my time at the school, and what Tommy has observed and shared with the board, we think..." She pauses, and Tommy turns his chair to me.

"We think you would be the perfect principal for Desert Grace, Emeline Jones," he says.

I snort.

Tommy squeezes my hand. "We mean it, Emmie."

"You're the best person for the job," Audrey adds.

"Me?" I gape at them, my mouth hanging open. "I'm a history teacher who occasionally convinces the board to let her teach a Latin class and is good at threatening kids in a way that gets them to listen. I am *not* the best person for the job."

Audrey gives me a kind, encouraging smile. "Emmie, you're already doing the job, and your own, and sometimes even a few other people's."

"I'm just doing what needs to be done. Anyone else would do the same."

"No, Em," Tommy says firmly. "They wouldn't, and they don't."

Audrey scoots a little closer. "Take some time to think about it, but also consider what you'd be able to accomplish in that role. What you could do for the teachers, the students, their families. We know you have ideas, Emmie, and they're good ones. We want to help you realize them."

Tommy puts a hand on my shoulder. "No one is as familiar with that school as you are. No one else could have written me a sixty-point list about things I should know on my first day. No one cares the way you do."

"I...I don't know what to say." I'm sure other candidates exist who could do an amazing job, but now that the seed is there, I'd like to try. Becoming the principal of Desert Grace—a place I've dedicated my heart and time to and love fully for countless reasons—would be a gift and an honor.

My pulse ratchets up as I consider, the refrain of my heartbeat hammering in my ears.

"It's okay to want it," Tommy whispers. His words topple the house of reasons my mind is building against me, and they are quickly washed away in a cascade of possibilities.

"I do," I say out loud. "I want it."

Tommy beams, and after a moment's hesitation, I beam back.

Audrey lets out a long breath through her smile. "I am so delighted to hear you say that."

Their excitement makes my eyes sting. "What happens next?" I ask against the tightness in my throat.

"The school has to make the job opening public, but Tommy and I intend to be clear from the beginning that we already have someone lined up. There may be a delay due to some restructuring, but we plan to have the board vote to finalize your role as soon as possible."

My stomach drops. "I have to convince the board to vote for me? Run some sort of campaign? You're both aware that the majority of the board either has no idea who I am or actively avoids my emails? Except you and Mr. Jain, I mean. You two are nice."

"We should have the board sorted out by then, but don't worry. We're working under special circumstances, and their vote is more for show than anything."

"How so?"

"The current board, including myself, has no idea how to run a principal search. When we brought Tommy on, they all agreed, in a surprising display of self-awareness, to put a stipulation in his contract that he would have full hiring power expressly to fill the position of principal."

"You mean..." I murmur.

Tommy tenses and takes a deep breath beside me.

"Yes," Audrey says, her lips tilting up in a reassuring smile. "Tommy has the final word. You have nothing to worry about."

Eighteen

I SOMEHOW KEEP MY hands from trembling for the rest of dinner. I answer Audrey's questions, more or less intelligibly, even though inside, my brain is raging a bitter battle.

I already know that however it plays out, triumph will come at a loss.

Yes, I tell them, smiling, I think it would be wonderful if we brought Micah on to teach gardening, or life skills, or something else I can't remember. Of course, I would love to meet with Mr. Jain and Audrey to get a better idea of our budget. No, that toilet on the second floor does not seem to be working any better since the plumbers came.

But all I can focus on is that Tommy—the man who has, in a mere week, helped me feel things I haven't felt maybe ever and consider things I never let myself consider—is the sole person responsible for filling the role of principal.

And I know, before dinner is over, what I have to do. I think Tommy senses it, too, because he's silent as we walk to the car.

I get in and shut the door, grateful for the darkness. Grateful that my face is cloaked in shadow, and he won't be able to read what's hiding there. He starts to drive, and I struggle to find the courage to say the things I need to say. Nobody speaks until we pull into his driveway.

"Emmie—"

And I know if I give him space to talk, I'll let myself be convinced that it's no big deal, that it's all okay. But it's not. "Don't," I interrupt, and the word is more of a ragged plea than I'd hoped for. "Tommy, this thing between us...it has to end."

He shakes his head. "It certainly does not. I have already—"

My mind shouts at me not to let him finish. "We *have* to stop seeing each other. It's the right thing to do."

"Emmie," he says, soothing, his voice almost a laugh. "If you'd just give me a half second to explain, you'd see this is not all that scandalous."

"There is nothing to explain. I can't be sleeping with the man who is offering—excuse me, basically *promising*—me a job when there are other qualified people out there who I'm sure want it just as badly as I do."

"You think that just because we aren't dating anymore, I won't still see you that way, Em? I can't just turn it off."

"You'll have to try."

"It's obviously not that simple. If you knew—"

"Tommy!" I shout, my voice raw. "No. I'll come in now, get my stuff, and email you later about Este. I'm still going to be her mom. You can have this back," I say, trying to pull Tommy's key off my key ring with shaking fingers.

Tommy leans his head back and sighs. "Keep the key. You'll need it to pick up Este when you want to take her out."

"Fine."

"Fine."

"I'm going in to get my things." I crack the door open, but Tommy's hand tugs my elbow, gentle but firm.

"I know you think this is over, Emmie, but I don't plan to give up so easily. I won't let you just slip out of my life again."

"You don't have a choice," I say, pushing the door wider.

"There is always a choice."

I stop, take a deep breath, and lean toward Tommy. "Well, I just made yours for you."

His chest rises and falls as we sit there, suspended over the center console, eyes locked.

He looks away first.

I win. My own Pyrrhic victory.

Back at the condo, I slip my key into the lock and open the door as quietly as possible, shushing Fib when he meows at me. I'm halfway down the hallway when Leila shuffles out of her room, yelping when we nearly collide.

"What the fuck are you doing?" she demands after catching her breath.

"Coming home," I say, pushing past her. "I live here."

"Do you? What's your name again? I definitely haven't had another roommate for at least a week."

"Sorry to disappoint, but it looks like I'm back."

"Shut up," she says, giving me a hug. "I missed you."

I hug her back, probably harder than necessary.

"But seriously," she says, "why are you here?"

I sigh. "Because the universe might officially hate me."

"Please, come. Tell me more." Leila drags me to the couch, and we sit cross-legged in front of each other.

"Benji?" I ask, glancing over her shoulder.

"Doing some renderings for an old church. It will be hours before he realizes I'm not in there. Spill it. What happened?"

I take a deep breath and spill all sorts of things: everything that has happened this past week, tears, some runny snot, even the literal tea she makes for me halfway through, and finally, what went down at dinner with Audrey.

Leila gets me tissues, holds my hand, and congratulates me. When I'm done but still sobbing, she says, "I don't get it, Em. All of this seems like a good thing."

"Don't you see, Lei? I told Tommy it's over."

"Why?"

I scowl at her, exasperated. "What do you mean, *why?*"

"You were already with him when he was your boss."

"*Interim* boss. But I can't be with him *and* be his candidate for principal."

"You can if you're the right person for the job, which everyone on the staff and faculty knows you are. Audrey and Tommy had clearly come to the same conclusion before you started hitting that. No one who matters, literally *no one*, would give a flying shit if you were dating the head of school."

"On principle, Leila!" I all but shout. "I cannot be with him *on principle.*"

She draws back a little, cocks an eyebrow. "That is the absolute dumbest fucking thing I've ever heard come out of your mouth, Emeline Jones."

"But—"

"If you don't want to help yourself, if you insist on self-sabotaging because of some obscure collection of ethical standards, that's fine. But it breaks my heart to see you do it. I know it's not easy, Em. I know that you're always fighting. But when something special and right falls into your lap, and based on what you've told me, Tommy is both these things, then you push it away? That's on you. That's a choice you're making."

"But if I don't have my principles..."

"What?" she asks, raising her arms above her head in question. I back further into the cushions. "You think the world will crumble, the dead will rise? The speed at which the oceans are warming will magically accelerate, and we will all get dengue fever?"

"No. But George—"

"George, what? George would only want you to be happy. I've met George. We had about thirty dinners with him and your mom freshman year and thirty more after everything happened, and I know that's not nearly as much time as you spent with him, but I think maybe you've been living under the false impression that George expected you to live up to some grand moral code, to be a certain kind of person in order for him to love you."

When I hear the words, they sound horrible. George never withheld his love. He never judged me. But I've been living this way for so long, trying to be good and do good, that it has become the one thing I can consistently lean on.

Though now I wonder if it's more that I've trapped myself in a box, and I'm not so much being supported as I am being contained. I'm not ready to find out. I'm not ready to break loose just to learn I can't stand on my own, that who I am deep inside is just as fragile and broken as my mom.

"George will always love you," Leila says, bending her forehead to mine. "And I will always love you. But goddammit, Emmie, one day I'd love to see *you* love you, too."

I SPEND ALL OF Sunday in bed watching videos of people slipping on ice, cats from Turkey with amputated limbs, and anything else I can think of that might elicit an emotion, that might help clear the anesthetized pressure from my chest. Leila brings me crackers and apple sauce like I'm a sick first-grader, and I nibble at them throughout the day.

At bedtime, I force myself up and into the bathroom so I can brush my teeth and floss—each tooth twice!—before crawling back under the covers, turning off the lights, and staring at the ceiling.

The dark corners of the room are all that exist until I suddenly think, *Este.*

Este.

I fumble for my laptop, squinting at the bright screen as I create a Google calendar and share it with Tommy so we can plan out my visits with the puppy. I send invitations for the days I think I'll be available to walk her, and others for days I'm hoping to work in.

Two minutes after wrapping up all of the invites for March and the rest of February, I receive an email that simply says: *Emmie, come see her whenever you want.*

And then, ten minutes after that, I receive sixteen *work* calendar invitations *from* Tommy: meetings with him and Audrey, meetings with him and Adesh, a preparatory meeting for my official introduction to the board as candidate for principal, and meetings to discuss filling my current position.

So. Many. Meetings. And the majority of them? Just me and Tommy. I go through them one by one.

I get to March seventeenth, the day of the talent show, and open the invitation. In the notes, he's written: *Prepare to have your (cashmere) socks knocked off, Ms. Jones.*

I shake my head but don't get mad at myself for smiling when I hit accept.

Leila follows me around the next morning, forcing a mug of coffee into my hand, pouring way too much syrup on my toaster waffle, and staring at me while I eat it. She makes me watch a video of a gazelle shaking to recalibrate its nervous system after being attacked by a cheetah and asks me if I want to try.

I take a pass. She accepts on the grounds that I agree to give it a shot after school.

Eventually, she coerces me into her car, where she blasts Cecily Prior's greatest hits.

When we enter the faculty lounge, Tommy is standing there with a coffee for both of us, seeming worryingly the same as he does every morning, like whatever happened two nights ago after dinner at Massa wasn't a total disaster. Like I wasn't an absolute jerk to him in the car.

"Good morning, ladies," he says, handing us our warm to-go cups of locally roasted coffee. "Ms. Jones, I thought, if you had a moment, I could brief you on the plan Audrey and I drew up for the next steps."

"He still wants to brief you, Emmie," Leila whispers.

Why is he acting so normal? I want to whisper back.

"My office?" he asks, and all I can manage is a panicked look at Leila and an okay before I follow him out of the lounge and into his office. There, he prints out a document, highlights some bullet points, and smiles at me.

Lopsided. Lovely. Perfect.

So this is how he's going to play it.

And I'm grateful because, at least this way, I can pretend. I can keep playing along, never having to acknowledge the precious slip of happiness that had taken root in my heart succumbing to the darkness before it ever had a chance to find the light.

Nineteen

WE NEED ALL HANDS on deck for our annual Valentine's Arcade Day, so Audrey joins us and drags along Adesh Jain, who smirks while Micah, who has accepted a position as our new activities coordinator, unabashedly hits on Audrey as they funnel students into one of the two buses we rented.

Tommy and I attempt to fill the other, wrangling overly excited kids up the stairs, all while I desperately avoid meeting his eyes.

"Bus two is locked and loaded," Leila calls from a window. Adesh pops in his sensory earplugs, gives a thumbs up, and climbs into the bus behind Micah.

"Closing up here, as well!" Tommy shouts back once our last student straggles in. "After you, Ms. Jones."

A pencil skirt probably wasn't the best choice for today, and I struggle to take the first step onto the bus. Tommy puts his hand out for me, and I take it, letting go as soon as my other hand is on the railing.

I hear him suck in a breath behind me, and I know he is eye-level with my butt. My heart pounds in all the wrong places as I squeeze down the aisle and find a spot next to a lone sophomore who seems more distressed to be sitting next to a teacher than he was to be alone.

Too bad, kid.

I've done an excellent job dodging Tommy on campus whenever he gets that look in his eye like he's about to pull a "Can we just talk?" or his lip tilts in a way that lets me know he's as unconvinced of my resolve to keep this up as I am.

I have my face trained on my phone, trying to look busy as I squeeze in a few NYT crossword answers when Audrey taps me on the shoulder. "May I?"

I glance up at her and back down the aisle. "Weren't you on the other bus?"

"Tommy needed to talk to Adesh, so we switched."

"Please, have a seat," I say, scootching the wide-eyed sophomore, Cyle, closer to the window.

He grimaces. "May I leave, please?"

I smile. Apparently, one teacher was bad, but being squashed in here with *two* adults is unbearable. I stand to let him out, and a row of kids further down the aisle waves him over.

"After you," I tell Audrey, ushering her into the window seat, mostly so I have access to the aisle in case I need to get up and yell at anyone.

She gives my hand a quick squeeze as I reach for my buckle. "Guess what?" she asks, grinning.

I sit up straighter. "You're going to tell me what the big St. Patrick's Day Talent Show announcement is?"

She winces, tugging her dark hair over her shoulder. "No."

"Weak sauce, Audrey."

"I know! And I can't even lie and say that what I'm about to tell you is better—even if it *is* pretty great—because the talent show news is *really, really* great." Audrey squeals, and her cheeks turn pink, and her eyes get sort of glassy all at once.

I flick her arm. "Then it is extra mean of you not to tell me." To think, I spent fourteen years being intimidated by this blushing weirdo when we could have been friends all along.

"It is," she says, resting a hand on her bouncing knee. It stills. "But I promised."

Tommy and I have not spoken much about St. Patrick's Day. Our meetings this week have primarily been filled with nailing down the plan for principal, but when it has come up, he's been cryptic.

"How come you get to know, and I"—I drop my voice to a whisper—"the possible future principal—"

"*Definite* future principal," she corrects.

"And I, the maybe, possibly, definite future principal, do not?"

"Tommy wants to surprise you."

"Surprise the faculty?"

She presses her lips together. "Sure, he wants to surprise *the faculty*. And he's so busy with…" She trails off and waves a hand. "*Stuff*, that I'm handling most of the details. But I can tell you one thing."

I cross my arms, waiting.

"It's confirmed," she says quietly. "Tommy was able to secure the arena at the convention center for the talent show."

"The whole arena?" I ask, wrinkling my nose. "What will we do with all that space? How will we pay for it?"

"The space was donated. And the special something Tommy has in the works will make it all make sense."

"Donated, of course." What isn't Tommy capable of accomplishing for our kids? "It must be *really* special if he expects five thousand people to show up." Traditionally hosted in our chapel, the talent show usually draws about two hundred guests, comprised almost entirely of our kids' families. Companies and wealthy patrons sponsor the show, which is how the school makes money, but they never come.

"Up to seven thousand, actually," she corrects.

"*Seven thousand?*"

"We're going to sell tickets, Emmie. Students, faculty, and their families get in free. But all those other seats? They're pure profit. This year's show could change everything for the school."

"And you really won't tell me what the surprise is?"

"I'm sorry, Em."

"I forgive you, especially if whatever *it* is means tons of money for the school."

"Oodles," she says, eyes bright.

I lean back in my seat and sigh in satisfaction. *Oodles* is good enough for me. "So what is this other great, but not *as* great, news you have for me?"

Audrey claps her hands together. "I persuaded one of the historical society's curators to help us compile a full compendium of the historic uses and archaeological findings of the Desert Grace building site."

"Amazing!" I say before dropping my shoulders as I remember the intimidating length of my to-do list these days. "I'd love to help, but with everything coming up, I don't know how I'd make it over there during the week."

"Well..." She beams. "I set up our appointment for a Sunday, so that won't be a problem. What do you say? You in?"

"Heck yes, Auds." We high-five, and it's almost like we *have* been friends since we were kids. "I'm so in."

A S SOON AS WE arrive at the arcade, I am reminded of just how overwhelming it is trying to keep tabs on one hundred adolescents hyped on freedom and annihilating aliens. "You are only allowed to throw the plastic axes at the target!" I yell, a slot machine game lighting up beside me. "Not the other students!"

Leila sidles up next to me. "I fucking hate this place."

"Really? Audiovisual overstimulation always makes me feel so relaxed."

"How was your bus ride?" she asks, her gaze trailing a pack of sophomores heading into the bathroom.

"Fine. I sat with Audrey, tried to get the dirt on the talent show, and failed."

"You and Audrey, huh?" She nudges me with her hip, a small smirk on her face.

I feel a sudden swoop of guilt in my stomach that maybe Leila thinks I'm going to make a new friend and forget about her. Like maybe, since Audrey and I talk a little more now, I haven't been a good friend to Leila.

"She had to switch buses, and there was nowhere else to sit so—"

"Em, she's cool. I'm glad you two are getting along so well." The zombie-hunting game behind us emits an emergency siren and we both cringe. "We should drag her to the Budgy Pony with us sometime."

My shoulders relax. "Yeah, we should. How was your bus ride?"

"Well, our new freshman Samuel"—she tilts her head to our right, where Samuel and some other boys are playing the most cutthroat round of Skee-Ball I've ever witnessed—"gave all of the senior girls homemade valentines that were incredibly explicit."

"He got here a month ago from Sierra Leone and only speaks French. What could he possibly have written on them?"

"Get this: he screenshotted and printed—likely in the school computer lab—a bunch of translations from Google Translate and stapled them onto paper hearts."

"A-plus for innovation." I click the red grading pen on my lanyard for emphasis.

"F for school-appropriate language." She looks at me from the corner of her eye when I open my mouth. "Don't even. My school-inappropriate language doesn't count. I'm a teacher."

"Can't argue with that logic."

"Hey, Ms. Jones," Harper calls to me as she strolls over. I resist the urge to tell her hay is for horses.

"Yes, Harper?"

"Mr. O'Connor claims he's unbeatable at that Auto Apex Raceway game. He's already destroyed all the science teachers. He said he'll buy an Icee for whoever finds a teacher who can beat him. So what do you say? Will you beat him for me? I really want an Icee."

"Ha," I bark. "That's kind of you to ask." Is it kind? What does this child think of me? "But I think Ms. Bashar might be a better bet. Ms. Bashar..." I turn, and Leila is gone, slinking off behind the Hungry Hippos.

Harper shrugs. "Looks like it's gotta be you."

"Fine," I mutter, following her to the bank of driving games.

Tommy gives Ms. Conn a hearty "good try" as she rises from beside him.

"Who's next?" Micah asks, scanning the crowd.

"Raise your hand," Harper orders.

I extend my arm halfway into the air—the classic *I'm raising my hand, but please don't call on me.*

"Ms. Jones, come on up!" Micah shouts.

Tommy turns to me, eyes glinting, mischievous yet endearing, as I step forward and claim the empty seat beside him. My feet don't reach the pedals.

"It's adjustable, you know," Tommy points out.

"I know," I shoot back.

"Here," he says, and before I know it, his hand is reaching for the bottom of my seat as he holds my gaze, and I am being propelled toward the steering wheel. "Better?"

I shift on the plastic in my pencil skirt, testing out the pedals and steering wheel. "This will do."

Micah signals to the gathering crowd of uniformed students to be quiet. "Are our contenders ready?" Tommy and I both nod. "Please swipe your cards and choose your vehicle. The students will choose the track."

The choosing of the track is very loud, but not as loud as nearly all of our students counting down three, two, one...

I slam my foot against the gas pedal, ignoring Tommy when he swings his head toward me, and my cute red Ferrari flies past his green Lamborghini on the screen.

"Hell yeah, Ms. Jones. Kick his ass!" Harper roars beside me, and I don't take the time to rebuke her choice of words because I'm coming up on a sharp curve, and there is a very large bus in my way. I swerve and overcorrect, and Tommy's next to me again, so I twist the wheel to the right and ram him into the wall.

"Oh, damn!" the kids all cry in unison. I hear Tommy mutter under his breath.

I fly up a ramp, launch my car off the back of a semi-truck, and land in second place behind a pink Porsche. Accelerating into a tight turn, I slide past the pretty little sports car, avoid an oncoming ambulance, and find myself at the head of the pack.

The rest of the course is smooth sailing, and by the time I'm gliding through the finish line, I haven't seen Tommy on my screen for at least fifteen seconds.

"What just happened?" he asks, gawking at me.

"I just won Harper an Icee." I stand and straighten my skirt.

The kids are chanting, "Ms. Jones! Ms. Jones!" Some are applauding. Mr. Duarte bows.

"I think you just won a lot more than that." Tommy smiles as he takes in the scene. He puts out his hand for me to shake. I steady myself before I grab it, and it's a good thing because when he speaks again, I feel so light-headed it's a miracle I don't sway on my feet.

"You never cease to amaze me, Emeline Jones."

After school, I drive home to change and head to Tommy's to take Este out.

His Tesla is in the driveway, and my nerves take a little excitement-fueled spin around my insides. Did his "you never cease to amaze me" comment leave me confused and breathless for the rest of the day? Yes. Did I refresh my makeup to come walk the dog? Also yes. Am I wearing the pair of yoga pants that made him go crazy during Brush and Bulky? Guilty.

I take a deep breath and stride up to the house, hesitating to use the key Tommy gave me until I hear Este whining on the other side of the door. I'm not sure Tommy's pet deposit will cover the damages our impatient puppy has inflicted on the wood—something else to add to the list of things I owe him for.

"Hello," I call softly as I open the door.

Este jumps up on me despite the hour we spent with the trainer Wednesday afternoon precisely to remedy this issue. The problem probably lies in Tommy and I finding her enthusiasm adorable. Even now, knowing I should be telling her "no" or "sit," my fingers dig into her shaggy (but clean) fur and scratch the spot she loves behind her ear.

"Where's Daddy?" I ask her, crouching so she can lick my face.

"I'm a da now, am I?" Tommy says, walking in from the kitchen. "My parents will be so excited to hear the news."

"The Dogfather," I joke in a high voice, nuzzling Este to hide the blush I feel scouring my face. I just called Tommy "Daddy."

He hands me her leash, and after I buckle that on, he passes me a little sack of treats and her clean-up bags. "I'm going to walk part of the river path," I tell him, forcing myself to focus on his face and not the cut of his shoulders in his gym shirt. "So I should be back here in less than an hour. If our best girl is up for it and not too tired, I thought I'd take her for a little ride to grab some dinner afterward."

"Remind me why it's called the river path?"

"Because it runs along the river, obviously."

"I'm quite familiar with rivers on account of all the rowing." He does me the disservice of actually miming rowing, and this time there is no avoiding the way his shoulders swell beneath the cotton. "And from my experience, they generally have water in them."

"Well, here, our rivers are seasonal. Ephemeral, if you favor the poetic. We don't like to do things like everyone else. That would be boring."

"Ah, yes. The risk of drought, on the other hand, is terribly thrilling." He grins, and it does that lopsided thing, and I'm grinning back in short order. I *amaze* him.

Este pulls at the leash.

"See you later then, maybe," I say, reaching for the door handle.

"One last question before you go." Tommy presses his hand to the door to keep me from leaving.

My pulse skyrockets. "Yes?" I rasp.

"What in the bloody hell is this Rodeo Break we have coming up?"

Este whimpers, spinning herself into a web of leash and legs and giving me an excuse to catch my breath until Tommy bends down to help untangle her. "It's not personal, Este," he says in what I assume is his Irish version of Michael Corleone from *The Godfather*. "It's strictly business."

Business. That helps settle me down right away. Tommy. Principal. Principles.

I have *principles*.

He stands back up, still very close, and I step back, tightening my hold on the leash.

"When you move to the Wild West, Mr. O'Connor, we might not have rivers that flow regularly, but there are other perks."

His eyes crinkle in a smile. "I'm well aware." His voice is low, and it takes a lot of effort and the relentless tug of Este against the leash to keep me from stepping closer to him again. "But this one sounds fake."

"I can assure you Rodeo Break, the rodeo, and the hundred-year-old parade preceding it are all very real. You should go."

"Do you?"

"Go to the rodeo? In high school, I saw a rodeo clown snap his leg in half falling out of a barrel while a Plummer bull charged him. One pickup rider had to drag him out on the back of his Morgan while the other unsuccessfully hazed the bull with a lasso."

He shakes his head. "And you think I don't make sense when I talk."

"The important takeaway is that I haven't been back since."

"So, what do you usually do over this Rodeo Break?"

"A lot of people go to Disneyland," I say, fiddling with my ponytail. "I'm pretty certain we are the only city in the entire U.S. that has those days off, so the park tends to be relatively quiet."

"Hm, yes," he says, pretending to consider. "A nearly thirty-three-year-old man alone at Disney doesn't sound disturbing at all."

Nearly thirty-three? Sometimes I forget that Tommy was making almost a million dollars a year by the time he was thirty. Thirty! When's his birthday? I bet Leila could make sense of it all if I can figure out his star sign. Can you just ask your boss their day of birth? How did this not come up during the week we were sleeping together?

"Any other suggestions?" he prompts, raising his eyebrows.

"San Diego is popular. That's where Leila and Benji are headed."

"You'll be in town alone?" he asks, crossing his arms.

"Well, not exactly *alone*," I lie. "But, yes, they are going to California."

He chews his lip for a second. "I think I'd prefer to get to know this area a little better."

"February is great for hiking."

"Any favorite spots?"

"Yes, and by then, there might even be water in the washes if it heats up enough for the snowpack to melt. *Rivers.* Este would have a blast on the trails."

"Let's do it," he says.

My traitorous eyes drop down his body: his snug, white shirt hugging his crew-sponsored chest muscles, black athletic pants slung low on his hips, and bare, confusingly sexy feet...that start to fidget.

My gaze snaps back to his eyes. "Do what, exactly?" I murmur.

Tommy tilts his head, a soft pink rising beneath his freckles. "Let's take Este for a hike or two if you're available and don't mind me tagging along."

"No. Yeah."

"Is that an American yes?"

I nod.

"Excellent," he says, opening the door for me. "Looking forward to it."

I step out, glancing back at the door when he closes it from inside. Some fight I put up about not spending time together outside of work. If I had to put my money on it, I'd say Tommy is a Taurus, so I can't be blamed for caving.

Twenty

TOMMY MEETS ME AT the condo with Este on the first day of Rodeo Break and drives us toward the low mountains east of town. Our conversation in the car revolves around Este and school, nothing that makes me skittish.

Our conversation is fine. But when I bend down to pick up a penny at the trailhead and misjudge Tommy's distance so he's forced to brace my hips with his huge hands to avoid smashing into me with his crotch? That provokes a touch of panic.

"Sorry," I mutter, straightening. Este leaps into a puddle, splashing our feet, and I take the opportunity to change the subject. Or, at least, the subject currently hijacking my mental function: our nearly aligned sexual organs. "The puppy loves puddles."

Tommy is smirking. "She sure does."

"Do you love puzzles, Este?" I ask the dog when she pounces into another shallow basin of old rainwater.

Did I just say *puzzles*?

Tommy regards me, a hint of concern on his face. "You okay, Em?"

"Yeah, of course." *Just flustered.* Like I always am when I'm near him alone lately. "Who doesn't get puddles and pretzels mixed up occasionally?"

I grimace.

Tommy scans me from head to toe, then looks into my eyes, probably assessing for signs of traumatic brain injury, and says, "I've hardly figured out the difference myself."

I laugh, thankful he's willing to play along, and follow him and Este down the trail. As we walk, Tommy repeats all the plant names I teach him.

"And this one is a Graham's Nipple Cactus." He chuckles, crouching to examine a five-inch-high plant with fishhook spines. "And some nipples they are."

"Hey," I say, poking him in the leg with my toe. "You're supposed to be taking your education of desert flora seriously."

"It's not my fault this alien world is filled with an assemblage of absurd, strangely sexual, and otherwise terrifyingly named plants. Scorpion weed, old man saltbush, hedgehog cactus, devil's claw."

"Fetid goosefoot," I add.

"Perfectly disgusting." He grins and rubs his hand over the deep red bark of a nearby shrub. "Let me guess, this one is called barbarous bloody bush."

"Oh, Tommy. No." I cross my arms. "Bloody bush?"

He winces. "I hadn't quite thought that through yet."

"This," I say, stepping closer to him and reaching for a bunch of pale pink flowers, "is a manzanita. And these pretty blossoms will turn into small red berries that look like little apples, thus the name."

He bends beside me to examine the flowers, and our shoulders press together. "Well, that's darling, and now I feel quite rude about my name-calling."

"As you should," I tease, straightening and continuing down the path and away from the warm call of his body.

We hike for a few minutes without speaking, the three of us in a line on the trail, Este leading the way, me behind her being dragged along by the leash.

"And what is this fuzzy assortment of sticks called?" Tommy asks behind me.

I turn back to him as he steps off the trail. "Teddy-bear cholla."

A thick lock of auburn hair blows across his forehead in the sun-warm breeze, the midday light making his eyes spark as green as the surrounding saguaros. "That," he says, "is the most adorable cactus I've met yet."

He moves closer to examine the plant, reaching out just as I tear myself from my revelry and shout, "Don't!"

Tommy whips his arm back, but it's too late. A piece of cholla half the length of his perfect forearm has implanted itself between his wrist and his shoulder, holding his arm hostage in a bend.

"The fecking thing attacked me!" He glances at me, wide-eyed.

"Teddy-bear cholla, also known around here as *jumping* cholla." I hurry over to him as I open my backpack. "Stay still."

"It's in two parts of my arm at once. It's like a finger trap made of deceptively benign-looking wickedness. Will I be stuck like this forever?" he asks, his face pale as he lifts his arm before flinching with a hiss.

"I told you not to move," I say, pulling the tongs from my pack.

"You carry tongs?"

"Only when I hike with newbies."

His breath hitches. "Dare I ask why?"

I wink at him before I close the tongs around the cholla in his arm and extract the six-inch piece of cactus from his skin, pinpricks of blood welling where the spines had been. He extends his arm, then reaches out with cautious fingers to prod the sore flesh.

I grab his wrist with my free hand before he can make another painful mistake.

"Don't touch it," I say, his pulse bouncing against my fingertips.

He studies my hand where it holds him, and I realize my thumb is caressing the back of his hand of its own volition. Stupid thumb.

I drop his wrist.

"And why can't I touch myself?" he asks. "Not, I mean... Lord, Emmie. What just happened?"

I assume, for both our sakes, that he is referring to the attack by cactus and nothing that happened after. "The tongs were step one. It's the hard-to-see little suckers still embedded in your skin that cause the real problems."

"It's still in me?" he asks, seeming both worried and confused.

"Don't worry," I assure him. "You happen to be looking at a professional glochid remover."

"Glochid is the scariest word you've used on the entire hike. What's step two? How many steps are there?"

"Let's get you home, and I'll explain as we go."

I DRIVE, MAKING A quick stop at the drugstore for supplies on the way. Every time Este gets excited and squirms in Tommy's arms, he scowls in pain.

I carry the dog and the shopping bag inside, opening the door wide for Tommy and ordering him to make himself comfortable at the kitchen island. I put Este out back and come back to find him with a glass of whiskey and a bowl of Nilla Wafers.

"I suppose you know what's coming," I say regretfully, sliding onto the stool beside him and stealing a cookie.

He lets his head drop. "I didn't know they sold bone saws at the corner store."

"It's the only way."

"Just like in the old country," Tommy says before throwing back his whiskey. "I'm ready. Do your worst."

I open the plastic bag on my lap and line up my tools: duct tape, tweezers, and Elmer's school glue. Tommy's brows crease.

"Trust me," I say, reaching for the duct tape.

"I'm trying, Emmie. Really, I am."

I laugh as I wrap the tape sticky side out around my fingers, then take Tommy's hand so I can hold his arm still while I dab at the impact sites. His fingers tighten on mine.

"Step one," I breathe, our heads close together. Removing nearly invisible hair-like spines with tape was not supposed to feel this intimate.

I clear my throat and grab the tweezers. "Step two."

Tommy is a good patient and lets me focus so I can pry out any glochids that escaped the duct tape. I tweeze out everything I can see.

"Step three?" he asks when I pick up the glue.

I twist the orange cap open. "Yep."

"How many people have you done this for before?" he asks, voice low as I smooth the glue over his skin, trying to be delicate but also firm enough that if I hit one of the spines, it won't send hellish electric shocks through his nerves.

"Minimum three a year. You saw what the kids were like at the arcade on Valentine's Day. Imagine how fun it is to take them out on Desert Days."

"An experience I'm sure none of them will forget."

"They have fun, I guess. Mostly it's a good way to wear them out when the end-of-the-year impulsivity hits."

"Not Desert Days." He tenses when I graze my gluey fingers over his wrist. "I meant you, doing this."

"Ew."

Tommy shakes his head. "Sorry. I just, I mean, I won't soon forget it. I've never had a woman use duct tape and glue on me all at once before."

I roll my eyes, but darn it, I'm definitely smiling. "We have to let this dry, and once it's off, we can rinse your arm and see if you feel anything else."

Tommy bites his lip. "Will you be very mad if I say something inappropriate right now?"

"Very," I warn. I go to the yard to get Este, and when we return to the kitchen, there is another thumb of whiskey in Tommy's glass even though I gave him very explicit instructions not to move. I cross my arms. "Bad, Tommy. Este listens better than you do."

"Lies."

"Sit, Este," I command, holding Tommy's gaze. He raises his eyebrows. Este climbs onto my shoes and rolls onto her back. "See? Just like I asked."

Tommy chuckles.

"Go ahead and drink that," I say, pointing to his glass. "The next part is the worst." I poke at the glue to confirm it is dry and start working up the edge.

"Oh, hells."

I pull up a corner slowly, his arm hairs coming with it. Tommy groans. "I can make this quick and easy," I say, " but I'm going to need you to tell me something."

"Anything."

"What's going on with the talent show?" I slide my tongue to the corner of my mouth, trying to secure my grip. "What's this big surprise Audrey keeps hinting at?"

"Damn her."

"Tell me," I say, pulling up another centimeter of glue as slowly as possible.

"It's a guest host!" he gasps out through clenched teeth.

"A surprise...guest host? Who's going to help us fill the entire arena?"

"She could probably help us fill SoFi."

"Who?" I demand, tugging at the glue.

His eyes are imploring. "I don't want to spoil it for you."

"Tommy," I say.

"Emmie," he pleads.

I pull at the glue in earnest.

"Okay, okay...it's..." I give a solid *yank,* and Tommy rasps, "Cecily Prior!" as I pull the sheet of glue off in one swift motion.

"That wasn't so hard, was it?"

He extends his arm and examines the skin. "Better than the bone saw."

"You're welcome." I throw the glue away and sit back down, grabbing his glass and drinking the splash of whiskey he didn't finish.

"Wait." I set the glass down and turn to Tommy. "Did you just say *Cecily Prior,* current Best Original Song Oscar nominee, is coming to *our* talent show?"

He grins all crooked and cute. "I certainly did."

Twenty-One

T HE WORDS "OH MY god" leave my mouth approximately fifty different ways: a gasp, a shout, a squeal, a cry. I make all the sounds as, in my head, I run through what this means for the school.

So many resources. So many opportunities.

So much freaking money.

"Can I tell Leila?" I ask, eyes wide. I have to tell her. I am physically incapable of not telling her. It is a testament to my shock, and maybe a little bit my respect for Tommy, that I didn't immediately run away to call her as soon as the words left his mouth.

"You can," he says, smiling at me and whatever face I'm making. Is there such a thing as an aggressively joyful grimace? "But if we can try to keep it only to Leila, it will give me and Audrey the time we need to sort the details."

"Deal. Yes, of course." I grab a clean, wet cloth and rub it over the spots where Tommy was impaled by the jumping cholla. "Is there anything I can do to help?"

He flinches. "Not at this point."

"Stray sticker?" I ask, pulling my hand away from his arm.

"I think so."

I grab the tweezers again and start searching, holding the back of his elbow in my free hand. "Well, when there *is* something, I'd like to support you however I can. I know I'm not the co-chair of the talent show anymore, but I'm here, and I'm available."

When I look up, he meets my eye, and my fingers tighten on his skin.

"Thank you." He brushes a piece of hair off my face. "With your permission, I'd like to take full advantage of your availability."

"Permission granted," I murmur.

He's so close, and it seems wickedly unfair that I was free to kiss that mouth just weeks ago. Not for the first time, I wonder if becoming the principal is worth everything else.

But it wouldn't matter. Tommy is doing things that no one else has ever managed for the school. When his contract expires, the board will offer him a permanent position. He will be our official, and no longer interim, head of school.

Tommy will always be off-limits as long as we're at Desert Grace together. I could never leave the school, and I'd never want him to because the place needs him. The kids deserve him, and the teachers deserve him. He's changing our school—for the better.

He's making a difference in the world, just like he told me he wanted to do in Vegas.

I swallow past the tightness in my throat and refocus on my efforts to find the sticker.

"Got it," I say, raising the near-invisible spine between us and trying to fill my voice with victory, not the emotional defeat that prowls around the edges of my heart.

Tommy runs a hesitant finger over his skin, meeting the tips of mine.

I shiver and grab the antibiotic cream. "Almost done. I just need to get you wrapped up."

He nods, chewing his lip as he studies me. I work in silence, smoothing the cream over his skin, blowing on it to help ease the sting. When it's time to bandage his arm, he turns a little on the stool and opens his legs so I can step into them to reach his shoulder. When I finish wrapping his arm, I step back, and I bite my lip as our eyes lock.

We are frozen like that for one breath. Two.

His hand flexes against the countertop.

I clear my throat, pivoting to collect the tweezers and leftover gauze. "How did you convince Cecily Prior to do the show? And how did you get the city to *give* you the convention center arena on a Friday night? What Celtic sorcery did you work?"

Probably his smile. Or his eyes.

He smiles at me, and they crinkle at the corners. Yeah, probably those.

"I asked them," he says, his gaze following me as I clear up my supplies. "And they said yes."

I stuff everything into a bag and turn my focus to Tommy. "You just...asked? Like, 'Hi, Cece, I live in your house and was wondering if you'd do this bonkers thing for me.'"

"In fact, she had called to talk about her plans for the house, and after that, we spoke a bit about why I'm in town. She seemed interested in the school, and so yes, I just asked."

"And she also said yes." I shake my head as I tape the end of the gauze at his wrist.

"She did."

I step back and cross my arms.

Tommy smirks. "You're the one who told me she was an advocate for education."

"Yes, at a *congressional* level, not a small, tuition-free private school with a leaky ceiling and reputation for breaking things on field trips level. I mean, it's *Cecily Prior. Time* Person of the Year, twice! Nobel Prize-winning poet. She probably invented Nilla Wafers. She's, like, magic."

Tommy shrugs. "My da always told me it never hurts to ask."

"Alas," I say, shaking my head and giving him a once-over, "if only we all had the confidence of a handsome Irishman. Imagine what the world would look like then." And yeah, I just called him handsome, but it's true, and it's still only one of the five thousand things I've come to love about him.

Tthe Monday after Rodeo Break, Tommy holds a faculty meeting in Desert Grace's chapel after school. When the other teachers and I arrive, Audrey, Adesh, and the rest of the board are already there—everyone, that is, except Mr. Edmonds.

No one seems to acknowledge or be troubled by his absence. Perhaps I'm not the only one who thinks he's a pretentious turd.

Tommy begins the meeting by reviewing some precursory information about spring testing and teacher retention incentives. You can almost hear the teachers' eyes roll. Last year, Mr. Edmonds gave us gift cards to Whole Foods. And don't get me wrong, teachers love food too, but we also love being able to buy lots of it for less money, so we have cash left for the classroom supplies we pay for *out of pocket*.

Most of the teachers only attended this last-minute, non-compulsory meeting today because they assumed we'd finally be getting the details about what our new head of school plans to do with the seven-thousand-person venue we've been offered for our talent show.

Incentive shmincentives. The staff just want the juicy goods about our St. Paddy's Day performance (and a gift card to Target).

I squirm in my seat because *I* know the news is worth the wait, and press my lips together to keep from shouting, "It's Cecily Prior, people!" at the top of my lungs.

Tommy glances at me and winks, then turns back to the rest of the faculty. "This year, we've decided to make some big changes to the retention incentives."

"He's going to keep kicking this horse?" Leila asks beside me.

"Maybe he's hoping that if he tells them our incentive this year is a week's supply of Costco-brand Keurig cups and then really quickly tells them about Cece, they won't have time to mutiny."

"Cece, eh?"

"Whatever." I nudge her with my shoulder. "That's what Tommy calls her."

Tommy, who still seems really hopeful for a man who's about to disappoint an entire room of teachers with another perfunctory gift from the board.

"I know it might not compare to pasture-raised beef," he says, a teasing smile playing on his lips, "but we've decided to take a new, more practical approach. This year, we will give each member of the faculty a stipend in the form of a prepaid credit card to be used for classroom stockpiles and whatever else you might need to do your job to the best of your ability."

"How much?" our art teacher questions, their tone understandably skeptical.

Tommy frowns and gives a small shrug. "Not as much as we'd hoped."

Crud. I tense, preparing for the uprising of our educators, the violent launching of lesson plans toward the stage.

"But," Tommy goes on, "we have managed to budget three hundred and fifty dollars per teacher. Per semester."

Holy *frittata*. My mouth hangs open as I stare at him. It's like he read my mind. But better.

Leila punches me in the shoulder. "Your lady parts made this happen," she whispers, not nearly quietly enough. "La Pasadita tacos don't hold a candle to your vagina."

I glare at her and shake my head. "I had nothing to do with this."

Tommy continues over the stunned hush of the crowd. "Teachers will receive their cards biannually, one before school begins in August and another after the New Year. Your first stipend for this year will be available in early March. The board has officially adopted the policy, and a majority vote will be required to change it. However—"

Someone groans.

"However"—Tommy raises his eyebrows—"the board will meet each summer to decide on an increase to the stipend to keep pace with inflation."

There are cheers. Some people cry.

Me. I cry.

Tommy gestures for Adesh to step forward. "Mr. Jain has something else to share."

"There's more?" Leila looks at me, stunned.

Adesh sits down at the edge of the stage platform. "As much as Desert Grace aims to prioritize the well-being of our students, there is one aspect in which we have failed. After some outreach, however, we are excited to tell you that we have secured funding to bring on a full-time school counselor. We are hoping to have the position filled in the next few months and would like to invite faculty to participate in interviews so we can guarantee the right match for our staff and students."

Leila pinches my arm.

"Ow!" I squeak, glaring at her.

She glances at my lap. "That thing is fucking magic."

"Stop," I warn. "My private parts are zero percent fairy dust."

"You're right." She raises her eyebrows. "They're a goddamn pot of gold. Your vagina is so compelling that all it took were a few lays to get us cash *and* counseling? You should exploit that gift in your pants more often. Use it to save the polar bears or something."

I glance at Tommy on the stage, my skin hot with a memory from Vegas. For mercy's sake, did I really call my genitals a pot of gold? And he still liked me after that?

He smiles at me.

"Thank you," I mouth. For so much.

He holds up a hand to quiet everyone down, a hand that implies *we aren't done yet.*

I panic.

What if he's about to announce my nomination for principal? The words that will be the final nails in the coffin of our fleeting and ostensibly already dead relationship.

"We know that this is way overdue," he says, and I squeeze my eyes shut, tensing as I prepare for the blow. "There are no excuses for the fact that you haven't had the access you should have in the past, but effective immediately, all of your insurance plans will fully cover therapy and other mental health services."

My eyes fly open, and I gape at him.

"No fucking way!" Leila and at least five other teachers shout.

"Yes way," Tommy says back, but his gaze doesn't waver from mine.

Leila narrows her eyes at me. "Are you *serious?* Em. Oh, Em. This is way bigger than your vagina. Do you see the way that man is looking at you? Shit."

I'm too shocked to tell her to zip it.

Tommy *did* it. He's doing it. He's making Desert Grace better.

Ms. Conn leans forward. "You ladies are hearing this, right? Or was that microdose I took this morning not so micro?"

"I think it's really happening, Denna," I tell her. "And don't take drugs before school."

"Well, now I won't have to, Emmie, because I'll finally be able to see a goddamn therapist."

"Touché."

I'll be able to see one too. The thought fills me with equal parts hope and dread. Because now, I will find out if what is wrong with me can be fixed, if I can mend the damaged pieces, or if I'm too broken—like my mom—to ever be whole.

What if all I find inside is darkness?

Leila grips my arm. "Here it comes," she says, and I turn my attention back to where Audrey has her hands clasped in front of her.

"Tickets will go on sale soon, and of course, you and your families and our students' families will all get free admission, but..." She pauses and takes a deep breath, and I suspect that Audrey, too, is a Cecily Prior fan by the way her cheeks get all rosy and her eyes sparkle. "We wanted you to be the first to know that for our talent show, we have a very special guest coming to help out. All proceeds will go to the school, but she'll—"

"Come on, Auds, tell us who it is!" Micah implores in his breezy, lighthearted way that somehow makes his outburst not make me want to throw a shoe at his head.

All the teachers second his request.

Audrey's hands shimmy a little before she fists them near her face. She rocks onto the balls of her feet. In fourteen years of knowing this person, I've never seen her like this. She is downright *giddy*.

"Cecily Prior!" she shouts, then covers her mouth like she can't even believe herself.

It takes about ten seconds for the faculty to recover enough to reach for their cellphones, but Tommy jumps in and asks us all to keep the news quiet until the board is able to issue an official press release and make tickets available.

"Good luck with that," Leila mutters.

Twenty-Two

I visit George after the meeting, stopping at a bakery in the
Mercado district on the way to pick up a Brazilian roll cake with
sugary guava jam, just like he taught Mom and me to make it.

This is how we celebrated my birthdays, George's promotion,
mom's sobriety, our pets' Gotcha Days, and my good report
cards—even when it became tedious because it was clear I'd rather
make everyone happy by doing well in school than have even the
semblance of a social life.

In the past ten years, there haven't been many occasions to
celebrate, but when one does come along, the little girl in me who
felt so safe and surrounded by love in those moments still craves
the company of my parents.

Seeing the school I treasure and believe in beginning to blossom? Knowing I'm supported there, financially and mentally, in
ways I never was before?

Probably, even, becoming the principal of that school?

I desperately want to share those things with someone who has
known me, been there for me, and whose support made it all
possible, from giving me and my mom a safe home and a family
to telling me to listen to my heart.

"George?" I whisper, pushing his door open.

He's sitting in a corduroy armchair in the corner, reading beside
an open window.

"Hello," he greets, and I can already tell by the way his voice is warm and friendly but not *mine,* not Emmie's hello, that he doesn't recognize me.

I swallow against the unbearable tightness in my throat, telling my heart it's not allowed to ache. Telling my eyes they don't have a right to fill with tears.

"Hi, Mr. Silva. I just came by to deliver a treat. A little bird mentioned you have a soft spot for Brazilian roll cake." I set the cake on a small table near the kitchenette and turn to grab a dinner knife—no one in George's wing of the care facility is allowed anything sharper—from the silverware drawer.

"Sweets before dinner?" he asks.

"Are you always such a rule follower?" I tease. Because George and his principles.

His grin is wide and beautiful. "Maybe just a taste." He comes to sit at the table, and I serve him a giant slice that would technically qualify as much more than "just a taste."

He doesn't protest. I cut a piece for myself and sit down across from him. George puts his book down on the table when he reaches for his fork and napkin.

"*How Democracies Die,*" I say, reading the title. "Have you ever heard of the *Jack Reacher* series? *Jason Bourne?* Probably the same amount of violence, but likely less depressing."

He laughs. "Ignoring the world's ugliness doesn't make it disappear. It just makes it more likely to catch you unaware when it rears its head."

The déjà vu of George: finding myself in the familiar, in repeated moments with the same person, but at the same time, impossibly alone. "So I've been told."

He eyes me in a way that makes my heart beat incoherently with hope and worry. Hope that he'll *see* me. Worry that he'll become confused, disoriented, when he tries to place my face and can't.

I hold my breath.

"And what is it that you do?" he asks, forking another bite of cake.

"I'm a teacher. History, mostly." And then I tell him everything else, because even though it is heartbreaking every time I see George, the only family I have left, and he doesn't know me, it gives me a chance to share my life with him in a way I usually can't. Today, I don't have to be eighteen-year-old Emmie. Today, I can tell George about all of the amazing things happening at school, about Este, about Leila and Benji.

I even tell him about Tommy.

George loves a good real-life romance, even if his reading tends toward the dismally nonfiction. He especially relishes a happy ending.

Which is why I leave out the part about Tommy and I being star-crossed lovers. Well, that, and I imagine it would sound even more preposterous to say out loud than it does in my head.

"This Mr. Tommy sounds like a good man," George says, raising his salt-and-pepper eyebrows.

I trace a finger along the woodgrain of the table, smiling to myself. "He is."

George swallows his last bite and leans back, patting his stomach like he has after every great piece of cake he's eaten for the past twenty years. "My heart is happy for you, senhorita," he tells me, his eyes kind and thoughtful.

I blink against the tears and stand to collect our plates so I can rinse them in the sink. "I appreciate that, George. You better get to dinner so we don't get in trouble. I'll be back with more cake, though, don't worry."

He tucks his book under his arm and thanks me, dipping his head as he leaves.

When the door closes, I let myself cry as I watch the crumbs and the bubbles swirl down the drain. I cry because I'm lucky—to still have George, to have a fulfilling job, to have amazing friends. I cry because I'm grateful, I tell myself.

I ignore the voice in my head that tries to argue otherwise.

I PULL OUT MY phone when I'm back in the car. I have a missed call from Leila and a text that says: Budgy Pony, ASAP.

I'm too tired and too desperate for a distraction to ask for details. But when I arrive, it seems I'm late to the party. Leila, Benji, Micah, Audrey, Adesh, and an untucked, slightly disheveled Tommy are all at a table together, a round of beers and burgers already half-devoured.

"What's going on?" I ask as I approach. Their energy seems to be teetering between panic and excitement, an emotional space I know very well.

Tommy turns to me first. "Emmie," he breathes, resting his bottle on the table and providing zero context for this little get-together.

"They serve Guinness at the Budgy Pony?" I ask, eyeing his drink.

"Yes, but not on draft, sadly."

Leila hands me a beer.

"Word already got out about Cecily's involvement in the talent show," Audrey tells me as I sit down between her and Micah, across from Tommy.

"And are we surprised?"

Leila snorts.

"No," Tommy answers, rubbing his hand along his stubbly jaw. I bite my lip. "We had anticipated this might happen. It just means we have to speed up our timeline: talk to our students and their families, establish ticket prices, schedule an official presser, those things."

"So we're holding a crisis management meeting?" My gaze sweeps over the others. "At the Budgy Pony?"

Leila rests her head on Benji's shoulder. "Actually, we came to make libations in honor of the day Desert Grace started getting its shit together."

"Thank you for the invitation."

Leila scoffs. "First of all, I did invite you. Second of all, they were already here when we arrived." She nods first to Tommy, then points to Adesh and Audrey.

"Tommy's idea," Audrey says. "I haven't been since they took my fake ID away when I was back for winter break in college."

Leila and I regard her appraisingly, the woman who I've never known to be anything but perfect, and spotless, and well-behaved in the decade and a half since we met. Audrey offers a shy smile and shrugs.

Tommy takes a sip of his Guinness and peers at me, then looks back at the table. "Seemed the place someone might come after a big day," he says. I don't miss Leila's smirk. "Anyway, the good part about the news being out regarding Cecily's participation in the talent show is that I've already received near a hundred emails from local businesses offering to donate goods and services."

"Restaurants and caterers, too?" Leila asks.

"Loads of them."

Leila reaches across the table to poke me. "Tell them that awesome idea of yours, that one you've been emailing the board about for years."

I lean back in my chair. "Six years of rejection would indicate it isn't so awesome. Mr. Edmonds made it very clear he was not interested. The food trucks have been just fine. Everyone loves pizza."

Adesh and Audrey share a look. "For argument's sake," he says, "let's take Mr. Edmonds out of the equation for the evening."

"We want to hear your idea," Tommy adds, resting his bare forearms on the table across from me.

I look away, take a sip of my beer and a deep breath, and then tell everyone at the table my dream about a post-talent show dinner that spotlights our families and their cultures. Community members could buy seats or bid on tables to attend.

Micah whistles low. "People would pay good money for that."

Audrey has her phone out and is typing. "How many people are we legally allowed to have in the Desert Grace building?"

"Max occupancy is three hundred and twenty." Benji taps a finger on the table. "But I don't know if the plumbing could take it."

Adesh nods. "We'll need a venue. Something close to the convention center. We could offer meet-and-greets with Cecily Prior after the show while we get everything set up for dinner."

"Yes," Tommy says. "I'll make some calls in the morning."

Audrey's hand shoots into the air. "Everyone okay with the Historic YWCA? Because they just accepted."

Tommy's foot finds mine under the table, and I glance up at him. "Amazing, Emmie, as always." His eyes are soft and mossy, and my chest tightens so much that it hurts to breathe.

"To the future principal of Desert Grace High School," Micah says, raising his bottle in the air.

I bury my face in my hands. "Oh, *sugar*," I whisper as heat rises to my cheeks.

He isn't supposed to know. I don't even know who does. But I am pretty sure this is not a good look in front of Audrey and Adesh. The board would not appreciate the thought of me advertising to the rest of the faculty that I am the chosen one. I, myself, do not appreciate that thought.

"To Emmie!" Leila and Benji shout in unison, and I drop my hands, my mouth still twisted in a grimace.

"To the principal Desert Grace deserves," Adesh adds.

Audrey clinks her beer against the others. "To the principal Desert Grace needs."

"To you." Tommy leans forward, holding my eyes, and taps his beer against mine.

Benji rests his face on his hand. "I wish someone would look at me that way," he says very loudly, his head tilted as he studies Tommy.

I gasp. *What?* Can they see it, too, then? That unreadable, impossible look? I don't dare check to find out.

I push out of my chair, backing away from the table, away from their cheers, and away from Tommy's face, which is so full of *something* that it makes me wonder if I need to pinch myself.

Leila reaches for me. "Don't get weird, Em. We're all—"

"Not being weird! Just hungry. Haven't had anything but cake, and..." I trail off with an awkward wave and turn for the bar, where I order a basket of chips and a burrito. Even though my insides are so knotted, I don't think there is any room for food.

Leila and Benji follow.

"What did I do?" Benji asks as they sidle up beside me.

Leila's fingers slide up to ruffle his hair. "I told you like a hundred times, babe. Emmie and Tommy aren't a thing."

"Right, but I thought it was a temporary bump—a little Emmie bump in the road of life. I mean, you've seen them together," he says to Leila like I'm not there. "It's obvious that—"

My hands fist at my sides. Nothing can be *obvious*. Nothing can be there. "It's not happening, Benji. It's over. Done. We're just friends."

"But why?" he asks as if it makes no sense why I wouldn't be dating my boss.

"On principle," Leila tells him, and I don't miss the sarcasm in her voice, the unspoken eye roll.

Benji chuckles. "On the principal sounds like exactly where Tommy should be."

Leila high-fives him.

"You guys stink," I mutter, rubbing my fingers over my heart. I glance back at the table, where Tommy has his hands curled around his bottle. His head is bent, and his gorgeous bottom lip is between his teeth.

I don't ask the universe for much, but it would have been nice if there'd been a way for things to work out. I wish there were a reality where Tommy and I had a chance, but unlike George, I know better than to still believe in happy endings.

Twenty-Three

I WALK INTO TOMMY's office Friday morning for a quick pre-first bell meeting scheduled to discuss how we'll play the principal angle with all the press attention the school is getting. Tommy wants me to be out there talking to reporters, but since the board still hasn't voted and I am not yet the principal, I am prepared to argue that it should be him, Audrey, Adesh, or literally anyone else (besides Mr. Edmonds) representing the school.

"Audrey is running a few minutes late," Tommy says, peering up at me before returning his attention to the computer screen.

"Should I…" I trail off. *Try to disappear? Hide outside the door until Audrey gets here? Avoid any possible opportunity to be alone with you?*

"Take a seat and get comfortable while we wait? Yes."

"Right." I nod, sitting on the edge of his desk so I don't have to face him and pulling out my phone to check on ticket sales.

Tickets officially opened to the public less than an hour ago, and every time I refresh my phone screen, I watch available seats for the talent show disappear almost as quickly as the donuts Tommy brought in for the faculty yesterday. The board is not wrong about needing a plan—and fast.

"One hundred left," I say, blinking.

Tommy doesn't lift his head as he continues typing. "I'm going to win."

"No way. You've only got eight minutes."

"Refresh it."

"Say 'please.'"

He chuckles and smiles up at me. "Please, Emmie." I shiver. Darn it, you'd think I'm trying to torture myself. "Refresh the ticket sales page."

"Since you asked nicely." When the screen reloads, my eyes just about pop out of my head. "Oh, *crows.*"

"I won?"

"No, another email from the art room about Ryker."

Tommy's head pops up, and he chews his lip for a second. "Ryker. Incredibly tall for a sophomore, but averse to playing sports that don't involve Xbox controllers. He also has a taste for classroom supplies. What was it this time?"

"School glue—a classic."

"Delicious, but better used for clearing glochids from the arms of unsuspecting immigrants."

"Indeed," I murmur. Ugh. Why does the memory of Tommy covered in cactus make my skin hot?

"Should the nurse refer him for pica testing?"

"On it."

"Are you actually messaging the nurse?" He tilts his head. "Or are you looking for excuses not to check the ticket page?"

"It is what I *should* be doing, but...what the frick! Twenty-three tickets remaining?"

"*And* I just won."

"You bet me that the tickets would sell out in the first hour, and there is still—"

"Check again." He smirks.

"Bossy," I murmur, mainly as a reminder to myself that he is, in fact, my boss. And after Tommy just brought in hundreds of thousands of dollars for our school, there is no way the board won't be completely desperate to renew his contract. "Holy *shirt.*"

"To think you didn't trust me."

"Seven thousand tickets in *one hour?*" I put my phone down and swing my head around to face him, brows knitted together. "All these people know that they will also have to watch partially-pubescent boys sing if they come to see Cecily, right?"

"The tickets are non-refundable."

"Good thing."

He presses a button on the keyboard and stands up as the printer starts whirring behind him. I watch him grab the paper, his eyes brightening as he looks it over.

"What are you working on over there, Mr. head of school? Another surprise? Did you convince the president to come have a talk in our chapel about the value of education and the importance of voting?"

"It's a mid-term election year, and this is a border state full of swing voters. He needed no convincing."

I narrow my eyes. "You know the president, don't you?"

"I met him once at a dinner, but he was just a senator then. He seemed like a smart, good-natured fellow, but he didn't cut his asparagus, which was uncomfortable for everyone. Like perhaps he intended to expel it later as a magician might with a sword."

I wrinkle my nose. "Just jammed the whole spear in there?"

"Hardly even chewed before swallowing." He stares at me over the top of the paper, and I press my lips together because I shouldn't be about to laugh for a thousand reasons.

"But the important question is: did he get your vote?"

"Alas, his wiles were wasted on me, as I've yet to naturalize." A sudden din reaches us from downstairs. The students arriving for breakfast. "However, I did tell my sisters, and they all have dual citizenship. You should ask them if the asparagus incident swayed their opinions."

"If I'm ever so lucky to meet them, it will be the absolute first thing I bring up."

I wince. Was that wistfulness in my voice?

Tommy gives me a lovely, lopsided grin and walks around the desk to hand me the paper he's holding. "This is for the teachers. I put together an index of all the mental health providers in the area who accept the school's insurance."

My eyes threaten to well up as I scan the names of providers, all listed with working hours, their distance from campus, and the issues they treat.

He leans against the desk beside me. "There are some great options nearby. And see here?" He shifts to point at something on the page. Our shoulders press together. "Everyone with an asterisk beside their name is currently accepting patients. These over here have waitlists. But there are plenty of choices, so people should hopefully be able to find a therapist who is a good fit."

"How do you know?" I ask.

"About the therapists? All of the information is available on the *Psychology Today* website. The email I'll be sending out to the faculty includes a link. It's an outstanding resource."

"No, I mean." My pulse makes my words feel wobbly. "How do you know when someone is a good fit?"

"Oh." Tommy smiles softly. "You've never...?"

I shake my head.

He crosses his arms, chewing his cheek. "Well, I guess it was just one of those things for me where you *feel* when it's right."

"I'm not sure I have those things," I whisper. I can feel Tommy's gaze on me. From the corner of my eye, I can see his chest rise and fall with his breaths. When I finally look up at his face, he's studying me, his eyes clearing like he's had an epiphany.

I reckon Tommy has, at last, come to the unfortunate but inevitable realization that I am deeply abnormal and messed up in ways he can't even begin to conceive of.

"I see," he says in a way that makes it sound like he understands much more of me than anyone else ever has. Goosebumps bloom on my arms as he holds my gaze. "I talked to a few providers and got to know how they worked and let them get to know me a bit. But when I met with Jacob, I knew he was my guy. It just clicked."

"Have you been with him a long time?"

"Since I left Boston. We Zoom now, mostly. Sometimes, we won't talk for months; other times, I book back-to-back sessions. He's been a constant in my life, though."

I shouldn't ask; it's none of my business, and it is rude and inappropriate. But I have to know if Tommy was once as broken as me. And if so, does that mean I can be as okay and complete as he is one day? "Why did—" I hesitate, knowing I'm overstepping, and not just professionally. "How come—"

"Why did I seek out a therapist in the first place?"

"Yeah. I'm sorry. I—"

"Hey," he says, bumping me with his shoulder. "I'm glad you feel comfortable asking me questions. Or at least trying to ask them."

I wrinkle my nose, and he chuckles.

"I told you a bit about my family. *Families*. My mum and my sisters. My da and my brothers. Cormac, my sisters' brother, who, in many ways, I was closest to, because, like me, he was a floater with no real place to land. I spent much of my childhood trying to understand my place in the world. I've always dreamed of a home, creating a space and a family where I could make sure everyone within the walls knew they belonged. That their place was there, that our togetherness wasn't contingent on custody agreements, no starting over every other week."

He shrugs, and with an unhealthy lack of deliberation, I rest my hand on Tommy's and squeeze.

His eyes drop to our hands, then he turns his over and laces our fingers together. "Jacob helped me realize that, as much as I wanted to offer those things, I had to do some work first. And I have been. He also helped me understand that for that dream to make sense, for it to function, I couldn't do it alone, but I probably also couldn't do it with Polly the defense attorney or Krista the governor's aide."

"Why not?"

"Because you can't forge a family with just anyone. Historically, I tended to go after not just any person but often the wrong person. I was pretty desperate to prove I could build this thing and keep it together, determined to a point where I, to an embarrassing extent, tried to make pieces fit that never would. As you might suspect, what I really needed to find was the right *person*. Someone who wants that dream, too. And that wasn't something I could just make happen, that I could force. So, I started focusing more on work and finding a purpose outside the fantasy I had created. And then..."

"And then?" I ask, peering up at him.

He meets my eyes, his face softening as the corners of his mouth turn up. "And then I ended up here."

Tommy's words are floating around in my head like heart-shaped balloons when Audrey opens the door. I pull my hand into my lap.

"You guys," she says, her cheeks pink, "I just got off the phone with Cece."

I raise my eyebrows. "At seven in the morning."

Her cheeks get a little darker. "We sold every single ticket, even the heinously overpriced ones."

I hop off the desk, away from Tommy, and sit down in one of his chairs. "I know, it's absolutely wild. And it all happened in less than an hour."

Tommy pulls out the chair beside mine for Audrey and then strides around to his own, leaning back when he sits and folding his arms over his chest. "Why am I, the only person in this room who doesn't have a massive crush on Cece, also the only one here who is not the least bit surprised about the tickets?"

Audrey rears back. "What kind of monster doesn't have a crush on Cecily Prior?"

"It's truly worrisome that they allow people like him to work in education." I smile at a very handsome and anything-but-monstrous Tommy.

He winks at me. "Thank god we have you, then."

"And hopefully, we'll be announcing your move to principal much sooner than we'd thought," Audrey adds.

I sit up straighter in my chair. "How soon?"

Tommy clears his throat. "Before the talent show."

"What about my replacement? And the board?"

"The board," Audrey says, turning her chair so she can face me, "is going to look a lot different by the end of next week."

"What do you mean?"

"My—Mr. Edmonds is stepping down, and Adesh will be assuming the role of president."

Happy chills race along my skin, and for an actual, countable minute, I am unable to form words.

Audrey's grin is enormous, her leg bouncing between us. "I thought you'd like that. We will also be announcing a few new members, but the important thing is that everyone is thrilled that you will be Desert Grace's new principal."

"When will we tell the faculty?"

"They were all consulted during the decision process," Tommy says. "They all know."

"Are you sure?"

"Positive," he confirms.

I put my hands on my hips. "And no one has quit yet?"

Audrey laughs. "No one is quitting, Emmie. Everyone on the faculty is ecstatic."

"Everyone?" I challenge.

"Mr. Romano did express some concern that, should you become the principal, there'd be no one to ensure that the dry-erase markers remained stocked in the classrooms between periods. But that was the extent of the pushback we received. To get back to your original question, we need to discuss your replacement."

"Nilo Lopez," Tommy and I say at the same time.

I stare at him. As far as I know, Tommy has only met Nilo once, at the graduate support meeting during his second week at school.

"What?" Tommy chuckles. "Nilo is perfect for the job."

"He is," I say, turning to Audrey. "Nilo will be completing his master's in education this May, so he's still finishing classes. But he and I could co-teach until then."

"Sure. Deal. Let's talk to him, and if he's interested, bring him in as soon as possible to meet with the board and get that ball rolling."

"Emmie?" Tommy asks, probably because I'm suddenly sniffling a lot and practically vibrating in my chair.

"Sorry, yeah, it's just that if he accepts the job, Nilo will be the first graduate we've ever hired to a full-time position, and he worked so darn hard to get where he is. I mean, a master's! After almost not finishing high school, after losing his dad. It makes me so..."

"Proud?" Tommy offers.

Audrey takes my hand. "Happy?"

"It makes me hopeful." I wipe a tear off my cheek.

I don't tell them the rest—that all of this, all these changes, also make me profoundly nervous because I don't know if this much luck, the myriad positive transformations, can be sustained. And I don't know how to trust that it won't all turn dark again—but by the way Tommy watches me, I think he might read some of it on my face.

Audrey hugs me before I leave for my first class, telling me she'll draft an email to Nilo.

Tommy walks me down the stairs to my office to get my things. "You know," he says, "sometimes good things *do* happen."

"Do they last, though?" I ask, looking up at him.

"I don't know, Emmie," he admits. "But I'm hopeful."

Twenty-Four

I SPEND EVERY FREE second during the rest of the day browsing the websites of all the therapists on Tommy's list and filling out their contact forms. Under the "What type of services are you looking for?" portion, I write, *IMMEDIATE.*

After what Tommy said this morning, the candor in his words about this thing he's yearned for since his childhood, and Audrey's news that they're hoping to have the board officially hire me as principal *before* the talent show—so, in less than seventeen days—a big, giant, scary rift has opened up inside me.

I need the guidance of a qualified professional more than ever before that rift grows deep enough to get lost in.

When I leave school, I barely remember to stop and say hi to Otis when I'm walking to my car. Then I toss him a maxi pad instead of the blueberry oat bar I brought him from the cafeteria. By the end of the exchange, I've somehow forced him to keep both. The drive home is an auditory blur of public radio pieces and my growling stomach, the only reason I'm aware that I forgot to eat lunch.

I open the door to the condo, dump my stuff in my room, and shuffle back out to the kitchen to put away the clean dishes. I *should* be ecstatic. And I think, in some part of my mind, I am. The school is offering me the one thing I've wanted since I've been there: the power to really change things and the resources to help at a level I was never able to before. An opportunity to make connections with our students and their families—with our community—that I didn't have time for as a teacher.

And yet, the things Tommy talked about this morning in his of-fice—his dream—kind of made me want to run away from Desert Grace just so we could see if I could be the person he can build that dream with, and not face the moral implications of dating my boss.

Which is absurd. Isn't it? To consider giving up everything I've worked for at the school. Possibly even insane.

I assume the therapist will be able to tell me.

The cabinet door opens with a loud creak, and I pull out all the old to-go containers and mismatched Tupperware, sorting them back onto the shelves. Then I scrub the counters with Benji's vinegar spray cleaner.

I've known Tommy for less than two months. (And ten hours, if you count Vegas.) I've never prioritized a man or a relationship, but the idea of throwing everything away for this hulking "what if" doesn't terrify me nearly as much as it should. Maybe because I crave family and a place of my own in the world as much as he does. Maybe because with Tommy, the weight of it all—the clouds, the loss, the loneliness—becomes easier to bear.

Fib rubs against my leg, and I dump out a little pile of his favorite treats on the floor. I grab a broom and sweep around him.

To the point of Tommy making things easier for me, is it fair of me to even consider being with him knowing that I'd be saddling him with a lifetime's worth of my own problems? It's selfish of me to entertain the idea of a relationship when I know he deserves better.

But what if I could *be* better?

Fib meows, and I sit down beside him on the tile, pulling him into my lap. He acts like my affection is horribly annoying, but his purr suggests otherwise. Maybe I didn't give him enough credit; maybe he and Este could be friends.

Este! Poor Este will be forced to face the same realities Tommy did growing up: two homes, two families, and never knowing where she belongs. What if Tommy gets another dog someday, with someone else, and Este starts to worry she's no longer special?

I sprawl out on the cold ground and sigh, staring at the dirty bottom half of the cabinets. I *love* my job—all of it; the good, the bad, the ugly—and I've poured everything into Desert Grace. It is a part of me, a whole chamber of my heart, and the kids, the faculty, and Leila have kept me going all these years. They've kept me alive, at the risk of sounding dramatic.

I hear the front door open, and Fib, who is now curled up on my tummy, digs his nails into my skin before he shoots off my body.

"*Fluffing* cat," I mutter, sitting up.

Leila drops her bag on the table and walks over to where I'm still cross-legged on the kitchen floor. "Existential crisis?"

"More of a conjectural crisis, really."

Her eyes roam over the countertops as she sniffs. "As your 'cleaning the kitchen' crises often are."

"I didn't have time to do the oven yet."

Leila sits down beside me and wraps her arms around my side, resting her head against mine. "You okay, Em?"

"Have I ever been okay?"

"It depends on whose standards we're going by, but in my opinion, which is the only one that really matters? Yeah."

"Says my best friend, the math teacher who also thinks having sex in hot tubs is okay."

"It was just once."

I shudder.

"But sweetie? You deserve so much more than *okay*."

She holds me while I cry. She asks if I want to talk about it—my current conjectural crisis.

I don't. All I want to do is close my eyes and forget about everything. I want to sleep for a thousand years and wake up in a world that makes sense. She ushers me to bed and tucks me in. Gives me permission not to floss.

My mind shuts up sometime around 3 a.m., the heat that had been fueling the hurricane cooled to a tepid ache, and with the company of exhausted numbness, I finally fall asleep.

I WAKE UP TO the phone ringing, which means it's much later than I usually get up because my automatic Sleep Focus has disengaged. Squinting at the screen, I quickly Google the phone number.

My heart rate speeds up when I discover it's one of the counselors I messaged between periods yesterday calling me back.

I consider not answering, sending the call straight to voicemail.

Because I'm afraid. So extremely terrified to face myself.

But I also know that I need help.

"Hello," I answer, praying my voice comes off bright but not manic. Friendly but not fake.

Me? Trying to be normal and likable for the person who, in order to help me, will have to witness the most questionable corners of my twisted soul, assuming I can find the courage to lay them bare? Who will learn how selfish and broken and dark I am inside?

Yep. Checks out.

Yasmin and I chat for a couple of minutes, during which I warn her that I am very messed up and ask about twelve times if she's sure she wants to take me on. She laughs, so I'm worried she thinks I'm joking, even though part of me is also pleased she thinks I'm funny.

When she offers an appointment that just became available for the following week, I accept and hope she's dealt with worse.

"Leila," I call, bursting out of my bedroom and into the kitchen.

"Yes?" She's doing the newspaper Sudoku at the kitchen table, and beside her Benji is flipping through an issue of *Architectural Digest*.

"Oh, *nuggets*," I huff. "Did we turn into real life grown-ups?"

Leila eyes Benji's bowl of colorful cereal and raises her eyebrows.

"Right, good. I'm sorry to interrupt, but do you guys think I'm going to traumatize my therapist?"

Benji shakes his head and closes the magazine. "You're not that fucked up, Em."

"Thank you?"

Leila cuts Benji a sharp look, jostling him with her shoulder. A spoonful of pink milk splashes into his bowl. "What Benji means is that these people are trained to address all types of issues. They are there to support you and provide tools and resources for dealing with your past and the day-to-day so you can be the healthiest, most confident version of yourself as you step into your future."

I clap my hands. "You made an appointment, too, didn't you?"

"Earliest I could get was three weeks from now."

"I go next week," I brag.

"Good. You need it more than I do."

Benji presses a hand to his chest. "Burn! Damn, Lei."

"To address her *principles,*" Leila clarifies, smirking.

She's not wrong, but I steal her pencil and sit down between them, filling in a bunch of empty spots on her puzzle with fours anyway.

"You even got one right," she muses, turning the newspaper around.

"It was bound to happen eventually." Benji pats my back. "Want to join us for brunch with my folks? These Fruity Pebbles are just an appetizer."

"What time?" I ask, my stomach growling at the thought of real food. "I'm supposed to be at Tommy's by nine-thirty to pick up Este. How do your parents feel about dogs at breakfast?"

"We're meeting them at ten, and the presence of pups is appreciated, even encouraged." Benji glances at his watch. "But Emeline, you're a bit behind schedule if you plan to be on time for this doggy date at your non-boyfriend boss's house."

Leila winks at me. "Better hurry. Wouldn't want Tommy to worry."

I glare at her as I jump out of the chair, rushing back into my room to get ready. I'm out of the condo in record time, and it's only ten minutes past nine-thirty when I pull up to Tommy's. But growing up with George and his strong displeasure at being late, ten minutes is still enough to make me squirm. I can thank him for my blossoming sweat stains.

I trip on my shoelace as I jog up to the front door, crouching to tie it before I knock. I haven't even had a chance to stand back up when the door swings open.

Tommy stops short. "What's the date?" he asks, eyebrows scrunching together as Este bounds between his legs.

"The what?" I ask, still kneeling, still frazzled, and wondering where I put my keys. The puppy puts her paws on my knee and tries to lick my face.

"Today's date. What is it?"

"The twenty-eighth of February," I answer, patting my pockets with one hand while petting Este with the other. "Is there a problem?"

"I thought maybe it was the twenty-ninth." He grins down at me. "And that I was about to get incredibly lucky."

I locate my keys, grab the puppy, and hurry to my feet. "I'm not sure what to say to that."

"It's not even a Leap Year, is it?" he asks.

"It is not," I reply, shaking my head.

He reaches out to ruffle Este's fur. "Should have known."

"Care to fill me in?"

"Old tradition. Don't worry about it."

"Oh! Oh. I've seen that movie." I readjust Este when she spots a lizard and tries to launch herself out of my arms. " That's real? Women really..."

Tommy nods.

"Wait." My heart is somewhere between my throat and my stomach. "You thought I was—"

He chuckles. "Nah, I'm just teasing. Though, maybe by next year, the idea won't be so upsetting as to make you go all pale and sweaty."

Next year?

"Tommy," I say, trying to sound stern. Trying to sound like a co-worker and not a girl who is seriously wondering, if I *had* come here to propose, in an oversized "Weird Teachers Build Character" tee and joggers, would he have considered saying yes?

There have been times, so many times these past few weeks, when we are alone, and the corners of his mouth dip down, the furrow in his brow deepens, and I know he's about to say something that will make everything more impossible. I can't handle the Emmie-if-you'd-just-let-me-explains and the there's-more-to-it-than-thats, so I leave. Or I interrupt him with something more pressing and upsetting. Or, like the adult I obviously am, I put my hands over my ears until he stops.

Tommy smiles at me now, soft and gentle, and I wish a world existed where one day I could let myself hear all the things he wants to tell me.

"You know, the legend behind the tradition is that on a Leap Day fifteen hundred years ago or so, St. Brigid proposed to St. Patrick, who happened to be a priest." He cocks an eyebrow. "I should never have thrown away that cassock."

Cassock. My face goes warm, and I press my lips together.

"I'll just grab Este's leash for you, then," Tommy says, winking as he turns away.

I step into the house behind him, still holding Este. "I should have her back in a couple of hours."

"You can use the key to put her in. I'm heading out in a bit and not certain when I'll be home."

"Sounds good." I scan the room to avoid focusing on his lips while he clips Este's leash on her collar. A big cardboard moving box is in the corner, and my heart squeezes.

"Jumping ship already?" I ask in a high voice.

Tommy glances up and follows my eyes to the box. "Ah, that. Right, that's..." He trails off, facing me. His deep green eyes light up in what feels like a challenge. "Would it matter if I were?"

"I don't understand. Do you mean you *are* leaving?" I ask, my pulse tearing sideways through my entire nervous system with the force of the emotional whiplash. Wasn't he just talking about next year?

"Would it matter, Emmie," he repeats, "if I were?" Tommy holds my eyes as he chews his lip.

I step closer, leaning back to glare into his face. "Of course, it would matter!"

"Why?"

"You know how they say there are no stupid questions? Well, Mr. O'Connor, *they* are wrong. That is a really stupid question."

"I disagree." He tilts his head, considering me as he crosses his arms. "I think it is a perfectly reasonable question. Why would it matter, Emmie?"

I take a ragged breath and feel my nostrils flare. "Because..."

"Yes?"

Because if you're gone, then I'm just me again. Me alone with the clouds. But you are the silver edges in the storm. You are the end of the rainbow. The promise of spring after rain.

You could be my family. And I would do everything I could to be yours, the one you deserve.

Because even though it makes no sense and is terribly inconvenient, I'm in love with you.

I love you, Thomas Flynn O'Connor.

"Because the school needs you!" I shout, squeezing Este in my arms.

"The school. Yes." Tommy drops his eyes to the ground, then glances out Cecily Prior's picture window, refusing to meet my gaze. "Well, rest assured, that"—he nods to the moving box—"is just a bunch of stuff I'd left in storage back east and had shipped out. But speaking of school, I best be off. You ladies enjoy your morning."

He grabs his keys and walks out the door, leaving Este and me staring after him.

Twenty-Five

WEDNESDAY, AFTER LAST PERIOD, I close the classroom door behind me and lean against it, smiling.

Tommy wasn't home when I brought Este back after brunch on Saturday, and I've barely seen him around school since we met with Audrey and Adesh on Monday morning. I'm not sure if he's avoiding me or I'm avoiding him, but our rate of success would imply it's mutual.

Mr. Edmonds will officially step down as board president this evening, and Adesh will take over. The board—and Tommy—will finalize my promotion to principal this week. They will make the announcement on Monday, at which point it will all be official.

Nilo accepted the job offer immediately and has been spending his free time, in between his own classes, at school with me. The kids already adore him.

There is a "Sale Pending" sign in the window of the building next door, and I'm a little terrified that just as I become principal, a bar or a strip club or a sex shop is going to open up beside us and make my job one thousand times harder. Nothing is inherently wrong with these sorts of establishments, but still, the donors wouldn't be thrilled if our parochial school's new neighbors were serving alcohol or selling bondage supplies, and even though our students would probably find it hilarious, our kids' guardians, not so much.

On the bright side? The sophomore history essays the kids just turned in look good—really good. They are titled and formatted correctly, and not a single one is written in Comic Sans. From what I've read so far, I'm impressed. The thesis statements make sense, and Harper even managed to sneak in a pun about a long sword that I am ninety percent confident is not about penises.

These kids are so amazing. Despite the hardships they face and the daily grind of being a teenager, trying to be optimistic about the trajectory of their life in a world full of bad news and endless crises, they are putting in the work. Sharpening their minds. These kids *are* hope. They are the dreams of our future.

A better world is possible, and their sweet, insightful minds will help us realize it.

I put my hand over my heart and exhale, my chest so full it's close to bursting.

"Hey, Ms. Jones," Kaira, one of my freshman students, says as she walks by. Naomi, beside her, flashes me a peace sign.

I smile at them, overwhelmed by the raw potential of our young people, and fall in behind them.

"Were those clementines or oranges at lunch today?" Naomi asks Kaira.

"They were oranges," Kaira answers. Then, in the quintessential know-it-all voice of youth, she adds, "Clementine is a language."

Naomi snorts. "You're such a dumbass," she says, and I wince, feeling a twinge of empathetic embarrassment for Kaira until Naomi goes on. "Clementines are a fruit. *Tangerine* is the language."

Okay.

Well, we will take the future one step at a time.

And that includes my future. I'm meeting Yasmin Ofori for my first therapy session in thirty minutes. She works out of a small studio downtown, so after depositing my things in my office, I tie my cardigan around my waist, square my shoulders, and march out the front doors of Desert Grace, ready to go get fixed.

Ready for her to tell me what to do to make everything better.

The walk only takes me ten minutes, so I linger by her building until I can go in—acceptably but not annoyingly early. The waiting room is what my students would call *aesthetic,* full of white and beige and bursts of color and patterns that feel energizing but not overwhelming. Potted plants—that, based on my examinations, prove to be real despite their perkiness and lack of browning edges—join hardcover novels on floating shelves and stand guard in the corners.

I sit on the edge of a shearling armchair and try to settle my breathing as the time passes. What's the protocol? Do I just assume she knows I'm here? Do I call? Knock on the door leading into the actual office?

Definitely not the last one. I'd rather sit here for the next five hours than knock and possibly disrupt her. And really, do I even *need* to be here? I've managed up to now, and what could Yasmin possibly tell me that I don't already know about what's wrong with me? She's not even legally allowed to prescribe me medication. I probably should have gone straight to a shrink. I'm just wasting our time by showing up here instead.

I check my phone and see that my appointment should have started one minute ago.

It's probably better if I just leave. Maybe Yasmin had an emergency. I don't want to bother.

Just as I start to stand, the door to her office opens. Two women emerge, both beaming. I recognize Yasmin from her photo on *Psychology Today.* She waves at me, and the other woman hugs her.

"First time?" the stranger asks as she walks by. She looks light. Happy.

She looks like she feels exactly how I want to.

"Yeah," I answer, trying to smile back with equal exuberance.

"I'm excited for you. Yasmin is damn good at her job."

Yasmin laughs and grins at me, and in that moment, I'm excited for me, too.

I follow Yasmin back into her office. Her natural curls are cut into a bob, and her clothes and accessories are even cooler than her waiting room. All I can think about is how excited all the kids at Desert Grace would be to go to the student counselor, and how little we'd have to force them to seek help, if we could find someone like her to take the position.

As soon as I've taken a seat on the camel-colored velvet couch—seriously, does she do interior design on the side?—I start digging in my shoulder bag for a Desert Grace card or pamphlet or tax receipt to give her, already determined to convince her that whatever good she is doing here would be amplified tenfold in our dilapidated building.

Maybe she can help us with a redesign, too, after all the talent show money comes in.

She clears her throat, the sound gentle, amused, and I turn to her.

"Hi, Emmie," she says.

"Hi, Yasmin." I pull my hand from my bag and give a guilty grin. It's fine. She'll be more inclined to take the card—if I can find one—once she's heard about the school. "Thank you for getting me in so quickly."

"I've been looking forward to meeting you in person since we spoke on the phone. And I know we touched on things a little during our conversation—"

"By the way, I was joking, mostly," I interrupt. "About being scarily messed up and worried you can't help me because I'm too broken for fixing." I laugh. It sounds hollow.

"I'd still be here if you thought those things were true." She crosses her legs and leans forward, bracing her arms on her knee. Her dark eyes, so sincere I feel it like a prick inside my heart, hold mine. "I don't believe anyone is too broken to be helped."

I glance at my hands, trembling in my lap, and then out the window. She's wrong.

My mom was.

And almost like she can read it in my body, in my mind, this reality I carry that maybe there is nothing beyond the clouds, she says, "With the right support and the proper treatment, I truly believe *anyone*"—she pauses and waits for me to look at her, and when I do, she smiles—"is capable of breaking out of cycles of disordered thinking. Anyone can create new patterns and build a life filled with the things they want instead of the things they feel they've been stuck with."

"Anyone?" I question, raising my eyebrows.

She nods. "*Anyone.* You, Emmie, can live whatever life you want. There's just some work to do first, and it might be work you have to continue doing for a good amount of time. But you won't be doing it alone."

My shoulders slip as my eyes fill with tears.

The way she says it, I believe her. I believe she can help me.

And I know the kids would believe her, too.

I clear my throat. "I'm a teacher."

Yasmin adjusts her notepad, clicks her pen, and waits for me to go on. Which I do. And once I get started, it's hard to stop. She asks questions about *me,* and how things at school affect *my* life. She quirks her eyebrow when I deflect, her mouth curving in a delicate smile, but I persevere.

Because I am going to be the principal of Desert Grace High School in less than a week, and I am going to find us the best school counselor this town has to offer.

With five minutes left on the Scandi wall clock behind Yasmin's shoulder, I wrap up my sales pitch and dive back into my purse. She leans back in her chair and watches me, and I ignore the gleam in her eye that says she sees a little too much, that she's putting pieces together she shouldn't even know exist.

Crumpled at the bottom of my bag, I find Tommy's business card from his first day as head of school. I pull it out, flatten it on my thigh, and feel my breath shudder as I inhale.

Desert Grace

Thomas F. O'Connor

Head of School

"I apologize this isn't in better shape," I say, handing the card to her, my fingers clinging a little too long when she reaches out to take it. "However, if you'd ever consider a change of scenery, please give us a call."

If she's put off that I just used our entire hour to sell her on a new job, she doesn't show it. Yasmin smiles at me and re-examines the card. "Who is Thomas?"

"Thomas? Tommy. Right, he's..." I trail off, then shake my head. "He's our head of school."

"I see," she says, and I think she might, actually.

What do you see, exactly? I want to ask. *And how do I make it disappear?*

Yasmin passes the card back. "You keep this." I hate the way I feel relieved when Tommy's semi-destroyed card is safely back between my fingers. "I'll make a note about the school, and if I think of anyone who might be interested and is a good fit, I will pass along the information."

"Oh," I say, looking at my feet. "Great. Thank you."

She stands and grabs a green planner from the desk, nodding to herself as she flips through the pages before shifting her attention back to me. "I have a client on vacation this week and next. All late afternoon appointments. If you think you'd like to come back, you can email me."

I stare up into her face. I think of Tommy, George, my mom, Leila, Este, the kids. Then I think of little Emmie, of all the things she saw and lived through, and how badly I want *her* to see the sunshine after the storm—to feel safe, loved, and happy. A tear rolls down my cheek, and I swallow.

I think about how badly I want that now, for me. For grown-up Emmie.

"Can I take them all?" I ask, sniffling.

"Let's start with Friday, same time, and see how you're feeling after that. I'll keep them open, though, if you decide you'd like some additional sessions."

"Thank you." The feeling in my chest almost hurts: a sense of grief that I didn't make this happen sooner, worry that it still won't work, worry that it *will,* and I won't like the person I am. And then, bright and burning: hope, hope, hope squeezing everything else to the edges.

"This was a good start, Emmie," she says, placing a hand over her heart like a small salute to the work we got done. "I loved hearing about how much you care about the school, and I'm really looking forward to our next visit."

"Me too." My smile wobbles, but it's real.

Twenty-Six

MY STOMACH ACHES ALL day, and it makes me angry.

I should be excited. Ecstatic. And I am. Leila and I danced with our coffees in the kitchen this morning, much to Fib's dismay, and I grinned at myself in the mirror as I got ready.

But when I slipped on my work heels—the pair I wore in Vegas—I felt a decade's worth of gloom coagulate, curdling in my chest, filling my lungs and my heart with sickening, suffocating darkness.

Right now, the board is locked in the auditorium, their makeshift conference room. Right now, the board is voting.

And any minute, I will be named principal, which is the most wonderful thing that has happened to me in years.

It is also achingly bittersweet. A door closed on a life that promised to be pretty good.

I hug my arms around my belly and tell myself that this is what I want, what I've wanted since I started at Desert Grace, really. The school and this life have been enough for years. I'll make do just like I always have. And now, as principal, I can find new ways to give the school and the kids more of my heart.

There's a soft knock on my office door at 4 p.m., and I hold my breath, hands pressed into the top of my desk. When Adesh enters, I'm both relieved and disappointed. It makes sense that the new board president would be the one to come and deliver the news. It's better than sending Tommy, but the impossible, selfish parts inside me wish I could share this moment with him, even if it would be a sort of self-imposed torture to see the crinkle at the corner of his green eyes and the sweet, smiling curve of his perfect bottom lip.

I stand up, and Adesh grins at me. "Good afternoon," he says. "And congratulations, Principal Jones."

My breath barrels through me, exiting my mouth as a throaty, eager, disbelieving laugh. *Life*—such a weird ride. "Are you all sure about this?" I ask, walking into the stiff hug he offers.

"Too late now," he says, bracing my shoulders and meeting my eyes. I bite my lip to keep it from quivering. "Shall I show you to your new office? You can start getting settled in now so you're ready to hit the ground running on Monday after we make the formal announcement to students and staff."

I step back. "New office?"

"You're the principal, Emmie. You get the principal's office." He tilts his head, amused. "Am I unsurprised, or am I worried, that this never occurred to you?"

The principal's office is directly across the hall from the head of school. The first and last thing I will see every day is Tommy's name on the plaque on his door, or worse: him, actual Tommy, mere feet away and yet impossibly out of reach—outside of work-based calendar invites and Este visits.

I grimace. "Do I have to move?"

Adesh laughs. "No one is going to force you, but it might be for the best. Nilo will need your desk, after all, and it's good for him to be with the other teachers and for you to have a quiet space where you can talk to kids and parents."

"Of course." I chew my lip. "I have an appointment at five, so I'll come in this weekend and—"

"We've got some time now," he interrupts, clearly worried that if he doesn't get me out of this office at this very moment I might never leave. "Here, I'll help with the first load."

"Thanks," I say, glancing around the room, mostly as an excuse to blink the tears from my eyes. For six years this office has been a sanctuary in the storms, and I didn't realize how hard it would be to walk away.

I climb onto a chair to peel the tape off the corner of one of Leila's math posters, rolling it up and tucking it under my arm while I sniffle.

"What can I carry?" Adesh asks, his smile gentle.

The head of school's door is thankfully closed as we come down the hall. Adesh adjusts the bin of binders he's hauling on his hip and reaches to open my new office. The door swings inward, and instead of the bleak emptiness I was expecting, the room is brimming with flowers and cards and balloons. Light streams in through a big window behind the desk, and the space is bathed in the soft sunshine of almost-spring.

"How does this all still look so good?" I wonder aloud. Adesh pushes aside a clover plant in a small gold pot so I can put down my planner and book bag.

He pauses by the door. "How should it look?"

"I mean, if someone's been coming in and watering since Ms. Bos left, the plants make sense." My eyes flick up to a squeaking congregation of multi-colored hearts hovering in the corner. "But I've never seen a foil balloon last longer than five days."

He shakes his head and looks, for the first time, like he is deeply questioning the board's decision to make me principal. Or my sanity. Probably both. "This is for *you*, Emmie." Adesh uses the plastic bin he's holding to prop the door open and gestures to the room. "This is all for you."

I stare at him. "Why?"

"Audrey," he calls, glancing at me from the corner of his eye like I'm completely bananas. "Can you come help, please?"

The door across the hall opens, and my heart catches, but it is Audrey, not Tommy, who appears. She smiles when she sees me. "What do you think, Principal Jones? Do you like your new office?"

Adesh leans against the door frame. "I think she's confused," he says in a loud whisper. "She doesn't seem to get that this is *her* office."

"That's just one of the things we adore about Emmie," she says to him reassuringly. "Her complete and total disinterest in things like big, bright office spaces and pay upgrades."

I cross my arms. "I told you, my teacher's salary is more than sufficient."

Adesh and Audrey share a look.

"Take it up with the board," she says with a shrug.

"You *are* the board," I argue.

Adesh glances at his watch. "Oh god, you're right, we are. And we have another meeting to get to."

Audrey wraps me in a quick hug. "I pushed our Historical Society meeting to early April, so you'll have this weekend to settle in a bit. Cece is going to be in town then, and said she wants to join us, maybe, if that's okay with you?"

I gape at her, my hands pressed into the sides of my face. "Cecily Prior wants to come with *us* to the Historical Society? Someone pinch me."

Audrey winks before rushing out the door behind Adesh.

"Expect to hear from me about the salary issue," I call down the hall after them before turning back to the room. The space is quiet and still, but not in a bad way. I can hear the echo of the kids on the floor below as they walk to study hall, the hum of the streetcar outside the window.

My appointment with Yasmin isn't for another forty minutes, so I unroll Leila's "I'm Just Here for the Pi" poster, smiling as I imagine her mock outrage when she sees it on my wall, and hang it by the door.

When I back up to admire my handywork, I bump into the desk. A card falls onto the faded brown carpet at my feet, my name scrawled across the envelope. I pick it up and delicately tear across the edge.

The front of the card says *CONGRATS* in big, embossed letters. I sit on the edge of the desk and open it.

Dear Emmie,

If it weren't for your grace and your generosity, I don't know how I would have survived the past three months. The worry of watching my daughter go through those tests in the hospital was eating me alive, and now with June on the mend, I can see how you made it all possible.

There is no one I'd rather see as principal.

Thank you for all you've done to help me professionally and person-ally. I am endlessly grateful and will do whatever I can to make this transition as seamless as possible for you.

Sincerely,

Joseph Duarte

I wipe the tears from my cheeks, my throat so tight it aches, and grab another card. A green envelope. The card says *Let's Taco About How Awesome You Are.* Inside, Leila has written: *We are so fucking proud of you.*

Benji signed his name next to Leila's. Leila wrote "Fib" underneath.

I put the card down and laugh—it sounds a little like a sob—and for the first time, really take in the number of letters and gifts sprawled across the desk and the top of the cabinet. I recognize the handwriting of my students on torn-out pieces of folded notebook paper, propped up like little tents, the edges covered in doodles, clearly decorated on class time. A row of mugs with principal puns written on their sides hold small bouquets and chocolate bars. Someone attached a sparkly balloon to a tiny teddy bear's arm, and it floats up and down like it's waving.

The gratitude I feel is so potent it makes me dizzy, so powerful I have to brace myself against the desk.

"Mama," I whisper into the air, squeezing my eyes closed as I hold the teddy bear to my chest. "I'm the principal of Desert Grace."

I LET MYSELF CRY, sinking to the floor as I cling to the little stuffed bear like a life raft. I let myself miss my mom and wish she were here. I let myself wish I could call George.

And then I get up and wipe my eyes, taking a deep breath. I square my shoulders. I have a school to run, a school I love, and an appointment with Yasmin in twenty minutes. There's no time to waste bawling my eyes out on the carpet.

I move the bin Adesh left by the door into a corner, linger for a moment to gape in wonder that this is real life, and then jog to my old office to get my phone and my sweater.

My breath pulls in on a sharp inhale when I push the door to my old office open. There's a ceramic bowl on my desk, cactus-green with lines scraped into the sides that give the impression of spines. It is filled to the top with coppery-red berries, an envelope tucked in amongst them.

I sit down in my chair and pull out the envelope. *Emeline Jones* is written on the back.

Tommy.

I consider stuffing it in a drawer, putting it back, pretending I never saw any of it, or dumping everything in the janitor's passing trash caddy. Instead, I pull it closer.

My fingers shake in time with my nerves as I work the seal back.

Dearest Emmie,

I recognize the irony of giving you more apples to carry—both figuratively with the new position and literally with the manzanitas. But I hope these will be the kinds of apples that nourish and restore. I hope for their weight to always be reassuring, calming, even, and never burdensome. More than anything, I hope that from their seeds sprout the life and beauty you deserve.

Because, Emeline Jones, you deserve everything wonderful.

Amazed, unceasingly,

Tommy

I toss the card across the room like it's on fire and wipe my clammy hands on my skirt before fisting them on the desk.

My breaths are ragged, and I can feel my nostrils flaring as I stare at the bowl of manzanita berries. I'm tempted to launch them across the room.

I pick one up and scoff. Seriously, where in the world did he even find these?

I shove the cactus dish in a drawer and slam it shut.

How dare he make this all harder than it already is? How dare he make it hurt worse?

Why is he doing this?

I want to scream. Roar. I want to corner Tommy. I want to shove him against a wall. I want to make him tell me why he insists on watching my heart break.

Twenty-Seven

I PRACTICALLY RUN OUT of my office. If Tommy left the manzanita berries here, we must have missed each other by minutes, and if I see him now, I don't know what I'll do.

Nothing good, though. I am very confident that it would be nothing good.

As I'm rounding the corner by the cafeteria, I smack directly into Leila, who grabs me, holds me still, and waits for me to take a solid breath before she says, "You have the most fucked up reactions to good news."

"To be fair—"

"Nope. You be on your way—straight to therapy you go." She spins me and smacks me lightly on the bottom. "Budgy Pony after. I'll congratulate you properly when you look less like you might punch me in the eye for saying something nice to you."

"I stole your poster!" I yell over my shoulder as I jog into a group of students heading for the door. *Man alive,* who thought it was okay to make me a principal?

I arrive at Yasmin's office four minutes late. She's watering the plants in the waiting room, and her face bursts into a huge smile when she sees me, falling quickly as she takes in my tacky, flushed skin, and the tight set of my jaw.

"Let's head inside," she says, reaching out. I realize too late she's going for my sweater, but when our hands meet, I hold on for dear life. "All right, Emmie. We got this." She guides me into her office, helps settle me on the couch, and sits down in front of me. "Why don't you tell me what's going on?"

I open my mouth, the stain of Tommy's words still at the front of my brain. But it feels too raw, like a fresh brand on my heart. So I go deeper. I dive right into the storm.

"My mom killed herself when I was eighteen." I say it like a threat, holding her eyes, willing her to wince or shy away so we can both escape what's coming.

Yasmin puts down her notebook and leans forward. "Do you want to talk about it?"

Apparently, I do. Because before I know what's happening, I'm describing the color of my mom's eyes, the double peanut butter and jelly sandwiches she'd pack me for lunch, cuddling on the couch after school watching *True Blood,* her telling me every five minutes how inappropriate it was for me but never turning it off.

I tell Yasmin about the sadness, too. The weeks it seemed my mom survived on tears and air, curled up in bed. The occasional outbursts, angry and wrathful, that always ended with her in a mess weeping on the floor and a deluge of apologies and promises.

At least when George came into the picture, I wasn't facing it alone.

The tears started for me in middle school. My birthright. The sadness offered me solace, though, an understanding—of my mother, of the darkness she faced inside. I could finally see that her battles weren't with us but with herself.

Yasmin chews her lip, her pen back in her hand, hovering over the paper. "Was there anything that happened at that time in your life, an incident at school or with your family? The loss of a pet?"

"You mean like a trigger?" I respond slowly, tugging at a strand of hair. "An event that brought the depression to the surface?"

"Something like that, yeah."

I press my lips together as I consider.

A flash of tile, a scream. Stomach pains and headaches and shaking hands.

I shiver, but nothing solid comes to me. In the end, it's just a lot of ill-collected memories from adolescence that didn't fully stick.

"I don't think so. I always blamed the hormones." I shrug.

Yasmin hums like she's not fully convinced.

"I think it's just who I am," I say. "The depression is part of me."

"Is that who you think you are, deep down?"

I slump in the seat, curling inward. "It's the only me I know."

"Is that who you want to be?" she asks gently.

I don't have to say anything; she sees the answer on my face, but she waits for me to speak anyway. I clear my throat. "Our time is almost up," I say, glancing at the clock, desperate to escape the truth pummeling the bars in my chest, the broken creature banging against its cage.

"I'm in no hurry."

I take a deep breath and pull my legs up on the couch so I have something to hold onto. "I'm so scared," I begin quietly. "I constantly feel like I'm riding a bike in traffic, and all at once, I might just lose control and swerve into the cars. Like I might step over the edge. I don't want that. I don't want to die. But I don't think my mom did either, and I'm worried that inside me is the same thing that was inside her, the thing that pushes or pulls without your consent. I'm scared I'll fall like she did."

Yasmin comes and crouches in front of me, taking my hand. "Emmie," she says, waiting for me to meet her eyes. "You are *not* your mother."

I repeat the words in my head. Once, twice, while Yasmin squeezes my fingers in hers.

I am not my mother.

The words are a balm.

Or a bomb. I can't decide through the buzzing under my skin, the choked sound of my breathing.

In either case, they are a break. They are a period in the longest run-on sentence, and a chance to write something different. Something new. Something that is only mine.

My eyes well, the tears charging down my cheeks, each one helping to corrode a belief I no longer choose to cling to.

"Tell me," Yasmin says a few minutes later, moving back to her chair when I'm finished decimating the contents of her tissue box. "In what aspects of your life do you feel like you are in charge of the narrative?"

"The whole narrative?" I snort. "None."

"Just as it pertains to you. Where you feel empowered to make the choices you believe are right."

Outside the window, the streetcar rumbles by. "I always try to make the right choices, do the good thing."

"Because of George." She raises an eyebrow. "And his principles."

We've been over this a couple of times now, but my lip twitches at the echo of Leila in Yasmin's statement. "That's a big part of it," I confirm.

"But when do you feel like it's *you*, and not George or your mom or the depression, driving the bus?"

Off a bridge, she doesn't add.

The answer is easy, though. "I don't know."

"Can you explain that more?"

I want to say it right, for myself as much as for Yasmin. I want to make sense of this voice that is so loud inside me but that I've never been able to fully identify. "I realized early on how much the little things matter, and I saw that by being kind and useful to people, I could make their lives better, even if just a tiny bit."

"Like people pleasing?"

I run the back of my nails along my lips as I think. "More like protecting, maybe? I could give them something good, or at least remove one bad or hard thing. Give them one less thing to worry about. It isn't about how they view me, but about making sure they are okay. I think that, with my mom, I thought enough good things, small efforts, hugs, and help, could counteract the bad."

"And you still exhibit this behavior." A statement.

I cross my arms. "If I can make someone's day a little better, is it really a problem?"

"That depends," she says, considering me. "Being that aware and empathetic is amazing and unusual, but the only person you are truly responsible for is yourself, Emmie."

Now I'm convinced Leila called and gave her pre-session talking points. "So I've heard."

"Where do you feel *most* yourself, like your actions aren't always driven by outside forces or beliefs?"

"When I'm teaching."

"Excellent. Let's start there. Why do you think you feel that way at school but not in other situations?"

"*Only* when I'm teaching," I correct. "Not at school in general. Especially not since Tommy came."

So much for avoiding that topic.

"Ah," Yasmin says, her expression unreadable. "Tell me about Tommy. The head of school, correct?"

When I first talked to Yasmin on the phone, I was worried that it was all the gnarled, tragic stuff that would make her think I was too messed up to be saved, but I'm pretty sure the most terrifying thing about me isn't how I've handled my past as much as how I'm handling my present: barebacking the ridiculous reality that I'm in love with my boss, and he doesn't know how to get out of his own way or mine. But that isn't right either, because Tommy has done nothing but empower me and look out for me, and between the two of us, it is me and my feelings that continue to be a problem.

"Yep. Desert Grace's head of school," I confirm. He's also my impetus for seeking therapy, a huge part of why I want to get better, and the reason I am able to actually be here. "And today, I was promoted to principal."

"Emmie, that's amazing news. Congratulations."

"Yeah. It's great." My voice quakes.

"And you and Tommy don't get along?"

I think of the bowl of manzanita berries on my desk, the perfect things he wrote to me. "Something like that."

"And what do you think the issue is?"

"Boundaries," I reply immediately, because I suddenly get why Tommy continues to be a problem. We need boundaries. Big, clear, unquestionable, unwavering boundaries—three feet deep with broken bottles cemented into the top.

Yasmin looks pleased. I should have known a therapist would love the idea of boundaries.

"Do you find yourself falling into your people-protecting behaviors with Tommy, too, then? Over-extending yourself, trying to make his life easier instead of focusing on your own work?"

My eyes widen as her question sinks in. "No," I say, confused by the realization. Have I even tried? Maybe, a little, but Tommy never let me. Or, perhaps, I never felt the need?

With Tommy, I let myself feel...safe.

"Are there other issues in your professional relationship that concern you?"

I peek at the clock—we've gone way over our time—and force a smile. "I'm supposed to be meeting my roommate soon to celebrate," I say, gathering my things. I don't want to risk sitting here long enough for her to ask me more questions. She is absolutely the kind of person who would see right through me, who would realize that when I use the word *boundaries,* I'm not referring to healthy professional limits so much as an unscalable wall around my heart.

"I'm proud of the hard work you put in today." She stands and follows me to the door. "I'll see you next week. In the meantime, let's see if you can find some other situations where you feel you can take more responsibility for yourself, be more in charge of the narrative."

"Got it. Will do." Homework. I've never not given my all on an assignment.

I thank Yasmin and walk to my car, already managing a detailed list of mental bullet points by the time I pull up to the Budgy Pony.

Tonight, I am going to be so responsible for myself no one is going to know what hit them.

I PULL INTO A space at the bar, put the car in park, and brace my hands on the steering wheel, taking a deep, steadying breath.

The feeling brewing in my blood is not happiness. It is not peaceful or calm, and it's definitely not kind. It burns and has sharp edges, and I let myself sink into it because it offers me protection and power and just the right amount of detachment. I open the door and step out of the Prius and onto the asphalt like I'm ready to take on the world and—

"Emmie!"

Tommy's voice hits my nerves like flower petals, like sunset light and summer rain. I frown, begging the sound of my name on his lips to stop pushing against the cracks in my armor.

It's too weak—*I'm* too weak—and we can't withstand more of him without caving. I turn on my heel to face him as he approaches me from his car.

"Hi, Tommy," I greet, my voice flat. "What are you doing here?"

My tone makes *me* shudder. I wasn't even this chilly to the students who hid Pop Pop Snappers under our end-of-the-year programs on the seats in the school chapel last June.

Something flashes across Tommy's face. Hurt? Confusion? A combination of both that feels like a sword to my gut, but he manages a smile. "I tried to catch you after school, but we must have crossed paths in the hall." He shifts his feet, scratching his jaw. "I left something on your desk. I don't know if—"

"I saw."

"Oh." He bites his lip. "Emmie, listen. I know that—"

"This has to stop, Tommy."

"But I—"

"Please, don't. This, whatever this is, it's got to end. For real. For me. I am the principal now, and I need to set boundaries."

He digs a hand into his hair, the auburn streaked with burnished copper in the parking lot lights. "If that is what you want, of course. I'll respect whatever boundaries you put in place. But if you'd just give me a chance to talk, if you'll give me five minutes, I think—I hope—you'd feel differently."

"It's not what I want," I say, my voice shaking. Shutting this door, stepping away from Tommy, is the very last thing I want. But if I am going to survive coming into work every day with him there…"It's what I *need*."

He drops his head, rubs his hands over his face, and makes the most frustrated noise I've ever heard come out of another human being.

"And," I force myself to say, shoulders sagging, "I don't think I should see Este anymore, either. I'll help cover her expenses, but I don't think the arrangement is going to work for me going forward." I swat a huge tear from my cheek and try to stand up straighter, but I feel like I just cut my own legs off. I hate boundaries, but I need to do this. I have to shut out Tommy and Este absolutely, lock them out of my heart, before the huge part of it they have taken over becomes necrotic with what-could-have-beens.

Tommy regards me like he's never heard anything sadder in his life. Then his face hardens, and he nods. "Have a good night, Emmie. I'll see you at work on Monday." He walks back to his car, opens the door, and then, over the roof, says, "You are going to be an incredible principal."

I watch him drive away.

I did it, I think numbly. I took charge of the narrative.

"Yo!" Leila shouts behind me. "Was that Tommy?"

I clear my throat and rub at my eyes before turning around. "He had to leave."

"I've been tracking you on FindMy and was getting worried you'd locked yourself in the car again."

"That isn't exactly what happened. It wasn't even my car, and we were nineteen, and if you recall—"

"Tomatoes, Emmie. Why have you been standing in the parking lot for the past ten minutes?"

And now, I'm going to take charge of another.

"I was talking to Tommy."

"Why the hell is he leaving already?" She squints, focusing into the darkness like she can bring him back with her mind. "He didn't even come in."

On his way home, probably, to call his therapist and rehash the possible reasons he has horrible taste in women. Officially adding me to the list.

I shrug.

She eyes me hard, which means I have to move fast. I see Benji wander out of the bar, searching for her, and strike while there's still time for me to run away without being waylaid by both of them.

"I'm moving out!" I blurt out, grinning.

Leila's mouth drops open in apparent disbelief, and then she whoops and does a little shimmy.

Ouch. "Okay, that hurts my feelings a little."

Leila pokes me. "Our girl finally got her head out of her ass," she says to Benji as he joins us. "The principal and the head of school will be holding office hours in *their* bedroom on the daily."

Oh, no. No no no no no.

Benji looks like he just got a pony for his birthday, but I don't know which of us he's more excited for.

"Good gravy, Lei," I say, my jaw so tight it hurts. "I am not moving in with Tommy. Are you nuts?"

She crosses her arms and steps closer. "Are *you?*" she counters.

"That has been well-established."

"Well, I'm not letting you move out."

I put my hands on my hips and lean into her face. "You can't stop me."

"I can try." She flicks my shoulder.

"Should I go order drinks?" Benji asks.

"Sure, babe," Leila answers, holding my gaze. "Coronas would be great."

I narrow my eyes at her. "Nothing for me, thanks."

"Stay," Leila says, her voice low and uncharacteristically gentle. "Please."

"It's time, Lei." Time for me to take control of my story, be responsible for myself. To find myself on the other side. And this is the only way I know how to make that happen.

Twenty-Eight

I WAKE UP SATURDAY morning to an email from Yasmin, almost disturbed by how deeply I slept. It is always exciting when I make it through a full six hours, but I might as well have blacked out last night. I battle to open my eyes, to extract myself from the covers.

And I know, as soon as I think back to the Budgy Pony parking lot, that my mind does not want to be awake because it does not want to acknowledge all the bridges I burned. The daylight makes the damage feel much, much starker.

Good morning, Emmie. Your session yesterday was rather intense, and we ended quite abruptly. I wanted to reach out and see how you are doing today and let you know you can always contact me between sessions.

Followed by: *I put you on the calendar for Monday at four. Let me know if that doesn't work for you.*

Perfect, I respond. *I'll be there.* No need to get into the rest of it and make her worry.

I press send and check the rest of my emails, hoping against reason that there will be something from Tommy. A calendar invite to discuss the upcoming contract renewal with the school's lunch company. A forwarded letter from an angry parent. A picture of Este looking as miserable as I feel after he broke the news that she is being abandoned by her loathsome human mother. *Anything.*

He's Tommy, though. He listened to me and respected my boundaries. I've never appreciated a person's integrity less.

Leila, however, *has* emailed me—a rental listing on Craigslist.

"What a boob," I mutter, pressing the link. For all the fronting and faces she made last night about me leaving, she's not putting up much of a fight.

The listing pops up, and damn her.

The title reads: *Housing available. For delusional principals only.*

A croaky laugh fights its way out of my tight throat.

One bedroom with unattached bath.

Must be into vindictive felines and Saturday crosswords.

Perks include afternoon wine on the balcony, plenty of tough love, and a third wheel with questionable taste in movies.

Best friends need only apply.

Good try, EJ, but you aren't going anywhere.

I don't bother getting angry that she posted an actual picture of my bedroom on the internet—possibly from this morning while I was still shrouded in the covers. The reply button leads me to a Craigslist-generated email address.

Do you offer month-to-month lease options?

P.S. In Benji's defense, The Big Lebowski *isn't a bad movie, but it does lose some of its charm when you are forced to watch it in perpetuity.*

It's not a joke. The part about Benji, of course, but also the question about month-to-month. I spent some time on the internet last night before passing out, and there's a lot I will need to figure out before I move, from basics like furniture to big things like how I will afford George's care and my own home at the same time.

For you? she emails back almost immediately. *Month-to-month, day-to-day, hour-to-hour. Whatever keeps you from making additional unfortunate life decisions. I'm holding your coffee hostage in the kitchen if you want to talk about Tommy.*

ME: I very much do not *want to talk about Tommy. Instead, I want to talk about how amazing you are and how I am such a butthole for always making you take care of me.*

LEILA: Don't do that shit, Em. You are my best friend. You've gotten me through so much...college and grad school and that guy I dated with the after-market car part addiction.

ME: Lance Chad.

LEILA: No!

ME: Yes.

LEILA: God, are you sure?

ME: Very. He drove a metallic purple Lancer, and his name was Lance Chad, and I will never forget that.

LEILA: See. You even remember upsetting things for me so I don't have to.

There's a knock on the door.

"I'm coming in with your coffee," Leila calls. She sets the mug on my nightstand and rolls into bed beside me. "Hey."

"Hey."

"You know you're my rock, right? And that any chance I get to help you out feels like a miracle—a rare but ravishing cosmic alignment where I get to be the good friend, for once. I don't get many opportunities to feel useful where you're concerned."

I turn and prop my head up on my hand. "What do you mean? You help me all the time! I literally would not have survived the past ten years without you."

"Shut up. You are the toughest person I know."

"Me?" I squeak. "Is there vodka in your coffee?"

"Now you're talking." She hands me my mug and forces me into a cheers. "How about some caffè corretto and a trip to Desert Grace to move your stuff into your new office?"

I take a sip of coffee. A splash of milk and maple. Just how I like it. No vodka. "So, I can't leave the house, but you are more than happy to kick me out of our shared school space?"

"I plan on spending all my free time in your new office, so really I'm excited for purely selfish reasons."

"In that case, I accept. Do you know who's on Saturday School?"

She eyes me over the top of her mug. "Not Tommy, since that's what you're asking."

I pinch her before resting my head on the pillow beside hers. "What if you're stuck with me forever?"

"I won't be that lucky."

"Don't bet on it."

"It's a sure thing, Emmie. I'd bet everything on it."

F OR OBVIOUS REASONS, WE don't actually drink before show-ing up at Desert Grace, but I do promise to buy Leila a beer afterward to thank her for her help—just not at the Budgy Pony. I'm not ready to return to the site of the emotional crime I committed against myself last night.

I use a plastic book bin to pack up my desk, smiling to myself as I go through my drawer of confiscated items: the Old Spice pomade I took from Marco on picture day, a B-12 vape pen, a bag of middle-finger party confetti, a Ziplock full of pencil shavings. I pop my bobblehead RBG on top and deliver everything to its new home. When I return to our shared office after finding a safe place for Ruth, I discover Leila on the floor beside her desk.

She looks up at me and sniffles, hiding her hands behind her back. "I wasn't snooping, I swear."

"What happened?" I ask, trying to get behind her to see what she's holding. She stands and backs up to the wall. "I was gone for five minutes." I ducked into the principal's office, dumped a box of books, and was out the door faster than a tall, handsome Irishman could down a Guinness, just in case.

Leila extends her hand, Tommy's letter pressed between her finger-tips. "It was on the floor under my chair." I recoil, and she pulls it to her chest protectively like I might tear the card to shreds if I get my hands on it. "I didn't mean to read it, but by the time I'd opened the card to see what it was, it was too late, and the words just flew into my eyes—"

"And they made you cry?" I ask incredulously. "You, Leila Bashar, are crying because of something my boss wrote in a card?"

"I am not an anthropomorphic sexy math doll, Emmie. I am a human being with feelings—not pretty ones like Tommy's, but feelings, nonetheless. So yes, the letter made me cry. Did you *not* cry when you read it?"

"No. I did not cry. I was really angry, actually, both when I read that and when I saw these—" I open my drawer and pull out the bowl of manzanitas "—I wanted to throw them at him."

"He found you manzanitas," she groans.

I rest my hands on my hips, feeling my face go hot. "Whose side are you on?"

"You idiot, I'm on your side. And right now, as your nearest and dearest friend, I must ask you what the fuck you think you are doing by pushing all of this away. *Manzanitas,* Emmie. Where does one even find fucking manzanitas?"

"*Cheez-its.* Am I the only one here who has any sense of right and wrong?" I demand.

She sighs dramatically. "Just wrong, I'd argue, based on the mounting, dismally irrefutable evidence."

I gape at her. A knock on the door interrupts our standoff.

"Bad time?" Audrey asks, looking genuinely frightened as she takes us in, closing the door behind her.

"Not at all," I say, shooting a quick glare at Leila. "I didn't know you were helping run Saturdays?"

"Oh, yeah. I'm just trying to get more acquainted with the school, so..." She trails off, her voice faltering like she's trying to come up with a good excuse for being an amazing person who is spending her Saturday with our unwilling students and not enjoying extravagantly priced mimosas.

"Thanks for being here, Audrey," I say to spare her the trouble.

She winces a little.

Leila nudges me with her hip as she joins us. "How are things going with the St. Paddy's Day show? Everything settled with the *talent?*" *Talent* surely implies Cecily Prior and not our junior-year beatboxers or the members of Desert Grace's improv club.

"I just got off the phone with Cece, and she gets in Wednesday," Audrey says, the words spilling out of her in a breathless jumble. "I'm trying to plan some small events for her to get to know the staff. Friday evening, we have a dress rehearsal at the arena, and then after, Tommy invited us all to Cece's house for cocktails and appetizers. Please. You two have to be there."

Leila punches the air. "I'm drinking margaritas with Cecily Prior!"

"Bring Benji, too."

"We'll see. I don't want to be distracted."

"Emmie?" Audrey turns to me.

"I, um, I'm still ironing out some details for the reception after the show. We have all the recipes ready to go, but I have to make sure the caterers can find the ingredients they need, and I'm meeting the event supply people Friday afternoon, so—"

"So, perfect! You'll be done in time to join."

Leila wraps an arm around my waist and squeezes a little too tightly. "Oh, don't worry, Audrey. I'll make sure she's there."

"Great. And can I just... Do you guys mind if maybe..." Audrey takes a deep breath. "May I just take a quick second in here to absolutely freak out that in four days, *Cecily Prior* is coming to town to be part of all this?"

"You absolutely may," I say, reaching for her hand and squeezing.

"I say we really go for it." Leila releases her hold on my waist to grab Audrey's other hand and then mine.

"What do we do?" Audrey asks.

Leila winks. "Cecily Fucking Prior is coming to our school!" she yells, followed by a loud whoop.

"Lei," I hiss. "The students are just down the hall."

"Holy shit, is this real life?" Audrey shouts, uncharacteristically ignoring the conventions of propriety *and* my reprimand. She wrenches our hands into the air in a cheer.

Okay, okay. It is pretty freaking cool.

"Cowabunga!" I cry out.

Leila snorts, and we all burst into giggles.

"I can't believe I slept in Cecily Prior's bed," I muse out loud, catching my breath as our laughter dwindles.

Audrey's eyes go wide, and I slap a hand over my mouth.

"Not fair," she says, nudging me with her shoulder.

"It really isn't," Leila agrees.

"If I can do it, anyone can," I reassure them in a high voice.

Leila shakes her head. "Not while Tommy's living there."

"He won't be there forever," I point out, eyeing the manzanitas in the drawer. All the air inside me balloons in an attempt to push the thought right out of my body.

When I glance up, Leila raises her brows at Audrey and shakes her head.

I narrow my eyes at her, but really, whatever it is, whatever is going on, I don't want to know. I don't deserve to know.

And as long as it isn't something that will interfere with me being the best possible principal for Desert Grace, I pretend it doesn't matter.

Twenty-Nine

T HE ANNOUNCEMENT IS MADE on Monday morning at the end of chapel before classes start. Our chaplain passes the microphone to Tommy, who hops up onstage, looking just like he did his first day at Desert Grace. Equally hopeful. Equally uncertain when our eyes lock.

"Today, I have the honor of introducing you to Desert Grace's new principal," he starts. "A person that everyone in this room admires, respects, and has come to love"—Leila kicks me on the ankle—"for her dedication, compassion, and strength. The school could not be in better hands, and we are all incredibly fortunate to have such an exceptional educator leading the Desert Grace family. Please give a round of applause to our very own Principal Jones."

The chapel erupts in cheers, and I erupt into tears that I hastily wipe from my eyes as I walk up to the stage.

I give the speech I prepared, thank the board and the staff, and at the end add an unscripted "I love you all, too," before instantly regretting it when I see five different people in the audience—namely Leila, Micah, Audrey, Adesh, and...Harper? What the heck?—exchange glances or make faces that imply they are reading way more into my comment than is necessary.

I do *not* look at Tommy.

The bell rings, and I head to my office to get my things for class, feeling extra grateful that I'll still be teaching and that not everything has to change all at once. I have three lessons this morning, and then

Nilo will come in after lunch to cover the afternoon. I'll spend that time finalizing all the plans and set up for the talent show's after-party, which, based on the amount of participation we've had from families and the excitement from the community, is going to be even more awesome than I ever could have imagined all those years I begged Mr. Edmonds to make it happen.

"Are you lost?" Leila asks at my shoulder as I stare into the room I've spent countless hours of my life in. It's where I grew up and where I grew into a teacher, where I cried and laughed so much and so often and so loudly that I imagine little disturbances etched in the paint by the sounds.

My stomach does something funny when I see Nilo's Baja Arizona tumbler filled with pens on my desk. "In all the ways that count."

She wraps her arms around my neck, resting her face on my shoulder. "You won't be lost for long, Em. You're good at finding your way."

"I can't even find my office."

Someone clears their throat behind us.

Not *someone*. A lovely, Irish, perfect head of school.

Deep breath.

"I'm quite familiar with that particular part of the building," Tommy says when we turn around. He smiles. "And would be happy to accompany you to your office. I happen to be heading that way myself."

"She's all yours," Leila says, pushing me by the shoulders toward Tommy. "I have to get to my Algebra I kids."

"Shall we?" Tommy says, and for a panicked moment, I worry he's going to offer me his arm, and I am going to take it, and that we are going to walk through the school with our sides pressed close together, right up to my office, where I will push him inside and lock the door—because I checked, and it definitely locks—and this will all play out the way it could have if I had zero scruples. If I never heard George utter the word "principles."

And I'd never resent George, but I do wonder what the point is of living by something that makes things a little worse instead of better.

I start down the hall, and Tommy steps in beside me, a respectable, average distance away. But I still catch myself grimacing as we pass the classrooms, even if I know it is perfectly normal for me to be walking with the head of school.

Oh, dear. People will probably expect to see us walking together a lot—and talking and meeting in our offices (alone!) and planning things.

I feel the swell of tears, a warm wave that surges all the way down to my toes—the kind of tears that don't feel specifically happy or sad but like something trying to get out, something bottled too long and shaken up, the pressure consuming your chest. The kind of tears that choke you.

The kind of tears that, if you take the time to shed them, leave you full of space for new things. Sometimes, even better things.

"Emmie?" Tommy asks, watching me chew my quivering lip as we approach our offices.

"I can do this," I say, my hands fisting at my sides.

"I know," he tells me, the corners of his eyes crinkling like his sheets bunched around us, the curve of his mouth the same arc as my back against his chest.

"Thank you, Tommy. I know that I could have handled everything better and that I haven't been very, well, you know. I've been really—"

"Hey," he says firmly, interrupting the rising of my voice and the frantic widening of my eyes. He is so calm, so confident, so kind for someone I've done my unholy best to shake. "No need to thank me. I'm happy to help you find your way back whenever the opportunity arises."

I look between our office doors, across the hall from one another. "Back here."

He tilts his head, holding my eyes. The green of his irises is a thousand blades of grass deep. "Back here," he repeats, his fingertips grazing my hand so lightly it feels like nothing more than the delicate rustle of an early spring breeze against my skin.

I shiver and slip into my office.

"ARE YOU FAMILIAR AT all with the concept of post-traumatic stress disorder?" Yasmin asks as soon as I've settled myself on her couch. There is a stack of books and pamphlets on the table that usually aren't there. I've read most of them.

"A little. I've tried to do some self-education on the topic," I say, pulling the improbably soft cable-knit pillow beside me onto my lap. "To better be able to engage with and assist a number of our students."

Yasmin smiles at me. "Those kids sure are lucky to have teachers who care so much."

"That's kind of you to say. But as well-intentioned as our teachers are, what the students *really* need to address these issues securely and appropriately is a trained and licensed school counselor." I cross my arms and shrug. "Seems they're hard to come by these days."

"I haven't forgotten." Yasmin chuckles. "I reached out to a former colleague. We can talk after our session."

I lean forward over the pillow, hands clasped, mostly to keep from shaking her. "Who are they? Are they good? Really good, I hope. How do you know them? When can they start?"

"After the session," she repeats, cocking an eyebrow.

I nod, relaxing into the cushions, but I'm still grinning as cartwheels of elated relief spin through my system. Desert Grace might have just found its school counselor, and not a second too soon.

"Fine." I glance at the clock. I can wait another fifty-three minutes. Probably. "After the session."

"Now tell me, Emmie, in your reading and research, what were your major takeaways about behaviors displayed by children who you believe might be experiencing PTSD?"

"I am obviously not qualified to make those kinds of diagnoses."

"I fully agree," Yasmin says, her smile amused. "But you are with the kids a lot, and you take the time to pay attention and get to know them. No one is going to judge you for sharing your observations."

My eyes shift to the door. "Do you promise that the armchair expert police aren't going to take me away for aiding and abetting the proliferation of non-empirically driven information pervading our society and driving the downfall of critical thinking?"

"I promise. I just want to know what you've seen."

"In that case..." I take a breath and start listing. "Mood changes are a big one. Feelings of sadness. Depression, hopelessness. I see a lot of worrying, a lot of overthinking, even some jumpiness. Often kids would rather be standing than sitting at their desks. Avoidance. Oh, oh, and self-sabotage. That's a *big* one."

"Interesting." She presses her lips together and watches me.

And watches and watches. I can literally hear the seconds tick by on the wall clock. Did she lie? Are the armchair expert police on their way right now to bust down the door and take me away for being a giant windbag and massive hypocrite?

I rearrange the pillow behind my back, waiting her out.

She writes something on her notepad.

I cave. "Interesting how, exactly?"

"Do any of those behaviors feel..." She twirls her pen and lets her gaze drift to the window, but I can see through her act. My muscles tense. I'm sure she's been working toward this since I sat down. I am a teacher, after all. I know when someone is about to drop a lesson on me. "I don't know, familiar to you, maybe?"

I gasp. "Oh my god."

"What?"

"You tricked me!"

Yasmin taps her fingers against the arm of her chair, cocking her head. "Did I?"

"No, maybe not tricked. You therapized me, like big time, and I fell right into your trap."

She laughs, raising her hands. "I promise, the last thing I am trying to do is trap you. You're just a lot more open when you're talking about your students."

"Clever."

"I try." She winks. "Now that you've found me out, let's just take it slow, all right?"

"All right," I agree with very pronounced hesitation.

She chews her cheek for a second. "Why don't you tell me what self-sabotage looks like."

I cringe.

"In regard to your students."

"Right, my students." Dang, she's good, always giving me the perfect turn off to get out of my own way and keep me talking. I should buy her a plant. "Sometimes it's skipping classes —which never works out for them because we have a closed campus and a staff that is highly knowledgeable about potential hiding places—or not turning in assignments when they're anxious about bad grades."

Yasmin nods.

"Other times, I've seen kids create drama with friends, conflict where there is none. The classic 'pushing people away before they can get pushed' behavior."

"And why do you think they do that?"

"It mostly seems to come from a need to maintain control, to feel a sense of power, when maybe they really have none." My eyes start to prick. "Like maybe by ensuring things go—or end—a certain way, there's no risk of surprise, no danger of an unexpected"—I hiccup—"an unexpected..."

Her eyes soften. "An unexpected what, Emmie?"

"Of an unexpected loss," I whisper.

"Like when you lost your mother," she says, handing me the tissues.

I take the whole box in confirmation.

"As we move forward," she says gently, "I'd like to examine your depression through the lens of PTSD a little bit more."

"But," I protest, blowing my nose before finishing, "I was *never* happy. Not even before I lost my mom. Not even before middle school. There were good moments with Mom and George, but I think the storm blocked out the sun long before anything bad happened. It just wasn't until middle school that the rain came, too, and I realized it was me who was gloomy and not the world."

I squeeze my eyes closed, recalling the heartbreak of realizing at eleven that my life was dark. And hard. And sad, so endlessly, impossibly sad. That the pressure in my chest would never ease.

I've been drowning ever since, struggling to stay afloat in a deluge of my own making.

"If you're up for it, and only if, and only when it feels good, I think we can conduct some emotional archaeology. Our minds and our hearts are really good at burying things when they think it's what's best for us. Unfortunately, they aren't always right. It can help for a while, but there comes a time when it's better for us to dig those pieces back up so we can give them a good rinse, tell them thank you for their service, and send them on their way."

"Or light a massive bonfire."

She gives her head a little shake. "Those parts, Emmie, they aren't bad. They aren't rotten. They are doing and have always done their best. You don't have to hate them or resent them, but you are definitely welcome to let them go."

"That sounds really nice."

"It will be. And we can take it slow, or fast, but for now, before you have to go, I'm curious about how you felt after Friday's session."

I scoff. "On the subject of self-sabotaging..."

"Let's hear it."

I tell Yasmin everything—pushing Tommy and Este out of my life in the parking lot of the Budgy Pony, threatening to move out of Leila's condo, all in the name of being responsible for myself and, of course, *principles*. She does me the kindness of not flinching.

"I'm still really curious about these principles." She studies me for a moment, tapping her pen against her chin. "From what you've shared about George, things aren't exactly lining up with this rigid adherence you stick to about what it means to be 'good,' or what it means to do the right thing."

"Yeah, I'm starting to wonder about that, too."

She eyes me, clicking the end of her pen once. "Then we are on the right track."

Thirty

I STARE AT MYSELF in the reflection of the four-by-six shatterproof plastic mirror I swiped from one of the science rooms when I got to school at six this morning, my face a Monet of blurred colors and indistinct shapes. I cannot believe I am sitting in my office putting on lipstick before the first bell.

Only two full days as principal under my belt and already circumstances force me to beg the question: *Who even am I?*

But I also caught Leila curling her hair at home before the sun was up, so clearly, I'm not the only one who is approaching today like an absolute maniac.

And is it really any surprise when the headliner of the highest-grossing international concert tour of all time and dedicated philanthropist *Cecily Prior* is coming to our school for a facility tour that I am supposed to be giving?

It was a pretty big assumption on Tommy's part that I won't asphyxiate on my own words as soon as I try to speak in her presence.

Yeah. I am freaking out.

But so is the rest of the staff.

And the students.

And the city bus employees outside who are yelling at Cecily's security to stop blocking the turn lane.

Everyone has been acting like the air vents in Desert Grace are pumping out nitrous oxide since we found out that she'd be coming to campus.

My door flies open, and Audrey is standing there, a drop of sweat rolling down her temple.

"What happened?" I ask, a million heinous scenarios already barreling through my mind. "Did someone poop on the front step of the school again?" The shame of Cecily Prior being greeted by human feces on her way into Desert Grace would be too great to bear.

"Again?" she asks, her face somehow more stricken than it was when she first opened the door.

My shoulders sag in relief. "*Heavens to Betsy*. For a second there, I thought I was going to have to leave town and change my name."

Leila slides into my office past Audrey, who is holding onto the door frame, and sits down in one of the chairs in front of my desk. "The phrase 'Heavens to Betsy' always makes me think of space porn."

"What is space porn?" Tommy walks out of his office and into mine, talking around the cap of a yellow highlighter. His gaze is focused on the papers he's holding, the highlighter clasped between his fingers.

"Ask Emmie," Leila says.

"What?" I gawk. "I don't—"

"Just teasing," she says. "You looked like you needed something else to freak out about for a second besides Ding Dong Doodies on the doorstep."

"Nice hair," I tell her.

"Thanks. I used your curling iron. Nice lips," she says back. I press my lipsticked lips together to try to hide them.

Tommy's eyes shoot up, and the quick jump of his brows when our gazes meet tells me I'm too late. His eyes drop back to my mouth and linger there. I swallow.

Luckily—for me, not so much for her—Audrey, who has not even blinked since Leila and Tommy arrived, stumbles as she steps into the room, dragging everyone's attention away from my face.

Tommy drops his marker and his papers, which flutter into a semi-circle on the carpet as he reaches for Audrey, the fabric of his linen-blend button-down straining against his flexed bicep. He settles her near the desk with the highlighter cap still clenched between his teeth before brushing a strand of auburn hair off his forehead.

Before she jumps out of her chair, Leila looks at me really quick to confirm with her eyes that whatever just happened was definitely sexier than space porn.

I'm around the desk in the next heartbeat, pressing my hand to Audrey's forehead. "Do you feel okay?"

She giggles, light and airy like she's two mimosas in, and the world is all sunshine and bubbles. Her hands open and close in her lap. "I'm fine. Just nerves."

Leila fluffs her big, brown waves. "Tell me about it."

I smell hairspray. Since when do we own hairspray? "I don't know what you guys are talking about," I say, leaning back against my desk beside Audrey and pursing my red lips. "What's the big deal?"

Tommy, who is hunched over collecting his papers, glances up at us all. "Cece is lovely. Audrey, you know that best of all. You've spoken with her more than anyone. No one has anything to be nervous about."

I squat in my skirt to help Tommy, but he turns his back to block me from the scattered sheets. "Thanks. I've got it," he says with a soft smile before peering at Leila and Audrey over his shoulder. "Everything will be just fine. The school speaks for itself."

"The horror!" Leila gasps.

Audrey giggles again and helps me stand up without flashing anyone.

The alarm on my phone goes off. "Ten minutes to showtime, friends," I say. Cecily is set to arrive just before our students start trickling in for breakfast at seven-fifteen in an attempt to mitigate the inevitable chaos. Of course, we did not tell our students she'd be here first thing in the morning. "Take your places!"

"Butterflies," Audrey ekes out before wandering out of the room.

"I'll keep an eye on her," Leila assures, following Audrey down the hall and presumably continuing on with her to the entrance of the school, where she is supposed to greet Cecily.

Tommy's standing by the door, still sorting through his papers. I lean against the wall beside him, wringing my hands. "Want to tag along on the tour?" I ask hopefully.

"You don't need me there, Em," he answers, turning the top sheet over. "You'll do great."

"But what if...I *want* you there?"

Tommy matches my gaze. "Cecily is coming today because she already admires the work you're doing here and wants to see it in action. This place is your budding magnum opus, Emmie, and there is no one better suited to show it off to her."

"But..." I bite my lip.

"But," he goes on, his eyes crinkling at the corners, "if you want me around for a while, I'll be there."

"Yes, please."

"We can have a signal for when you're ready for me to leave."

"Like this?" I ask, giving him the middle finger before quickly balling my fist and hiding it behind my back.

"Principal Jones, are we going to need to wash that hand out with soap?" he asks, and my chest heaves on an inhale. "I was thinking more like a secret word, a code phrase."

"'Bananas.'"

"Too obvious."

"'Captain, this is madness!'"

Tommy grins, and I am obliged by the undisciplined muscles in my face to grin back. "*Odyssey*. Book ten?" I nod. "I like it. A lot. But it might set the wrong tone. How about we go with something simple." He scans the room, then up to the cabinet where I keep my obligatory comfort snacks.

"Nilla Wafer," we say at the same time.

And just like that, Tommy and I have a safe word.

"I'm going to set this stuff down across the hall," Tommy says, indicating the pile of paper in his arms. "And then I'll see you down there."

"I'll be waiting," I warn to his back as he strides across the hall. I take one last look in the wonky plastic mirror, stick my phone in my pocket, and head out after him, pausing at the door. A piece of paper has drifted under the cabinet. I bend awkwardly to pull it out, turning it over to see if it's one Tommy missed.

I stand back up, stiffening as my eyes scan the words.

It's some sort of contract, or maybe an application, with Tommy's name listed in bold in the middle of the page beside what I believe is a woman's name, Roisin Mahon. Underneath is a Dublin address.

The word *URGENT* is highlighted in yellow.

I let the paper fall out of my fingers and use the toe of my shoe to push it back under the cabinet.

W HEN I COME DOWN the stairs, Cecily Prior is being herded through the front doors of Desert Grace by a man who is a solid foot taller than she is. And that is saying something because Cecily, even in her heel-free Oxfords, is really, really tall.

She is one part California cool with her highlighted hair tossed back in a loose ponytail of beachy waves and another part New York City collected in her black vest suit.

Leila and I stand, gaping, fifteen feet away.

"She's so awesome," I whisper. I'm pretty sure there was something I was supposed to do, like welcome her to Desert Grace. But when Cecily raises her sunglasses onto the top of her head and smiles at us, four security guards fanning out behind her like the army of a one-woman nation, my mind goes blank.

"Do you think she got a perm?" Leila asks. "I'm getting a perm if she did."

"Perms for everyone," I agree. "And sexy suits, too."

Fortunately, someone amongst us is an actual professional. Bumbling Audrey from my office is no longer, and in her place is a complete MBA from Kellogg boss lady—all business, no blushing. When Audrey approaches, Cecily looks like she's going in for a hug, but Audrey offers her hand for a shake instead, cool and aloof.

"I'll never let her live that down," Leila murmurs beside me as Audrey directs Cecily's attention to us.

"And this," Audrey says as they approach, resting her hand briefly on my arm, "is our principal, Ms. Emmie Jones."

Cecily's grin is pure sunshine. "I can't tell you how excited I am to speak with you and learn more about the school and your students." Her honey-colored eyes shine with emotion. I stare stupidly into them. "It's all I've been able to talk about for days. Audrey is probably sick of hearing me go on about it. Right, Auddie?" She bumps Audrey with her hip, and I'm frankly surprised Audrey doesn't tip straight over. She's so still I'm not sure she's breathing.

But also, *Auddie?*

Cecily gives her a soft, questioning smile and then returns her attention to me. "Thank you so much for letting me visit, Principal Jones. I'm really grateful to be here."

"*New* principal," I hurry to say, offering my hand. "Fresh out of the principal egg, in fact. Just a baby principal...named Emmie. You can call me Emmie."

Yikes.

I feel the reassuring warmth of a hand against my back and relax into the touch. "Emmie has been here for six years," Tommy says over my shoulder. "She's the beating heart of Desert Grace."

Cecily raises her arms in the air, smiling. "Tommy O'Connor, get over here."

Tommy's hand squeezes lightly between my shoulder blades as he steps past me and Leila and into Cecily Prior's hug. Leila makes a face at Audrey, who has her lip pressed hard between her teeth.

We ogle as they chat, their hands finding purchase between them as they come out of the hug, like old friends.

"Goddess," Leila states.

I hum. "Like for real, maybe?"

Audrey whimpers.

Cecily is less than an inch shorter than Tommy. She looks like she was born and raised on Themyscira—lean, powerful muscles. Sexy and intimidating all at once.

Tommy introduces her to Leila, who he calls the leader of our math department, eliciting the goofiest noise I've ever heard her make before she excuses herself to monitor breakfast in the cafeteria.

"Come on, scholars," she calls to the gawking students starting to arrive while ushering them up the stairs ahead of her. "Move your butts."

I wince at the casual use of *butts*. Cecily, however, is grinning as she watches them stumble over each other to get a glimpse of her on their way upstairs, so I don't immediately plan the lecture I am going to give my roommate this evening when we get home.

In the vacuum that Leila and the kids leave behind, Audrey clears her throat and says she has some board business to attend to. She ducks out, not giving anyone a chance to respond, leaving me, Tommy, and Cecily—and Cecily's troops—alone in the front hall.

Tommy winks at me, a viridescent arrow that hits right where it's meant to. I let my hands relax at my sides.

"Shall we?" I say.

I've witnessed Mr. Edmonds give many tours in my time, courting donations and showing benefactors where their dollars were going. I still shudder thinking about how he talked about the students, parading their stories down the halls, each its own Dickensian tragedy.

I promised myself this tour would be different. Our kids are more than their circumstances, and they prove that every day they come to school. I want Cecily to *see* them—the students and their interests, their resiliency, humor, hearts—the way Tommy has. I want her to behold each unique student and not have her view already hemmed by their situation.

Cecily says she doesn't want to miss chapel, so I decide we will begin our tour on the roof so we can be on the third floor by eight. As we walk, I ask her about her time in D.C., and she talks about how depressing it was to be forced to convince old rich people about the value of education and the need to improve systems in low-income communities. She is much better versed in education legislation at a federal level than I am, and I beam at her the whole time she's speaking. Imagining Cecily Prior arguing with salty politicians gives me goosebumps.

Tommy trails behind us with two of her bodyguards, and when I turn back, he's smiling at me.

On the roof, I tell her about Micah's veggie garden and the school's new collaboration with one of our local farmers markets, where the kids will sell our organic produce and plant starts this spring. When I show her our vermicompost bin, tucked away in a shady corner, she does not hesitate to dip a hand in and admire our red wigglers.

"Cecily Prior isn't scared of worms, then?" Tommy asks.

"I love all critters," she says, placing the worm she's holding back in the box before shutting the lid and rubbing her hands together to brush off the soil.

"Tommy," I say. "I don't have my phone, but you should show her—" I cut myself off, my heart beating so high in my chest I probably couldn't speak anyway.

"A picture of Este?" he asks, his voice bright like me bringing up the dog I deserted—as if I have any claim on her outside of the gaping hole in my chest where her cuddles and whiskers and ginger curls are meant to be—is no big deal.

I nod.

"Oh, Emmie," Cecily gushes, placing a hand on my shoulder and bending down to meet my eyes. "I have seen photos. That is one weird-looking mutt, but I love her already and can't wait to meet her Friday evening."

My insides warm at the thought of Tommy sending photos of Este to Cecily Prior, and I chuckle, wondering how Cecily makes spending time with her feel so surprisingly normal.

We all walk to the edge of the roof to take in the view of the valley, the mountains rolling like an embrace in every direction. We discover that from up here, we can pick out the pink of her house in the barrio southwest of campus.

"Sometimes I forget how special this town is," Cecily says, her voice holding something nostalgic, almost fragile. "I'm excited to be spending more time here."

I straighten, my heartbeat quickening. "Are you staying for a while, then?"

"That's the plan," she says in a way that implies I should already know. She glances back at Tommy, standing at the herb planter on the other side of the roof with his cell phone out.

I swallow the bile rising in my throat. "That's great to hear! Did you notice the university's new ecology building? Look, right over there past the stadium."

While Cecily and her bodyguard admire the solar-panel-covered tower, I slip over to Tommy. "Nilla Wafer," I hiss.

He frowns at me like he doesn't get it.

"Captain, this is madness," I try, hoping that one gets the point across.

"I heard you the first time," he says, raising his hands.

I wince. "Sorry."

"For what?" He smiles at me before calling out to Cecily, "I have to head down to my office for a bit, Cece. Emmie will bring you by when the tour wraps up."

"Sounds good," Cecily calls back, barely having time to turn around before I'm beside her.

"How exciting that you're moving back," I say, pressing a point I have no right to press.

"I'm ready to feel settled somewhere again, to feel at home. I don't have that anywhere else. Something about that pink adobe." She shrugs and rubs her fingers at a spot just below her collar bone. "I didn't think the move would happen so fast, but when something's meant to be, you know?"

So fast? What is a pop star's definition of *fast*?

"Yeah," I say. But no. I have no idea. What happens when something is meant to be? In Cecily's alternate reality, clearly it means things just—*poof*—work out.

My reality is the opposite. I have to hear from a famous pop star whom I have no right to question further that the man who is everything I could have dreamed of finding in another person is moving out of his house, and soon, by the sound of it. The same man who was reviewing a document this morning covered in another woman's name and an Irish mailing address.

I scheduled with Yasmin for the Monday after the talent show. In my pragmatism, I decided there wouldn't be the proper room this week to sort through my feelings, much less dig through repressed childhood traumas and current romantic ones, given everything we have going on.

How was I supposed to focus on healing my inner child when the possibly coolest, least problematic famous person in the history of people is *here?*

But after Cecily's news, I'm worried there won't be time after, either. There won't be a chance to figure this all out, to figure *me* out, before it's too late.

Thirty-One

THE TOUR IS A huge success. Cece—who insisted I *also* call her Cece during lunch (where she sat down with us in our cafeteria and ate off a paper plate on a crumb-covered, plasticized tablecloth) and again while she helped pack boxes in the Family Pantry—asked if we'd be open to her helping out with music lessons in the future.

Kicking off my tenure as principal by bringing on a famous, caring, talented assistant music teacher? Psh. No biggie.

"Takes the whole *per ardua ad astra* school motto to a whole new level," Leila jokes when I tell her.

"Desert Grace, through hardship"—I bust out my best jazz hands—"to the *stars*."

Cece spends time with the kids during study hall and asks them about their plans for the future. Their eyes glint with excitement while mine well with tears.

"I was raised by a single mom, too," I hear Cece say to Harper after reading a haiku she wrote for the state poetry competition, and I suck in a breath.

The words kill something in me. Something that needed to die. Something that should have been put out of its misery years ago: the quaking belief that who I am is bound by where I came from, by the sadness and stories that trail behind me like rusty, tetanus-ridden cans.

How can I expect my kids to overcome their stories when I let myself be limited by my own? How many excuses will I find not to try because

I am afraid? How many excuses have I already used to avoid the risks of living fully?

I stay at Desert Grace until the very end of the day and am the last person to leave campus, setting the alarm and locking the door behind me. Leila invited me to eat Sonoran hot dogs and watch a movie that is not *The Big Lebowski* with her and Benji, but when I pull out of the parking garage, I turn the other direction. I head straight for George.

"Emminha," he calls as soon as I open the door to his room. He stands from his seat by the window, sets down his book, and opens his arms to me.

His smile—my smile, familiar, warm, everything I need right now—erupts across his face, and I throw myself into his hug. The way I did for years after bad days at school. The way I did when I received my scholarship to college. The way I did when Mom died.

I hold on so hard I'm worried I'll hurt him. He's not the same man who used to catch me when I fell. He's fallen, too, and it shows in the slimness of his arms and the shadows under his eyes.

I should be the one holding him up, but I can't let go.

George chuckles into my hair, his embrace steady and warm. "I've missed you, filhota."

"Sorry I haven't been by." I pull away and smile at him. He frowns at my quivering lips. "Things have been busy."

"At school?" he asks, leading me to the table and pulling out a chair.

I sigh. "Yeah, at school." It's not a lie, but if he presses, I don't know if I have the energy to play along today. To be the Emmie I was ten years ago. I glance at my bag, where it's hanging by the door, and start working on an excuse.

When George was first diagnosed with dementia, I met with countless doctors and read all the books. I know that trying to reorient George in the present wouldn't just be futile; it would also be a little bit evil.

I don't ever plan to undo his world again.

Since I don't have the emotional resources today to keep up the charade, it's probably best for me to make sure he has everything he needs and then leave as soon as possible.

I feel his hand land on mine, stilling my tapping fingers. "Is that nice fellow still the head of school?"

My eyes widen as I swing my head to look at him, my hand tensing under his fingers. "What?" I whisper.

George shakes his head. "I know I get a bit muddled, but I seem to recall you telling me about a handsome young man who has taken quite a liking to my Emminha."

"You remember that?" My eyebrows furrow as I think back to when I told George about Tommy. George didn't even know who *I* was that day. "How...?"

His eyes well up, the tears deep as lakes, like they've been dammed for years. Maybe they have been.

George's head drops, and I scoot my chair beside him, wrapping my arms around his shoulders. He swallows, and it sounds like he's choking.

"Are you okay?" I ask, frantic, trying to raise his face to mine now, my other hand feeling for the space above his heart. "Should I go get help?"

He reaches up, finding both my hands and pulling them to his chest. A tear spills from the corner of his eye, leaving a glassy trail down his dark cheek.

"George?"

"I'm so sorry," he says, his voice rough and strained.

"No." I shake my head. "You have nothing to be sorry for. Everything is fine. *We* are fine."

"Your mother was my world," he says.

The words are a broken absolute, an atom torn asunder. My throat closes, my breath trapped between my mouth and my lungs and the wild beating of my heart.

"I know," I sob, trying to open my palms, to shush him, reassure him. I don't want him here, in this reality. I don't want to see him hurt.

"But you, sweet child, you were my world, too. And I left you alone. I left..." His head bends forward, and our brows meet, and we weep against each other. Shaking. Damaged. But together. "I'm so sorry," he repeats when he's caught his breath.

"Please, don't say that."

He looks at me, almost surprised. "But it is true, filhota. It does not make it better, but being your father was the greatest gift your mother gave me, and I've missed so much. I've missed watching you grow up."

I rest my head on his shoulder. "You gave me everything I needed to get here."

"I should have been around to give you more."

"You gave me your principles," I say, sitting up to face him. "I'll always have those."

"Did I, though?" he asks, and something in me sinks.

George's principles are what I bear of him, what made me good, the thing that binds us. He is my father in every way that counts, and his principles are the expression of that. We will never share the same face shape, or skin tone, or eye color, but I can *be* like George.

My hands tremble as I start listing things out loud: "Being late is disrespectful. Always shake someone's hand like you mean it. Bad words are a substitute for thoughtfulness. Be a good person."

He laughs lightly. "You were always a good person, filhota. Handshakes and timeliness are just extra, but they are not principles."

My forehead wrinkles. "They aren't?"

He shakes his head.

"But I was a good person because you taught me how to be," I insist. "You knew I could be."

He chews his lip. "You're giving me too much credit. My principles were for me, Emmie. I knew that if I stuck to them, I could find peace, happiness, in almost any situation. Even after we lost Lara—and even now, on grey days—they can help me find the sunshine."

"Happiness?"

"Happiness is not a catchall feeling, but it is one that sustains me. It can be a burst, a flutter, one spark on a dark day. It can look like a million different things, come a million different ways." He tilts his head back and closes his eyes, taking a deep breath. "You just have to know how to see it, and how to find it. You don't even need a lot. Just enough to remind yourself there is something beyond the clouds."

He stays like that for a minute, and I think of his childhood, the family he left behind, the ways he fought to build a life here only to see so much of it fall apart. But through it all, he sought happiness. And he found it. He still does.

"George, was I ever happy?" I ask. The question is urgent. Did I once know how to see the sparks? As far back as I can remember, my heart was filled with shadows, doubts, worries. Was there a time when it knew the light?

George's grin is so bright that I see it then, the one burst that could sustain me, and I feel it like a reminder of something I once knew well. "When I met you, sweet girl, you were the happiest. As a child, you were joy incarnate, bright enough to light a thousand dark days."

I snort. "Okay, George. But if you were to look back as someone who *didn't* raise me, would you say the same?"

His shoulders rise and fall with a breath. "If I was more aware then, I would have seen it. I would have done more."

My eyebrows knit. "Seen what?"

Guilt flashes across his face, and my stomach flips. "The autumn of sixth grade, after your mother's knee surgery. You found her after school. They had prescribed opiates and..." He looks up at me, touches my cheek, and I can feel under his fingers how clammy my skin has become. "I don't think she meant to, but the pain had been so hard for her to manage, and she took too many. I was at work and couldn't get back before the ambulance arrived."

I pull back, shaking my head. "I would remember that. I would..."

A bunch of snapshots flash through my mind, images I've been waking up to in the middle of the night for years.

Oh, god. The bad dreams.

They are memories.

"I failed you, Emminha. I saw you pull away from your friends. I saw the changes, right there happening before my eyes. I hoped we'd get your mom better and you'd feel better too. I didn't realize how deeply it had hit, how much damage it had done inside. Once I did, I felt useless. I allowed myself to believe that it was normal teenage stuff, that you'd grow out of it."

I whimper, a sound like a wounded baby rabbit—tragic and fragile and maimed. But, though I sound it, I don't feel like I'm any of those things right now.

Instead, I am uncaged, escaping, realizing that this feeling that's haunted me is a part of me, but maybe not all of me. "I was happy," I say. A fact. *I was* happy.

The sensation in my chest is like warmth seeping into ice-cold toes, the gnawing burn of coming back to life. And maybe the depression would have come either way, but there is a moment I can return to, that I can turn over. I can see what I lost on that bathroom floor—shaking my mother, begging her to wake up—and maybe I can try to find it again. Maybe that piece is one of many that I can call back and build up again.

"Very happy," George confirms.

"George," I ask, suddenly very aware of something else I might have gotten wrong all this time. "What *are* your principles?"

He leans back in his chair, his expression thoughtful. "You don't need to worry about those old things. Look at you, my Emminha, doing such wonderful things for this world."

I narrow my eyes at him, playful but dead serious. "Don't flatter me. I need to know."

George tilts his head. "Why's that?"

"I think," I start, and my shoulders drop. "I think I've been principle-ing wrong."

"I doubt that." He grins at me.

I cross my arms, waiting.

"Tá bom, tá bom," he says in resignation as he rubs his chin. "They are quite simple, really, nothing profound: practice gratitude, be of service to others, love your family and friends without conditions."

"Good. Right." Nothing about being a good person in the traditional sense—cheating, stealing, sleeping with the man who is responsible for the future of your career—but implied, surely.

"And," he continues, raising an eyebrow, "always follow your heart."

I scowl. "That one seems fake."

"That one is most important of all."

"*Flapjacks*, George." I drop my head into my hands and groan. "I'm such a mess."

He chuckles. "Want to talk about it?"

"Just to clarify, all those times you told me I was good and always did the right thing, did you mean from a moral perspective or, you know, that last part? Did you mean because I followed my heart?"

"Is there anything more moral than that?"

"Not dating someone you're in love with because he's your boss, and it's not fair to everyone else?" I try, my voice going high at the end.

George appears like he's considering but is definitely not convinced. "Does he make you feel good?"

"Yes."

"Supported?"

"Very."

"Does he make you happy, Emminha?"

"He makes me hopeful that I can be. Not because I'm with him, but because he wants to help me get there. He isn't afraid of my dark."

"So, he loves you back, then?"

"I don't—" I sputter.

He smiles and squeezes my arm before I can stammer my way through an entire *maybe he was close, but he shouldn't, not after how I've treated him.*

"You deserve to be loved by a good person. But I think you are right, my girl. I think, perhaps, you have been principle-ing wrong."

Thirty-Two

W E TALK AS THE sun sets outside the window—about Tommy, about Este, about Leila.

"You've never dragged Ms. Bashar here for a visit?" George asks, scrolling through the photos on my phone.

"Of course I have. She's the one who slipped all those Danielle Steel novels onto your bookcase."

He huffs. "All this time, I thought it was the night nurse trying to send a message."

I give him a pointed look. "That you need more romance and less depressing non-fiction before bed?"

"Or," he says, waggling his eyebrows, "that I need more cute night nurse in my bed."

"George!" I exclaim, pretending to cover my ears. "Not in front of your daughter."

He chuckles and sets the phone down.

"But you know," I say, giving him a nudge with my shoulder. "You deserve that, too—to be loved like that again by a good person."

George's mouth opens, and I know he's about to argue, but a nurse interrupts us, popping in to check on George since he's late for dinner. I eye him when her back is to me, and he shakes his head. She is not the cute night nurse, then, but she does come back five minutes later with two meals so that I can eat with him.

We laugh and toast our ginger ales. We talk about Mom. We smile through the memories, even while we cry.

A part of my mind keeps telling me this might never happen again. That this might be the last time I have George with me lucid and fully present. But that part of my mind can shut up and bugger off because, at this moment, I am home. I am with my dad.

I won't let my mind steal this moment that my heart needs.

"Will you bring Este by to visit?" he asks, folding his paper napkin into tiny, neat squares.

"Of course." I stack his empty plate on top of mine. "I just have to fix a few things first."

"And then Tommy, too, perhaps?"

My pulse gallops at the thought, and I fumble the plastic forks I'm holding. "Yeah, and Tommy, too. I hope."

He nods. We talked about how dating my boss might not be the worst thing for the school. I can speak to the board, which is now comprised of two of my favorite people, and we can come up with a plan. A plan that is fair and equitable for the entire staff and faculty. A plan that would make everything okay. That would let me have Tommy.

If Tommy will have *me*.

God, why was I such a jerk?

"He'll understand, Emminha," George assures, his voice quiet. "Love isn't always easy, but it's worth it. And he knows you are worth it."

"Does he?" I grimace. I've pushed and pushed, and now he's leaving Cece's house and moving who knows where.

"If he is as smart and wonderful as you've told me he is, then yes, he does."

Tommy *is* that smart and wonderful. And I don't care if I have to dress up like a leprechaun and sing U2 songs a capella at the talent show in front of seven thousand people. I'm going to make sure he knows how amazing I think he is.

But first, I need to get some of my own business in order.

I email Yasmin on my way home and ask if she could squeeze me in before the weekend. I tell her I am even willing to miss one of my morning classes, which I have never, ever done in the six years I've worked at Desert Grace. But I love those kids, and if giving them the best version of me means missing second period on a Thursday despite my perfect attendance record, so be it.

Nevertheless, when she emails back a time for tomorrow that doesn't interfere with any lessons or meetings, I sigh in relief.

I wonder if this is what Cece meant when she was talking about things that are meant to be. Is this feeling of everything coming together what I was supposed to instinctually call to mind when she asked, "You know?"

Is this the *poof*?

I'm going with yes.

I listen to Cece's second album on the way home, singing along to all my favorite songs from ten years ago with the windows down.

"There's a hot dog for you on the counter," Leila calls to me when I enter the condo, not tearing her eyes away from the TV screen.

"Thanks," I say, grabbing the Sonoran hot dog in its to-go box and sitting down on the couch beside Benji. "How does it feel to be watching something new?"

Benji turns to me, his face a mask of horror as I take a bite out of my roasted chile güero. "I'm fucking terrified."

I turn to the screen, chewing. "*Fear*, Leila. *Really?*"

She reaches behind Benji's head to flick me in the ear. "He's never seen it."

"I think she hates me," Benji whispers.

"Don't take it personally," I tell him. "The first time we watched a movie together, it was the second night in our dorm room, and she put on *Single White Female*. Lei just has a thing for screwed up movies from the nineties."

"Can you please give Mark Wahlberg the respect he deserves?" Leila demands, glaring at us. "And kindly shut the fuck up."

I get up, waving at Benji when he begs me with his eyes to stay, and put my hot dog in the fridge—because my stomach isn't exactly in second-dinner mode this evening—before walking straight to my computer in my bedroom.

Tommy can't leave yet. He's probably never even had a Sonoran hot dog, or been to that old western film set where you can pan for fake gold, or seen a venomous snake up close enough to pee your pants a little.

I can't let him go, not without giving it all a fair shot.

In the school calendar app, I add a meeting for tomorrow afternoon and send him an invitation to *discuss the future*. Vague enough to prevent scaring him away, and late enough in the day that I will have a chance to talk to Yasmin first and make sure my head is on straight.

He accepts the invite immediately.

Poof.

B Y MID-DAY THURSDAY, THE *poof* declines into whatever the sound is that a balloon makes as it deflates. By fifth period, it's Munch's silent scream.

The police arrive at school after lunch. Santi, one of our juniors, was supposedly posting incendiary comments in a dark web forum about hurting people and hating his classmates. They patted him down in the middle of the hallway and escorted him out to a patrol car. It's a miracle I'm not sick all over the sidewalk when he presses his hand to the window glass before they drive him away.

Tommy leads the officers to his office, where he cancels all of his talent show-related appointments for the day (of which there are many), and I reschedule with Yasmin for after school as I simultaneously delete my meeting with Tommy from the calendar.

We spend the rest of the afternoon sitting around Tommy's desk with a few rotating officers. Santi's guardian, Ximena, is called in, but she tells us she can't get away from work. The police sigh. I don't mention to the officers that she's not documented. That if she shows up, she's probably terrified that she'll be detained, or worse, sent away, and then Santi will have no one.

I wish I could talk to him. It is nearly impossible for me to believe that the boy who keeps his table laughing all through lunch, who I lent my copy of *Pride and Prejudice* at the beginning of the month to, and who quoted Austen back to me between periods a week ago, is capable of such sad and frightening thoughts. But the pain we hold on the inside wins out sometimes, in different ways.

Still, *Santi?*

No, I don't buy it.

"How do you even know it was him?" I demand of one of the officers, leaning forward to read his name. "Detective Moore? The screen name? It's asinine. Topedayger69er. Seriously? Santi would *never*. Last year, he wrote a six-page essay on the modern usage of Zapotec, for *chips' sakes.*"

"Zapotec?" one of them asks Tommy.

I shift over so he has to look at me instead. "It's a group of languages indigenous to Mesoamerica." I shake my head. "But that is not the point! Santi is a great student. He has never exhibited any behavioral issues or worrisome conduct. Ever."

"Has he been evaluated by a school therapist?" the one who is rocking back in his chair asks, raising his arrogant eyebrows at me. We have already been over this.

I clench my teeth together. *"Fiddlestick fudgemuffin hole balls."*

Tommy stands up. "Gentlemen, thank you for spending your afternoon with us. If we can be of any service or provide any additional information, please get in touch. You have our cards"—he glances at me, the faint hint of a situationally-appropriate smile on his lips—"and you can contact us at any time. We'd appreciate it if you were to keep us apprised of Santi's case. But I think I speak for both of us, and the entire staff, when I say that we have no reason to believe that Santi was responsible for those comments."

They stream out, shaking Tommy's hand as they go. I keep my trembling fists at my sides. I know George would understand.

When Tommy shuts the door behind them, I let out my breath, and it sounds like I'm trying to breathe fire. "I know they're trying to protect the community. To keep the students, and us, and the school safe, but for crying out loud, why do they refuse to listen?"

Tommy nods. "I'm calling a lawyer. I'll have someone with Santi as soon as possible."

"Oh," I murmur. "Crud. Tommy. Lawyers are really expens—"

He runs his thumb along my mouth, and dang it if that pad of skin isn't the best weapon in the world. I'm so surprised that I stand there staring at him with my lips open.

"Sorry," he says, his cheeks flushed. "You had a little piece of paper stuck there."

"I had paper—*paper*—stuck on my lip this entire time? While I was yelling at policemen?"

"Small. Nearly invisible. No way they noticed."

"*You* noticed!"

He shrugs and walks around his desk, where he opens the top drawer. My heart is singing, *Tommy noticed, Tommy noticed,* as he pulls out a small white box.

"For you," he says as he passes it to me across the top of his desk.

I take it and slide the lid off, pulling out a card. My lip quivers as I read it.

Desert Grace

Emeline Jones

Principal

"I have my own card?" I ask, staring up at Tommy's very pleased face.

"Do you like it?"

"I love it," I say, holding the box to my chest.

"Me too." He leans onto his hands as I step closer to the desk. His eyes flick to my mouth.

"More paper?" I ask.

"No paper."

"How's Este?"

"Still misses you."

I chew my lip. He watches.

I could do this. Right now, I could lay it all out.

But I'm not ready. I know I'm not, because as our eyes hold, something plunging and powerful inside of me says *run,* says *don't,* as claws of sorrow dig into the edges of my heart.

"I have an appointment," I blurt out.

"Should I reschedule our meeting?" he offers.

"I'll get something on the calendar."

"I'll keep my eyes open for the invite."

Neither of us move until my phone starts buzzing. It's Yasmin checking in. I'm late.

I run across the hall and grab my things and am a sweaty mess by the time I get to her office.

"I need to be fixed. Am I close?" I ask, bursting into her session room. "Can we do it this afternoon?"

Yasmin settles into her chair and gestures for me to be seated. "Why the sudden urgency?"

"I think we can both agree I've needed to be fixed for a long time." I clasp my hands in my lap and sit up straight. "But I'm already so much better, and it's only been a few weeks. I'm pretty sure we can get me all the way there by tomorrow."

She raises one eyebrow. "What's tomorrow?"

I tell her about my talk with George and how everyone was more or less correct—which I am loath to admit but which is also too obvious to deny—about my use of principles as a crutch and a cage and an excuse.

"Wow," she says.

"I know. Record growth. My parents always said that when I put my mind to something, it was best to get out of the way."

"I'm all for it." Yasmin steeples her fingers and studies me. "But you are the only one who can say whether or not you are 'fixed.'"

"There's not like a therapy report card? Or achievement chart we can rank me against?"

"I think you know it doesn't work that way."

I flop back on the couch. "I do. But for Tommy, I just wanted to be as good as possible, to be easy and healed and happy."

"What do you think Tommy wants?"

I think of the dark green of his eyes as his thumb grazed my mouth, the tension in his arms as he leaned toward me over his desk. The endless hope in his endless smiles.

"I think maybe..." I can't say it. It sounds vain and obnoxious, and god, if it's not true, if it's not possible, I don't know if I'll care about putting all the pieces of me together.

"That maybe," Yasmin hedges, "he wants *you*."

I press my lips together and don't respond in case my words suck the air out of the chance she's right. Puncture a hole in the delicate casing that is keeping my faith afloat.

"Emmie, have you considered that he'd be happy with you just as you are?"

"He deserves better," I protest, dropping my head against the back of the couch.

"Emmie," Yasmin says, I hear her shift forward in her seat.

I raise my face enough to peek at her. "Yes?"

"*Tommy* gets to decide what is best for him." Her tone is kind but unyielding.

I sit up. "Is it fair, though? What if I try to push him away again? What if he gets tired of my darkness, of the tears? What if Este develops contact-depression and forgets how to wag her tail?"

"We could spend the rest of the hour drowning in what-ifs, Emmie. In fact, let's do that. Let's make a list of what-ifs. I'll start." Yasmin grabs her notebook and turns to a fresh page. "Ready?"

"I think you're underestimating how good I am at this game. Forty minutes of what-ifs is nothing."

"There's a twist." She comes and sits beside me on the couch. "One," she says out loud as she writes. She smiles at me before going on. "What if everything works out?"

I take a deep breath, letting the question sink in, paying attention to the feeling in my belly at the thought.

Sunshine.

I've obviously never played this version before, but I clear my throat and give it my best. Because I'm ready to imagine a world where things work out.

Thirty-Three

Stepping out of Yasmin's building, I immediately call Tommy, leaning against the warm brick wall while the phone rings, smiling at the sky.

I have one hundred and twenty-four wonderful what-ifs up my sleeve.

Once I got going, thinking about all the things that could go right, that could be good, that could work out, it was hard to stop.

Who knew?

"Hello?" Tommy answers. His voice sounds far away.

"Tommy. Hi..."

"Hi. Sorry, I'm—"

The call cuts out, and I stare at my phone screen. I guess I should have added good cell reception to the what-if list. His name pops up on the screen, the phone vibrating in my hand, and I swipe the answer button.

"Hey." I take a deep breath. "There's something I need—"

"Em, can you hear me? I'm..." His voice fades out, then back in. "And the parking was... Are you there?"

I guess the universe is making sure I really want this. "I need to talk to you. I know I bailed—"

"Oh, god. I'm sorry. I should have messaged. Santi's...great lawyer...home... I think he'll..."

"Santi's home?" I yell so loud that everyone at the crosswalk turns to look at me. The busker at the corner scowls. I drop my voice just enough to avoid another dirty stare. "They let him go?"

"Yes. Home. Sorry, I've got to..." There is yelling in the background as his voice wanes again. "I'll call later," he says, the words cutting out.

The call goes dead.

All right, universe, I say in my head. *Let's do this.*

Yasmin made it clear that some what-ifs need a little more care and effort. I'm willing to give this one whatever it takes. And it's not like Tommy is leaving next week. He's still the head of school at Desert Grace. He can't just pack up and check out.

I have time to do this right.

As I walk to the parking garage, the street is loud with the usual downtown evening street things: honking, light laughter flowing from the sidewalk bars, music booming out of open car windows, and construction. At the building next door to Desert Grace.

I stop a guy in a hard hat heading for the door and ask if he knows what kind of business is going into the space, while in my head, I beg for a library—which was coincidentally one of my what-ifs of things that could end up going really well.

He shrugs. "Some kind of place for people who need, like, continued support, or something."

"What kind of support?"

"I don't know, miss. But they can come here and get it when they need it, I think."

Crud. "Do you mean a methadone clinic?"

"Maybe? They teach things, too."

"So, some sort of reintegration or reentry program?" A sudden influx of formerly incarcerated people hanging out next door to a high school? I'd fully support the organization in nearly literally any other context. But not here. Not attached to Desert Grace. "They would have had to tell us if that's the case, right? The city? Someone? There must be some sort of permitting process for these kinds of things. No one could possibly think a bunch of erstwhile convicts and teenagers are a good—"

"Ex-cons? Look," he scoffs, lifting his hard hat and wiping a hand across his forehead. "I don't think they'd be putting in the good tile if that was the case."

"Good tile?" I ask, narrowing my eyes. "How good?"

"I've got to get back to work. Take it easy, ma'am."

Ma'am!

I deserve that.

As I approach the parking garage, Otis is sitting in his usual spot near the stairwell. I sit down next to him. "Where've you been the last couple of weeks? I've hardly seen you."

He points to the sign he's decorating. His beautiful doodles tell an entire story around the short text: *No change? Spare kindness.* "Just working on my art." He grins. "In my apartment."

"Apartment?" I look around and realize that, though he is here with his cardboard and his markers, he doesn't have his bag or blanket.

"That's right, Ms. Jones."

"Congratulations." I high-five him. "But, I must know, why'd you decide to come hang out in the parking garage if you've got your own place now?"

"I missed my landing. And the company."

I squeeze his shoulder. "The company missed you too. Got any plans this Saturday?"

"Nothing that counts."

"Want to be my date to the Desert Grace Talent Show? There will be dinner after."

"I don't want to step on any toes," he says, winking.

I blush, thinking of the things this man has seen. Me and Tommy before and after class for that one glorious week where we couldn't keep our hands off of each other off campus, and I didn't give a flying squirrel. Yep. I want that again.

I give him a little nudge. "The show starts at five at the arena. Should I pick you up?"

"I can make it."

"There will be a ticket for you at the will-call window if I'm not out front," I say, standing. "I don't know if you're a Cecily Prior fan, but—"

"Would you believe me if I told you I met her yesterday?"

I put my hands on my hips, considering the probability of Cecily and Otis meeting. Based on what I saw of her at school, it's not so surprising. "You know what? I would. She'll be at the show, and I'm sure she'd be thrilled to see you again."

"Thanks, Ms. Jones."

"Have a good night, Otis."

"You too. And good work today."

Later, when I'm crawling into bed, Tommy texts and apologizes again for the shoddy reception.

I text back and thank him for taking care of the Santi situation.

Did you have something else you needed to talk about? Things are wild here, but I can sneak out for a call. Apologies for earlier. I had a pick-up at the airport.

It can wait:) I'll see you tomorrow.

Tomorrow, then. Good night, Emmie.

He sends a picture of Este with her head tilted to the side and her ears raised. I chuckle.

Good night, you two, I type back with tingling fingers.

Things are going to be okay.

T HE FIRST EXTRAORDINARY THING that happens when I get to work is a visit from Detective Moore, one of the officers who was at Desert Grace yesterday morning.

"You were right, Ms. Jones," he says, standing behind one of the chairs in front of my desk with his arms crossed.

I stay standing, too, my hands gripping the back of my chair. "In what sense?"

"Santiago Reyes was not responsible for the comments in the forum."

My knuckles go white as I squeeze the chair harder in an attempt to thwart the smug grin battling for purchase on my face. "I can't tell you how happy I am to hear that." And also, *duh*.

"Sorry for taking up your time."

That's the second extraordinary thing—this uniformed man apologizing.

"Thank you for your service," I respond, reaching out my hand. I give him my very best shake and eye Tommy's closed door over Detective Moore's shoulder. "Anything I can help you with while you're here?"

He clears his throat, pulling a little policeman notepad from a pocket.
"This is my cell number," he says.

I take the paper from his fingers. "For emergencies only? Or should we call you instead of our previous liaison, Officer Anus?" My face heats. "Officer *Janus*," I correct.

"Officer Janus"—he grins; Leila would love that dimple—"has been transferred. The number was more for..." He trails off when I run past him and out the office door to Tommy, who is standing in the hallway. Moore follows me out, shakes Tommy's hand, takes in the grip I have on Tommy's arm for a couple of seconds, and mumbles, "Never mind," as he walks away.

"Did I miss something?" Tommy asks, scanning my face before his gaze settles on my fingers where they still cling to his arm.

I let go, my hand dropping to my side. "Santi was let off. They were wrong. Detective Moore even apologized."

"Did he?" Tommy asks, his eyes wandering down the hall after the officer.

"And he gave me his cell phone number. Officer Anus was transferred."

"His cell number, Emmie?"

"Here, put it somewhere safe." I jam the piece of paper into his shirt pocket. He smiles, tucking the last bit in when I'm done. "How are things going at the arena?"

"I'm headed down there now. Just popped by to check on something next door."

"The hopefully-not-a-methadone clinic?" I ask, wincing with guilt. "Not that there is anything wrong with a methadone clinic. I'm so grateful there are places where people are able to receive assistance and so proud of them for—"

He chuckles softly. "Emmie, it's not a methadone clinic."

"How do you know?"

"I—" He raises his eyebrows. "I have a source."

"Who?" I ask very loudly.

Tommy's lips quirk up. "Handsome fellow. Tall, funny accent, has a dog that matches his hair."

"You giant weirdo, *you* are your own source? About the building next door?"

"Look at the time." He grabs his keys off his desk. "I've got to run. See you this evening after rehearsal. Cecily's house, seven p.m. sharp."

"*Your* house," I correct, daring him to tell me more about his move.

He regards me, his gaze surprisingly serious, before tossing his keys once and catching them. "Don't be late."

"I'll be there as soon as I'm finished helping the caterers set up at the Historic Y." And because the bubbles are too big now to keep them in, I add, laying a hand on my hip, "And don't forget, I still need to talk to you, Mr. O'Connor."

He twirls the keys on his finger. Is he intentionally drawing attention to his hands? Does he know all I can think about is sticking that finger in my mouth? "Can't wait to find out what kind of talk you need to have surrounded by Cece's team, a select few members of the press, and our entire faculty. I bet it's good stuff."

Mashed potatoes.

"After the talent show," I clarify.

"Works for me. I'll have a lot more time on my hands when this is all over." He glances around his office, his shoulders dropping on a long exhale as he leaves.

I don't like it. It looked like a goodbye.

Thirty-Four

DURING THE TWO HOURS I spend unfolding chairs and draping tablecloths, directing the party supply people, and setting up chafing dishes, I decide I do not give one single hoot about who is at the party tonight.

I'm sure I can find a quiet moment to steal Tommy away from the crowd, maybe find a quiet spot in the magic yard under the string lights.

And what? Drop an emotional bomb on him that he has to deal with for the rest of the night? Surrounded by people?

Maybe it's not my best plan, but the thought of maybe being lucky enough to kiss that beautiful bottom lip again sooner rather than later makes me sort of not care. I can at least start rebuilding the bridge.

I leave the Historic Y as soon as humanly possible so I can shower and arrive at Tommy's before seven, just in case. And so I can have time to grab Este an apology bag of Snickerpoodles on the way.

Less than an hour later, I'm parked down the street after taking two laps around the neighborhood, grateful that my car is a hybrid, so I didn't have to feel as bad about wasting gas.

Showing up fifty minutes early to a party is just as rude as arriving at an appointment late. But he must need reinforcements, right? Tommy's probably trying to get all the last-minute stuff set up. Geez, how does one even throw a party that Cecily Prior is coming to? Where will he put Este?

I should be helping. Helping isn't rude.

I manage to kill another ten minutes bouncing between horribly anxious what-ifs and some pretty solid ones, like what if it doesn't matter who is here tonight? What if there is no wrong time to tell someone you love them and beg them not to leave?

Cool your jets, Em. I'm going to take this nice and easy.

Which for me means busting out the calendar app and sending an invite for an 8 a.m. meeting in my office on Monday. No better way to start the day, to start the week, in fact, than delivering a fully unhinged admission of love to a co-worker who you can't escape for the next ten hours.

There is a valet kiosk outside the house and big black vans in the driveway with the back doors open. Inside, they're filled with trays and bottles of expensive-looking prosecco and flowers.

"Need help?" I ask, jogging up to hold the back door of the van wide for a young woman pulling out a chest full of ice.

"Are you a guest?" she asks, eyeing my clothes.

Great. I match the caterers. "I'm a teacher."

She blinks at me and shakes her head. "I'm good, thanks. By the way, this is a private party. They have security."

"Oh, I'm…" Even better, she thinks I'm trying to crash a party at Cecily Prior's house by disguising myself as the staff. Maybe Leila was right, and I should have gotten myself a new outfit for the pre-game party and not just the talent show. But the button-down and black skirt didn't fail me in Vegas.

"Emeline Jones," Tommy says, jogging up to the driveway. His shirt is damp and clinging to his chest, and I'm tempted to reach for a handful of ice to cool myself off. "You made it. And, you're even early."

"I came to see if you needed any help."

"Luckily," he says, walking up to the door, smiling for me to follow, "we have professionals taking care of all the hard stuff. I was just dropping Este off for a playdate so she's not totally out of her mind when she meets the guests."

Gosh, he's a good dog daddy.

"I'll get to see her later?" I ask, worrying my lip.

"Maybe you can duck out with me to pick her up."

Perfect.

"Sounds like a plan." We pause at the front door. "Should I come back then? At seven. I don't want to—"

"To what?"

I frown, shifting my feet. "Intrude?"

"You know what, I do have a job for you. If you're up for it." The green of Tommy's irises flares, and my fingers tingle with warmth.

I press my lips together. "Lay it on me."

"I just got back from the gym and have to take a quick shower—"

"Yes."

"Yes?"

"Sorry." I bite my lip. "You weren't done talking."

He grins the biggest lopsided grin yet, and my stomach tilts with the curve of it. "I have to take a quick shower," he repeats, and his grin suddenly looks a little like a smirk. "But I have these five absolutely lunatic women in here who could use some supervision, especially if, heaven forbid, anyone arrives before I'm out."

I take a step back. "You have five women in there?" I whisper.

He pushes the door open and shouts, "*A chailíní,* I have some-one out here who has a question for ya!"

"Oi, Thomas, do you always have to be fecking yellin'? The babe's just gone down to sleep finally!" a short, curvy woman with fire-red hair shouts back from down the hall, surely doing more to interrupt that baby's nap than Tommy did.

I gape at Tommy, eyes wide. "There's a baby in your house?"

Two other women come out of the kitchen with a young girl, no more than three years old. One of the women is tall and slender with pitch-black waves pinned back around her face. The other is young, with short bleach-blond hair and a tattoo of a small, winged heart beneath her ear.

"Emmie, I'd like you to meet my sisters," Tommy says.

And there is no way. None of these people look related. I refuse to believe that these women are Tommy's sisters and not some Irish fairy tale coven come to life.

Though, I suppose both could be true. I shake their hands in the order they appeared, repeating their names back as we are introduced.

Ro the redhead. Neeve with the raven hair. Fia the blond.

Little, adorable Eloise, who clings to Tommy's leg.

I smile, facing them where we stand on the front porch. I don't know what they know about me and Tommy, and I don't want to sound like an idiot for not knowing they were coming—why did he not tell me? Why does he not tell me *anything?*—so I simply say, "How lovely that you're able to be here for the talent show."

"We try to never spend a St. Paddy's Day away from our big brothers," Neeve says while Ro and Tommy hug her between them like there's more to the story, but that part is just for family.

"Cormac is running a bit late," Ro explains. "But we'll all be together."

"Plus, ya know, Cecily Prior," Fia adds, twirling a strand of short, light hair around her finger.

Tommy clears his throat. "These girls just needed a good excuse to get off the island. Hopefully for a while, this time." He studies each of them in turn.

Neeve drops her gaze to her toes, but Ro nods. Fia sticks her tongue out.

"A good while," Ro concurs, and the way she says it makes my mind start whirring.

Are they moving back to the States? Is Tommy leaving Cecily's house so he can be closer to his sisters? Am I the kind of person who is capable of doing *this* level of relative-ing? The closeness of them, the warmth, the way they exude the feeling of family, would I even know how to be a part of that? Would I just get in the way? Would Tommy even want me there?

Tommy gets to decide that, Yasmin's voice recites in my head.

And I have to give him that choice, because what if he does? My shoulders relax.

Fia leans against the door frame, studying me in a way that gives me definite Harper vibes. I'd guess she's not much older. "So," she says. "Tommy says you have a question for us."

I see it then, in her eyes. In all their eyes, as they regard me expectantly. That little sparkle. A touch of mischief.

"I do?" I ask, glancing at Tommy for help.

"Ah, you sure do," Tommy says, extricating his leg from Eloise's grasp and passing behind his sisters and into the house. "About the asparagus."

"And the president?" I ask after him, but he's already making his way down the hall to his shower.

"If it weren't for his ability to swallow asparagus spears whole," Ro says, letting go of Neeve and wrapping her arm through mine instead, "the man wouldn't have much to recommend him."

Fia pushes the door wide, and Neeve bends to pick up Eloise before Ro let's go of me and scoops the toddler into her own arms. We all walk inside together.

"So that's a no, then?" I ask. "His secret talent didn't sway you to vote for him?"

"Course we did," Ro answers. "The other fella was an absolute dry shite."

"I think I agree," I say. "Pending a definition of the words *dry shite*."

Neeve laughs. Fia grabs a bottle of prosecco out of the freezer and pours us all a glass from the rack of crystal the bar catering set up in the corner.

"To Tommy," Neeve says.

"To Tommy," we all repeat.

I

HELP TO WELCOME the guests as they arrive and drink probably one too many glasses of prosecco with Fia in the process. Ro keeps supplying, and I learn quickly that you don't say no to Ro.

The thing about being with Tommy's sisters? It's comfortable.

Maybe that's because we aren't offloading our problems onto each other as family often does or guarding or protecting each other, I realize, but maybe if I eased into it, even those parts wouldn't feel overwhelming.

Once everyone on the guest list has been greeted, I stand against the wall, tucked away where the hall meets the living room, and take in the scene.

Cecily is sitting beside Audrey on the couch, bent toward her as she gesticulates with her hands. Audrey's silky hair slides over her shoulders when she shakes her head. She is composed as always, cool, verging on aloof almost except for the semi-frantic way she keeps smiling and then pressing her lips together like she didn't mean to.

Neeve's baby is awake and being passed around by faculty members while Neeve watches from an armchair. Eloise is building magnetic castles with Micah and Benji on the dining room table, while Leila has Cece's heretofore standoffish assistant, Rayne, clutching her middle with laughter on the other side of the room. Ro is arguing with one of our more conservative board members, and I love the way she's backed him into a literal corner while Adesh observes with his arms crossed. But at least he's smiling.

"Quite the party," Tommy says by my ear. He's standing behind me. Close. Close enough that I can smell him, that I can almost feel him in that small gap between our bodies, in the space between memory and the present moment.

"Sure is."

"I'd hate for Este to miss it."

I turn and smile up at him. "She'd never forgive us." I can almost hear the word *us* echoing in his brain. Or maybe that's in mine.

"Time to bring her home," he says, taking my hand. I don't argue as he leads me through the crowd that only he can see over and out the front door.

The night is brisk, desert-dry. The stars and the moon are out, showing off in the otherwise empty sky.

"It's not far," Tommy says, letting my hand go.

I cradle it against my belly. "Does she have many playdates?" How does Este have a whole secret life when it's only been a week since I've seen her?

"No. Just happened to meet a neighbor who was happy to help out for the evening."

He guides me up a stone walkway, his hand flat against my lower back, and presses the doorbell beside the gate.

I hear the door open, and the sound of Este's paws tearing across concrete. The gate lock pops, and Tommy swings it open. Este and I lock eyes right before she leaps into my arms.

"How was she, Mrs. De Vries?" Tommy calls to the person standing in the lit doorway, a small, hunched silhouette against the bright light.

"A delight, Thomas. Bring her by again. Any time."

He thanks her and says he will, shutting the gate as I lead Este down the walk.

I shake my head when he's beside me. "How do you do that?"

"Do what?"

"Get people to do all the things."

"I told you, Em." He meets my eyes, the perfect night sky framing his perfect face. "All you've got to do is ask."

As soon as we re-enter the house, Cece leaps off the couch and comes over to meet Este. She studies her collar between pets, a new fancy leather number with a brass nameplate that I have never seen before.

"Este," Cece reads out loud. "A dog. Probably."

She laughs, and when Tommy's lips turn up while he watches me, I have to blink to keep the tears at bay.

"I forgot I brought her treats," I say, feeling guilty and completely head over heels in love all at the same time.

"Fia put your purse in the guest room," Neeve says from a few feet away, where she's now rocking the baby in her arms. "I can—"

"I'll grab it," I interrupt, backing out of the living room.

I need a second.

I *need* a plan. Something even better than the leprechaun costume idea. And Tommy definitely deserves more than a work morning meeting confessional. I open my phone to cancel the invite, but he's already declined it.

"Huh," I murmur, bumping into the small desk as I walk into the guest room, my fingers fumbling to turn on the reading lamp. I find my purse on the bed and dig through for the bag of Snickerpoodles.

There is a ton of luggage in the room, but I haven't seen any moving boxes in the house. Not even the one Tommy had shipped out.

Then again, everything in the house belongs to Cece. I check the tag on the luggage just to be sure Tommy's move doesn't include an imminent flight somewhere away from me.

Roisin Mahon.

Roisin. The same name from the document Tommy was zealously highlighting in my office the day of Cece's tour.

"Ro is a chronic over-packer. Overthinker. Overachiever," Tommy says, watching me from the doorway. "If you can over-something, she probably does."

Roisin is Ro.

I laugh and drop the tag. "You ready for tomorrow?" I ask, glad he can't see the heat on my cheeks in the low lighting.

"Are you?" he asks back, his eyes bright like he knows something I don't.

I cross my arms. "I think so."

He chuckles. "It's going to be grand. I promise."

You have no idea, Tommy Flynn.

Thirty-Five

T HE ARENA IS HUGE and smells a lot like corndogs. I stand at the sound booth and look up into the buzzing seats. Rows and rows of people—about seven thousand, to be exact—talk and laugh while they wait for the show to start. The teachers and their families and the students' families are all seated on the floor in front of the stage where a bunch of teenage faces peak out from the wings. Some seek their families in the audience and wave. Others are pointing up at the jumbotrons or trying to get the cameraman's attention.

A few of the students seem like they aren't sure if they're excited or about to be sick. I empathize with those students the most.

Nilo gives me a thumbs up from where he's tucked in with the mariachi kids waiting to open the show. I nod and give the go-ahead to the sound booth. Tommy takes the stage while I jog back to my seat at the front of the floor, smiling at Tommy's sisters and Cormac, who I met briefly this morning, when I pass. Micah is sitting with them, Eloise on his lap.

From the crowd, I see Tommy the way everyone else in this stadium sees him. He's all tousled auburn hair, bright eyes, bitable lips, and, *oy*, his body in that moss-green button-down and those slim-fit trousers make him look like he should be seducing someone on an Italian beach and not corralling a bunch of questionably talented youngsters for a variety show.

"How is that man still single?" I mutter to Leila.

She sighs. "Don't ask stupid questions, Emmie. Silly doesn't suit you."

"You know what suits me?" I ask, and she nods because it's about the twentieth time I've forced her to admire my outfit. I bought myself a green Anthropologie jumpsuit that not only matches Tommy's eyes (coincidence) but makes me look like I should *also* be seducing someone on an Italian beach.

"It goes especially well with your lanyard. You know people will realize you work at the school even if you're not wearing that thing, right?"

I wrinkle my nose, clicking my red pen at her.

I talked to Cece before the show, and she was more than happy to help me with my plan. But none of that will happen until later, until dinner at the Historic Y. And it won't be *everything* because for that, I need Tommy alone. I need to apologize—a lot. And I might need to beg a little, maybe find ways to convince him.

Those are things that are better done in private.

But it's a real start, and even though he never rescheduled or asked about the meeting I'd tried to arrange for Monday morning, I've planned everything. Cormac and Tommy's sisters will be dining on tacos at La Pasadita with Leila and Audrey for lunch tomorrow, and I will have Tommy all to myself in an empty house.

Cece's performance at the dinner later will just be setting the stage for all the things I need to tell him.

The lights turn low, and I search for Otis in the seats behind me. He waves from where he's tucked in with the Campos family, and I wave back. Tommy returns from the stage and finds his spot, Leila and Benji between us. We smile at each other.

The mariachi kids nail the opening number, and Marco looks like a movie star playing the guitarrón in his charro suit. The sheer amount of squealing in the audience when the band saunters off the stage confirms a number of new crushes have been established.

Cyle and Amari perform next, a hip-hop cover of "Imagine."

"They aren't half bad," I whisper to Tommy, leaning forward past Leila and Benji. I saw Tommy talking them down when the pre-show jitters hit.

"No, not half," he teases.

A few sets later, Ryker walks onto the stage with a papier mâché cow as big as he is and conducts a sort of live-action art installation in which he helps the cow jump over a moon, also constructed from papier mâché.

Tommy gapes at me with huge eyes.

"Oh my god, he wasn't eating the glue!" I squeal.

"How much Elmer's were we missing?" Tommy asks.

"Lord, here," Leila says, grabbing Benji's hand. She pulls him to my other side and pushes me out of my chair and into the seat closest to Tommy.

"Hi," I say, tucking my arms in close to my sides.

"Hey." He smiles down at me. "You look nice in green."

I shrug. "I *am* one-twenty-eighth Irish."

"Em." He winces. "You've set me up. The joke. I can't..."

If there were a poster child for doofy grins, it would be me, right now, as I watch Tommy force himself not to ask me if I want a little *more* Irish in me.

But also, the answer is obviously yes.

And for a couple of middling dance numbers, I think about little else until Harper gets on stage and reads two of her original poems. Tommy tucks me into his side when the tears start squirting out of my eyes like I'm a cartoon baby.

Cece plays a few sets before all our students join her to end the show. They sing "Hallelujah" together, holding hands, arms draped over shoulders, beautiful, bright, and promising—and guaranteeing not a single person in the arena leaves with dry eyes, so at least I won't be the only one all puffy-faced.

I turn to Tommy during the applause. "You did a really great job with the show. And to think you were so worried when you started."

"Incredible what the participation of a world-famous pop star can do to secure a good turnout."

"It was more than that."

"You're right. It was. I get it, Em. Why you care so much. The show needed to be a success for the kids, for the school." He brushes a knuckle down my arm. "For y—"

"Tommy, man," Benji says from the seat beside me. "They need you on the stage."

And I can't even be mad at Benji, because literally everyone in the arena seems to be staring right at Tommy, waiting for him to get up there.

I sneak out while Tommy is talking because I have to get to the dinner venue before the guests and also because he threatened to make me come up on stage with him and say a few words.

I'll say my words at dinner.

In front of just under four hundred people and not seven thousand, thank you very much.

W E HAD THIRTY-TWO FAMILIES of fourteen different cultural backgrounds provide recipes for the dinner, and at the edges of the hall, in front of every silver chafing dish, is a framed photo that tells a story about the dish and lists the ingredients.

Each guest will receive a recipe book designed and illustrated by our students. All proceeds from the dinner will go to the Family Pantry, and all of our students' families will receive a credit to special-order anything they want: shatta, cola nuts, chermoula, cassava, za'atar. Trader Joe's and the food bank are amazing at keeping us supplied, but it's hard for our families to find the flavors they miss, that remind them of family or connect our students to places they've never been but that are part of their stories, their history, nonetheless.

I take a deep breath, my hand pressed to my heart—which right now is so full of sunshine that the shadows are just hints of darkness in the deepest corners.

I'm pretty chuffed with how it all turned out.

Guests begin arriving around seven, and others stagger in later, after the meet-and-greet with Cece wraps up. Tommy is with them.

"You left," he says, coming to stand next to me by the West African food tables where I am devouring a slice of tapalapa between table visits.

"I had to be here," I say, gesturing with my free hand. "Did I miss anything?"

"No, because I decided to finish my speech here, after dinner, instead."

The mayor interrupts us, a plate in either hand. We thank her for coming and watch as she takes a seat at the student table. She asks them questions about the food. They answer thoughtfully. They make her laugh.

"It's just too good," I say in a weepy voice to Tommy.

"It's just right," he responds as Cece walks in the door with her guitar in her arms.

My heart pounds, and I take a deep breath, shoving my crust into Tommy's hand. "I've got to go."

I grab the wireless microphone off the table where Benji left it for me. Leila gives me a thumbs up as I walk, hyperventilating, to the front of the room. I offer her a grimace in return.

"Good evening, everyone," I say, my mouth too far from the mic to make a dent in the din of conversation. "Good evening, everyone!" I try again, this time too close, but it gets their attention. "Thank you all for being here. If you weren't familiar with the mission of our school before this evening, I am confident you are now, after having it hammered into you by countless staff and faculty members. The last two and a half months have been a time of huge growth and change in our little Desert Grace community, and we've been able to conceive of things for our school that we never thought possible, thanks, in large part, to our new head of school."

I smile and glance at Tommy, who has found his way to a table right in front of me.

And oh, no, he looks horrified.

So do his sisters.

What is happening?

"Um," I go on, shaking my head. "Well, we just, all of us, not just me"—my giggle is manic—"wanted to thank him for all of the energy and positive change he's brought to our school. For all of the dreams he's helped us realize and for all of the dreams we hope to build together."

The last part, yeah, that's personal.

Cece starts strumming on her guitar, "Dreams" by the Cranberries. Yeah, that part's all about me too.

"Oi, does no one in this country realize that the Irish continued recording new music after the nineteen hundreds?" Fia whisper-shouts at Cormac.

Neeve shushes her and stares at me, her eyes big and round and cow-like wells of sympathy.

Ouch.

I work my way around the edge of the room until I find Leila.

"Ballsy," she says, patting me on the back.

"Huge mistake," I counter.

"It's not like you were totally obvious about trying to ingratiate yourself to your Irish boss, whom you are hoping to win back after taking him on the emotional roller coaster ride of his life, I promise. Not unless you already knew."

Audrey glances back at me from where she's seated by the South American food. She looks as pale and nauseous as I feel. "I'm sorry," she mouths.

"Reassuring," I mutter, massaging my temples.

The song ends, and Tommy, whose head has been down for the entire song, stands up. He gives Cece a hug and asks for the microphone.

"Thank you for that, Cecily. And Principal Jones..." He searches the room, finding me in the crowd. "I would argue that you were the one to put all the pieces into place at school. I just happened to show up at the right time. And on that note, I have some news." He gives a soft, lopsided smile.

My heart sinks, dragging my breath into the floor with it.

"I am incredibly grateful for my time at Desert Grace. Watching the school blossom and step into its own has been the best professional experience of my life. I have learned so much from this community, and the lessons are something I will carry forward with me into my next endeavor."

He bites his lip. Our eyes lock.

"I am honored to share with you all that Audrey Edmonds will be taking over my position as head of school, effective immediately."

Leila wraps her arms around me just as the ground goes out from under my feet.

"I know this is short notice and a surprise to many of you." Tommy pauses and clears his throat. Leila holds me tighter. "But between Ms. Edmonds and Ms. Jones, I am confident that I am leaving the school in the very best of hands and hearts. Thank you, to the students, the staff, the faculty, for letting me be a part of your world."

People start clapping. Why are they clapping?

Do they not realize what just happened?

Thirty-Six

"Excuse me?" I say as he approaches. Or shout, maybe, if the number of eyes that turn to look at me is any indication of the volume of my voice. The only pair of eyes I care about right now are Tommy's, though. I march up to him, closing the distance between us, and declare, inches from his face, "You can't leave," as calmly as I am able. Which isn't saying much.

"Maybe it's about time we have that meeting?" he says, his voice quiet and confusingly cool.

I put my hands on my hips and get my face as close to his as I can. "You think?"

"Check your phone," he says.

I narrow my eyes at him and reach a hand into my pocket (all the best jumpsuits have pockets). On the screen is a calendar invite from Tommy. Sent ten minutes ago, while Cecily was singing.

I accept and immediately receive a notification that the meeting began one minute ago. I frown at the screen. Great. I'm already late to the event that will dictate the trajectory of my entire existence. "I hate being late."

"I know you do," Tommy says, smiling at me. "Want to go for a walk?"

I glance around the room. Dinner is wrapping up. Guests will be leaving soon. I know Leila and Audrey can take care of things.

"We can wait," Tommy says, reading the hesitation in my face.

It's hard for me to walk away, to let things go, to trust that someone else will make sure everything is okay. But I'm going to have to learn sometime. I shake my head. "No, now is good."

I grab my cardigan, pulling it tight as I trail him out the door into the cool night. He seems to have a direction in mind, so I follow, trying to steady my breath, my nerves, my heart.

Two minutes pass, the rustling of palm trees and distant barking of a dog filling the silence. Is he waiting for me to say something? Fine. I gulp in the air and open my mouth and prepare to really give it to him.

"Why didn't you tell me?" I whimper.

Tommy considers me, eyebrows raised. "Em, you didn't want to hear it. Do you not recall all the times you'd feign a sudden need to pee or magically receive an urgent, silent, phone call whenever I tried to talk to you? Once you even duck-duck-goosed me and ran away."

I grimace, adding a solid dose of self-directed anger to the outrage already brewing in my belly.

"There's more, Emmie," he says softly.

My stomach roils. "You mean you're not just stepping down as head of school? Let me guess. You've booked one of those rich people seats on a spaceship and have to go away for training."

"Nope."

"You are actually three leprechauns in a trench coat."

"Not that, either."

The walls we walk past transform into giant works of art, the bright colors of the Warehouse District murals muted by the honey glow of streetlamps. The painted papel picado now spans the brick in shades of late sunset, the illustrated javelina a shadow beside pads of amber prickly pear.

I rub my chin. "You secretly *hate* tacos."

"That's really where your mind went?"

"Listen, Tommy, I'm not even going to pretend this is about the school anymore."

"What's it about, then?" he asks, leading us across the train tracks.

"It's about…" I let the word sit in my heart for a second. "Us, Tommy. It's about us."

He nods.

His lack of reaction makes me want to poke him. Did he not hear me? Does he not care? Too bad. I'm not running away this time. I'm not running away from this.

"I don't want you to leave," I say, loudly, firmly.

"Desert Grace?"

"No, you goober. *Town.* I don't want you to leave town. Ever, really. I want you to be stuck here, with me. Forever." I feel my skin flush. That was a lot.

"That's excellent news, Emmie." Smiling, he pulls a key out of his pocket and keeps walking.

"Are you sure?" I ask, furrowing my brows. "I was really mean to you."

"I didn't notice."

I want to shake him. "As you've already mentioned, I literally fled any time you tried to talk to me about us. I hid in classrooms to avoid having an adult conversation. Tommy, I was rotten. I was so, so unkind." I have to swallow down the tightness in my throat.

"You were never cruel just for the sake of being mean." He puts his hand on my lower back when someone passes us on the sidewalk, then keeps it there. I shiver. "You were doing what you thought was right, Em. You always do, and I love that about you."

I duck my head. "You should have been the one running away."

"I was never going to run." He stops, forcing me to face him.

A bird startles and flaps out of a Tombstone rose bush spilling over the adobe wall beside us. I use the interruption to step out of Tommy's touch. I need to make sure he realizes what he's choosing. *Who* he is choosing. "As soon as I heard the news about becoming principal, I set everything we had on fire. I told you there wasn't a choice. In fact, after dinner at Massa, I told you I was making the choice for you."

"I'd made my decision long before you could have made it for me. I'd been looking for you for a long time, Emmie. Looking for *this.*" He rests one hand on his heart and the other on mine. "I was happy to take my time."

"So, you're not leaving town?" I ask, pressing my hand over his where it rests on my chest.

"I'm not."

The streetlight flickers above us. "But then why did you step down as head of school?"

"You know that building next door to Desert Grace?" he says, grazing my neck as he pushes a strand of hair behind my ear. His touch lingers.

"I'm familiar with it," I murmur.

"I made an offer in early February." His fingers sweep along my jaw, and I tilt my face up. "The sale went through ten days ago."

"I don't understand," I say, searching his eyes. "Why'd you buy it?"

He shrugs, laughing. "At first, I wasn't entirely sure. I saw how much you loved Desert Grace and thought maybe I could turn the space into something that would make you happy. Impress you with more classrooms, or maybe a whole eighth grade."

It's really hard not to kiss him right now.

"But then I started to fall in love with Desert Grace, too. And after our first graduate support meeting, something kept nagging at my mind, and that little thought wouldn't let go. After dinner at Massa, once I realized that your exemplary principles"—he winks —"left zero room for compromise, I knew exactly what I needed to do."

My chest constricts. "I forced you out of Desert Grace?"

"I did everything they hired me to do to at Desert Grace, Em."

"Which was?"

"My job. I cut the extra weight."

"Mr. Edmonds," I realize.

"I straightened out the budget."

"With a bazillion dollars from the talent show."

"Managed staffing issues." He gestures to me.

"Thank you?"

"Emmie, you helped me discover what it is I really want to be doing with my life. After talking to Nilo and other alums, I realized there was an opportunity to provide services to our students after they left Desert Grace, and to other students from similar circumstances and backgrounds to make higher education more accessible, to increase college graduation rates or find jobs and training opportunities. The school does an amazing job, but the real world can be rough, and I want to help them navigate that space."

Tears streak down my face. "How are you so good?" I say as Tommy wraps me in his arms.

"I'm not. But I wanted to be worthy."

"Of what?" I ask against his chest, the feeling of being in this space again, the relief, the certainty, the bliss of it so overwhelming I shudder—my nervous system resetting just like Leila's gazelle. "A Nobel Peace Prize?"

He kisses the top of my head. "Of you."

Something in me bends, expands, rearranges. The cages where I keep the dark things flood with light, so much more than a spark. A sun bursts to life inside me, to see myself by, to find myself by. A sun that I know will be there even when the storms roll in, that I'll find in the golden edges of the clouds, in the hint of a rainbow tracing through the gray sky.

"Ro?" I prompt, my voice thick. "Is she staying to help?"

"She's the CFO of Old Pueblo Graduate Extension."

"And the others?"

"I'm hoping they'll all spend some time out here."

"Of course they will. They love you." I wonder if Tommy knows how much he means to them. To all of us. I don't ever want him to question that, his place, how important he is to his family. And to me. "A lot."

"Come on," he says, releasing me enough to take my hand and pull me past a low stone wall, through an iron gate, and up three steps onto a small porch.

I peek inside the dark window. "Where are we?"

Tommy flips a switch on the wall, and rows of string lights burst to life. The house is a white stucco territorial with a pale green door and Victorian accents. Probably not as old as Cece's place, which was built in the 1880s, but darn close. The front yard is filled with fruit trees. I can smell orange blossoms.

Tommy opens my hand and places the key he's been holding in my palm. "Home. If you want it."

My fingers tremble as I unlock the door.

I want it.

The floors are covered in plastic sheeting, and the space smells a little bit like fresh paint. It's adorable. It's perfect.

I turn to Tommy. "I love you."

He kisses me, finally, the sweetest tingle of rightness bubbling between us.

"I'm going to do the work," I promise, as much to myself as to Tommy. I'm ready to live a new story. "I want the dream."

"We'll do it together."

"I don't want you carrying all my apples, though." I square my shoulders as his hands run down my arms, electricity riding in the wake of his fingers. "I don't want this to be one-sided. I already have too much making up to do."

"Making up to do? At the risk of going overboard with the corny analogies, I need to tell you that before I met you, I didn't realize how many stickers I still had in me. I didn't know how to get the ones I was aware of out or understand that even the invisible ones can keep hurting."

"I'll make sure we always have some glue and duct tape on hand," I say, my voice cracking.

"And a pair of tongs at the ready, for emergencies." He cups my face, running his thumb over my cheek, before nodding into the house. "What do you think? Leila mentioned you weren't committed to renewing your lease."

"Este is going to absolutely terrorize these oak floors."

"We've had some talks about it."

I chuckle, turning to take in the space. Tommy's arms come around me, holding me close, his body a wall behind me. I melt into him, the musky, warm smell of his skin, and I can see it, the life we could have here.

"Hey, Tommy," I say, peering back at him.

"Yes?"

"Will you be my boyfriend?"

His shoulders relax, and he grins at me, spinning me in his arms. I trace the crinkle at the corner of his eyes with my finger and the dip of his lip with my eyes. "I thought you'd never ask," he says, his voice deep and lovely. "And in case it wasn't obvious, I love you, Emeline Jones. I'm all in."

"Me too. All in." I beam, hooking my fingers through his belt loops. "Is that our couch? We have a couch already?"

"That's all we have, in fact, in terms of furniture. To be fully transparent, I spent nearly all my money on the building downtown and the house."

I drag him with me as I walk backward, letting myself fall onto the couch when it hits the back of my knees, and pulling him over me. He buries his face in my neck, and I moan as he trails kisses down to my collarbone, the weight of his body pinning me in place beneath him.

"A couch is enough," I murmur as we fumble with buttons and belts.

"For now," he breathes against the swell of my breast.

I wrap my arms around his neck and arch against him. "There's a Brush and Bulky coming up next month, so we should be okay."

He hums against my ear, and goosebumps erupt across my skin. "Will you wear those blue pants again?"

"If you wear your Boston College Crew shirt."

"Whatever you want, always, *a leipreacháin álainn*."

"I want all of it." I push him up, backing him into the arm of the couch, and straddle his lap. "But right now, Tommy Flynn, I'm just after your lucky charms."

Better Late

A DESERT GRACE NOVEL

COMING SPRING 2025

Acknowledgements

I love this part, but since I wrote a dang essay in my last acknowledg-ments, I'm going to try to keep things (a little) tighter.

First, thank you to my readers. To everyone who took a risk on a book a couple of years ago and stuck around. To everyone who has shared this journey with me, I love and appreciate you all so much. Thank you for being my friend. (How'd I get so lucky?)

Thanks to Rebecca and Danielle for being the best critique partners a girl could ask for. Thank you to my three new mamas who have somehow made so much time for this story: Caitlin for book stuff and moon stuff and all the endless stream of other stuff two other-ly-brained girls get themselves into way too often, including italics. Gia, for sharing her this year and creating this beautiful, perfect cover. And Dana, I could never have pulled this off without you. You are all nailing the mom thing. Thanks for letting me hitch my cart to your incredibly capable wagons. Dee! You are a great friend, and I love how you show up for people. To my editor, Clara, your work is *chef's kiss*. To Kristen, your developmental comments (the hahahas especially) gave me life. To everyone else who I am definitely forgetting who had a hand in making this book come true, I am full of gratitude for all of you. And that includes all my dear friends who read this book before it was fully ready to fly and still said nice things.

Thank you to my family, the whole lot of you—by blood, by choice, by friendship, by...force? I will never not be grateful for the way we love each other and for the delight of family-ing together. It was a privilege to grow up seeing how people with so many different kinds of brains and passions and careers can always find ways to laugh and love and listen to each other.

Mama and Kate, thanks for still liking me (or pretending SO well).

To my babies, G and E, you are my whole heart, and I am so lucky to share my days with you and learn from you. It is such a gift being your mama, and when I say I love you more, I win now officially because it's printed in a book. I am so proud of your bravery and kindness and your incredible ability to be unabashedly yourselves.

V, I couldn't have cooked up a better partner if I'd tried (and not just because I'm pretty questionable in a kitchen). Your support means more to me than I could ever express. Thanks for being tender and strong and such a great papá. And dare I say, for challenging me? Ti amo infinitissimo, fino alle stelle, piú veloce della luce. A tutte le avventure che verranno...sciamanin!

And to Roo. You are a one-in-a-million kind of friend and human. There is no one else I would have worn an "Are you my lifemate shirt?" my first week of college, or planned a whole Democlican debate with, or have let convince me to make only BIG or little faces in photos. You are the best of the best, and I love you so much it should definitely make Cam nervous. Your strength and your humor and your fight never cease to amaze me, Bump. Thanks so much for sharing.

Anyone out there struggling, I'm holding you so tight in my heart. Here's to a tomorrow with just the right amount of clouds.

BONNIE CALLAHAN was born in Tucson, where she went on to study Classics and Italian at the University of Arizona. After seven years in Italy, she is back in the Sonoran Desert, where she lives with her Italian study abroad sweetheart, their two kids, and a few bilingual pets.

CONNECT ONLINE

bonniecallahanbooks.com
◯ authorbonniecallahan

DESERT GRACE

www.ingramcontent.com/pod-product-compliance
Lightning Source LLC
Chambersburg PA
CBHW022026310726
48972CB00006B/1831